# A Small
# Flirtation

# A Small Flirtation

## Buff Brazy Given

Copyright © 2000 by Buff Brazy Given .

Library of Congress Number:   00-191909
ISBN #:      Hardcover        0-7388-3440-8
             Softcover        0-7388-3441-6

All rights reserved. No part of this book may be reproduced or transmitted in any form or by any means, electronic or mechanical, including photocopying, recording, or by any information storage and retrieval system, without permission in writing from the copyright owner.

This is a work of fiction. Names, characters, places and incidents either are the product of the author's imagination or are used fictitiously, and any resemblance to any actual persons, living or dead, events, or locales is entirely coincidental.
Cover art by Jim Warren - www.JimWarren.com
phone # 727-461-2039

This book was printed in the United States of America.

**To order additional copies of this book, contact:**
Xlibris Corporation
1-888-7-XLIBRIS
www.Xlibris.com
Orders@Xlibris.com

"Is this her fault or mine? The tempter or the tempted, who sins the most?"

    Wm. Shakespeare—Measure for Measure

To all of you who encouraged, pushed and prodded me to write this book, my heartfelt thanks. To all of you who read the early drafts and continued to push me, more thanks. To my editor Pat Golbitz, I owe a tremendous debt for her wisdom and insights as well as pushing and prodding. To mi amor Bert my enduring love.

To all of you who encouraged, pushed and prodded me to write this book, my heartfelt thanks. To all of you who read the early drafts and continued to push me, more thanks. To my editor Pat Golbitz, I owe a tremendous debt for her wisdom and insights as well as pushing and prodding. To mi amor Bert my enduring love.

# PART 1

# PROLOGUE

I saw him for the first time in the book stalls at O'Hare. I almost dropped the cup of ice cream I was juggling, along with the usual traveling paraphernalia—jacket, purse, portfolio. There he was, my cowboy, my guide, come to life.

I almost ran up to him. Restrain yourself, girl. So I casually sauntered by, was about to say, "Don't bother to buy that one; it's really lousy," when he put it back and turned away—away from me.

Well, what did I expect?

I'd been alone so long and was so isolated, I rarely even thought about men anymore. Hadn't I had enough? All I had—or wanted now—were fantasies. But just walk into an airport and find him? I was startled by the sudden queasy kind of rush I felt as I stood and watched him for a moment. There was a sense of casual elegance about him—tall, attractive, well put together. He exuded an air of confidence as he strode off. My heart sank.

He's off to another part of the world. He could be going anywhere from Beloit to Bangkok. And I'm going home to San Francisco. I hurried to my gate to check in.

Everyone looked disgruntled, standing in groups, shaking heads, some loud protests . . . "Sorry, but there's been a delay."

"How much?"

"Don't know yet."

"What's the problem?"

"Well . . ."

"What's the problem?"

"Something in New York . . ."

"Something in New York?"

"The equipment hasn't become airborne yet."

"By 'equipment' do you mean 'airplane'? The plane that's supposed to take me across the country hasn't left New York yet?"

"Well, yes."

"As New York is a rather large center, how about sending a different 'piece of equipment'?"

"It's being considered. But in the meantime there's a plane getting ready to leave for Los Angeles and then we'll fly you on to SFO."

"What about other airlines; after all, this is O'Hare and you do have other airlines here."

"We're considering that, too."

Good grief. Here we are, entering the new millenium and no one seems able to figure out how to put another plane into service at the busiest airport in the country.

And on and on. Eventually they re-routed as many of us as wanted to be. I stood by and waited. The new "piece of equipment" was on its way.

"Have lunch on us . . ." So I teamed up with a woman who'd come up from Washington for a couple of days of U.S. business and was en route to a conference in Oakland. I didn't tell her Oakland is not San Francisco, and good luck getting there. We all had enough irritations for the day.

"We'll begin boarding immediately. Please line up at the gate." The new equipment had arrived and there he was. I couldn't

## A Small Flirtation

believe it. He caught my eye and gave me a quick little half smile and nod.

He walked down the aisle past me; didn't even see where I was sitting. As is my pattern I fall asleep on take-off—some kind of self-protection, against fear. I was told at eighteen by a Navy flyer that take off and landing are the most dangerous times in an aircraft. Since that day I nod off at both ends of a flight. Not too good if there ever is an emergency—'Wake up, dear, its time to jump into the slide.'

Anyway, I dozed off to be awakened by, "Would you like something to drink?" The flight attendant had drawn the cart next to my seat and was speaking to me. She handed me a coke and moved on. I glanced across the aisle. The woman I'd had lunch with had been seated there when we first boarded the plane. Now *he* was in her seat! He raised his glass in a toast, smiled, opened his brief case and began to work.

I don't remember how much time elapsed before we actually spoke. It seems a long time. I remember a child was playing in the aisle and dropped a toy near his feet. He retrieved it with a laugh, and looked up at me. We said—something.

Thus began the saga.

# 1

We talked a bit and returned to work and reading. The meal was served. We looked at each other and both began talking at the same time. " I watched you at the counter after the delay was announced. You really put that agent through her paces."

"I didn't see you."

"I know. You were too busy. You were awesome." We both laughed.

"You changed your seat," I said.

"Yes. I was supposed to be on the aisle. It was a lucky move," he grinned.

What did we talk about for the next three hours? Who knows or remembers or even cares? We just talked—simply, easily, naturally. He told me he was a structural engineer and wanted to know what I was "involved in." I told him I shoot pictures and no, not as a hobby. I'm a professional photographer.

"Tell me, do you design buildings as a hobby?" I tried to keep a straight face as I asked. He almost choked on a piece of chicken he laughed so hard.

"Not exactly. But I do happen to love my work."

We talked on as though we were old friends. That's it. It was natural to be talking with him. Easy. And we laughed. A lot.

Later I came to realize that our entire time together was natural and easy—the two operative words. Like nothing I'd ever experienced before. I was to think this many, many times in the future.

When we landed he asked, "Are you being met?"

"No," I said slowly, hoping against hope.

"My car's parked here. I'll drive you to town."

"That's all right, thanks, but it's not necessary."

"I want to."

By now we were in the aisle being pushed along. He was suddenly very protective and took my portfolio. "Here, I'll carry that."

On the way to baggage claim I felt a strange sense of disquiet creeping into me and began to panic. Who was this person? And why was he persisting? Taking charge of me? There was an intimacy to this behavior and an insistence that I go along with it—with his idea to take me to town.

I acquiesced to the point of showing him which bags were mine. Before we left the airport, I rushed to phone my friend TJ whom I was visiting for the weekend. I whispered to her, "This terribly attractive stranger wants to drive me to town and I don't know what to do."

"Good lord, girl, what do you expect to happen? Obviously, he must be a perfectly divine man for you to sound so flustered. I'll see you when you get here." And hung up.

What are friends for?

I didn't direct him to her house immediately. We literally crisscrossed San Francisco laughing and joking all the way. It was a glorious summer day—sunny, bright. The flowers in the park in full bloom—children, puppy dogs, even horses. The works. What a set up!

Finally I told him to head up to Sea Cliff, one of San Francisco's prime residential look-out-over-the-water areas...the place TJ calls home.

"Was that so hard?" he asked.

"Yes."

"What's made you decide to let me take you to your friend?"

"I decided you're not an ax murderer."

He chuckled, turned to me, "No, I'm Paul Crowley," and asked, "Are you married?" This question came before I introduced myself.

"No, not now. And I'm Jenny Matthews. Are you? Married, that is?"

"Yes, as a matter of fact, I am."

"Oh!" We rode in silence for a few moments. "You don't seem the type."

"I'm not. I've never done such a thing before, but I'm having too much fun to let this end abruptly. So I decided one way to continue is to drive you into town." He looked over at me. "Anything wrong with that?"

"No, of course not."

I hesitated, suddenly embarrassed by my statement and his. I mean, it sounded like some kind of *fait* à *compli.* All we were doing was driving into town and I was to be dropped off at a friend's house and...and . . . thank-you, good-bye.

My sense of disquiet returned. He was calling all the shots—definitely in control of each of his moves while putting me on notice, no matter how subtly, that if I went on with this game I'd have no cause for complaint—hadn't he told me he was married from the out-set? A neat trick to transfer any guilt directly onto me. Strange. Notwithstanding, I opted to push those feelings aside. What the heck—it was only a ride into town.

# 2

TJ had been out front ostensibly walking her dog when we drove up. As we got out of the car, she gave me a hug and said, "Honestly, I was beginning to doubt myself and wonder if I should have told you to drop the lout and come straight here!" She was smiling broadly. "I'm TJ—Jenny's friend of many lifetimes."

He took her outstretched hand and smiled, "I'm Paul Crowley."

Then she said laughing at him, "Would you like to join us for a glass of wine?"

He came in happily, looked out at the spectacular view, sighed and sank into the deep couch by the fireplace. TJ had already laid a fire. It was a typical late August evening getting more beautiful by the minute, and chilly.

"You remember Mark Twain's wonderful comment, don't you? 'The coldest winter I ever spent was a summer in San Francisco'." She was addressing us both.

"He was right." I sat down next to Paul and began to shiver. I mean the teeth-chattering kind.

# A Small Flirtation

He took my hand and held onto it. "You're freezing."

"Not really. It's just the drop in temperature. Chicago was so steaming—like walking around in cotton candy. It's good to be back."

"Cheers!"

He had another glass of wine. I excused myself for a moment—to compose myself. He was so damned at ease and I was a wreck. What's he doing here? Why hasn't he left for home and his wife? Where's home anyway? He hadn't bothered to say.

"I don't know about you guys," TJ said, looking at her watch. "It's getting late and I'm getting hungry. How about corned beef and cabbage? There's a local eatery that serves it every Thursday night and the last time I looked, it was still Thursday."

Paul looked at me and then at TJ. "I'd like to join you if that's all right. I mean if you don't mind?"

I burst out laughing excited by the idea, "Why not?" I answered, "Come." TJ doesn't drive—ergo, she has no car. His car was a two-seater. We were a sight to behold. Like the VW bug in the circus—but we managed.

Half way through dinner and two non-alcoholic beers later, I turned to him and said, "OK, tell me what you're going to tell her—your wife, that is. Run your story by me. If you can convince me, you're OK. But I doubt you will."

He was laughing so hard, I'm sure he didn't hear half of what I said.

"It's OK. Believe me, it's OK."

"Aren't you supposed to be back yet? I mean today?"

"Yes."

"Later?"

"No."

"Did you phone when we weren't looking?"

"No." More laughter. He took off his glasses and rubbed his eyes. "You're a persistent little thing, aren't you?"

"I haven't been called 'little' since I was twelve and stood head and shoulders above my class-mates." It was a nice feeling to be called that—almost an endearment.

But still no explanation. The rest of the evening was spent quoting baseball statistics, the state of the wine industry in California and other trivia. We closed the restaurant as the help began to clean up the place for the night. It was well after 10:00 by the time we drove back to Sea Cliff. I've always loved that particular area. It is as romantic as it sounds—high on a windy hill, spectacular seascape, golden daffodils, all the rest of it and me, with my fantasies in high gear.

We said good night in front of the house. At least I tried to say good night. He lingered after saying what a great time he'd had. He added that he hadn't had so much fun in twenty years. I found the remark a bit odd, but didn't pick up on it. Why make anything of a casual throwaway line?

Then: "I want to see you again. Will you please have dinner with me tomorrow?" I began to protest. "I'm here to see TJ. We have plans."

"For tomorrow?"

"Yes."

"Not really," TJ chimed in. I could have slugged her! "Go ahead. I've got work to catch up on anyway. That'll leave me free during the day to play, and I'll work tomorrow night while you're out."

Did you ever want to clobber your best friend? She turned to go inside. I grabbed her:

"Don't you dare leave me out here with this crazy man." I said.

"What crazy? He just wants to go to dinner." TJ was grinning like a Chessy cat.

"Swell, you go then," I retorted.

"He didn't ask me."

"No!" I turned to Paul. "How can I leave my hostess?"

"How about Saturday?" he asked, obviously amused at the by-play between TJ and me.

"Saturday, we are busy," TJ said. "Go on, Jenny. It's OK. I really do have a lot of work to catch up on." TJ was urging me.

"I really don't think so. This was great fun. I admit it, but tomorrow, on purpose? I don't think so." I was getting cold feet.

"Please don't say no, not now." He backed off. "I'll call you tomorrow. In the meantime, think about where you'd like to have dinner. I'll call you. Good night."

He bent down and brushed his lips against my cheek in a quick kiss. My cheeks were on fire.

I went inside and picked up a sofa pillow and threw it at TJ. "Some pal you turned out to be."

"Oh, for heaven's sake; it's only for dinner. He didn't ask you to run away with him—not yet! Anyway, you've already decided he's not an ax murderer. What are you afraid of now—that he's a rapist?"

"He's married."

"Oh, that!"

"Yes, that." I answered emphatically.

TJ was stoking the fire and added a log. The room was bathed in flickering light. She turned and looked at me and shook her head again. "He's the genuine article. I'll bet on it."

"Me too."

"Yes, he's a straight arrow. When he said he never speaks to anyone on a trip, I believe him."

"Why, exactly?" I asked.

"He's too open, too friendly, and obviously was having the time of his life. There was nothing phony. Nothing held back."

"Except explaining the time lag at home." I reminded her.

"Too true. But there is some logical explanation for that."

"We'll see."

She turned on the television and we watched a late re-run of Star *Trek*. Whenever we're together that's our routine. Dinner, conversation, a little wine, a fire and either Star *Trek* or some old black and white romantic/tragic comedy. You know Cary Grant stuff. All terribly uplifting. All back to our school chum days during the sixties.

Later TJ and her pooch went for a walk. I retired to 'my' room and called home. My son, Max, hadn't yet returned to his post at

Santa Clara College and was dog and housesitting for me. "Was it a good trip, Jen? Did you get great reviews? Better still, did you have any fun?" He and his twin brother, Nicky, were always on my case to have fun. At twenty-eight, they were each becoming serious about lasting relationships.

"Yes to all your questions," I answered laughing. "I'm staying with TJ for the weekend, OK? I'll be back Sunday afternoon."

"Sounds like a plan. I'll see you then."

Some sort of miracle was taking shape around me that was to change my life. I was totally unaware of the lasting impact these few hours would have as I fell blissfully asleep.

# 3

The morning was brisk and clear, downright nippy. I did my best to keep busy while at the same time staying close to the phone. I skipped taking a walk, and then berated myself for being so jittery. Finally it came.

"Have you decided to have dinner with me? Of course, you have. I'll call again when I'm on my way up the coast."

"I'm not sure. I'm thinking about it."

"Don't say anything more. Don't think anymore. Just say yes and wait for me, please. Don't go away, please." The urgency in his voice was palpable.

And so I said, "Yes."

I waited and waited, some more. Traffic, combined with nervous tension, caused him to take a wrong turn. I almost did go out. It was too much, too fast.

I sat and stared out the window, finally turned away and got up . . ."A watched kettle never boils."

Eventually he arrived, flushed with anticipation and in high good humor. He had some sort of paper tucked under his arm.

"Look here you two; look at this. This is where we drove from the airport, through town, through the park, the Embarcadero, the Presidio, Fisherman's Wharf—a city tour would have taken less time. And finally out here."

He had drawn the route with a green felt pen on a map he picked up at a gas station.

TJ looked over his shoulder, " No wonder it took you an hour and a half to get here from the airport yesterday. You could have been here in twenty minutes!"

"Tell me!" he said as he took me by the elbow and guided me to the front door. "Shall we go then?" He smiled down at me.

"I won't be late." That from me to TJ.

"Take this house key anyway. I may just turn in early." TJ, with a sweet, knowing smile.

Paul helped me fold up into his little red sports car. It really was a red one.

I've thought so many times as this whole thing unfolded how trite it might sound if and when I told it.

Of course, all love stories are the same: Fantasy and reality hopelessly co-mingled. It's almost impossible to see the true object of affection clearly, ever.

"I'd like to stop for a drink and watch the sunset," Paul said as he drove.

"We could have stayed at the house."

"I want to be with you."

I was starting to get nervous again. What in the world was the matter with me? He sensed this mood shift. I was very quiet. He reached over, took my hand and smiled. What a meltdown inside of me!

"I'm heading out to Cliff House. How's that?"

"Good Choice," I nodded. He turned on a tape. We drove in silence.

Cliff House. I'd been there so many times with my husband,

# A Small Flirtation

Tom. It was one of our favorite places and after the accident it was literally years before I could go back comfortably. It is a house, a big one, and it does stand on a cliff overlooking the ocean crashing powerfully against the rocks below. Next to it are remnants and ruins of what once had been bathhouses—the old fashioned natatorium from turn of the century.

Each of its two restaurants offers great views and wonderful seafood. Tourists love it and crowd the gift shop. Yet for those of us who virtually grew up there, they are no distraction from the grand decor, the great wall mirrors, tiered seating and always the view of the sea. Spectacular.

Yes, it was a good choice. In fact, the thought of being there with this man I was so unaccountably attracted to excited me.

It's not easy to park there. We drove into the lot further up the hill across the road from Mario's Ristorante. He came around as I was, typically, struggling with the shoulder belt, helped me out and stood there very close. He bent down and kissed me, this time fully on the mouth. He tucked my hand under his arm and guided me across the road.

I was disarmed and on guard at the same time. Who was this Paul, so sure of himself, so unselfconscious, so full of light and so familiar to me?

The questions kept coming. If he had never done this before, how is it that he seems so practiced and so amused by it all?

We were given a table by a window, of course. The view was breathtakingly beautiful, of course. He sat with his back to it.

"I thought you wanted to see the sunset, the view?"

"I'm seeing exactly the view I want."

He was looking directly into my eyes. That kind of remark has always left me feeling just a bit uncomfortable. I said nothing.

We managed to get through the cocktail hour. Cliff House is a busy place, especially on weekends. I spent much of my half of the conversation commenting on the seascape outside and the people inside. In my head I wondered just exactly what I was doing. When I recall how we talked non-stop for three hours on the plane just the day before, (Was it really only the day before?) and all that time driving around town and then the entire evening at TJ's and the restaurant. It's curious to note how the climate was changed by our statements of wanting to be together and that kiss at the car.

Suddenly, we were serious, still joking; still lots of laughter, but the underlying feelings were serious. I felt as though I was on tiptoe inside, holding my breath. I was still trying to come to terms with my very strong attraction to this stranger.

Once more we made it across the road and up the grade to the car. It was getting quite dark now. Again, he held my hand, guided me to the car and helped me in. I found later that I was always to have a quick kiss before tucking me inside.

"There's a place in Sausalito I like; want to try it? The crab is great."

"That's quite a ride," I said.

"Only over the bridge. It's virtually at the very beginning of Marin County. We've got all night."

I looked at him. He laughed. "I mean I have no time restrictions and you do have a key."

"Sure, why not? It's still early and it's a nice night." Pause. "Are you ever going to break down and tell me about the ability to simply be out without your wife? TJ and I speculated that you're not really married."

He laughed. "I guess I'd better tell you or you'll think of nothing else all night. Can you wait until we're at dinner? I want to look at your face when I do tell you."

"OK. Yes, sure, OK, but it had better be good!"

He still didn't know where my home was or that I lived in Marin myself. He knew it was "up the coast." I had the crazy notion to tell him to just keep driving, that we'd be there in another thirty minutes. After all, I had no serious relationship in my life. Not even a not-so-serious one. I had purposely isolated myself from the single scene. This wasn't my thing. And hadn't he told me he had the whole night? Maybe I'd have considered it if Max weren't staying there during my absence.

No matter how many times I drive across the bridge, I find it thrilling—enveloped by fog, creeping through a rush hour traffic jam, under any conditions. Is there any other sight, any other place in the world, as romantic?

"What? What did you just say?"

"I asked you," Paul said, "if you can think of any other sight, any other place in the world, as romantic as driving across the Golden Gate Bridge? Especially on a moonlit night with someone you want to have next to you?"

I feigned shock.

"I mean sitting next to you." A bit of a pause. "I meant what I said the first time."

"I know."

We found the restaurant. Don't ask me the name. It's enough that I know what town we were in.

Paul barely looked at the waiter when we ordered. He had to glance at the crab on his plate from time to time while we ate or he'd have broken a finger cracking the claws. Other than that he didn't take his eyes off me.

I've heard about light coming from within; read glowing, passionate passages of this in novels. Now he was telling me my eyes were shining so that he couldn't stop staring.

Another time for me to stammer. I simply smiled and stared back.

"How do we know each other so well? We seemed to know it all when we first said hello."

He nodded. "Let me tell you more about me . . . where I'm coming from, that is."

I kept quiet. I was riveted by curiosity.

"Yes, I'm married. No, I'm not unhappy in the conventional sense. We have a companionable relationship that goes back to high school. We even like doing many of the same things. What we have never had is an intimate relationship. Over time I have fantasized one. Don't look so surprised. You must realize that men do this as well as women."

More silence on my part. I nodded.

He continued: "You told me I seemed so practiced even after I assured you this was my first step, if you will, into this kind of adventure and it's true. My actions, my responses are all being stimulated by you. You see, *you* are my *fantasy* come to life." He took a sip of his wine. "I seem practiced because I am. I've been practicing this encounter for years. Not the exact words, of course, but the feelings. I promised the gods I'd respond to every one of my feelings honestly—whatever was to happen."

I started to speak. He reached across the table and took my hand to stop me.

"No, please let me finish." He looked at me and looked away for a few moments. He seemed to need to compose himself. He was revealing a lot, very fast. "When my wife and I were young and starting careers and a family, we were enthusiastic about life and everything in it." He paused again and asked, "Am I talking too much? I don't want to bore you."

"Bore me? Impossible. Please go on, I'm mesmerized."

"We were like all the young couples I've known. We were so busy just keeping our heads above water, we didn't have time to wonder whether we were happy on not—with each other, I mean. Our daughter, Beth, was born after three years. Kathy had had a tough time during her pregnancy. She'd had a couple of false starts and was naturally apprehensive. I'd hoped after she gave birth to a perfect baby, she might begin to enjoy life again in a more relaxed way. It never happened. She became obsessed with every little thing about the baby and refused to have anything to do with me—physically, I mean."

He turned away again and then said he had just a little more to say on the matter of his marriage and was that OK.

"Certainly. I'm fascinated. Carry on."

"For years I've heard men talk about the women in their lives, extra marital affairs, one night stands, whatever. I've always known that wasn't for me. I couldn't live that way, but I could have my dreams, my fantasies and I could still go home to my wife and sleep nights."

"There is one thing I want to say at this point. I may be able to make all this easier for you." Now he was silent. It was my turn to speak "I wasn't surprised at your having created a fantasy woman to love. You see, I have a fantasy, too: my guide, my cowboy. When I saw you at O'Hare, I almost ran up to you. I wanted to say, I'm here. Thank God, I've finally found you. What took you so long to appear?"

He threw his head back and laughed so hard I thought he'd fall over backwards. "Maybe now you understand why I stuck to you like glue at the airport. When you jumped up and started down the aisle brushing aside my offers to take you to town, I very nearly grabbed you to keep you from getting away."

"I wasn't going to 'get away' very fast. We were standing still. The aisle was jammed. Besides you did grab."

"I grabbed?"

"My 'folio. I certainly wasn't going far without it."

He looked serious again. "I couldn't let you go. I knew if I didn't stay close by, you'd walk out of my life forever. Just like that. You'd hail a cab and I'd never see you again. No, it would have been impossible for me to have let that happen. That's really why I took your portfolio . . . to slow you down."

I was shaken by the sudden depth of feeling he was betraying. What was there to say except the truth? "I wanted to stay with you, too, be driven to TJ's, the whole thing. I guess I just panicked. Suddenly afraid my fantasies had finally got the upper hand and I was imagining things." It was my turn to look away. Paul waited. "I felt so excited and conflicted. I didn't know what to do. That's why I called TJ to stall for time. And believe me, she was no help!"

"What did she say?"

"Oh, she said something like, 'He must be a perfectly divine man for you to sound so flustered.' And then she added, 'I'll see you when you get here.' And hung up! What a pal!"

"She was my pal."

I smiled in agreement and then asked, "Weren't you being a little unfair to your wife? I mean not to talk about your relationship and seek some help, some advice?"

"I tired of trying. There was no way to break down that barrier. And I don't just mean about sex. There is so much more to an intimate relationship than sex. In fact, once I realized I was making matters worse by attempting to discuss the possibility, I dropped the whole notion and turned up the volume on my dreams"

There was nothing I could say to that.

It was getting late. Time to leave the restaurant and head back over the bridge. Besides, I wasn't thrilled by all the revelations. They made me a bit uncomfortable. The way he talked, sometimes a little offhand, sometimes with a sad intensity. I don't know.

Paul had made his marriage sound hopeless. And yet there was no indication that he had any intention of changing the situation—that is, of getting a divorce or even separating. I couldn't help wonder why he hadn't called a halt to the whole thing. Divorce may be a rough go; still, neither do I think of marriage as an endurance contest. As I said, somehow all the explanations, the disclaimers had made me wary. I brushed the feelings aside. After all, we barely knew each other—as yet, he owed me nothing.

He took my hand on the way to the car and pulled me closer. I stopped pondering as he stopped and took me into his arms. Our first real embrace. We were both shaken by the impact. He continued to hold me close, looked down and smiled.

"Don't think you can distract me the entire night," I said. "What's the explanation?"

"Oh, we're still there, are we? I thought maybe you had forgotten!" He released me.

"Never!"

"OK. It's really very simple. She's out of town."

"That's it?"

"That's it."

"And you've kept me dangling all this time wondering, and she's out of town? You are a . . ."

"I couldn't help it. You and TJ were so funny with the questions. When you told me to run my story past you, I just couldn't resist the temptation of stringing you along."

"Some temptation. And we thought you were so smooth. I can't believe it!"

"You two were hilarious. It just had to be something complex. I don't think it ever occurred to either of you that my wife is simply out of town.

"Oh just get in the car," I laughed.

We both did.

He took my hand and kissed it again. "OK. Tell me more."

"We were in Wisconsin at a reunion of her family. She has stayed on for a few more days and I came back, as you might have noticed, to meet my fantasy woman in the flesh, so to speak." He was sounding smug and self-satisfied.

"Just that simple."

"Yes, just that simple." He was grinning broadly. I was becoming irritated.

"Paul, what would you have done if Kathy had been in town? Would you have risked last night and tonight to be with me?"

"Fortunately, Jenny, I didn't have to. The powers-that-be have been on my side this week-end."

There could be no real answer—at best speculation and the temptation to lie just to be nice. I let it drop.

"I'm tied up with my daughter tomorrow during the day, but I am free for dinner. How about it, Jenny?" He was back on track

"No, I'm not," I answered.

"Really?"

"Yes."

"You can't get out of it?" he queried.

"No, as TJ told you yesterday . . . Good Lord, was it only yesterday? We do have plans—with other friends. I simply can't change that."

"How about Sunday?"

"After breakfast, I'm going home."

"I'll drive you home. I am free in the late morning. We'll stop for lunch and have some more time together before I have to meet Kathy's plane."

For a brief moment my heart sank. Reality had just moved into the car and sat between us. I pushed past my feelings and said, "I'll agree to your driving me to Larkspur. We can have lunch at the old brick kiln near the ferry dock. That's where I've left my car."

"Great. Except, I was hoping I could drive you all the way. I'd like to see your house, meet your dog. You know just 'hang out' for awhile, as the kids say. In fact, how about now? We have the whole night, Jenny. I'll come stay with you." Paul was so enthusiastic; I could hardly resist him.

"I'm afraid that's impossible, Paul. You see, you'd meet more than my dog. My son, Max, is there and I don't think either one of us is anywhere near ready for that confrontation!"

"I thought you said your sons have returned to school already."

"No, no. Just Nicky. He's back in Boston getting resettled. Max doesn't return to Santa Clara for another two weeks and I miss them both already."

We headed back across the bridge into San Francisco. Both of us were quiet. Silent. Immersed in our own thoughts. I for one was suddenly shy again. We'd exposed ourselves a great deal this evening. More, I dare say, than either one of us had in a long, long time, if ever. Sharing the sunset, the drive across the bridge up to Sausalito, with fantasies running ahead of us—it was all a dream. We could pretend a little that we could just go on from there, forever.

# 4

Big, black, handsome Poochie took TJ and me for a walk in the morning. We carried our coffee mugs with us and sipped and talked of the happenings during the last thirty-six hours, while Poochie picked up his messages at every bush and tree. He left a few himself.

"Well, tell me. Is he really married? And what's the story on these past few days?"

"She's out of town."

"She's out of town?"

"Yes, she's out of town at some sort of family reunion in Wisconsin. He left. She stayed. That's the long and short of it."

"Oh, for heaven's sake. That didn't occur to either of us."

"I don't know, TJ. He is still married."

"I know."

"He's *married* TJ, this really isn't my cup of tea. True, I feel as though I've known him forever." I shook my head. "It really feels like an old love. It's so strange at times."

"Like ancient memories coming through?" she asked.

"Exactly. God knows, I don't know what all this means, but I feel as though when we parted the last time in another life, we vowed we'd find each other in the future when we truly needed one another."

TJ nodded. "Well, we both agree that reincarnation is the only belief system that makes any sense of life at all and times like this only make it more real. Ancient memory, of course. It absolutely explains souls recognizing one another. That's what you two have done. There's no doubt about it in my mind."

We got into one of our conversations about continuous life cycles. Through her studies, TJ had come to these beliefs long before I had. We talked and I questioned everything. She dragged me with her to lectures, insisting I hear from scholars both religious and secular. She gave me books and then would query me on what I'd read. I took a course in comparative religions only to discover all major religions believe in some form of afterlife. I even learned Sufi dancing and meditation and yoga. All the while we talked and have continued through the years to broaden and deepen our firm belief in reincarnation.

I asked yet again one of life's imponderable questions: "Why would an all-knowing Creator put us here once—only? To struggle for a few yeas and then die."

"What would be gained? Who would benefit? What would be the point? Meaningless," TJ shook her head, "No. I firmly believe in reincarnation." We smiled at each other. There is such comfort in this kind of friendship. We, too, must have been close in one way or another for many lifetimes. A real blessing, one for which each of us is grateful.

Saturday with TJ is always busy, and as she was having friends in to dinner, there was marketing as well as the usual, including a trip to the bookstore to pick up some volume she'd ordered—another one on esoteric psychology or astrology—her consuming interest.

## A Small Flirtation

We toyed with the idea of letting my cowboy come to dinner—introduce him as a cousin. And we decided that was too juvenile and downright dangerous. After all, although he grew up down South, he'd been in the bay area all of his adult life. Also, as principal in a very successful firm, he's prominent in his field and whoever knows who knows whoever? Not smart.

"You'd better never stand next to each other under any circumstances where you're supposedly strangers. I've already told you the charge between you could light up the city."

And so the day went. He did call as promised, and I was hard pressed not to tell him to join us. It was such a whimsical idea, I'm certain he'd have accepted.

It was a short call. He actually was going to a flick with his sister and brother-in-law. Not exactly the people he'd want to confide in about me: "Guess what happened to me day before yesterday . . ." Not exactly!

We agreed to talk in the morning and make our plans.

I managed to put him out of my mind for the rest of the day. After all, didn't I say I had a well-ordered life, or some such? The dinner was great fun. Everyone commented on how well I looked. I, for one, wished Paul was there regardless of consequences.

Sunday began like Saturday—Poochie, TJ and I walked. We retraced our steps and entered the house, just as the phone was ringing. My level of anxiety took a quantum leap. What was I anxious about? TJ talks to her daughter and my Goddaughter Cara every Sunday about this time.

"Jenny's here and about to go up the coast. Do you have time for a cup of coffee? No? Well, maybe we'll plan it better for next time. Of course. I'll tell her about your new love. Talk to you later, sweetie. Bye."

The phone rang immediately after she hung up. I jumped a foot inside.

"Hello."

"Hi, TJ. It's Paul. Is Jenny there?"

"Hold on, Paul. She's here." TJ signaled to me to take the phone.

"Hello." I was suddenly short of breath.

"Good morning, Jenny. Are you ready to be picked up? I can be there in about fifteen minutes."

"Not quite, but come ahead. I won't be much longer."

"Great. See you soon. And Jenny, Friday night was great."

TJ looked up from the paper. "I take it you're about to leave? Well, good luck in the next phase of the adventure."

"What do you mean?"

"Do you really believe he'll take you at your word and leave you in Larkspur?"

" I told him Max is at home. He agreed this is not the time for that kind of meeting."

"I forgot Max was there. When does he return to Santa Clara?"

"In two weeks."

"Tell him to call me and stop by on the way down. I don't see enough of that young man. My, but he's a doll. Remind him he's got a bunk here if he needs one when he comes to town."

I assured her he knows that, and will take full advantage of a night in San Francisco staying in Sea Cliff. He loved it there and he's crazy about TJ. They've been buddies since he was a little boy.

I finished gathering my things together as I heard the little red car pull up in front.

TJ invited him in. By now he was feeling quite at home. This was his fifth trip to the house in sixty hours by my count. In fact, she had some loose connection in a kitchen thing that he tackled and fixed, while we stood by in utter amazement and watched. Well, he is an engineer.

"Coffee?"

"Sure, thanks. Black."

He seemed relaxed and content to stay put for awhile. It was just fine with me. I was getting shaky again and needed some time. I went into the garden and picked a few daisies while he and TJ had some time to get better acquainted. I was happy about that. After all, she had been made a party to this whole

## A Small Flirtation

shenanigan—unwittingly, at first. It had been a lark, now it was rapidly turning serious.

It was still great fun. Lots of laughter and good-natured teasing. I was the only one who seemed to be affected by nerves.

"We're off. TJ, thanks for being my pal. I've had the time of my life. I'll be seeing you again, I know." Paul held her hand in both of his.

"Anytime. You're welcome. There's always coffee on the stove and wine in the fridge. Come by."

"Thanks, darling." I said. "As always, I've loved every minute of it. Come up soon with the pooch. Max will be leaving, and with Nicky gone already, the house well be very empty and very big." I waved out of the car window as we drove away.

There we were again; in the little red car, again; holding hands, again.

"I want to show you my favorite view of San Francisco. What kind of shoes are you wearing?" He looked down.

"I've got walking shoes in my suitcase. Why?"

"Want to climb a bit?"

"Sure, where?"

He pulled over near the viewpoint and then swung across to the road that leads up the mountain behind the bridge. I was twisting around to see the view.

"Just wait. We're almost there."

He parked the car off the road and came around to give me his hand and pulled me out. He fished out my shoes and I wobbled my way into them. In the meantime, he had opened his attaché case and extracted a Polaroid camera and was, unbeknownst to me at the moment, taking pictures of me.

"Don't you dare!" I lunged for the camera. He backed up laughing, waved me off and took another one.

"Who's the photographer around here, anyway?"

He pulled out the last one and lined them up on a rock: Me, taking off my shoes. Me, wiggling into shoes. Me, grabbing for the camera. I looked happy. I was happy. Happy, with a thin overlay of uncertainty and apprehension.

"See what I have now? I've captured you—my real life fantasy come true." He opened his arms and I walked in. "I want to kiss you."

I did. He did. We were ready for much more. Some young hikers and bikers were watching and nodding and laughing with approval.

"Gives me hope." One darling youngster called to us, saluted and waved with thumbs up.

You bet, and hope springs eternal. We waved back and kissed some more. He held my face and stared into my eyes and brushed my cheek with his finger tips; then a tiny kiss and let me go.

"Come on with me, just over that rise over there. Now stop and close your eyes. I'll guide. Careful. Step to the left. Now, open."

"Good Lord!" I was speechless. We were standing above the bridge looking across the Bay at the city, the islands, the boats. As far as the eye could see was beauty. It was hard to believe I'd never seen this view before. I had often wondered about that road, but never investigated it.

"OK, that's enough for this time." He was pulling me away. "One day I'll plan better and we'll have a picnic up here."

"What a splendid idea. Call ahead and I'll meet you."

"No you won't, Jenny. I'll come across and fetch you right and proper. One day, you'll see." He was wistful for just a moment.

We left our magic place.

We talked and talked as we drove across my gorgeous bridge into Marin County on the way to Larkspur. Throughout lunch we kept up the mad pace of talk, stumbling over each other's words, eager to learn more of each other's daily lives. I told him about my house. It's on the coast side of the road up on a bit of a rise. I, too, had a sensational view even on misty, foggy days . . . sand dunes and grasses, with a cultivated garden in the courtyard.

Wool pants, a thick sweater and walking shoes were my early morning uniform. I'd keep something hot in the studio—soup or tea, sometimes coffee to have after my walk. Then came work. Drafting new ideas, talking over progress with clients, etc. Music on, humming—a happy and thoroughly satisfying life.

As I started to ask Paul about his daily life, he said, "Tell me about your work, your photography. I want to know everything—about the double images and double exposures you mentioned before. Do they apply to life as well as photography?" Paul sounded eager, inquisitive.

"I've always been fascinated by the juxtaposition of image on top of image, and so I played with them endlessly for a time. In the good old days it was easy to make the mistake of double exposures."

He nodded. "Sure. Simply become distracted and forget to advance the film."

"Yes, it was as simple as that. But now, today's cameras make it virtually impossible to do it. I have, in fact, kept a very old, very small Olympus for that reason. I can click away to my heart's content and double and triple expose on purpose for the fun of it. Sometimes I even get something worthwhile."

He smiled and kept urging me to talk on while he watched me intently, as though he was absorbing the very look and the sound of me. And so I went on, all the while observing him observing me.

"I remember my first day in a darkroom alone. I remember so well what a thrilling time that was. Discovery every day. Have you ever worked in a darkroom?" I asked.

"No."

"I've never lost my fascination for the place. It's also a perfect socially acceptable place to hide from an intrusive world. Many days I've emerged with a stack of fresh prints only to encounter an annoyed dog (She's truly the soul of patience.) and an already dark house. It had been bright and sunny when I entered with my sandwich and soup on a tray."

"You stay at it all day? Really?"

" I do try to break every couple of hours, take a walk outside, get some fresh air and leave the darkroom door open so it can air out. It's much safer in the long run and better for one's work."

"You mean the business of falling in love with your own work?" Paul queried. "I know that syndrome well."

And so the luncheon continued. We lingered over coffee. We both were suddenly deflated—subdued.

"I don't want to let you go. This has been the most wonderful time I've had in years." He reached for my hand.

"Wonderful and sobering," I answered.

"How's that?"

"I don't quite believe it's happened . . ."

"Happening."

"OK. Happening. But what was it? Just one of those things, or something much more?" I stopped and stared for a moment. "Only time will tell, Stranger."

He looked sober. "Stranger. How strange that sounds when I already feel so much, and feel I know so much." He guided me out of the restaurant and to his car. As always, we drove holding hands. We embraced in the bright sunlight in the parking lot at the ferry dock as though no one else were around. So far it hadn't occurred to either one of us that we were being seen.

"By the way, didn't you say you live in Stinson Beach?" Another 180° shift away from what we were both feeling so intensely. "Isn't Tiburon closer than Larkspur?"

"You're right. It is. But there's no long term parking in Tiburon. It's all a bit confusing, I'm sure; but, you see, my car needed some work and so my mechanic took care of it while I was in Chicago and then left it in the long term parking lot for me to pick up when I got back. Ergo, Larkspur."

"You're right, girl. It's confusing, but I think I can sort it out from here: You shuttled from the mechanic to SFO airport, I grabbed you up and spirited you off to TJ's upon your return, relieving you of taxiing or shuttling to her for the week-end..." I was nodding and laughing, "And now, with me bringing you here, you didn't have to hassle the shuttle again, right?"

"Perfectly right. Wasn't that clever of me? Plus, I might add, a great lunch."

"And a longer time for me to be with you."

"Right, again. And a longer way to the airport to pick up your wife." I was reminding myself that he was married.

"Yes, and I'm going to need every bit of the time to calm myself and be ready to greet her at the gate."

"I imagined you would."

"What? Need the time to compose myself?"

"Yes, that too. But I was referring to your meeting her at the gate. I simply presumed you wouldn't meet her at the curb outside of baggage. I was right; it's not your style."

"I like being met myself, although it doesn't often happen. I guess, that's why I do it." A shrug and a hug goodbye.

"I'll be in touch very soon." And so we parted, reluctantly.

He turned back once more and strode over to me. "Jenny, we need to be together again. At least, I need to be with you." His manner was very sober.

"With your wife back, Paul, I don't know how you'll make it happen." I was losing my cool rapidly. I really didn't want to let him go either.

"It's not your worry, Jen. It's up to me to make it happen. And believe me, I will. You just have to be willing to continue our adventure. You simply have to say yes."

"Yes." Another embrace and we parted.

It was going to be tough, really tough to sort all of this out—impact, ramifications, raw emotions, deep feelings—the future. Was there to be one for us?

# 5

On the way home, I thought of what all I'd told Paul and wondered if the life I described sounded lonely and isolated. I told him about my life at Stinson Beach—how and why it worked for me.

I told him about Max, and how he comes up from school to visit, launder clothes, bum a meal and take 'mother cares' packages back to his digs: about our great and sometimes rowdy conversations. Max, quoting from the Greeks—Heraclitus, Thucydides, even Herodotus; how I'm much happier and at ease with the likes of C.G. Jung and C.M. Rilke and that the older I get, the more I understand them both and take comfort in their writings.

More and more I just "live the questions" and understand more deeply Jung's statement "the story of a life begins somewhere at some particular point we happen to remember; and even then it was already highly complex."

All in all, I said, I have been content—more than at any time in the last ten years. I didn't explain that further. In reality, I felt it was unnecessary if not inappropriate at this stage. There would be time during this time of discovery—if there is to be time.

It has taken all of these years to even contemplate another relationship for nothing could have prepared me for the collision with reality I experienced when my husband Tom was killed. Now, a stranger has insinuated himself into my life, and I have let him do it. Now what? Now I'm unsettled—maybe unnerved is a better word. My well ordered life has just had another trauma.

I realized I was already planning to see Paul again. I needed to pull myself together. I may not have had to face a husband, but I did have to face a very intuitive, grown son who knows me well.

I turned on the radio to try to drown out my thoughts. I snapped it off. I didn't want to drown out my thoughts. They were too exciting. I pushed the problems that were only too apparent to the back of my mind. I'd deal with those issues later. Better still, he'd deal with them later. And I simply wallowed in the sheer excitement and enjoyment of the past few days.

Max and Honey, my golden retriever, greeted me "You're just in time. Honey and I are going for a walk. Care to join us and tell us what's been going on in your life?"

I was startled out of my skin. What was he feeling? Or was it just me?

"No thanks, dear. I've already had a walk with TJ and Poochie. I'll just get unpacked and unwind a bit. Are we having dinner together?"

"Sure. I'll barbecue lamb chops. Thought you'd like them and corn on the cob, OK?"

He gave me a companionable hug with one arm as he lifted my bag out of the car. I watched as he and the dog trotted away and was filled with the simple joy of being with him. What a really nice young man, this son of mine.

I certainly did need some time to myself. I hadn't realized just how deeply immersed I was in my fantasies until Max said he wanted to know what had been going on. I really over reacted inside.

I almost told him! That was to be the hardest part. Not telling anyone. Thank God for TJ. At least I would be able to 'carry on' about this crazy thing with her.

Try as I did, my innards were still shaken up. Paul was the answer to all my dreams. Or so it seemed. I'd sent a message to the universe to find him. I had failed to add to my list of requisites that he be available.

Later, Max and I cooked and ate and talked. Fortunately for me, he had lots to tell me about the coming year, giving me time to refocus and to concentrate on him. He's an assistant professor. Classics are his field. He's ruggedly handsome with a shock of unruly golden-red hair, has winning ways and is as bright as hell. He is also a twin. His 'older brother' Nick is at MIT in Boston. Max, the classicist—Nick, the engineer, what a great pair. I'm also biased.

I had told TJ he wasn't returning to Santa Clara for another two weeks. Now it sounded like he was leaving in a few days.

"I've had a chance to lease a small house, Jen, and I think it makes sense." Whenever one of my sons calls me "Jen" it either means something important is to be said, or, I'm about to be teased. In either case it's a signal to pay attention.

"Tell me more. I've a feeling you have a plan."

He launched into a description of his deepening relationship with his best girl, Bridget. They had been talking about living together—giving it a try—then when the house came on the market, they took it as a portent of good things and decided to take the plunge. And, by the way, what did I think?

"I think TJ will be thrilled that you two are looking at signs of support from the universe." We both got a laugh out of that as I was right on target. "Seriously, Max, you two seem up for this next step. I say go for it."

"I knew you'd feel that way. It's just good to have you say so."

"It's even better to be asked. Speaking of asking, what does Nick think?"

I knew without asking the boys had spoken. They talk about everything. They are extremely close—never mind being three thousand miles apart. Before I studied about twins, I was under the misapprehension that, as they are fraternal not identical, they might be totally different and not be as close. In the case of my sons, not so.

"He's all for it, as you might expect. After all, he and Diane have been together about six months now, isn't it? You know he wouldn't want his baby brother walking around free as a bird for much longer. Now would he?"

It was a family joke. Nicky always lorded it over his twin that he was born seventeen minutes before Max, thus becoming Big Brother.

"It may sound a bit trite; however, I am very happy about you boys and your special women."

"I wish you'd let yourself find some nice guy, Jen. You don't even try." How did the conversation take such a turn? "You live a very encapsulated life. Nick and I have talked about it—especially, with both of us kind of settling down. Well, we just thought it would be nice for you, too."

"My life may seem encapsulated, Max, but it isn't insulated and isolated. That would be awful."

"I know, M'am. You have your work and us, the rest of the family and friends and, of course, Honey and the house, but...I don't know, sometimes your sons worry about you"

He did have a kind of worried, turned inside sort of look—very dear, very touching. I assured him my life, while routinized, is not dull and pedantic—that I've become content.

"I still don't see how you can ever meet anyone up here being so isolated."

"You'd be surprised!" I said over my shoulder as I got up to clear the table "Anyway, be assured, should the right man appear, he'll whistle and I'll hear." He chuckled at that one.

We sat outside wrapped in a comfortable silence watching the beautiful summer sunset. I was left to think of my stranger and how he looked, looking at me in the soft last light of the sun, just three days earlier. I shivered slightly. Max noticed.

"Someone walk on your grave, Jen?"

"No, just a summer shiver. The temperature drops as quickly as the sun." That, too, was true.

We spent the rest of the evening talking about Bridget and their plans. "Can you come down next week and see the house?"

"And help you move? Just kidding!" I laughed, so pleased to be included in this new phase of life Max was entering. "I'd love to and I will take a load of your stuff from here if you'd like me to."

"Great! Listen, Jen, I don't want you to feel abandoned. I mean, if we don't come up as often as I have before...It's just with Nick so far away, I don't know, it kind of bothers me"

"Sounds like you're suffering a little bit of separation anxiety yourself, my boy. You'll get over it and so will I. You can still order 'Mother cares' packages. I'll even deliver sometimes!"

"Honestly, Jen, I really am excited about all this; but, I'm also a bit apprehensive. What if it doesn't work? That would be awful."

"Certainly not pleasant but not the end of the world either. You'd chalk it up as another life experience. But don't dwell on the possibility of a failed relationship. Personally, I'd rather be excited together about this grand new adventure for you two."

I stood up and gave him a quick pat and a little hug. I seemed to have hugged quite a lot this weekend.

"Listen, old boy, I'm going to call it a day—or a week or whatever. See you in the morning, OK? Don't forget to lock up"

"Good night. M'am. Sweet dreams"

"You too, son. Good night."

He wished me sweet dreams as we always do. Tonight I hoped I could sleep at all. Thoughts of Paul were making my head swirl. I finally decided to call him in hopes he, not his wife, would answer the phone. But then what? What was I to say—'Oh, hello'?

And if she answered—'Sorry, wrong number'? For sure, I was losing it. Finally, I jumped into bed and pulled the covers over my head and laughed out loud. What a moronic idea. I was thinking like a pre-adolescent with a crush on the school jock!

# 6

Breakfast at my house when either of my sons is there is a ritual. Out of the fridge come eggs and butter, milk, orange juice (freshly squeezed), yogurt, Bisquick and bacon. Then granola, raisins, sliced bananas and anything else that isn't tied down.

Honey stands at attention; surely she'll have something more than two large milk bones with Max around. Poor thing, never gets anything extra! Golden Retrievers have a way of bringing their brows together and up in the middle in such a pathetic way. Of course, they can't maintain that sorrowful demeanor for long. They are far too sweet natured and happy. I managed a glass of juice, some coffee and nibbled on a biscuit.

"What's up, Jen? Did you eat too much while you were away?"

"Not really. I'll eat more when I get back from the gym. By the way, how long will you be staying before heading south?"

"Oh, a day or so. I want to check out the house and the lease again, but I'm ninety percent certain we'll take it. Why? Do you need me for something?"

"No, no. Just an idle question. I will plan to come down when you're ready to have me haul things. Just give me a day or two notice. OK? Well, I'm off. Will I see you later?"

"I'll be here. So long."

I don't know when I'd worked out harder at the gym. My trainer was impressed.

"A few days away and you're really whipping along. What's inspired you?"

"Oh, I just felt like it's time to move on up the scale of my development. Can't let things go slack."

What silly small talk. I really wanted to tell him the truth: I've met this extraordinary man and I don't want an extra ounce on me anywhere. Never mind the old tired "she's broad where a broad should be broad." I've never settled for "letting go" and excusing it because I'm over fifty and single. I'm fortunate that, by nature, I'm slim. Of course, with enough over indulgences when I'm on the road working, even that can change.

Concentration and focus have always been strong points of mine. Single minded effort—put on blinders and just stick to the task at hand. Well, so much for that. I couldn't concentrate on anything worth a damn.

I lived and relived the past days. Over and over I sought to gain some insight, some message from it all. What was I to learn? Or was it all just the proverbial cosmic joke? I kept coming back to that: Here's your perfect mate, your true other half. Oops, sorry—look, but don't touch—he's not available.

I had to sit on my hands to keep from reaching for the phone, especially after my near miss Sunday night. I heard nothing and the days were slipping by. Hadn't he said, "I'll be in touch"? Yes, but he didn't say when. He couldn't have meant all he said and did and then have a sudden attack of remorse? Or could he? And seeing Kathy? Back to his reality.

I was slowly becoming obsessed and embarrassed at the same time. I was convinced I'd made a fool of myself playing around with Paul and this was the pay-off. No contact. What was I thinking of? A total stranger picked me up on a plane. We had some fun and now I'm ready to serve myself up to him on a platter. Thank God I hadn't.

I was being whipped-sawed by conflicting emotions. Paul had dropped sexy innuendoes about coming up to my house because he had the whole night—no mistaking the message in that—or about the console in the car being in the way and on and on. I had flirted with the idea of suggesting a quiet place in Larkspur for a couple of hours of love-making instead of lunch; but I had held back, not wanting this to turn into nothing more than a happenstancial week-end fling.

Fortunately for my peace of mind, Max kept me busy as he and I went through things I'd kept in storage for him.

These last few days I've been more than grateful that he's been here. Good humor and good company, a winning combination—plus a distraction as I waited for the phone to ring. And now my son is ready to leave.

"You'll be having Thanksgiving here, won't you?" he asked. "Aren't Nick and Diane planning to come?"

"Oh sure. Of course. I'll just be working steadily on the Smithsonian project until then."

"The one on the migrating waterfowl?"

"Yes. I'll be doing the north-west section of North America."

Max looked surprised, "So you did get the assignment? That's great! I didn't know."

"I was sure I told you."

"You must have told Nick twice."

We both laughed at that old one. It used to happen all the time when they were growing up and, obviously, it was still happening. We finished loading his van. I was having a terrible tug at my heart. And yet, I was sincerely pleased. It was 'appropriate timing', as my mother would have said.

She would have been so proud of her grandsons. How she loved them. They were 'her boys.' And they adored her. She died when they were fourteen. They were bereft. Now they are twenty-eight—half a lifetime later, and their memories of her are as vivid as if she were still alive. For me, too.

What a waste—to have died so young. All that grace and beauty and talent. We have all felt deprived. Another reason for my strong belief in reincarnation. She had to move to a higher plane. Her work here was complete. We, who were left, felt very incomplete. We all speak of her and quote her often—her legacy of immortality to all of the family.

"You're looking pensive, M'am. You OK?"

"Yes, just thinking of your grandmother for a moment. It's times like these that she seems so close at hand."

"I wish she were, Jen, for me and Nick, and for you, too."

"Well, you get going now, kiddo. You've a bit of a drive. Give my fond regards to Bridget. Tell her I'm excited for both of you. And let me know when you need me down there."

"You can count on it. Probably within the next couple of weeks. I'll give you plenty of notice."

"Anyway, get going, now. Drive carefully. I love you, Max."

"Me too, Jen," in a serious voice. "I'll see you soon."

# 7

He called on day five—Friday. T.G.I.F. "I couldn't wait any longer to hear from you. Can you talk?"

Oh God, he sounded good. "Yes, I can talk," but I could hardly breathe.

"Your son. I didn't know if you wanted me to call while he's home. I forgot to ask, and so I waited, hoping I'd hear from you."

His tone revealed so much, I winced.

"Oh no, and I was afraid that you'd come to your senses."

"What?"

"You know . . . had a change of heart."

"No. Never. Why'd you think I'd do that?"

"Oh, a large dose of reality setting in, I guess. Something like that." I shrugged mentally.

"You're very real. I can attest to that. In fact, I want to test that again, soon."

He wasn't going to get into the other subject. Not now. Not over the phone. He was right of course. We'd have to face that but not now, not so soon. Right now it was premature.

"Speaking of reality, I want to do some testing myself," I said.

"Tell me more. Do I sense the beginnings of a plan?"

"Half formed, but yes."

"When will the other half be formed?" he asked.

"When you agree to the first half, I guess."

"Which is?"

"I'll be in Santa Clara with my son, Max, for a few days, soon. From there I'll return to pick up TJ and the dogs before heading back up here."

"The dogs? Is that plural? She acquired another one this week?"

"No, I'll be dropping Honey off with her and continue on. Max is moving and Honey's useless at such times. That's the first half of my plan."

"The second half I can come up with in a flash. I'll meet you at TJ's and we'll have dinner, at least. Will TJ mind if I spirit you off for a few hours?"

"Did she mind before she ever knew you? I hardly think she'd object now. Anyway, she'll be busy herself packing up a few things for her and Poochie."

"No, no," he said, "my plan is to meet you at TJ's on your way to Max—that's the first half. Then, And then I'll meet you at TJ's again when you stop to get her and the dogs on your way back. That's the second half," he explained.

"You're way ahead of me, mister. But then, you always were in all of our lifetimes together."

"Yeah. That's just the way I like it, too. Ahead of you, around you, as long as it's with you."

"There you go again, saying all the right things." A light self-conscious laugh.

"I told you the other night—I've practiced these conversations in my head for years."

"So they're just lines." A flat statement.

"You know better. They're what we both said we wanted to be. Honest. Open and honest." His voice was firm.

"You're right. No games. No subterfuge. I'm just not used to it yet."

"I'm being straight, lady."

"Yes." I agreed.

"And you're guarded a little." Not a question.

"I'll practice, " I assured him.

"Great."

"I'm very glad you called. I was beginning to stew,"

"Don't do that. Just call, anytime." He sounded enthusiastic, so upbeat. I was beyond pleased. Well beyond. I was so relieved; if I were the crying kind, I think I would have. Again, so easy, so real, so thrilling to experience this kind of a man. I shocked myself with the depth of my excitement.

"And you mustn't feel inhibited," I told him. "Feel free to call whenever. I do hear from friends. Even if someone else answers. You'll think of a message and some name, so I'll know."

"And as I said, anytime is OK. There's no problem here. Please call anytime." Emphatic.

"You, too." We were repeating ourselves.

"I will. Talk to you soon. And Jenny, it's so good to hear your voice."

# 8

The days flew by. Admittedly, not fast enough to suit me. I walked around in a kind of miasma thick with thoughts of Paul. I wanted to phone him constantly just to hear his voice. Luckily, my less emotional self saved me. I had a surprise planned for him and could hardly wait to start working on it.

There was more research to do on my new project, too. I'd done some preparatory work prior to seeking the assignment. Now I was feeling so great, so energetic. The work flowed freely and easily.

Back to my surprise. I drove to the city without letting anyone know. Did what I had to do. Bought supplies and began. It was such fun. I felt excited—girlish. Just thinking about what his reaction would be kept me working until the wee small hours. Romantic music playing, humming along. I hadn't had so much fun in years either. Honey was disgruntled. She never really settles down for the night until I do. She kept handing me her paw. When that didn't work, she'd bring her toys out of her nighttime basket. Finally—the ultimate demand. One impatient WOOF!

"All right, Honey. You have more sense than I do. I'm coming, and I promise we'll have a good romp on the beach in the morning to make up for all of this."

And we did. It was a glorious day. After breakfast Honey and I got in the Jeep and went to market—minimally. We were about to head south in a day or so.

The phone was ringing as I was unloading the groceries. "Hello."

"I love your 'Hello'. The way you say it, it's a four syllable word." Paul was laughing.

"Four syllables?"

"Hel-oh-oh-oh. I've just heard it twice in a row and I'm right."

"Twice?"

"I didn't leave a message. I called a few minutes ago and someone came into my office just as your machine went 'beep', so I hung up. Where have you been?"

"Out with Honey running errands. Nothing terribly exciting. What's up?"

"That's why I'm calling. What's up? When are you coming down? Tomorrow or Thursday?"

"Thursday. Is that OK? I mean is tomorrow better? I could push and do it."

"No. Not necessary. No need to push. I just want to firm up my plans at this end. What time do you plan to get to TJ's?"

"I'll finally finish up here around noon, grab a quick bite and head on down."

"That should bring you to Sea Cliff by 2:00 or 2:30."

"Absolutely. And you?"

"As soon as I can. Early. Around 4:00. I hope. Maybe earlier. I want us to have as much time together as possible."

"Sounds good to me."

"I also thought we might have corned beef and cabbage again with TJ. What do you think of that idea? We'll have Monday to ourselves without feeling too selfish."

"She'd never think that. When you know her better, you'll see. Anyway, she says we're a thousand giggles. You must know she's a terrible romantic."

"Outstanding!"

"I'm anxious to see you. I have a surprise for you, too."

"A surprise? What kind of a surprise?"

"A surprise. I'm sure you'll be pleased."

"I am already."

"Well, back to work." We were both reluctant to hang up.

The phone rang again as I was finishing putting things away. This time it was Nick.

"Mom, Hi!" I'm glad I caught you."

"Oh, hello dear. It's been ages. How's everything in Boston? How's Diane?"

"We're great. How about you? Max tells me you're heading down to Santa Clara in a couple of days."

"That's right. I'm about to put some of his things in the Jeep."

"Well, we haven't talked since he and Bridget sprang the news of their moving in together. We think it's great. How about you?"

"Of course, I do, too. I haven't disapproved of you guys since you went to the midnight movies in high school and didn't show up at home until 3:00 a.m."

"Boy, you sure do have a long memory. I thought you'd forgotten about that by now."

"Never, my boy. Wait until you have children of your own. Those things you don't forget, along with first words and the first night of sleeping dry." We both laughed at that one.

"Seriously, Jen, what I really want to say is, Max and I have been talking about you."

"You guys, really . . . I . . ."

"Don't protest. We know you've got a lot going on in your life, but we also know there are big changes going on within the family and we've been wondering if you're alright with all of it? Max told me you seem a bit tense and somewhat distracted, lately."

"There is a lot going on, for sure, but I'm really fine, Nicky.

Maybe it's that you're both more focused on women's reactions now that you have each made a commitment. Have you thought of that?"

"Maybe so. That is a thought. But that doesn't alter the fact that we care a lot about you, specifically."

"Nicky, dear…"

"OK. I'll drop the subject for now. What's next in the work department? Have you started on the bird project yet?"

"I'm doing more research now and will begin to plot and map the whole course soon. Guy and I'll go north first and then follow the route to Morro Bay and on south. We should be finished with the rough shooting by Thanksgiving and complete before December 15$^{th}$. Listen, dear boy, I've really got to run. I'm on my way to Max now. I love you, Nick and thanks" My sons were being perceptive and I was dodging the real issue like mad.

# 9

We piled into the car—Honey and I—and hit the road. She, of course, liked nothing better. We had two rules for being in the car: One, if she wanted to sit up front in the passenger seat, she had to wear her seat belt. Two, no head hanging out the window on the freeway. It was worth being compliant. This was special time together, and we both enjoyed it.

The ride down to the city was beautiful. End of summer, a hint of fall in the light. My favorite season to shoot outdoors. Oh, lush spring and summer have their own appeal as does barren winter and snow, but somehow I'm partial to September. Maybe it's because it's my natal month.

We arrived in Sea Cliff as planned around 2:30. The dogs were happy to see each other. So were TJ and I.

"What time is our new friend arriving?"

"He'll call when he's on his way. Sometime around 4:00," I answered.

"Perfect. That gives us some time to talk before he gets here. How about an iced coffee?"

We went out on the terrace with our glasses, got comfortable and sat in silence for a few moments enjoying the view.

"I never tire of it. I love the series you did from here for me last year; a real treasure." TJ smiled.

"Speaking of series, I've just had the best time. I've made an album for Paul."

"You must really be smitten! I mean to have completed a series in this length of time. Or are they works from your own collection?"

"No, wait till I tell you."

"Can't I see them?"

"Of course." I got up to fetch the album and answer the ringing phone. "Hello."

"You're there already? Great! It's Paul."

"Oh, hi. When will you be here?"

"Can't say exactly. I'd hoped to get away early, but there's been a meeting called for 3:00. Should be a short one and I'll be on my way immediately. I'm clearing off my desk now."

"We'll be here. Don't worry. Get here when you can."

"Is my surprise there?"

"You bet," I laughed. "Can't wait to see your face."

"You'll see it soon. Have you mentioned corned beef and cabbage to TJ? Is she available?"

"I haven't yet. I really just got here, but I'll do it as soon as I hang up."

"What will you do as soon as you hang up?" TJ was walking in from the terrace.

"Paul wanted to know if corned beef and cabbage is on your agenda for tonight? He wants a repeat of last week."

"Sure you don't want to be alone?"

"I think it'll be more fun to be together."

"Safety in numbers?" She looked amused.

"Maybe. Something like that. Funny thing is he sounded nervous just now, and I'm feeling reasonably relaxed for the first time."

TJ said that it was probably true. She pointed out that Paul was at his office surrounded by his colleagues and staff. People he's known well and who've known him well over a period of years. And now he was going to have to cover his tracks. For the first time according to him.

"And he's about to see you. That in itself could make him anxious. It's like you said it's reality-testing time for each of you. And, yes, I'd love to have corned beef and cabbage tonight. I'll retire to my end of the house early, and you can have some time together—alone."

We went back outside. I laid the boxed album on the table. TJ was hovering. "Open it up already. I'm dying to see what you've done."

"Look!"

The cover page was the map Paul drew our circuitous route on. She turned one page after another.

"The airport baggage area, telephone, the parking lot, Golden Gate Park . . ." She continued turning the pages.

"What do you think?" I was anxious for approval.

"He's going to flip! Your work is beautiful, Jen. That alone will please him. The subject matter is icing on the cake." I was delighted with her reaction. "I still don't know when you found the time to do it all and by the way, have you given any thought to where he'll stash this rather over-sized object?"

"Ask Honey about the timing. She'll tell you. I worked all night and she didn't like it." We laughed as I tied it with raffia and dried seagrass. "As for stashing, Paul will think of something. He has Polaroid's of me so they will probably go into the same place—presumably not in his sweater drawer."

"Tell me, ten days later, does it still seem so impossible? That it's happened, I mean. Love at first sight?" TJ was watching me closely.

She's always had the ability to look into someone's eyes with such penetration, I swear she sees into one's soul.

"I can't answer that question yet. Maybe after tonight and Monday, I'll be closer to an answer. Maybe I won't. You know, TJ, it's too easy to call it love at first sight and then act on it in a way we might be sorry for in the long run." I shook my head, "I really don't know yet."

She was still quiet, and then said in a very serious tone, "I still think you two are coming to grips with an ancient memory scenario remake. Call it what you will. I, for one, say enjoy it, treasure it and don't, for God's sake, talk it to death!"

"How come you're so damn smart? That's precisely what I've been worrying about. How to 'play' it, and I don't mean 'play-act' it."

"Just be the real person you are. You don't have to dwell on the handicap to this relationship; that's not your responsibility. It's his."

"But, TJ," I interrupted, "he is married…"

"I know. I also know you're no home wrecker, nor are you a back street wife type. So far, this has been light-hearted and amusing. If you look ahead too much and have misgivings, well then I say give it up. Otherwise, why don't you simply play along with it? Don't be premature about dealing with heavy life-choice issues, at this point, Jenny. They may never come up. Wait and see."

"How'd you get so smart?"

"It's an accumulation of knowledge from all those lifetimes."

"What's happened to my 'accumulated' knowledge?"

"It's in a different field! I don't know about you, but I'm getting cleaned up a bit. Before you know it, your knight-in-shiny-red-sports-car will be arriving. At least, I want to be ready." She moved off toward her room, leaving me standing in the hall.

He arrived at 4:15, along with the cooling afternoon sea breeze.

I watched him unfold from the car, straighten his jacket after buttoning it and reach back inside for something. He emerged with a bunch of Gerbera daisies. I was very excited to see him.

*A Small Flirtation* | 63

"The Gerberas are beautiful, thank you." I reached for them, but he drew his hand back.

"They're not for you; they're for TJ for being my new best pal." He presented them to her and planted a kiss on her cheek at the same time.

"Well for heaven's sake; how nice. These and corned beef and cabbage, too. I'm overcome. Want a drink? Help yourself while I put these pretty things in water."

"Here, this is for you." Paul drew out a small package from his pocket and handed it to me with a smile.

It was a gold pin—a cowboy with a thin twisted gold lariat. I was speechless. I looked up at him and back at the pin. "Thank you. It's wonderful," was all I could muster.

"Let me pin it on you. You now have your cowboy with you everyday. Do you like it?"

"I'm overcome. It's perfect."

"TJ told me your birthday's coming up soon and . . . well, you'll see. I don't telegraph my surprises—the way others do. Now, where's mine?"

He ripped off the paper, took the album out of the box and opened it. He saw the map first and started turning the pages. "I don't believe this! It's fantastic!"

"It was great fun to do."

"When in the world did you find the time to shoot all these?"

"I asked the same question. She had to have worked day and night," TJ said.

"I was motivated." I was delighted, too.

"I'm very pleased. It's impressive, Jenny. Your work is outstanding—sensitive and intelligent, not just pretty and sentimental."

A rave review would not have made me happier. My surprise gift to him was a four star hit. And I was overwhelmed by his surprise, his gift.

This newly founded friendship was moving along at a fair clip.

We jammed ourselves into the car and went off to dinner early.

We settled in the booth with our beers and awaited the steaming plates of succulent food.

"Jenny, I'm knocked out by your work, and touched beyond words at the amount of time and effort you put into my gift. The only thing missing . . ."

"Is what?"

"The pictures I took of you."

"How perfectly appropriate, and then TJ can take one of the two of us, and we'll add it to make the perfect coffee table book!" We were laughing again. TJ didn't join in as much as she had been doing. I was to reflect on that later. All through dinner she was observing us.

We were getting silly over nothing—drunk on happiness, just being together. Nothing much of note was said, if I recall correctly. We just had fun. We returned to TJ's. It was still early, but true to her word, she started to excuse herself. Paul stopped her.

"I'm going to take this girl out for a coffee," he said as he picked up his gift. "This goes into my 'eyes only' file tomorrow under lock and key."

"What a great idea. See you guys later."

"That was a swift move." I fell into the car. "Graceful as the bird they call the elephant, my grandmother would have said."

"I'll have to teach you how to do that more easily. I'm 6'4", and if I can do it; you should be able to."

"I can use all the help I can get."

"I sensed you were willing to go out for a bit. I don't usually just swoop people up without asking first."

"Yes, I was willing. And yes, I believe you do. I have experienced it! It's good just to be with you, Paul. The last two weeks have been murderously busy."

"Busy and difficult for me, Jenny. My head has been

everyplace but at work. You can't imagine how you've affected my life already. I want to be with you all the time. I know it's crazy; I know we've just met and, yes, I know I'm married."

"That's the hardest part, Paul, everything else about us is so easy...everything but that." I shook my head, "I can't bring myself to tell you how I feel, not the way you can. When we're together you seem so at ease...so comfortable. I don't know how you do it."

Paul said nothing. He merely let me get it all out "You're ready to take me off to bed and without a thought of afterward...consequences...whatever. I want to, too, Paul. I'm simply not able to—at least not yet." I stopped, caught my breath and plunged on: "Adulterer has a nasty ring to it and until I'm willing to accept that fact..."

"No, Jenny, please don't do that to yourself." He thought a moment and then went on, "It all seemed so harmless—a small flirtation, a few hours of light hearted fun and suddenly everything about it has changed. You're right, I do want to make love to you—now—tonight."

"Paul, I..."

"It's OK Jenny, I understand."

I was very silent. I'm not sure what that means—'very silent'. Silent is silent! How much more noiseless can you be than silent? Still, I was very silent.

He continued, "You wouldn't be here if you weren't single, would you?"

"No,no, I wouldn't be."

He let go of my hand in order to park the car. He didn't get out immediately. Instead, he turned to me and said, "I didn't think so. Jenny, can we continue like this? See each other from time to time? Stay in touch? Keep it light? And enjoy each other in ways that don't make you uncomfortable?"

"I hope so, Paul. I'd hate to have to let go of you now, so soon, without more time."

"Then let's do it! And not let anything spoil it." He sounded so young and enthusiastic—and unrealistic.

"It's a deal as long as it doesn't complicate your life or mine. No strings. No promises." I added.

"No expectations beyond friendship."

We were so naive—in our mid-fifties and dreaming like children in a fairy tale. There was something terribly bittersweet in our unspoken wish to love one another. But how could we ever live "happily-ever-after"? We weren't able to touch that or to look beyond the tomorrow of our next meeting. We promised not to hurt anyone, and actually believed we could carry it off.

I had already convinced myself that I wasn't taking anything away from Kathy that she hadn't given away years before. What Paul had to give was all that had been lost in his marriage.

And I'm the one who always has said I didn't like living a life of illusion! Reality was for me. "Keep it light" was to become my mantra for some time to come.

We got out of the car. Paul came around and put his arms around me. He was smiling and tender. He took my face in his hands, smoothed back my hair and just pulled me close. So close I could feel his heart pound.

"Thank you, my Jenny. Thank you. Thank you." He let me go and kissed me on the tip of my nose.

We went off for coffee, spoke of inconsequential things, and yet everything we had said told us something new about the other and seemed to bring us closer together with greater understanding.

He drove us back to the house at Sea Cliff, and glanced at his watch. "I'm terribly sorry, but it's later than I thought, and it's a long ride to Atherton. I hate to say good-bye like this, but I must."

We both felt a sense of disappointment and knew we'd face these moments many, many more times in the future. We were right. We did. More often than I like to remember.

He walked me to the door.

"Please say good night to TJ. Call me. No, I'll call you here in the morning, early, and we'll plan Monday. I'd better be going. Good night, Jenny."

I braced myself for the sense of loss I felt coming. It was crazy to feel it so keenly. We had known each other two weeks.

"Good night my stranger, my fantasy."

We embraced quickly and he left.

Another leave-taking.

TJ was reading in the living room. She hadn't come to the door. She sensed there was a bit of tension.

"Hi, kid. Problems?"

"No, not really. Only the one big problem which will be there always and which I might just as well start to get used to right now if I'm ever going to enjoy this time." I felt disgruntled. "Let's take the dogs out."

It was a brisk night. We let the dogs run ahead a bit and didn't stay out long. We returned to the kitchen, made coffee and settled down by the fire. We weren't back fifteen minutes when the phone rang. TJ looked at me. "Why don't you answer it? It's probably for you."

And it was.

"Hi, M'am." It was Max. I was appalled at my intense disappointment. What is this, anyway? I chastised myself. This is your beloved son. Pull yourself together!

"Max, oh . . . hi, dear. How's it going?"

"Fine, M'am. Bridget and I are plotting the best way to use your talents. How do you feel about taking on the hanging pictures project? Or is that too much of a bus-person's holiday?"

We both chuckled at his use of the politically correct term. I told him I'd love to do anything as long as they hadn't asked me to line cupboards or drawers. He laughed. We talked on for a few minutes more, planned a bit more for the use of my time, and signed off.

"How's my young boyfriend? Sounds like they want you to hang pictures, by your response?"

"Right. I really am flattered; that's no joke. To have your kid appreciate your subjective ability is pretty nifty," I responded.

"I thought it might have been Paul calling from his car," said TJ.

"Are you disappointed?" I said rather haughtily.

"Are you?"

"I hate to admit it—it's so unrealistic, and yes, I am. Here I go again, TJ. I know I'm repeating myself, but I really don't think this is such a good idea. I'll be utterly selfish, and add 'for me.' I'm too drawn to him and to what avail?"

"Jenny, I promised myself I wouldn't say anything about all this, just watch and wait—you've been having such a good time."

"And now?"

"Well, you could say I'm about to break my word to me."

"Speak up TJ. What's on your mind?" I was still unnerved by my confrontation with Paul.

"You just called it 'the one big problem'."

"Yes, that's so...and?"

"We've been together, what is it four times? And I've seen you two move from 'isn't this a kick' to 'where do we go from here?'—from fun and frolic to dead serious. You're acting like a couple of lovesick kids. I've been watching this develop at breakneck speed and, yes, I've had fun too going along with it. But now, tonight, Jenny, it's taken a different turn."

"How so?"

"The carefully crafted gifts for one thing—your album, his pin. Then the frivolity—no sense of responsibility, no caution. You two look like you're heading straight to bed and yet, Jenny, what do you actually know about this man? Nothing. Oh sure, he's got his name on the door of a big engineering firm, but who is *he*?"

"TJ, Paul and I just had a put-on-the-brakes kind of conversation."

"Timely, I'd say."

"Is there more?"

"Yes. The questions that kept bothering me as I observed you tonight were how does he manage the nights out—what's with his wife? Oh, you've shared his stories with me—his explanations about his marriage. Admittedly, they do sound plausible, but they don't give me any answers to my questions. I don't know, Jen, I'm getting a bit uncomfortable in my gut. It's—well, you seem so accepting, too content to go along with everything and be happy when you're with him. Then later, you turn on yourself and question the whole relationship."

"The truth is it isn't even a relationship at this point. We're still very much in the period of discovery," I rejoined.

"True. I'd say slow down until you're past that period, at which point you'll know whether or not you'll want to go further. He is a terribly attractive man, there's no denying it."

We both agreed to that. "He's also very bright and fun to be around," I added.

"Let that be satisfying for now, Jen, The future comes fast enough, as it is. Don't run for it and miss the present on the way."

"Sage advice, TJ. Do you think I'll live long enough to learn that?"

"As it is said, my friend: It takes as long as it takes." TJ looked at her watch. "Hey, it's getting late. I'm going to bed, and I suggest you do, too. Don't stay awake thinking; you know it's bad for you."

This time when I threw a pillow at her, it connected.

"Gosh, you really are still a kid. Come on. I'm turning out the lights."

A fine mist shrouded the area in the morning. The sun had yet to climb high enough to burn it off. It was mysterious and silent. I pulled out a camera and was shooting long before breakfast. A perfect setting for romantic, dream-like shots. Not my usual genre. My black and whites are more stark, more structural. For the moment, my focus was slightly blurry around the edges. That might be said for other areas of my life, as well.

"Thanks for everything, dear. See you sometime Monday."

"Work hard and fast. Get lots done with the young ones, and hurry back. By the way, if you can you stay here an extra day, it would make life simpler for me. Remember, I said I'm busy Monday and Tuesday nights. I really am. Otherwise, I'll catch the shuttle bus Wednesday."

"No, no you won't. I'm in no rush. So plan on it."

"Great. Drive carefully. Tell Max I'm expecting him and Bridget soon. See you Monday."

They were driving up as I pulled into their driveway. Two glorious-looking young people. He, with his shock of unruly golden-red hair—a true strawberry blond; she, a raven-hair, blue-eyed beauty.

The two of them greeted me at the same time. "Welcome, Jenny. Come on in," they chorused.

The house was within a fifteen-minute walk of campus. A not so small, bright bungalow with a rather untended, fixable, sunny garden. Enough room for them to have an office-at-home apiece, and a spacious kitchen-cum-dining room. Altogether pleasant.

"We've been thinking about taking the so-called master-bedroom and making an office for two out of it. What do you think, M'am?" Max is so bright-eyed. I have trouble not grinning like a simpleton at him all the time.

"Why not? If you two think you can get any work done being in the same room."

"Personally, I'll like it better," Bridget said. "That way we'll be in each other's company when we need to work at home, instead of being apart all day and night, too."

"Sure, we can sleep in one of the smaller bedrooms. Make it kind of a cozy space. You know, lots of pillows and maybe my rocking chair. My old small TV doesn't take any space," Max chimed in.

"And we can use all the closets and have a guestroom, too, for you, Nick and Diane, whoever comes to stay," Bridget added.

They were so excited. It was wonderful to see. I envied the simplicity of their relationship.

"It makes at lot of sense to me, too. It really maximizes the use of space. It will give you an extra room and you'll end up feeling less crowded, when people stay over. No giving up one of the offices to accommodate someone and having your work-privacy invaded."

"Exactly what we figured out. Of course, our houseguests will be right next door. But we can be quiet for a few nights." Max was laughing and turning bright red at the same time.

My grown-up son.

After we toured the entire house, we returned to the spare bedroom. Everything unpacked and undecided was there.

"Are you ready to start working? We've got lots to do and it's getting late," Max said.

"Sure. Why don't you show me what you want hung in each room, and I'll start right in? You've already placed your furniture, so it won't be hard."

"Well, Jenny, we're not so sure what of mine goes with Max's, though we do have some ideas."

"That's OK. Just show me the pictures. And after I select what I think will be best in each room, you two will make the final decisions. How's that? By the way, if either of you has any favorites that must be hung regardless, point them out to me now, OK?"

It took me over an hour to make the selections for each room, and by then, it was time to break for lunch.

With only a couple of exchanges, they were satisfied with my choices and placement, and said they'd help me hang them after we ate.

And so it went. Three delightful days. We even had dinner out and went to a "flick" Sunday night. I loved being with them, and reluctantly bade them good-bye the following day.

"Thanks, Jenny. Thanks a lot. It was fun having you here." Bridget gave me a small kiss on the cheek.

"It was more fun for me than you know. You're most welcome."

"Is TJ going up to the beach with you?" Max inquired.

"Yes, and I'm looking forward to her spending the rest of the week with me. Then it's off following the birds. I'll fax you a rough itinerary, and we'll talk before I take off."

"Is Guy working with you on this one?" Max was pressing his point about my solitary life.

"Oh yes, always. At least always for as long as he wants to, and I hope that means 'always'."

They helped me pack the car. Max was sending some things back to the house for awhile longer. I was amused. Seems he hadn't calculated the storage space to include things Bridget was bringing. Typical. Even the best of them. God Bless the gender gap!

"By the way, I forgot to ask about your class at Berkeley this fall."

"I'm covered, Max. I don't have to be back until after the first of the year. Got to go. Stay happy and well. I love you. Bye." It seems I'm always saying good-bye to someone I love.

# 10

Paul had said he'd like me to meet him downtown, but changed his mind when I phoned him from my car. I told him I'd be at TJ's and ready by 4:30. He'd get over as soon as he could after that.

I'd had a truly relaxed time with the kids. I thought about them during the run up the coast. Maybe I had said too much. I didn't want to pre-empt their decision by speaking of the future, and yet I was sincere in my wishes. I was certain they'd marry probably sooner than they thought at the time. My hunch was correct.

The closer I got to San Francisco, the more excited I became. Another evening together. TJ was going out very early. That meant Paul and I would have the entire evening to ourselves. I was excited and nervous again.

My escape from my thoughts was to play a Willie Nelson tape, "Angel Flying Too Close to the Ground." I didn't need that. I fast-forwarded the tape. A duet—Julio and Willie: "Of All the Girls I've Loved Before." I certainly didn't need that one. I flipped on the radio and caught an early broadcast of the "Jim Lehrer News Hour." It was neutral, benign and informative. Exactly what was called for.

TJ and I had a few minutes to talk before she had to leave. "Paul phoned twenty minutes ago."
"Oh?"
"He called to say there was a foul up on some important document that he had the responsibility to unscramble, and he'd get here as fast as he could after he 'unscrews the damn mess,' if I quote him correctly. He didn't sound too happy."
"Any idea how long?"
"Only that he'd hoped to be here by 5:00, and that looked impossible now. He'll call again."
"Damn is right. Oh well, under those conditions, maybe I should make dinner here. What do you think?"
"Not a bad idea and you'll have the entire house to yourselves. Couldn't be all bad," she said with her best innocent smile. "Anyway, it'll keep you occupied until he gets here. You go to the market. I've got time to set the table and feed the dogs."
"Splendid idea. Very smart. Honestly, TJ, I could never have made it in life without you."
"You never have had to. We've been together in one configuration or another for millennia; you well know that."
"Whatever you say, I'm continually grateful to you."
"Give me twenty-five words on the not-so-young and then get going."
"They are simply splendid together. It was joyous to be there with them. The place is very nice, very livable. They'll probably get married soon. I think that's twenty-five."
"I figured as much. Especially as they called you to come down. That's very good news. You are pleased, aren't you?"
"Extremely. They'll be great. I predict it. Well, I'm off. What can I get for you?"
"Some freshly squeezed orange juice and two small lo-fat

yogurts will do the trick. I've got everything else we'll need for a couple of days. Thanks."

"Be right back."

"Any news?" I called out as I carried in the groceries.

"He called not five minutes after you left. Sounded distracted as hell, and asked that you phone him before six at his desk on his private number."

"Anything else?"

"Yes. He'd be here if it was midnight, and to please stay put."

"Where does he think I'll go?"

"It's not specifically where that bothers him, it's the fact of doing it at all. I think he's very in tune with your flight syndrome. Remember that he's witnessed it first hand. Both at the airport and later—much later I might add—here. It's enough to make one tremble." She was laughing, but serious.

"I'll call now and get the suspense over with."

He picked it up on the first ring, "Paul Crowley."

"Paul? It's Jenny. Anything the matter?"

"Plenty, and I'm so frustrated. It's this new assistant of mine, again. He's got to go. I can't have him screwing up like this all the time. Anyway, he's at his computer and should have something for me to see by six." I'd never heard him agitated before. "I'm so sorry, Jenny, I wanted us to have a long, peaceful evening."

"It's OK. We will have a peaceful evening. I'm preparing dinner here"

"Super. I should be there by seven. I'll call when I'm on the way—from the car that is. Right now, I've got to go and breathe down his neck. See you soon." He hung up without further ado.

TJ was being quiet and looking quizzical.

"Everything's OK; just a prolonged foul-up at the office. Paul's new assistant isn't long for this world I'm afraid." I did what I could in the kitchen and was off to take a bath and relax. That would take up some slack and calm me at the same time.

"Mind you, there's a big, thick terry robe in your bathroom

in case you're not dressed in time." TJ's parting shot. She was out the door before I thought of a good answer.

The doorbell rang at exactly 7:07. From the sound of things at the office, I didn't think he had a prayer of getting out of there for hours. The dogs and I greeted him in what was fast becoming the usual way: They, anxious for a pat; we, anxious to be in each other's arms.

He felt so good, so strong, so lean—and lean I did. It had come to feel secure there with my head on his chest. We were developing a little greeting form—we embrace for several moments. He, holding my head against him, and then I, lifting my face up for the kiss.

Tonight was different; we were at home, even if the home was TJ's. I had 'slipped into something more comfortable'—a soft buttery silk blouse in a candlelight color over wide, black silk jacquard palazzo pants. The effect was very good—flattering and fairly seductive. I had wound a very long strand of Biwa pearls around my neck. He took hold of them and very gently pulled us together.

I smiled and backed away from him. "Come on in the kitchen with me. I'm being domestic and I don't want you to miss a single minute of it! Come, have a beer. How do you like your steak? Rare, I hope. I don't know how to fix them any other way."

"Sounds good to me." Small talk. So much small talk. We were safe if we stayed in the realm of the inconsequential.

"More coffee or ice cream or something else?" I asked.

"Jenny, come to me—that's the something else I want." He was serious.

I dropped down beside him on the couch and we all but wrapped around each other immediately. The air was getting thick with passion when I suddenly heard a car door slam. TJ was being brought home. I could hardly sit up we were so tangled up in my Palazzo pants and the long rope of pearls. It would have been hilarious under different circumstances.

I managed somehow to straighten myself, running my fingers through my hair, feeling like a school girl being caught necking on the couch. Which was precisely what was happening.

We looked at each other. I was amused and relieved. Paul was not. Frustration and annoyance were more to his point.

"Well, if I'm not going to be allowed to make love to you, I might just as well go home."

I looked stunned, I guess, because he continued: "I mean it, Jenny. This is no good. I can't do it. I can't just play at making out on the couch. It's impossible. I've said I would keep it light and I'm having a hell of a time keeping my word." He was up, pacing.

"It's awful for me, too, Paul. I'm sorry. I'm fighting a terrible battle within myself."

"I know that, Jenny, and I'm sorry too. Maybe we shouldn't meet here anymore for awhile." I sat in dumbfounded silence. "I don't mean not see each other. I mean meet out in public where this can't happen. At least until we reach a decision. I can pick you up here, but not hang around when TJ's not here. It's . . . it's just too tempting." He sounded miserable and looked worse.

TJ came in with a call to us—in case we hadn't heard her, I suppose—just in case. That made us both laugh and broke the tension.

"Hi, TJ. I'm just leaving."

"Don't let me chase you away."

"No, no. I was so late getting here that I'm later now than I should be. However, I did say I'd help with the clean up. Jenny made a super supper." He was making a valiant effort to return to social conversation.

"No need, Paul, I don't want to spend my last minutes with you elbow deep in sudsy water!"

"Boy, she's really letting you off the hook." TJ was greeting a pair of sleepy dogs and friends who were embarrassingly 'revved up.' "You two have a nice dinner? Jenny's usually a good cook."

"As I said, she made a super supper. By the way, are you two going up to Jenny's tomorrow?"

"No, not until Wednesday. I have a full day and evening here tomorrow."

"How about lunch tomorrow, Jenny. Are you free? I can make myself be. I'm sorry I can't say we'll have dinner, but I'm tied up with the family."

"Let's talk in the morning, Paul. I'm not sure about lunch right now." When he mentioned his family, I was left with a sinking feeling; otherwise I'd have jumped at the chance to be with him.

"OK. Well, I've got to go. Thanks for a great evening. I'll call you in the morning and see if we can make a plan."

The magic of the moment, before TJ came home, was lost. We'd straightened ourselves up too much. So much so we seemed very remote to each other—polite.

I walked out to the car with him. I slipped my arms around him wanting to recapture the moment. We kissed lightly and smiled at each other. "Good night, Jenny. Thank you for being so patient."

"Good night, stranger. You're the one who is being patient. Thank you." He folded up once again into the car and drove off.

I was relieved we'd been interrupted—sorry, too. I felt like a foolish virgin who had saved her virginity and hated doing it. I stared at the little red car until it disappeared and remained standing outside for a few more moments composing myself. Nothing terrible had happened, and yet, it felt that way.

The real life story of our lives was intruding yet again. I let out a deep sigh and reminded myself to breathe. I took another deep breath and finally felt ready to re-enter the house and face TJ's queries.

"Did I hear the soft sound of a bubble bursting out there?" TJ had put on walking shoes and was holding the dogs' leads. "Why don't you change and join me in a short walk before we have a nice cappuccino in front of the fire?"

"That's the best offer I've had in forty-five minutes." I was feeling better already. "I'll be ready in two minutes." As we walked,

TJ told me about her evening and her plans for the following day. I "hummed" at times and made other appropriate noises and said virtually nothing.

Back at the house, I busied myself plumping up couch pillows and gathering things Paul and I had left on the bar. TJ was preparing coffee. "I made them doubles. I have the feeling this could be a long night."

"How about a drop of Kahlua in them? In fact, how about a rather good-sized splash?"

"What good will it do to make them doubles? The Kahlua will put you right to sleep."

"That's not a bad idea either. Anyway, I'd like some. How about you?"

"Of course. Would I let you drink alone?"

"Never!"

We settled in front of the fireplace, but instead of clicking on TV right away, TJ turned and looked at me. "Want to talk?"

"Yes, but not now. Mind if I wait until the morning? I'm bushed and I'd just like to enjoy this delicious coffee and *Star Trek* with you and turn in."

"I couldn't agree more. It's just if you needed me now—well, you know, I'd listen."

"I know."

## 11

My orange juice was poured and the coffee brewing when I made my entrance the following morning. I must have slept hard, because I hadn't heard a sound.

"Well, good morning, sleepyhead. It's almost 9:00 o'clock. What time am I hitching a ride into town?"

"I saw the clock and couldn't believe it. Have you had breakfast?"

"Yes, over an hour ago."

"I'll be ready to leave the house by 10:30. Will that get you downtown in time to run your errands before your meeting?"

"I'll be ready." TJ was already on the way to her room.

Paul called as I was blowing my hair dry. We exchanged the usual niceties, then, "Jen, will you join me for lunch today? I want to see you again before you take off on your field trip."

"Right now I don't know when. I'm bringing TJ in this morning. In fact, within the hour. What time can you meet me and where?" I felt distracted and tense.

*A Small Flirtation*

"Would it be possible for you to pick me up? I had to leave my car at the garage this morning. It's developed some kind of pinging sound I don't like."

"Of course, I can. When?"

"I'll be in front of the building at 11:45 come hell or high water and wait for you."

"You can reach me on my beeper if something comes up," I said. This time I was smiling. Something always seemed to come up to delay him.

"Nothing's going to delay me today. I promise you."

"Isn't it a little obvious to be picked up by me?" I wondered if he had even thought of that.

"No. It happens from time to time. I'll just have to remember to bring my briefcase along, and try not to look so happy at the prospect of meeting some client."

TJ got out of my Jeep at Union Square in front of what used to be I. Magnin's.

"I'll grab a cab and see you at my place after dinner." She stuck her hand through the open window and patted my shoulder "Don't forget, Jenny, keep it light." I felt like a little kid who had just received parental instructions.

After a couple of quick stops, I headed straight to Paul. What a rush I felt when I saw him coming toward the car. He reached for my hand and gave it a quick squeeze.

"How's my Jenny? You look mighty pretty."

"You look mighty nifty yourself. Also, I'm impressed. You really did get out here on the minute. Where are we going?"

"Do you know the Japan Center on Geary?"

"You mean where the little pagoda is?"

"Yes, that's it. There's a unique sushi place there. You do like sushi, don't you?"

"Indeed I do. I grew up on it. We had Japanese help in the house when I was a child. In fact, I'm pretty good at making it myself."

"Prove it to me." He challenged.

"I will sometime. You'll see."

"I don't know—walks on the beach with you and Honey, spending time in the darkroom, learning about developing film and printing pictures, of course, and making sushi together. It all sounds like an idyllic life to me. One I'd like a lot." He turned his head away and stared out the car window for a few moments and then continued, "It simply isn't possible, not now at least." His banter had turned serious. He took my hand again. This time he kissed my palm and folded my fingers over it. "Keep it safe."

There didn't seem to be any way to avoid, even obliquely, the subject of Paul's marital status. It intruded on everything we said. Every action we took was shaded, no matter how subtly, by this fact. Neither could we gloss over the fact we had already been drawn into an intensely emotional situation.

As we walked into the restaurant, Paul, as usual, tucked my arm under his and we were in 'lock step'.

When I look back on those days, on all of those early times together, I marvel at how oblivious we were to the world around us. Over and over again, we acted as though we were invisible, or at least, encased in a bubble, where nothing and no one could penetrate. It was wonderful. We were out of our minds. We were lucky, too. I shudder to think of it today.

We got settled at the bar in front of a steady little stream of water in which tiny boats laden with sushi and sashimi floated by. We chose our dishes and ate. Made more selections and ate some more. We ordered a large bottle of Chinese beer and drank and ate silently, simply enjoying being together.

"It's time I got back to the office. Where are you going now?"

"I'm meeting Guy Meadows to go over some last minute details about our plans before he comes up. We're leaving Monday. Remember?"

"Guy Meadows? Who's he?"

"My associate and traveling companion. Surely, I've mentioned him to you."

"Only as an associate, never by name." Paul looked puzzled. "I simply presumed that the associate was another woman."

This tickled me and I laughed much to his discomfort.

"Am I detecting sounds of jealousy?"

"Should I be?" He was trying to sound light-hearted.

"Only if you want to be. Guy has traveled with me for years, and, personally, I hope he will for years more." I was sounding unnecessarily defiant, and continued in the same vein. "We have a very special relationship. I find him invaluable. He has sound judgment and a keen eye. And a great sense of humor to boot. He really lightens my load, both literally and figuratively, especially when we travel abroad."

"He travels abroad with you? That's interesting. I'd like to meet him sometime." He was failing miserably at his nonchalant act.

"Sometime, maybe you will." I was amused.

We were leaving the restaurant when Paul asked, "How did you find each other? Was he a student of yours?"

I stood by the car before we got in and thought a moment. I made up my mind to explain in a serious, but light way, the role Guy played and still plays in my life.

"Paul get in and I'll tell you about Guy as I drive."

"Sure, I'm curious."

"I know you are. To start with, no. Guy was never an actual student of mine, nor I of his; although we've certainly learned much from one another over the years."

"Go on." Paul was encouraging me now.

"He and my husband grew up together and were best friends all through school as well as college. He's "Unc" to the boys to this day. He was great with them. As they were two times as much to handle, Guy and Tom shared many activities with the twins."

Paul sounded testy. "And since you're single this lifelong friend of your husband has stayed on your side? Is that the deal?"

"Oh Paul, I haven't told you, have I?" We'd spoken so much, and yet this subject had never seemed germane to our previous conversations.

"No. I'm afraid you haven't. I really don't know anything about Tom, what he does or what kind of person he is."

"Was. Tom is dead. He died when the boys were eighteen. Ten years ago. Guy was a lifesaver. It all happened so fast. Nicky and Max were getting ready to leave for college. I don't know how they or I would have managed without him."

"Good Lord, Jenny, I had no idea. There's so much I don't know about you."

"And this isn't the time to go into it all. We'll continue at some point—some point in the future." There was nothing to be done about his gaffe. How could he have known? And I didn't want to put a damper on our today.

"This is not the way I want to say good-bye to you, Jenny. You're going to be away for weeks." He was getting out of the car. "I'll call you tomorrow night at your house."

"OK, dear. I'm sorry. I know what a surprise all of this must be for you. We'll talk tomorrow." He waved. I pulled into traffic. What a day!

## 12

Guy and I met in the small office he kept in the city. We finalized the itinerary for the first leg of the trip, which would probably take two weeks.

I had a terrible time keeping my mouth shut about Paul and me. After all, Guy had been my friend forever and my confidante since Tom's death. Somehow it seemed dishonest not to tell him. I was lying by omission, not commission. Is there any difference? I consoled myself by answering 'yes' to my own question. It wasn't as though he had asked me any direct questions. He didn't know anything to ask. I knew one day I'd tell him about Paul. It just wasn't timely now, and we had other work to do.

"You're looking especially delightful today, Ms. Jenny. Might it be because you're happy to be planning our next adventure?" Guy always flattered me a bit, and flirted a bit, too. It was expected and fun.

"Not only happy, Guy, but excited about the project. It will also be good to have some uninterrupted time with you." I meant what I said.

"Well, I did come by a couple of times when the boys were here. They both look great and sound happy."

"I'll catch you up on their respective love lives while we're on the road."

"And what about your love life, Jenny? Anything interesting in the wind?" More of the usual banter I could expect from Guy. Only this time I blushed. I turned away quickly and began gathering my things together, but not quickly enough.

"Was that a blush I saw on your face, Jenny?"

"Oh, come on, Guy. That's enough teasing for one day." I gave him a little peck on the cheek. "Got to run. I'm about to be late for the bank."

That was a near miss. I told myself I'd have to be more careful than I thought. I now knew he'd know about my dalliance sooner than I had originally planned to tell it.

The weather was fogging up a bit; it looked like rain. "Let it. I'll build a fire and be quiet and cozy for the evening," I told myself as I drove the Jeep into TJ's garage.

The first drops started to fall as I entered the house. I dropped my things and headed for the kitchen.

I poked around in the refrigerator and pulled out an artichoke left over from last night's dinner with Paul plus half a cooked crab. Suddenly, I was very glad to be alone. I put dinner on a tray, built a fire, turned on some music and settled down.

There had been an awful lot going on in the past three weeks. I needed a breather badly. And these few hours alone with no conversation were truly welcome. They gave me a chance to think through all the revelations I made today at lunch.

One thing was nagging at me. Before being told about Tom, Paul had seemed possessive and snide when referring to Guy. That attitude didn't sit well with me, and admittedly made me apprehensive. It was a side of Paul I didn't know—hadn't experienced. Hopefully, it was related to our mutual frustration and not some character flaw. I felt a bit testy and pugnacious myself from time to time, although I kept it to myself...mostly. We simply had no one to blame and so took it out on each other at odd times.

TJ arrived home in a downpour. "Jenny," she called. "Boy, that fire looks good." I stretched and yawned—glad she was back. I'd been doing enough thinking—enough pondering and analyzing.

"It's really coming down. Sorry you got caught in it and I'm very glad I didn't have to drive all the way up to Stinson tonight. What can I get for you?"

"Any coffee left? I'd love a cup."

"Coming up."

We plopped down by the fire—our special, favorite spot.

TJ turned to me and said, "Jenny dear, do you mind terribly if I don't come up to the beach with you tomorrow? I really do need another day here at my house."

"I'd stay over if I could, TJ, but I'm pressed already. I've done too much goofing off lately."

"Goofing off? That's a new name for it." TJ suppressed a giggle.

"Call it by any other name; it's blown my time schedule to hell in a basket."

"Then it's set. Unless it's still pouring." I told her I'd heard the forecast and it was expected the storm would abate during the night.

I yawned and stretched again. "Well, I'm ready to turn in. How about you?"

"Me too, Jenny. I'll just close up. 'Night, dear."

"Good night. Sweet dreams."

The storm did abate, though it was still a bit windy. Clouds scudded across the sky. Some yellow light was penetrating the gray, casting a beautiful patchwork of golden glow and shadows everywhere. It bode well for a great weather day.

As I was leaving her house, I told TJ to phone me from Mill Valley or Tiburon or wherever she landed, and I'd come pick her up. What with her not driving, we always have to consider various ways of getting her to and from places not served by public transport.

She'd hoped to be up in time for a walk on the beach before dinner.

The air was fresh and clean, and although there had been a heavy rain, once it stopped, everything dried as though no weather front had passed through. The miracle of California! Don't mention fires followed by rainstorms and mudslides or earthquakes for that matter. I'm a Californian, and that's all that need be said.

Crossing the Golden Gate Bridge on that kind of a day is nothing short of spectacular. I don't know a city anywhere in the world that doesn't benefit from a face-washing rain. San Francisco, because of the hills and valleys, bay and ocean vistas and the bridges, is shining and sparkling even when it's half-cloudy, like Jerusalem with its golden aura. It was good to be home for a few days.

Mail. How does it pile up so fast? I swear I've thrown out an entire forest in my lifetime, so far. At least I had taken phone messages while I was away, so I didn't have that to deal with, too.

Honey took a run on the beach, and I did laundry and started assembling my clothes for the trip. Pack. Unpack. Pack again. It seems that's all I had done since early summer.

Well, when this assignment was over and I got through to the New Year, I intended to turn off the phone, close the shutters and put my feet up for a month. I've had this same fantasy for years.

By late afternoon I was feeling a sense of increased tension and wondered what it was all about. Of course. Paul had said he'd call me here today to say a proper farewell.

Well, he either could or couldn't, would or wouldn't, and that was that. I didn't feel comfortable with my phoning him. I scolded myself for dreaming and decided it was time to take a break. Even take a little nap. I'd been at it steadily for days.

Honey curled up, too. We both slept peacefully for close to two hours. Not unheard of, but certainly a rare occurrence.

The ringing telephone shattered the silence. I fumbled for the receiver, and by the time I got it right side up to my ear, I could hear Paul saying, "Jenny, are you there? Are you all right?"

"I'm here, Paul." Yawning. "Just sound asleep."

"Oh sorry; but, what are you doing asleep? It's 6:00 o'clock. I imagined you and TJ busy in the kitchen by now."

I told him I'd come home without her and that she'd be coming up tomorrow barring rain. "How are you?" I'd awakened enough to be polite. "Did you have a nice evening with the family?"

"Yes, as a matter of fact. It was exceptionally nice. My daughter, Beth, and her boyfriend, Dan, announced their engagement. They want a June wedding."

"You must approve of the young man. You sound enthusiastic." Personally, I was less than enthusiastic talking about his family life.

"I am for sure. They've known each other for two years, so I've had a good look at him over time. He wears well. Kathy's another subject."

I kept still and waited. He went on about Beth and Kathy and how close they are in spite of their differences.

"Beth is very much like me, and yet, I think Kathy can talk to her better than to any other person in her life. Beth understands and is considerate of her mother in a very touching way. Maybe it's because they're two women. I think that's why Kathy's having a hard time with the thought of losing her. I sometimes think she sees Beth as being the person she herself would like to be."

"Too bad," for whom? I added under my breath. For Kathy or Beth, or me having to listen to all this?

"Yeah, and Beth is doing her best. But, damn it, Jenny, I really won't tolerate Kathy acting in anyway to spoil Beth's time."

I had listened to enough. "Well, they'll work it out one way or another. People always do... somehow." A limp, disinterested and accurate response.

"So much for that, Jenny." I guess he got my not very subtle message. "I called to talk to you and to say how much I'll miss you these next few weeks and not to go into the Crowley family hour."

"I'll miss you, too, Paul."

"Not as much as I will. I mean it. Don't you know the one who is leaving is going onto an adventure, while the one left behind is just that—left behind, doing the same old thing." He, sounding much more like the Paul I knew.

"I thought you loved your work," I said.

"Yes, I do. And you know just exactly what I'm talking about. I wish I were able to go with you."

"Me, too."

"About yesterday, Jenny. I want to hear more, but not over the phone. It's too important. I want to be with you when you talk about it."

"Thanks, Paul. I agree. It'll wait. It's been ten years already."

"Jenny, dear Jenny. You sound so sad." So did he.

"No, not really. It's just when I say ten years, it rather overwhelms me. I mean ten years is a long time. But I'm really OK. And Paul, I know you were terribly surprised when I told you about Tom. It was an awkward moment and I blurted it out without any thought. It's just that I haven't had a need to talk about what happened for years. It *is* a very important part of my past but that's exactly what it is—the past. What we have now is all present and I didn't want you to feel constrained by the information. It just hasn't seemed appropriate, some how, to bring the subject up." I sighed—another hurdle overcome no matter how badly.

"Forgive me for bringing it up at all, when I simply called to say a proper good-bye, safe journey and have a successful trip."

"Thanks. But you left out have fun."

"OK, have fun, but not too much."

"You're still curious about Guy, and that'll have to wait, too." He was fun to tease, and why not?

"Sure, that too. E-mail me your itinerary, OK? So I can have an idea where you are?"

"I would, Paul, but it's rather amorphous. How 'bout me calling you end of next week?"
"If that's the best you can do."
"Till next week, then. Take care of yourself, Paul."
"You too, Jenny."

Were we destined forever to be saying good-bye? It still was unfathomable to me that in three weeks this stranger had become so important to me. And, if what I was hearing was real, I to him.

The sound of the disconnect on the line had the same effect on me as a train whistle in the night. Click. And he was gone. So tenuous was the connection. Just 'click.' I shuddered. It had happened before. A phone call, a click and he was gone.

I shook myself. I mustn't react like that. It's too melodramatic. It doesn't fit my style. Still . . .

"Come on, Honey. Let's see what we can whip up for dinner." It was still light, thank heavens. And soon the gloom I felt a few moments before was dispelled. Instead, I concentrated on the phone call. In spite of all the family references, the sweetness and lightness of the man enchanted me. Suddenly I found myself humming.

A lot got accomplished that night—phone calls, mail, I even paid some bills. All the time I was thinking ahead deciding how far to go on the first day out. Guy, of course, would have ideas of his own. We'd have plenty of time to compare notes and make our decisions. I was becoming excited. I was ready to sink my teeth into a new project. I sorely needed both the balance and perspective it would bring back to my life.

## 13

It was cool and comfortable in the morning. I started the day early in anticipation of TJ's arrival. Did a little marketing and spent the remainder of the time pushing forward with completing the tasks at hand. Just as I was about to break and get ready to pick her up, she phoned.

"I'm here at the drugstore in Mill Valley, but I've already made arrangements to be driven over, so stay put."

"Great. Terrific. Who's bringing you?"

"Someone here has a delivery to make in Stinson Beach and so I'm on my way. Need anything?"

"No, thanks."

"OK, dear, see you soon." She rang off without further comment.

That was a break. I went into the living room to lay a fire. I was standing at the kitchen counter rinsing romaine when I heard a car stop in the drive. The door was unlocked, and so I kept on with salad fixings.

Poochie bounded into the kitchen and straight out the pet

door to join Honey. I called out: "I'm in the kitchen elbow deep in salad. Thank whoever brought you for me."

"Thank him yourself."

I turned around and dropped the salad bowl. My jaw dropped, too. It was Paul. TJ was standing next to him, grinning like a cat.

"Well, I told you someone at the drugstore had a delivery to make in Stinson Beach. I didn't lie."

"You never do. However, you occasionally, conveniently rearrange the truth." I was wiping my hands. Fortunately the salad bowl hadn't been filled yet. "You two are too much for me." I was astonished and laughing and happy all at the same time.

Paul hadn't moved. He was waiting to hear my reaction before coming over to me. We met in the middle of the room and had one of our lovely, warm hugs and face pets and kisses.

"Aren't you even going to say 'hello' to me? And tell me how clever I am—or I should say 'we' are? Hey, you two, break it up!"

"Now, tell me what this is all about. How did it happen? Did you bump into each other or what? Come one, tell me!"

They looked at each other a bit sheepishly. "We planned it. I confess," Paul said.

"Planned it?"

"Yes," TJ answered. "Paul phoned me last night after he heard that I wasn't coming up until today."

"I decided to bring her up. You sounded sad and a bit too remote for my taste. I wanted to suggest coming up last night, but thought the better part of valor would be to check with TJ."

"You mean run it past her first?"

"Yes, and then we agreed it would be a great lark to surprise you. You are, aren't you—surprised?"

"Very." I just shook my head and smiled.

"Can I look around?"

"Not until we've had our walk. I'll show you everything. Did you bring proper clothes?"

"I have a sweater and shoes. Hold on a minute and I'll get them." He went out to his car.

I turned to TJ. "What is all this about?"

"He told you the truth. He was kicking himself for bringing both his wife and Tom into the conversation when all he wanted to do was have a nice, easy conversation with you."

"And . . .?"

"And when he called me, he stumbled for a moment, and then asked what I thought of his bringing me up—would you be upset, feel put upon, whatever. I assured him you'd be delighted after the initial shock, that is. You are, aren't you—delighted?" TJ was serious.

"I am. Honestly. I'm also pleased to see you. I wasn't tired of being with you yet, when I left yesterday." I said, laughing.

"Here, now what's with you two gals, hugging and laughing?" Paul was back and properly shod.

"We always do. Don't tell me you're jealous of TJ, too? Come on, let's go!"

During our walk on the beach, I wondered about which way to approach the evening. Obviously, Paul expected to stay for awhile. Did 'awhile' mean all night or what? I was determined not to ask the 'hows' of that. I knew the 'why'.

Paul ran. Honey and Poochie trotted. TJ and I sauntered. Honey had carried her Frisbee part of the way and dropped it. Paul retrieved it and was playing with her. They both were having a great time.

"I think this is as good a time as any to finish the story of Tom's death and Guy's role. What to you think, TJ? He's curious about Guy, you know."

"Yes, I agree. Let's do it before dinner while we're relaxing over a drink."

"I'm awfully glad you're here. You realize I haven't talked about what happened in years—there's been no need. I was fascinated by my reaction to Paul's mentioning it over the phone."

"How so?"

"Well, after we hung up, I really sagged emotionally. There

was that final click of disconnection. I suddenly remembered that other phone call as though it had just happened."

"Poor kid."

"Come on, let's head back." I started to jog.

Ten years later and I was still reacting. Funny. Well I guess I always will, and why not? After all, with Tom everything was a first, and I don't think any woman forgets that man—ever.

"That was great. Just what I needed. Now, do I get the house tour?"

"In a moment. I just want to start a couple of things in the kitchen. You are staying for dinner?"

"May I? I know I wasn't expected."

"Certainly. You're more than welcome." I was sounding a bit stiff—a bit formal and wasn't sure why.

"What can I do to help? I set a mean table and make a superior martini. How's that?"

"Perfect. Here, TJ, snip the points off the artichokes, will you? Paul, the flatware's in that drawer and the plates are in the cupboard above. I'll feed the hounds."

I was beginning to feel better. A little organizing of the troops put me back in charge of myself in some odd way. Whatever it was, it was working. The rest of dinner could wait awhile now.

"Come on ladies, take your glasses. Here's to my newest best friends." We all clinked glasses and sipped the best martini I'd had in years.

"What in the world did you do to these? They're gorgeous!"

"An old English friend of mine taught me his secret years ago. I, of course, have improved on his formula, and *voilà!* The superior martini!"

We all clinked again.

"No stirring, no shaking, no bruising the gin; those prohibitions we all know—what's your technique?" TJ asked.

"It's a very special secret. I only tell people I trust not to spread it around."

"Oh, we're very trustworthy, aren't we, Jenny?"

"Be sure you don't tell Poochie and Honey. They're terrible gossips. It'll be all over the neighborhood by morning." I admonished. I felt light-hearted again.

"Maybe I'll tell you next time I make them for you. Right now, I still want you to be impressed."

"OK. Bring your glass and I'll show you around. Where do you want to begin?"

"Your studio and the darkroom. Is that permitted?"

"Yes, indeed. They are an integral part of the house. Really the heart of the house after the kitchen."

"They are an integral part of you, Jenny. That's the part I'm most interested in." He and his smile.

I carried on. He said all the right things. Made all the right sounds as I let him look through some of my pictures.

"You've got quite a set-up here. Are you taking all that video equipment you have packed up over there?"

"Why, yes. That and more. Guy will be bringing some, too. Why?"

"I guess after hearing about the show in Chicago and then the photo journal you did for me and these pictures I've just been looking through, I don't know, I presumed you were shooting stills."

"I'll do some of each. Guy, too. We'll take slides and prints as well as videos. Then we'll sort it all out a few times. He's great help in that department. That's the hard part—making the tough cuts. The final decisions are made by the client, of course."

"Of course," Paul agreed.

"I told you the other day that Guy has sound judgment and a keen eye; add to that impeccable taste, and I've got a winner on my team." I fervently hoped he'd get past his obsession about Guy.

We returned to the great room—that is, the combination kitchen, dining and living room.

"Well, what do you think? Isn't it perfect?" TJ had her back to the fire. She'd built it while I showed Paul around.

"Very impressive. The whole place is great. It becomes you, Jenny."

"Thank you. I really do enjoy living here. It's been quite a change from Palo Alto. A very beneficial change, I think."

"How long have you been here? It seems the rework is quite new."

"You're right. I moved in three years ago plus a couple of months. Work on it started as soon as escrow closed. So I've owned it virtually three and a half years. That's right, isn't it, TJ? I forget exactly."

"Yes, that's right. The Palo Alto house sold almost immediately. You had a push to get in here early."

"The house you left . . . ?" Paul asked.

"It was Tom's and mine. In the early days, we dubbed it 'the big white mortgage with the red tile roof.' The boys grew up there and I wanted them to continue having it as home base, while they were still in school." I paused for a few moments lost in thoughts of Tom and the twins and of me, too. The perfect nuclear family in the perfect setting only we had a stucco wall instead of a white picket fence around the house.

"Jenny, there's no need if you don't want to continue," Paul interjected.

"What? Oh no, I'm fine. Honestly. I think I'd like to continue, now that I've started. TJ, please fill in as you see fit. After all, you do know it all."

She and I smiled at each other and raised our glasses.

"Tom was killed in a routine flight to one of the outlying labs in Silicon Valley. They were in a helicopter. He and the pilot both died." I stopped.

"Jenny received a phone call from the police," TJ added. "The boys weren't at home at the moment. She was picked up in a squad car and taken to the hospital. She phoned me from there.

I taxied to her. In the meantime, somehow the boys were located, and Guy, too. They all came to the hospital together."

"There was never a chance that Tom would live," I said, "But they went through the motions of trying to save him. It was a grim seven hours. Guy and the twins drove TJ and me back to the house to sit out the surgery."

"It came as we were getting ready to return," TJ interposed.

"The call, that is. It was over. The phone disconnected, and so did I."

"Guy caught Jenny before she hit the floor . . ."

"And he's been catching me ever since," I added with a small smile and little shrug.

Paul had remained silent throughout the telling. He was transfixed for a moment and then spoke. "What a ghastly, cruel experience for all of you."

"Tom Matthews was a terrific man. He was bright and funny and serious all at the same time, and loved me and his sons. He had a brilliant future. Yes. It was a cruel act of fate. The boys and I needed all the help we could get to overcome it."

TJ took over telling the story, "That's where Guy came in, Paul. Jenny's other friends and her Dad were all wonderful, but Guy had special areas of concern to cover. Guy always had special feelings for Jenny. So when tragedy struck her life, he was the logical one to take her under his wing."

"His wing seemed the most attractive," I interjected, "the strongest, and he persisted. While all this was going on, Paul, during this entire time, it was TJ who hovered over everything, keeping an eagle eye on each one of us."

TJ smiled. "If I ever needed to drive, I did then."

"You almost broke down and took lessons. Remember? We all decided one tragedy was enough." The heavy moment passed, and we were once more able to laugh.

"Well, that's the story. Now, I'm heading back to work in the kitchen. The artichokes must be done by now. I'll get the rest of the dinner going. You two pick out some discs; I could use a bit of music, OK?"

# A Small Flirtation

TJ got the message. I needed to be alone for a few minutes. Whipping up a sauce for the fish I was about to cook, steaming some rice and melting butter was just what I needed to clear the head.

I also knew TJ would continue on with the tale: Guy and his mentoring the boys—helping them get off to college. I've often thought what a blessing it was the twins had decided to stay together during undergraduate school. It would have devastated them to have been separated at that time. As I look back, I'm not certain they would have started school that year had they been going to two different institutions.

Guy spent the rest of his time holding me together. I shall forever be grateful to him for that.

He'd had a short stormy marriage that ended in divorce and no children. Caring for the boys and me during those dreadful days, as we worked at reconstructing our lives, helped to fill a void in Guy's life He was crazy about the twins. It was Tom and Guy who corralled them and played ball and surfed and camped with them.

After Tom died, he was as needy as I and we fell into the easy pattern of consolation, not to be confused with love. Although from time from time over the years, we wandered over that line and considered having an affair, in the end, we opted for a life-long friendship.

"Come on, you two. Dinner's ready. What do you want to drink?"

"Coffee for me."

"And for me, too, Jenny." Paul walked straight over to me and put his hands on my shoulders. He stood there looking down at me for several moments and then took me into his arms. A big sigh.

"Jenny's quite a girl!"

"And she smells good, too!" I finished it for him.

I liked the way Paul fit in. He didn't usurp or take over; he was simply in charge of himself and completely at ease. I loved watching him. He moved like an athlete. Light on his feet. Graceful.

Hold on. You're one step away from other fantasies. Be careful, I warned myself. You don't need complications, not at this moment.

"Where are you and Guy heading first?" Paul was filling our coffee cups and reaching for a brownie at the same time.

"We're not going far on Monday; actually, only up to Sonoma. Does either of you know about the waterfowl preserve at Sebastiani Winery?

"No, not really," TJ replied. "I've only heard of it in passing."

"The Sabastianis have been very big environmentalists for generations. Particularly interested in birds. Did you know they've developed ninety acres of wetlands as a sanctuary for migrating waterfowl, and have actually logged over 130 species of waterfowl? Seems the logical place to begin. Guy agrees. They are expecting us Monday afternoon. After we drop TJ and the dogs at the Ferry."

"Jenny, that's been changed," TJ interrupted.

"How, TJ?" I asked.

"Paul's taking me back tonight with the dogs. It makes eminently more sense."

I began to protest when TJ stopped me.

"You've no idea how behind I am, Jen. The syllabus for my Esoteric Psych class is barely in outline form and you know how department heads are. They want it all in and ready weeks before I begin the seminar. I really would love to stay, but this time it's better all around to take Paul up on his offer."

Paul hadn't uttered a sound until now. "I hope I haven't wrecked any plans by my offer."

"Not really. I was simply going to put her to work. I'm only disappointed that you two aren't staying over."

"I am, too. And I'm going to have to leave now, Jenny. Are you ready, TJ? Come on animals. Let's see if we all fit!"

We strolled to his car. "I'm glad you came up. It was a glorious surprise."

"I'm very glad, Jenny. I wanted to see you and it was a chance

*A Small Flirtation*

to add your home to my images of you." He gave me a quick hug and light kiss. "Have a terrific trip. Good luck. And please keep in touch . . . And, Jenny, most important—thank you for allowing me into your life." This time he held me very close. We stood there for a few moments just holding each other quietly. Absorbed in our own thoughts and feelings. We parted and smiled. He got into his car and left. Yet again—he left. This time with TJ by his side and the dogs in back. I had to smile in spite of myself. At least Honey would be happily ensconced with Poochie and TJ in the city, all the while Guy and I were off chasing the birds.

I sighed, watched him drive off and returned to the house. Boy, it sure felt empty. Two minutes ago it was filled with beloved people and happy dogs, and now I was unexpectedly alone. I waded into the job of cleaning up the dinner debris and had no sooner sunk onto the couch in my favorite spot by the fire, when the phone rang. It was TJ. My friend.

"You OK, kid? I mean, it's been quite an evening."

"I'm OK and, yes, it has been. I'm still a little shaken and puzzled, too, by my intense reaction to retelling the story of that time."

"But as you said earlier, Jen, you haven't really had to tell it in years. And that bit with the phone call and disconnect—your reaction to that was almost bizarre."

"I just hope to God I'm not feeling something that's already in the future."

"You mean some sort of prescience? Oh, Jenny! Don't make yourself crazy with thoughts like that."

"It's just—I don't know. We always seem to be saying goodbye."

"That's nonsense. Every time you leave me or the boys or even the grocer, you say 'good-bye.' Come on, don't borrow trouble."

"You're right, of course. It's just . . . tonight was hard."

"Now I'm sorry I encouraged him to come up with me. All of that could have waited. In fact, it may never need to have been said."

"No, I'm not sorry, because at some point it would have come out one way or another. And frankly, I'd rather have been in control of the way it happened, than not, and of what was said, et cetera. It's fine, and it's over. I hardly feel it will have to be addressed any further."

"You mean I don't have to feel guilty? What a relief. You know how I hate having the 'guilts'; it doesn't become me. I'm not the type."

We both laughed and then she grew serious. Apparently Paul was terribly moved by my story. He asked questions all the way back to the city and wanted TJ to fill in the gaps for him. He was hungry for someone to talk to about his feelings for me and needed confirmation of mine.

"He's so conflicted, it was almost painful to hear him. I tell you Jenny, as ambivalent as you are about having a love affair with a married man, that's how certain he is you are the beginning and the end for him."

"How do you mean that?" I was intrigued.

"You are the beginning of reality and the end of fantasy for this man."

After we hung up, I stared at the fire for a long time as I was, once more, beset by images of the past. I remember it all in excruciating detail. . . . Tom, Tom. . . .

. . . ."So long, Babe. I'll call you if it looks like I'll be late." You chucked me under the chin as always and I lifted my head for the goodbye kiss. Oh God, how was I to know it would be our last? You could have prepared me. I stood at the door of the car holding the window frame reluctant to let you leave. Did I know someplace deep inside?

Coming home after the your funeral—entering the house, our house knowing I'd have to do it over and over again day after day alone. Empty. No joy. No more merriment. No more love. Over twenty years of a fairytale marriage. We couldn't have more. The jealous gods wouldn't let us.

Everyone important to us was there helping, coping, hand-under-the-elbow, worried expressions: "Are you all right?" "Yes." What was I to say, to do? Scream—that's what I wanted to do: Wail, keen—but the boys, our sons, I still had to think of them. Eighteen and readying themselves to go off to college. I simply could not collapse and I didn't, not until they left.

I kept thinking you'd be proud of me! Oh God, Tom, how could I have clung to such a thought, to have found even a modicum of comfort in it? I recoiled at the image of myself so broken and desperate, trying and failing utterly to make any sense out of the tragedy that had happened to our family. We had been too happy.

Later, I came to realize I had fooled no one with my pathetically brave front. I turned away from everyone and found some peace and quiet in my darkroom, only to be startled back to reality every time I stepped out of it. What gloomy pictures I took that first year. You would have hated them. I shot every angle of every dark and dreary landscape all in stark contrast of black and white. I roamed alleyways and empty buildings clicking away at an array of rusted, broken and smashed remnants of things that once had been useful and were now abandoned. The flotsam and jetsam of life. The symbolism was not lost to me.

Gradually under the watchful eye of Guy and the patient persistence of TJ, I began to turn around. There was no understanding the events, only acceptance of what could never be changed. Nick and Max somehow managed their first year. They got very little help from me, God knows. Thank God they had each other and the ever-available Guy and TJ.

Now, fully a decade later, I still love you and long for our easy kind of intimacy, never taking for granted, but always able to count on each other. Is that still available? That kind of love? Am I ever to experience it again?

I roused myself from my reverie and realized I had been sitting in the same spot for over two hours. The fire just embers, my cheeks still damp with tears. I found several crumpled tissues in my lap. The trance I had been in allowed me to travel backward in time, to experience once again the sweetness of our life together, to taste the final farewell kiss and smile the last smile at you. My beloved first love, precious man, partner in all my dreams, God bless you.

Between my reveries and TJ's phone call about Paul, I was so shaken I don't even remember what all I did the following days. Mostly, I walked on the beach and worked. I packed and re-packed the Jeep—and I thought again and again of what was evolving into a major change in my life.

Monday was clear and cool. Some clouds lay offshore at the horizon. I hadn't yet checked the weather channel, but as the day passed, they seemed to dissipate. Perhaps it had rained at sea.

Guy had arrived early morning for what was to be a non-stop session, going over our gear and talking through the next three or four weeks in more specific terms than before. "What's the farthest north we'll be going? Do we know yet?" I asked. Once more we were in the kitchen preparing food. This time we were packing it in an ice chest.

"I want to go to Vancouver and Vancouver Island." Guy was chopping onions. "Then we'll be in the San Juan's for a couple of days, at least. Friday Harbor is probably where we'll stay. Right?"

"Right," Guy responded. "Orcas and the entire area is so beautiful. It'll be fun for us, too." He sounded happy and enthusiastic. "But right now I'm interested in food." Guy was fishing in the refrigerator and came up with some Port Salut.

After lunch there was last minute checking the house, locking up and piling into the Jeep.

"Onward and upward!" Guy sang out.

"Good-bye house. Be safe. And protect all the love and warmth for my return," I prayed silently.

# PART II

## 14

Days became weeks—a collage and montage of color, images and texture. Luck and the weather was with us.

Suddenly we were in Victoria contemplating our return trip via ferryboats, at least as far as Seattle. The turn around to Stinson Beach would only take a few days.

The birds were fascinating and magnificent. We planned to turn inland, eastward to the Sacramento River after leaving Oregon. We were heading for the Central Valley wetlands where the Canada geese, among many other waterfowl, spend the winter.

I called Paul as promised after we'd been out five days. It began as a brief, light-hearted chat—nothing heavy, no reference to our talk that last night at my house.

"I'm going to Vancouver for the firm soon. Probably within the next few days. Where will you be?"

"Gosh, Paul, I really can't say. Are you staying over?"

"I would if it meant seeing you. Otherwise I'll go up and back in the same day."

"I wish I could say yes, but we've been out less than a week and I don't honestly see us up there so soon. I really wish I could, but I'm afraid I can't. Damn."

"Too bad. But it was worth a try."

"It's probably just as well. How would I explain you to Guy?"

"Oh, that's right. Guy. Yeah well, it was a nice idea. I had it all figured out in my head, a perfect plan."

"Mark it up to another one of those great ideas that didn't work, Paul. And I'm really so sorry."

"When do you think you'll be back?" He asked, disappointment in his voice

"No idea right now. Probably as close as we can figure, it's going to be at least two weeks for this segment of the trip."

"That long, really?"

"Yes. I really think so." I went on to explain briefly what all we'd do when we got to Vancouver, including using a lab there to see what we'd got, what we missed, etc. Then we'd judge how much more we'd need. All of that.

"How's Guy"

"Fine. We always enjoy our time together."

"Good." He was attempting to sound interested.

"And you? How's everything in your life?"

"Business is great. We'll be bidding on the Vancouver job. It's a nice one. Keep your fingers crossed for me."

"I will, though it'll make using a camera a little tricky."

We both chuckled. He wasn't going to say anything about 'hearth and home,' and I certainly wasn't going to push it.

"Well, thanks for keeping in touch, Jenny. Call again." A very abrupt change.

"Did someone just come into your office?" I asked.

"No" He told me that he just had to run What had started as a light-hearted conversation had deteriorated rapidly. In the end it was an unsatisfactory call—no real warmth. Each of us suddenly at arms length from the other. The emotional thread connecting us was very fragile indeed. We said good-bye. I hung up first. He had waited for me to do so.

I thought and rethought my response to Paul's invitation and called myself a fool for not, at least, making an effort to work something out. Too late. Next time, maybe. If there was to be a next time.

I had a hard time putting his cool tone out of my ears. Was that the way he treated his wife? I mean to say, is that what happens when he doesn't get his way? Thus far, and I was well aware of the short time we'd known each other, I had acquiesced to every request he'd made. I began to believe this separation was a good way to slow things down between us—Take your time, Jenny old girl. Cool it.

There was much to learn about this man, his life and most certainly, his marriage. Funny, he asked all the questions most of the time. All about me, my friendship with TJ, my past, my boys and most recently my relationship with Guy. I hadn't liked his tone of voice when he asked about it. It clearly implied Guy and I were having an affair. What business was it of his, anyway even if we were? He was, as would be expected, very embarrassed and apologetic when he learned about Tom and Guy's true role in my life. Still, it was some kind of possessive attitude which troubled me. Hadn't he displayed it from the very start at the airport?

If, in fact, this was the 'modus operandi' of his marriage, I could readily understand Kathy's attitude. It would be impossible to be intimate and entrust ones emotional life to a controlling man, no matter how bright and attractive. I'd have to stay on the alert and pay attention to more than my yearnings. Clearly, I'd grown too close too fast and could no longer see him clearly. There would be other times for thinking about all of that later. Right now, I had to get back to Guy and our joint assignment.

The ferry boat rides down to Seattle were fascinating and great fun. We hopped from island to island and boat to boat. Guy was busy watching people and scenery. I scanned for birds. Late afternoon convocations of fowl along shorelines have always fascinated me. What do they do there? They seem to simply stand. Is that the way they bed down for the night? Curious.

I once caught two sea gulls wing tip to wing-tip soaring in front of the setting sun just as it hit the water and flared way up into the sky. Nicky and Max called it my "God shot." I called it "if you shoot enough film, you may just catch an extraordinary picture once in a while . . . if you're lucky!"

We "B and B'd" it in the Central Valley—stayed an extra day to pick up additional data on the wetlands and headed back toward the coast. It was getting colder in the evenings now. Guy and I were happy we'd booked into motels with fireplaces and decent dining rooms.

"When do you want to head south, Jenny?" He asked while we were sipping coffee, I'll take my cue from you."

"I'm willing to combine both parts of the trip and continue south from here. How about it, Guy?" I was anxious to finish and get home to Paul. Home to Paul. My heart ached when I said it even to myself. "Let's talk about it in the morning. I'm ready to turn in."

Guy pulled me up from the chair. "Good night, sweet girl. I really love you. You know that, don't you? It should have been you and me all along." He looked so serious.

"Dear Guy. I love you, too. I truly do. It would have been fun; I'm certain of that. Who knows, maybe in the next life."

"Right. Maybe in the next life." He kissed me lightly on the lips and smiled half sardonically. "I should have spoken up years ago." He was being light-hearted . . . sort of. "Nonetheless, I hold to my little fantasy that one day we'll have our own roll in the hay."

"Even though you're the one who has always said if you don't do 'it' by the time you've known someone six months, you never will."

"For you, my darling, I'll make an exception!"

"Come on. Let's go to bed."

*A Small Flirtation*  111

"My pleasure."

"Guy! Behave yourself!"

I thought about those early years of our friendship as I got ready for bed. Everyone but me was aware of Guy's feelings for me. I was too deeply involved with Tom to take his flirtatiousness seriously and Guy was Tom's best friend.

We talked in the car about the next leg of our journey. "We should cover this part in much less time I think, Jen, don't you?"

"Yes. Monterey-Carmel, Big Sur, the little sea coast towns right down to Morro Bay and Cambria. That shouldn't take too long. The waterfowl further south isn't migrating."

"We should wrap that in five or six days."

"I agree. Are you getting anxious to finish? Do you have a time deadline, Guy?"

"No. No more than you, Jenny. I know our date to finish is Thanksgiving with our final package in the client's hand by December 15—just doing a flow chart in my head."

" I think we're ahead of schedule. But even so, I do feel we could use a break and then head out again, fresh." And so it was decided. We'd head back to the Bay area for a few days of R&R.

We were both silent for a long time. "Tuppence ha'penny for your thoughts, Guy."

"Just thinking how much I always enjoy this—working with you and being together. It's remarkably gratifying. You're such a pro—so cool, knowing what you're doing all the way. I admire you, Jenny—your integrity, your honesty. You're one terrific female type person."

"My gosh, Guy, what brought all that on? Not that I didn't love hearing every word of it."

"I was ruminating on the past few years and appreciating all over again what wonderful adventures we've had together."

"We've also done some darn fine work together, Guy. Don't forget that."

"Never. I guess after my declaration last night, I was forced to think about you and me in a different light. If we had played at sex, it would have cast our friendship in a very different light. Murky at best."

"You're probably right, Guy. I would have hated that happening."

It would certainly have muddied the waters. To mix all of that with our professional judgment would have been the end of one and maybe the end of both. It's not as though we hadn't talked about it and even played at it a bit years ago.

"I just don't want you to ever think I take you for granted after all these years, Jenny. Kind of a reaffirmation of our friendship."

"That's the beauty of us, Guy. The love is real, the devotion deep, as I said last night. For my part I pledge to you nothing will harm it. I'll never let it!" It was time to take a break, blessedly. More of this talk and we'd become maudlin and embarrass ourselves. Neither of us wanted that.

# 15

One more night, one more day and we were winding down the circuitous road that leads to Stinson Beach. It was a bit windy, but also fresh and clear. It was good to see the house over the rise.

Smoke was coming out of the chimney. I was startled for a moment and then remembered it was Celestina's day. How nice to be greeted by a roaring fire. A stockpot sat on the back of the stove. I lifted the lid and peeked into thick soup. The aroma filled the kitchen.

Celestina appeared at the back door. She greeted me with an armload of fragrant leaves—laurel, I think, and eucalyptus and feathery acacia.

"*Hola*, Celestina. Haven't seen you in a long time. You're as pretty as ever." Always a sweet comment from Guy.

"*Gracias*. I hope your trip was good. I have salad in the refrigerator, too. Do you want me to stay?"

"No, thanks. I'll see you Friday before I go to San Francisco though, won't I?"

"Yes, I come Friday at 8:00."

"Good. I'll see you then. Anything happen I need to know about before you go?"

"Only a Mr. Paul call you and say to call him by 6:00."

"Thank you, Celestina, for making my homecoming so nice. See you Friday morning. Drive carefully. It's getting a bit windy."

Guy was unloading the car and didn't hear the message from Paul. It was only 3:00 o'clock. I still had plenty of time to call him from the privacy of my room.

We put everything to do with the job into the studio. The rest was dumped in the kitchen. I carried my bag to my room.

We got to work almost immediately and worked solidly for a couple of hours.

By 5:00 o'clock I was ready for a bath, a call to Paul and an early supper. I intended to do no more than sit by the fire and listen to a little music before retiring very early.

I hoped Guy felt the same. If not, he was free to stay up and work or whatever.

"Jenny, it's early. I have the time to shift my gear into my car and head back to town tonight. What do you think? That'll give me a head start on things at my place."

"Makes sense to me, Guy. I'm going to bathe and freshen up and we can have a bite of supper early. How's that?"

"Great. I'll do the same. See you in a bit."

I tried not to dash to my room. In fact, I walked to the bath and turned on the water taps and added soaking salts before placing the call—drown out conversation by leaving the water run. How quickly the good friend and talented pro melted away.

"Paul Crowley."

"Hi, Paul Crowley. Jenny, the photographer, here."

"Oh, Hi." His voice rose an octave. "You're back! You are, aren't you?"

"I'm here. We arrived a couple of hours ago."

"Is Guy still there? I mean is he staying on?"

"Just through an early supper. He decided to go home instead of staying over."

"Jenny, I want to see you . . ." he hesitated, "tonight. That's why I left the message to call by 6:00. I'm glad you made it back on schedule."

I thought only women sounded breathless. I was wrong. Paul sounded breathless when there was a sense of urgency about something. He rushed to say what's on his mind. He was doing it now.

"I can be there by 7:00. Will he be gone by then? I'll call you from the car to make certain. All you have to do is say yes, and I'll be there."

I was overwhelmed. I'd no idea I'd see him so soon after getting back. I was thrilled and excited and couldn't hold back my feelings. I really missed him.

"Yes, I'll be here," I said it as calmly as I could, "and yes, please call from the car."

"Terrific. Save some supper for me."

"It's windy here, Paul. Be careful on that crazy road."

Again he waited for me to hang up first.

He hadn't said how he could get away. I hadn't asked. I vowed I wouldn't, ever. If he wanted me to know, he'd tell me.

I slid into the warm, scented water and closed my eyes.

"Soup's hot, the salad's mixed." Guy's booming voice brought me out of my reverie. "Shall I pour you a beer? I've made coffee, too."

"No beer, just coffee. Thanks, dear. I'll be out a.s.a.p."

Guy and I supped and talked. As the time slipped by I became agitated, wanting to continue and yet, increasingly aware of the duplicity of the situation, wanting him to leave. My beloved Guy, who had only just told me how he admired my honesty and integrity. Here I was, less than forty-eight hours later, deceiving him. Oh, I know he respected my privacy as I did his. It's just that right on the heels of his declaration of admiration, I felt like a heel. I knew then, I'd tell him about Paul soon. More out of the fact that we'd be working closely together for the next several weeks than a need to tell all.

I didn't want to have to hide. Doing so would kill my relationship with Paul faster than anything else. I needed to be able to make and receive calls and I needed Guy's steady hand and head. He'd guided me before. I simply hadn't heeded his warnings.

Was I setting him up to be my alter ego? That didn't seem quite fair. I convinced myself I only wanted to be open and honest with my best male friend. I'd listen to his opinion. He wouldn't offer advice.

"You really *are* tired. I am leaving, and I hope you go straight to bed!"

"I'm sorry dear. I guess my mind was elsewhere. You go. Mind the windy road. We'll talk tomorrow."

"Don't come outside, Jenny. It's turning quite nippy. There's the phone, anyway. Go back inside. We'll talk tomorrow afternoon. Bye, dear."

"Bye . . . Hello?" Now I was breathless.

"For a moment I was afraid you had gone away."

"No way. Guy was just leaving. I'm here and getting ready to heat the soup for you."

"I'm in Mill Valley and will be there very soon."

"I can hardly wait."

"Nor I, Jenny. Nor I."

I stood by the phone for a moment. Suddenly, I felt every fiber of my being resonating to the urgency in his voice. The sound of it made me catch my breath. My head began to throb. My cheeks were burning. What was happening to me? I hadn't felt like this in years. The pent-up emotions, the feeling of being starved for intimacy. All of it was unleashed by the sound of Paul's voice. What was I going to say to him? I heard the car come into the driveway. Paul jumped out and slammed the door. He got to my door as I opened it.

He took one look at me and grabbed me up in his arms and carried me to the couch—kissing me all the way. No words, only moans. He flung off his jacket and I opened my arms.

I'd not dressed. I'd hurried to join Guy at the table and had slipped into a thick velour robe. My hair was tied back with a blue ribbon. I had no makeup on.

"My God, you look beautiful. Sexy eyes, shining face; what have you got on under the robe?" He began unzipping it. I thought I'd go through the ceiling. I fumbled and struggled to undo his clothes. All the silly things people do in the throes of passion. They're all true, and we did them all.

There were no further comments, just hurried, awkward, clutching and clinging amid exploding emotions.

He lay back and sighed and laughed.

"Not exactly the lingering, languid way I imagined it would be the first time, Jenny. I guess it took too long to drive here and the preliminaries were over by the time you answered the door." He was laughing a bit self-consciously.

"We'll make up for it later." I laughed, too. "Come on. Let's get you some soup and quiet down a little."

"For now."

We were, happily, past the first hurdle.

"I'm here for the night if you'll have me, Jen. I've got till noon tomorrow before I head up north again."

"How wonderful! Seventeen whole uninterrupted hours! You're some genius, Mister."

"And you're some dish, lady."

He ate the soup with gusto. Also with chunks of bread and cheese. He carried his coffee mug to the sink as I prepared to clean up.

"That can wait. This can't." No more soft sweet kisses. Not this time. Not now. Deep passionate kisses. Our bodies crushed against each other.

"I think my bed will be more comfortable," I offered when I could speak.

We made our way to my room and tumbled onto the thick down comforter.

"We'll drown in down, Jen. Let's pull it back."

We did. And climbed in laughing. My God, how we laughed.

I guess it's the laughter, the giggling that really got me—so lighthearted; everything is fun and amusing . . . and serious. Probably the most serious relationship of my life, because of the awareness of the pitfalls we had to avoid.

Nothing was 'made-up' with us. No pretense. No 'making nice' or 'making do'. No man but Tom had ever been with me—stayed with me in the way we were together. Until now, no man but Tom had ever given himself to me in this manner. Totally trusting, expecting and accepting being trusted in return. He was complete with me. I was, once again, complete with him.

Our fingers were intertwined, and I turned our hands over lightly kissing his finger.

"Did I kiss yours or mine?" I couldn't tell the difference.

He pulled me to him again. And surrendered himself with utter openness and a great deep passion. He took me with him on an incredible journey. Not a word was uttered, and yet everything was understood. Acknowledged by a deep sigh, a racking shudder. Held so closely, so tenderly—our very breath was the same.

"Where are you going?" I had started to get untangled.

"Just getting comfortable so I can sleep. I'm right here."

"Roll over if you must, but I'm coming with you."

And we slept.

I heard the shower, but could neither move nor speak. He'd not have heard me anyway. He was bellowing some great, happy tune as he splashed.

He came into the room partially draped in a bath sheet. Such a beautiful person and a body that was perfection. I knew what it was like, even fully clothed, and I was right. Long, lean, supple—long firm muscles and beautifully tan.

"You're so beautiful. There's not an extra ounce on you. Almost nothing to pinch."

"Don't think I haven't been working on that." He grinned impishly. "Happily, you have wonderful, girlie things to pinch. Here, I'll show you."

By the time I got to the kitchen, coffee was brewing and everything was out of the fridge that remotely resembled breakfast. Like having the twins home.

The thought of the boys made me burst out laughing.

"What's so funny? Share please." He handed me a glass of orange juice. "Drink it first. You need the energy. Now what made you laugh so?"

"I was thinking of my sons."

"Oh? Would they disapprove?" He paused in the middle of beating eggs.

"I must tell you I really don't think so. They would probably be both surprised and delighted. You see, they've been talking about me between themselves and each of them, in his own way, expressed concern that I didn't have a 'nice guy,' I think Max said, in my life. They're feeling a bit sorry for me. I think because they each have made serious commitments in the last several months. Anyway, the whole scene just suddenly struck me very funny."

"I like those boys already. They've got the right idea about their mother. We'll have to tell them they can relax now."

Every time Paul said something like that my heart lurched. Here we were living out a fantasy with no apparent foundation to build upon. For a structural engineer it seemed a mite tricky.

We had breakfast on the terrace. The sun was burning off the mist and everything was shining and clear.

I rose and went to my studio to get a camera. I had to have a picture of him and, maybe, one of the two of us.

He looked up at me with that wonderful smile draped across his face as I clicked away. He took the camera and placed it on the rail, set the timer and pulled me onto his lap. We made faces at the camera just as it flashed.

"I have no words, Jenny; at least not adequate ones to tell you what being here with you like this means to me."

"I'm at a loss for words myself."

"You're beautiful, talented and wise; what a potent combination, my girl." He stood up and stretched. "How about a trot on the beach before I have to leave?"

We walked for about an hour—holding hands; stopping for a kiss; picking up a sand dollar—just being together. No pretense, no "trying," just being who we really are. Pleasing each other automatically—perfectly harmonious. What a blessing.

Too soon we were back at the house. Too soon he would have to leave. He had a plane to catch for Vancouver.

"How I wish you were coming along."

"Don't tempt me."

"Sometime we'll do it."

"Wouldn't that be glorious?" I squeezed the arm that was around me.

"When will you be back . . . ?"

"When will you be in town?"

We stumbled over each other's questions.

"You first," I said.

"I return tomorrow afternoon . . . and you?"

"I'm driving to TJ's tomorrow afternoon. I'll be with her until Monday or Tuesday."

"Then you're coming back here?"

"Yes. Guy will come up to my place. We'll have a live-in work session for a few days. Then he and I will reorganize for the second part of the trip. It should take a week at the most to finish the project."

Paul nodded and asked, "Will you be having Thanksgiving dinner here?"

"Oh, yes. Both the boys and their young women will be here. Doesn't it crack you up not to be able to say 'girls' anymore? They'd be so insulted! Soon they'll simply be my four 'kids,' like it or not."

"Yes, in the outside world 'woman' or 'young woman' seems easy and right. It's awkward in the family, though, I agree. Beth gives it to me, too, when I refer to her girlfriends as just that. And I've known most of them since they were squirts."

"They'd certainly like being called squirts! And you? Will you have a family dinner at home?"

"Yes, it's our turn this holiday. We do the usual one year here and one year at another family member's home. Thanksgiving's ours this year. And I might add, I have a whole lot extra to be thankful for this time."

He never misses an opportunity to say something nice. To include me in any way possible. It didn't go unnoticed.

"Call me at TJ's if you're able. Otherwise, I'll be back here for certain by Tuesday."

"With a house full!"

"That's true. I won't be terribly accessible," I conceded.

"I'll find a way. You can count on that. I'll see you before you go, in any case."

"Will you be able to?" I wasn't ever going to ask that question. Never.

"I'll make it happen. I promise."

"Don't, Paul. Don't promise. You may not be able to keep it."

"That's for me to handle, Jenny. You're not to concern yourself with my situation. I repeat: I promise I'll be with you—long before you leave."

By now he had to leave. It was difficult beyond words to part. I felt ragged inside. Paul embraced me at the door and again at his car.

Again and again. I worried about the good-byes.

"I want copies of those pictures," he called out as he drove off.

"Bye. Bye."

How I wished Honey were with me. I needed her to confide in.

# 16

When I went into the kitchen and saw the chaos only a creative happy man can make, I laughed and poured myself a cup of coffee. I'd never finished the first one. We were too busy.

I strolled out to the terrace and sat down in his chair. I sipped the coffee with my eyes closed and relived the past 17-½ hours of perfection in the minutest detail. I was warm all over again. Blissful and happy, at least for now. And who wanted to spoil it by thinking about the possibility of 'not now'? Life happens now. Not in the past, and there may be no future. Now!

I must have dozed a bit. Admittedly, I'd had little sleep. The ringing phone awakened me but by the time I reached it, the answering machine had picked up. I let it. The mood I was in, I wasn't prepared to talk to anyone.

I went into the darkroom and enlarged a few of the first pictures I'd taken and I thought of what TJ had said earlier: "Be happy . . . it's the only decent thing to do."

The phone rang again. This time it was my neighbor, Laura, the writer of children's books.

"Hi, Jen. Glad you're back. How'd you like to have a bite of dinner tonight? I could use a little diversion and some adult conversation."

"Oh, hello Laura, what a good idea, sure. I can use a little diversion myself. It's been a rather intense time for me, too." What a magnificent understatement.

We settled on potluck. I'd bring Celestina's great soup and she'd supply the rest.

Nice dinner, nice company, an altogether satisfying way to spend a few hours. It also gave me a little time to separate myself from the racking emotions I'd felt all day.

"I've enjoyed being with you, Laura. It's been much too long since we've done this." We were thoroughly relaxed sitting on the floor in front of her fireplace, talking of inconsequential things. I suddenly had an overwhelming desire to mention Paul to her. It would have been so easy. Luckily an alarm bell went off in her garage. A perfect warning for me.

"It sometimes happens in windy weather," she said. "Excuse me while I turn the darn thing off."

"Speaking of turning off, I'm about to leave and turn off my day." I rose and walked out with her.

"Thanks for tonight, Laura. It was just perfect. Just what I needed to clear my head."

I slipped into a warm tub before climbing back under the covers. Was it just twenty-four hours ago? What was it with this man? So much in such a short time. A world of living in 17 ½ hours. Can this be real? Happiness, passion, fun—all the emotions wrapped up in so few moments? He comes and goes like a puff of smoke. I go about my daily life calm and directed, focused on the job at hand; yet, there is an underlying tension, anticipation mixed with anxiety.

Can he be feeling the same? I somehow doubted that. After all, wasn't I simply the frosting on the cake of his life? And since I was his fantasy-come-to-life person, he could compartmentalize me and not feel guilty. Hadn't he dreamed of me forever? Played out the scenes—spoken the words; acted the acts of love? I was no stranger to him. Therefore, no guilt.

My thoughts were getting fuzzy. The moment I relaxed into sleep the telephone rang. "Hello . . . ?"

"Jenny, did I awaken you? I did. I'm so sorry."

"Paul?" Yawn and sigh.

"Yes. It's me. Are you all right? It's not very late; only 10:00."

"I'm fine, really. I just fell asleep thinking about you—about us in this very bed so few hours ago."

"I wish I was with you right now. I just got back from a meeting with the clients. It's cold, and I miss you. What did you do today?"

"Not a whole lot." I sat up in bed and turned on a light. "Did a bit of printing; took a nap." I laughed, and so did he. "And had dinner with Laura at her house. I brought over the rest of the soup."

"Laura? Who's she?"

"My next-door neighbor. I think I mentioned her. She's a writer."

"Yes, you did. Sounds like a very pleasant unenergetic day."

"Exactly—unenergetic."

"You expended enough energy for a few days! Get rested up. I approve." He was chuckling.

"Well, I do have a restful weekend planned; although, it does entail some work."

"I'm tired myself. It's been an intense day for me at every level." Big sigh. "I'm about to crash. I just wanted to say how incredible our time together was. More than I can say. It was the greatest night of my life, Jenny—by any measure you want to use. Thank you."

He was doing it again. Saying such perfect things to me. I didn't know how to respond. I wanted to say: "Please don't be married. Tell me that was just a joke. Please." Instead, I said something unmemorable. He said all the memorable things.

"Sweet dreams to you, my Jenny."

*A Small Flirtation*

I fell asleep wondering how he could be so candid about his feelings—expressing them so freely and fully; how he could be so seemingly untouched by the reality of our lives. When it came to us, he was able to keep it separate somehow.

I was terribly wrong.

The day dawned fresh and clear. I was up early and took advantage of the morning light to shoot some coastal views that were spectacular. They might be useful later. Anyway, it was a way to focus myself on the work at hand.

I was sitting at my desk when Guy phoned. He was excited by the first look at our work and asked me to bring everything I had with me.

"Come here and we'll take a look at all of it together. I'll even take you to lunch. By the way, TJ invited me to dinner tonight."

"Thank heavens we've got our next meals lined up!" He chuckled at that one. My friends all tease me about my love of food—it is a sacred subject to me. " Fine, Guy. I'm finishing up at my desk now. I'll come straight to you. See you soon."

## 17

The house was too quiet. Ordinarily I loved the peacefulness of it, but this time it felt deserted—kind of like when the twins leave, though in truth, this place has never been their home, they've made a definite mark on it.

But it wasn't the boys I was missing. It was the man who had filled the house with his being so few hours ago that made it feel so empty, now he was gone.

The rush of feelings was so strong when I thought of him, it made me slightly weak in my stomach, as though I'd had my breath knocked out of me.

I hadn't felt this way since the years with Tom. He, too, filled a room when he entered, and I was excited in the same kind of way. When he died and the boys went off to college, the void inside of me was so great, I didn't believe I could function. Family and friends were wonderful, saying all the wrong things, but that didn't matter so much. I understood. They were in shock, too. Most importantly, they were there.

Gradually life righted itself. My interior gyroscope was doing its job—keeping me in balance. I got through the chaotic interlude, which somehow brought me to this place and dropped me on this beautiful shore to compose myself and continue on. I must have had an awful lot of life's lessons to learn. It certainly has taken me long enough to do it.

Now it was time to see if the learning was only intellectual or had I internalized the answers and was I now able to live them? God knows I'd lived the questions long enough! And it surely isn't God's fault I'm such a slow learner!

I shook myself out of my ruminations and took a long look at my reaction to this deep sense of loss I had begun to feel every time I said good-bye to Paul. I finally admitted I was becoming terrified of losing him, as I had Tom. All the admonitions to drive carefully, to take care of himself were more than the commonplace niceties people spoke these days. They were prayers sent directly to Heaven to protect this wonderful stranger who the Fates had brought to me.

Leaving the house sooner than planned was a blessing. I was happy to put all of the soul searching aside, to get back to work and join my old friends for the weekend.

By the time I closed up and took off I was humming again. The beautiful early morning weather held, and I was off.

Guy greeted me with great exuberance. He was obviously more than pleased with what we'd done.

"Hi, Kiddo. Come on in." Kiss on the cheek. "Wait till you see what we got—some really good stuff!"

I followed him into his studio. He had already printed a few things, as had I. We lined them up and took a critical look.

"They really are quite good. If the rest reach this level, we're home free, Guy."

"Here's hoping the trip south is as fruitful." He raised his glass of water in a toast. "To the birds!"

I said we'd undoubtedly have plenty of good shots left over, what did he think of putting a book together?

"And call it *To the Birds*." I laughed at his idea.

"Why not?" We could turn our notes over to TJ and have her work on the text." He was warming to the subject. "Let's mention it tonight. But for now, Jen, I'm getting hungry. How about you?"

"You know me, Guy, I'm always ready to eat. Where shall we go?" We were out the door already.

He turned to me and asked... "Sushi?" I held my breath. "There's that place around the corner we can walk to, or we can ride over to the Japan Center. You know the place I'm sure. It has really great food."

"Yes, I've been there. It is good, but can we afford the time?" I wasn't ready to go back there so soon.

"Listen, Jen, we've been working nonstop for weeks. I think we can take an extra thirty minutes for lunch. Since when did you become such a slave driver?"

We were stopped at a signal when Guy turned to me smiling, "By the way, you're looking exceptionally lovely today. What's different? Your hair? You don't usually tie it back like that."

"No. It was still damp from my shower. It seemed the easiest and fastest thing to do."

"You had it like that the other night. It's quite fetching, if I do say so."

"Go ahead and say so. I love the compliments."

"You sure were 'out of it' by the time I left the other night. Did you go to bed early?"

"Yes." I didn't dare elaborate, not now. Not about that night. Later I'd tell him about Paul. Sooner or later—but not about that night. That was mine.

Luckily he was distracted by the traffic and parking. I sighed in relief. The moment passed—for the moment. I'd face it another time. Guy knew me too well and was a keen observer as I've noted before. We talked of nothing more important than the food and brought up the book idea again.

Then I saw him.

He was standing in the doorway looking for a place to sit. He

*A Small Flirtation*

was with another man who I recognized. They were heading my way when Paul spotted me. He almost waved, then he realized I was with someone else, and he wasn't alone either.

"Hi, Jenny. Hi, Guy. How's it going on the Bird Project?" Tim Rawlins owned the professional lab we worked with.

I held onto the counter as I turned toward him. "Oh, hi Tim." It was all I could manage.

"We're gearing up for the second half," Guy answered, as he rose and shook hands.

I was looking over his shoulder at Paul. Paul was looking at Guy. I could only see the back of Guy's head, so I didn't know where the heck he was looking.

Tim saw me glance at Paul. "Oh, this is Paul Crowley. I'm trying to make a customer of him. Jenny Matthews, Guy Meadows, Paul."

"Hello."

"Guy." Paul stuck out his hand.

"Hi, Tim. Hello, Paul." They shook hands.

As luck would have it, two seats opened up next to Guy, and they took them. Tim turned to Paul saying, "These two, they're the greatest photographers you'll ever meet."

And so the charade continued. Tim explained our project to Paul. Paul and Guy trying to connect and unable to because of the seating arrangement. Guy had moved so Tim and I were in the middle leaving the other two out completely.

We finished first, said our good-byes and made our way out of the restaurant after promising to stop in before we took off again to look at some outdoor filters he'd just got in.

"Paul Crowley didn't take his eyes off you." Guy looked over at me as he maneuvered into the traffic. "Did you notice?"

"I was too busy talking to Tim about the new filter I need." I blushed. I could feel my face get hot.

"Jenny, old pal, am I sensing there was more to that scene than meets the naked eye?"

"Now, Guy, what kind of a scenario are you cooking up? Other than Tim explaining who I was, I didn't notice any particular interest in me."

"Then why are you blushing?" Guy persisted.

"Why did you move to the other side of me?"

"To get a better view of the whole scene. I had a feeling something was happening. There was another dynamic at work there. Come on, Jen, fess up."

"Guy, come on. You're going to drive me up a wall with your dreaming up situations to entangle me."

"You're right. I do—it's fun. However, this time I smell a rat. Something's going on you're not telling me. No wonder you're looking so enticing lately. I'll get the truth out of you yet."

Blessedly we both laughed and dropped it. Well, almost.

"I'll get it out of TJ. She can't resist me. Besides, she's a terrible liar—can't keep a straight face worth a damn. Don't know how she keeps winning at bridge."

We were back at Guy's, busily at work when TJ called, "Hi, dear. What's up?" As Guy was out of the room, I answered.

TJ sounded serious. "Paul just phoned and told me what happened. He sounded like grim death."

"Oh? Why?" I was trying to stay neutral.

"He couldn't believe that neither of you had the presence of mind to admit to knowing each other from Berkeley." TJ sighed. "Meeting Guy that way makes everything more awkward in that department."

"It probably would have been easy," I admitted. "But we both were in shock. We've never rehearsed that scene."

"One more thing, Paul was planning to come by for a drink before heading home tonight. Now, he doesn't see how he can unless we pretend he's coming to see me. And that sure as the devil won't fly, not with Guy."

"Good lord no."

"Have you thought about telling Guy? I mean right now?" TJ asked.

"No, I haven't, though it might be the easiest thing to do. But not here—later, with you."

"For moral support?"

"Something like that." I'm a devout coward.

"In any event, this isn't the right time to have Paul drop in," TJ stated flatly.

"No way. Even if I were to go into it here, now, I don't think it would be a good idea."

"I agree," TJ replied firmly.

And so I left it for the moment. Knowing full well the issue of Paul would be addressed sometime that weekend. There was no easy way. Frankly, I felt it would be a relief.

TJ was anxious to talk to me alone. As soon as we arrived, she dragged me into her bedroom ostensibly to show me something. Guy didn't have a clue. He busied himself with the dogs and said he'd pull out something from the fridge to have before dinner. He was content to be with the two of us for a few hours.

"Paul called again after I spoke to you. I told him you felt it wasn't the right time to talk to Guy. You didn't want to force the issue as it could come about easily when you were traveling."

"Exactly."

"He said he wants to come over anyway. Now that he knows who Guy is in your life, he feels he might as well face up to the 'situation,' I believe he called it."

"Now, we're a situation? An item maybe; but, I never quite thought of us as a 'situation'." I smiled to myself.

"He sounded like a kid about to meet the in-laws." TJ was amused.

Oh brother. What did I get myself into? More of Paul wants to control every situation. "Guy is already smelling a rat. He said so after lunch. He was teasing, but . . ."

"But, he was kidding on the square. That's his style. You know that, Jen."

"What shall I tell Paul when he calls?"

"I can't tell you what to do on that score, Jenny. But I will say, in sum, I honestly don't think it will make one iota of difference to anyone which way you go. So, dear, make yourself comfortable. Play it anyway you like. I'll go along."

"You mean in the long run it won't matter one way or the other?"

"Precisely."

I was silent for a moment thinking the 'situation' through. TJ didn't say another word, but stood looking at me expectantly.

"I agree totally. Twenty years from now who will even remember? What I am worried about is how Guy will feel tomorrow. We do have a lot of work to finish. Weeks worth. Will knowing about Paul and me make a difference?"

"You must be joking. No way will Guy be affected by this nor will it change his feelings for you. However, he is so accustomed to his special role in your life, what he might be is a little jealous. I doubt he would take kindly to the idea of being replaced by Paul. You must know he's crazy about you and always has been." TJ was serious again.

I told her he'd spoken to me about his feelings, and that he and I agreed our lifelong friendship is more important than a love life together which could spoil everything.

"That's crazy, and also true. You two would never make it married. Your friendship may have survived a roll in the hay or so, but marriage, no way! I've always told you: You must never marry your Saturn. No one who wants a long, happy marriage should do that."

"I forgot. I can't remember all of that. Must be why I rely on you so totally."

"Uh, huh. Must be!"

The phone rang. TJ looked at me as she grabbed it. "Hello?" It was Paul.

I turned my hands over, palms up in defeat, and nodded yes.

"Outside the house? Here? Now?"

"Good Lord!"

"Jenny's very uncertain. She's right here. Let me put her

on." TJ handed me the phone and left the room to join Guy. She obviously wanted to give us privacy.

"Paul, hello."

"Hello, Jenny. That was really wild, wasn't it?"

"It worked OK with Tim, I think. Don't you?"

"Oh, absolutely. He thinks you're terrific. I heard about you all the way back to my office."

"Flattery will get you what you want. Come on in. It's not the way I wanted you and Guy to meet; but, what the hell!"

"Look Jen, if you honestly think it's a lousy idea, I'll go along with that. I'm sorry. I know I'm pushing." At least he admitted it.

"It's OK. How can I say no to seeing you when you're outside the door? That's impossible, on the face of it. Just hang up and come on in. We'll make it work."

"I like the sound of that. Now get ready to look surprised."

"No, Paul. Wait. Not surprised. I want Guy to understand that we've talked and decided to be up front with him. It's much more respectful of our relationship. His and mine, I mean."

"You're right. I wasn't thinking of Guy. Hang up, Jenny. I'm coming in!"

I laughed as I went into TJ's bathroom. I brushed my hair, retied it and put a touch of lipstick on. There. That would have to do. The doorbell rang. Guy was busy in the kitchen getting a bucket of ice. I came out into the foyer as TJ opened the door. I hadn't had a chance to tell her not to be surprised.

"Paul! What a nice surprise. Come in, join us. We're just about to have a glass of wine."

Luckily, Guy hadn't heard what she'd said. I quickly told her our decision to handle this straight on. Based on our meeting at lunchtime, it would not be good to pretend we didn't know Paul was coming—not to Guy. She nodded in approval and said she'd follow our lead, and then proceeded into the living room ahead of us.

"Guy, pour another glass of wine. We have company." TJ

had Paul in tow. "I hear you met my friend, Paul Crowley today." TJ was wearing one of her most beguiling smiles.

Guy was coming toward us. "Paul Crowley. Your friend, TJ? You mean you and he? Hello again, Paul." Guy put out his hand. Paul took it. He was grinning.

"Not exactly, Guy. It's Paul and Jenny." TJ wasn't going to leave me out on a limb all by myself. Guy directed his attention to me and waited to hear more.

"That's it, Guy. What you've been feeling is true." I turned to Paul. "Guy's been watching and wondering out loud, what's been going on with me. I've been putting him off, but he's got the best sniffer in town. He knew I'd confide in him soon." I emphasized the word 'confide.'

Guy's eye caught mine and he nodded, barely. He had got it all in one breath. He'd watch it carefully. He'd guard me fiercely, as he had done all the years since Tom died. My special protector. I can't imagine why I was reluctant to tell him. Probably because Paul was married—Guy would hate that for me. Also, it was premature.

There was nothing but the barest bones; the barest outline to this relationship. It could still go nowhere. Or it could go everywhere. We'd just have to let it unfold. "We'll see" was my father's answer to many pleas of mine. And "we'll see" still fit.

"Now I understand. I was observing you watching Jenny at lunch, Paul." Guy was genuinely engaged by now in understanding the dynamics of the earlier meeting. "Well, now that the mystery of why Jenny's been looking so delectable lately has been revealed, let's have a drink together and some real conversation."

Guy was being gracious beyond gracious. I was beginning to be skeptical. Was he going to pounce? If so, when?

TJ was obviously relieved. Guy was right about her. She's a terrible liar and deceiving him would have been an awful burden. Sins of omission were as great as sins of commission to her. Lessons of childhood die hard, if at all, for most of us.

My skepticism was short lived. Guy and Paul were soon finding common interests beyond TJ and me. Guy was talking about our recent trip, the project and the next leg coming up, while Paul described his work and teaching at Cal.

"You're at Cal, too? I'm surprised you and Jenny hadn't met before."

"Yes, me too. Now we're planning to look at our courses and maybe team teach for part of the spring term."

TJ and I exchanged glances, and in one lock-step-move left for the kitchen.

"Would you believe...?" I was dumbfounded and delighted.

"How often must I remind you, men are such simple creatures? We worry about everything—every word, every nuance. And men, do they not do that, too? Nonsense! They say 'Oh? Is that so? Well, hum.' And that's it. On to the next subject. Look at them, and tell me I'm wrong."

"Never." I answered fervently.

"And to think you were ready to clunk me in this very house over that very man just a few weeks ago. Am I not most forgiving and gracious to my slightly wayward friend?"

"What you are is incorrigible. Let's make dinner."

"I don't think he's staying, Jenny. At least he didn't say anything other than wanting to come by for a few minutes."

"It's nearly 6:00. I think I'll just go in and begin to light the fire. That should break up their conversation for a moment. Then I'll mention dinner." I left TJ in the kitchen.

The two men had gone outside. Even though it was still sunny, it was getting quite nippy, but they didn't appear to notice.

"How about a fire? I could use some help."

"Sure, Jen. We're coming. It's getting to feel wintry out there." Guy was already crumpling paper.

Paul stopped me with his arm. "There. And now it's done, right?"

"Right." I smiled and lifted my face He touched the tip of my nose. "Are you OK with it now?"

"Yes. I am. Thanks for the push."

"It didn't take much. Now did it?"

"Didn't take much what?" Guy looked up from the fireplace at us.

"Jenny had wanted to tell you about us during your trip," Paul answered.

"And I would have, but the timing was somehow off," I interrupted.

"The serendipitous luncheon today did it. I convinced her now was the time and this was the place." Paul was being pleased with himself.

"And it didn't take much convincing, is that it?"

"Right. She wanted to and didn't know it." Paul looked at me grinning.

"God bless men! You've got it all worked out so simply. You're simply wonderful, or is it that you're wonderfully simple?" I was laughing and TJ had heard me, too.

"Smart girl. I always had confidence in you. I knew one day you'd figure it out!" TJ joined in.

"Now that we've got that straight, I'm going to have to break away from this sage group," Paul broke in. "Sorry guys, but you know Friday traffic heading down the peninsula As always, TJ, thanks for the open door. Guy, I'm glad we've met. Very glad." He slipped his arm around my waist in a protective manner—or was it a possessive move? "Now, I really can be jealous of you and all the time you have with Jenny. Before it was just the idea of a friend traveling with her and sharing work. I envy you."

Guy and Paul shook hands and looked at each other very soberly as though they were making a pledge to each other.

"Thanks, Paul. I'm glad we've met, too. Now, I'll have something new to tease Jen about."

"I'll walk you to the car, Paul." I moved between them.

"It's too cold, Jenny. Stay in. They'll go to the kitchen and leave us alone for two minutes."

TJ and Guy left us. Over his shoulder Guy said, "Did you hear that, TJ? Two minutes." We hugged and held each other tenderly and kissed and parted and smiled and kissed again with such a fierce intensity we both stumbled and caught ourselves before we crashed into the door.

"Not again. Not now. How funny we are." I held his arm for balance. "We need time, Jenny."

Another embrace. He tore himself away from me. "I'm sorry. I really do have to go."

"I know, Paul. I know. Good night, dear friend."

"Good night, my Jenny." And he was out the door. I stood in the doorway until he was gone. I'd have to stop doing that; it cast an overlay of sadness on the pure joy I felt being with him.

Inside I could hear the clatter of preparations in the kitchen. I was very glad my beloved friends were here with me. For now, all was well in my world.

# 18

"He's married." Not a question. Guy was watching me.

"Yes, as a matter of fact he is—very. Complete with childhood sweetheart and young adult daughter."

"Be careful, dear one. He's a nice man. He's not going to mean to hurt you, but he very well might. That's all I'm going to say. Just don't ever think you can't tell me something. That's nonsense. We're here for each other. Remember that."

"And now that the high drama is over, do you suppose we could have some music, stoke the fire, throw the steaks on and pour some wine? All this climbing over hurdles has made me very hungry." TJ had finished tossing the salad and was seasoning the meat.

"I'm famished myself. And frankly, with the tension at lunch, I don't remember eating much. Garlic toast anyone?" I bit into a crispy piece, picked up my glass and headed for the couch

I was wiped out. Satisfied with the way things went I began to relax and think about what had happened. The men got along extremely well, and that pleased me. We were rapidly becoming a happy little family. I caught myself on that one. My fantasies were working overtime again. Guy was right. I'd have to be careful.

I dropped the subject of Paul. There was nothing more to be said. Both of my friends had warned me, each one in a different way. TJ was being girly and light-hearted in her admonitions of 'keep it light.' It was her way of telling me not to take all of this too seriously. After all, there was no place for it to go that could possibly suit me—not at this time, under these conditions. What she admonished made good sense—it was also terribly difficult to do.

Guy, to whom all of this was brand new news, was much more direct, much more to the point. He was also a man, talking from a man's perspective. "Be careful! You could get hurt!"

Keeping my emotions in check was a whole lot more difficult than letting them run free in fantasy.

We spent the rest of the evening talking over plans for the remainder of our bird trip and then began with the first sketchy ideas of how to spend the various holidays, which were rapidly coming upon us.

"By the time you two get back and settle down, it'll be Thanksgiving." TJ was piling mashed potatoes on my plate. "Will the boys and girls both be here?"

"Absolutely. Nicky and Diane are coming for a week; part of it, they'll be in Santa Clara."

"I'd 'do dinner' here for them one night, or shall I have Thanksgiving here?" TJ was addressing me.

"Dinner one night here would be great. You can do one of your fabulous numbers—candles, flowers, music, the works. I'll have Thanksgiving as planned. I know Nicky wants Diane to experience a holiday dinner at the beach."

Guy was quiet letting 'the girls' work it out, knowing full well he'd be at both events no matter what else he had on his agenda or with his own family. We three were inseparable and that was that.

That settled, we moved onto Christmas vacation.

"How about renting a big house someplace, and all of us go skiing?" Guy is a very good athlete. He is shorter than Paul is and wirier. His muscular strength came from his life on the family ranch. His dark curly hair and blue eyes bespeak of his family heritage when the Irish and Spanish fraternized centuries ago. His idea of fun always includes some sort of sport. "We could have Christmas in town and go up for the week after or vice versa."

"Vice versa is too complicated. Hauling skis and Christmas goodies is too much of a good thing in my book," TJ grimaced. "Can't you see taking ornaments and gifts and all that jazz?"

"Not I. No, Guy. I like the idea of all of us together after, and then staying over New Year's Eve." I seconded TJ's grimace.

We talked on a bit more, sketching out our holiday plan and looking forward to all 'the young' joining in yet again. We mused over Nick and Diane moving west and joined in a conspiracy to woo Diane from her eastern establishment life.

"It's set, then and now I'm going to leave you two elegant female creatures and head home. Thanks, TJ. It was a lovely dinner, as always. And to you, Jenny, I say once more and only once more, he's a very nice man. I understand where you're coming from and be careful. Remember, I love you very much. Good night."

I was wordless. I gave him a quick kiss on the cheek and smiled and nodded.

TJ locked up, made her special cappuccino laced with Kahlua, and we flopped down by the fireplace in our usual places.

"TJ, I must say you and Guy are right. I just don't know how to do it. To keep it light. I thought I could try willing myself to do so. Maybe I'll get used to it and be able to, yet. It's just, I've never had any experience in this sort of thing—you know, treachery."

"Treachery! My God, Jenny. Is that what you think? If so, stop right now—right this minute!" TJ looked sorrowful. "I only encouraged you because it's been so long since you've had any real boy-girl fun. And because you're so good at it, I thought you'd enjoy it for awhile. I had no idea you thought of it in such a damning way." And she shook her head.

"I swear the word just slipped out. I wasn't thinking about it in that way. It literally slipped out of my mouth. What do you think that means?"

She said I was becoming too serious too soon and needed to back off. "I'm very glad you won't have much chance to see him for a few weeks. Then the holidays and then who knows."

"I know, it's becoming the busiest season now for both of us. It's probably better that way." I reached for a biscotti and continued, "I can count on nothing, except for the very real fact, that I can count on nothing. It's all so frustrating. How could I have been so foolish?"

"You and many, many others have asked that question. Don't be hard on yourself, Jen."

"I'm not referring to the romance, I'm loving that part of it; I'm referring to the order I placed out there in the universe for this man. In the order, I foolishly forgot to add that he be available. Oh, TJ, I'm such a . . . what was it Scarlett called herself? Oh yes, I'm such a ninny."

"You certainly are."

"Oh, let's change the subject. It's getting boring, and you and I have had years of conversations without ever boring each other."

We went right back to planning Christmas and our skiing holiday. TJ took on the job of finding the best place with the best deal anywhere from Tahoe to Teluride. No small task. It was agreed that we would have something in motion before Guy and I took off again.

"I'm anxious to see Cara and meet her new beau. Gosh, how I dreamed of having her for my daughter. It never mattered which of the boys—just one of them." I said wistfully.

"They spent so much time growing up together, I think they all consider each other siblings."

"You're right, I'm sure, TJ. They'd be horrified. The idea probably seemed like incest to them."

"No doubt about it. Well it won't hurt for them to have a life-long, loving, sister-brothers relationship. Each one has missed out on that total experience."

We were deeply devoted to each other's children. They truly have been reared by us both, impartially, before and after we became single parents.

TJ's husband fell in love with a Vietnamese nurse while overseas. Hank Phillips was Air Force. He asked for a divorce. Got it, and married his nurse. They've been relatively happy as far as any of us knows. He's been good to Cara and OK to TJ. They were never the best match. Hank was a nice guy, but in no way equal to my stunning 'black Irish' friend—neither intellectually nor any other way.

She's had a fling or two. Nothing terribly exciting or particularly fulfilling. Frankly, I think being a single parent suits her. She's been free to pursue her esoteric interests, unhampered by the time constraints and obligations of house-wifery. She adores Cara and vice versa. Their relationship is, at once, devoted and honest. They are a singularly rare pair.

"Just one thing more about Paul and me before we turn in. Enough of the soul searching part. I want to tell you our being together was perfection's self from every aspect."

"I told you I could tell in your voice over the phone. Then when I saw you, I was positive. I reiterate, don't stand too close together in public, you'll friz people's hair!"

"We are pretty electric, aren't we?"

"Yeah. And I'm delighted about that part of it. That's why I keep saying enjoy it and stop imaging the future. I'm certain you've heard 'don't push the river, it flows by itself.' Our friend Fritz Perls' contribution to Truisms-To-Live-By?"

We laughed and turned everything off. It was more than time to 'turn-it-off.' I'd had a very busy two days. Jam-packed, thrilling and exhausting. By extension, I'm sure my dear, true and loyal friend was exhausted by it, too.

I thought little, sighed a lot and slept soundly.

# 19

The weekend was spent working with Guy at his studio. I was extremely grateful to be emersed in a complex project. Every aspect was studied with critical eyes. Rough-cuts were made, some editing done, and while we worked we talked a great deal about our lives and the world at large. Nothing and nobody was sacred with one important exception: not one word was spoken about Paul.

"Well, that about wraps it up for now, I think. When will you leave TJ's for the beach?" Guy began to clean up the studio and close shop.

"As it's so early, I may just go up after dinner with TJ and get a jump on tomorrow." I reminded him autumn was definitely in the air, that it had turned quite chilly in the late afternoons. And to bring something warm if he wanted to run on the beach.

He walked me to my car, made certain I had everything and leaned down to give me a peck on the cheek.

"You're still my favorite girl, and I don't care who knows it" He chucked me under the chin and backed away from the car. "Paul's jealous. That's obvious, and he should be. It'll make a better man of him." The only mention tossed off over his shoulder as he walked away.

All the years since Tom's death, Guy had shown his devotion and affection in a myriad of ways to the twins and me. Now with Paul in the picture, he'd begun verbalizing his feelings almost every time we were together. I was becoming slightly unnerved by this turn of events and wondered how it would affect our time together on the road. I found out in ways I hadn't imagined in years.

TJ and I went out for Chinese food at a marvelous little place we'd frequented for years. The owner was always pleased to see us.

"You honor us by your presence in our humble establishment." Wu Yee bowed down and smiled, led us to a table, handed us menus and started to laugh. We had been so dumbfounded by the performance we couldn't speak.

"How was that, TJ? What'd you think, Jenny? I've been practicing."

"For what, for heaven's sake?" I asked.

"For a minute I thought I was in the wrong place." TJ was looking puzzled.

"For a part in a TV series," Wu Yee explained. "The Production Company scouting locations liked the place. They're working on an offer now and asked if I'd be interested in acting as owner-manager. What the heck!"

"As you are the owner-manager, I don't think it will be much of a stretch." TJ was already nibbling noodles.

"No stretch, but should be fun, and the money won't be bad. They'll paint the place and do whatever's necessary. My cousin will look at the contract. Stop worrying."

"Who's worrying? The look you're mistaking for concern is just hunger." I was smiling, sincerely.

"Oh golly, so solly!"

"Cut it out, Yee, you're giving being Chinese a bad name." TJ was cracking up. "Just order us some hot and sour soup to start, will you?"

Yee backed away bowing and grinning. He turned and snapped his finger at a waiter and pointed to us, all the while speaking Mandarin to the young man. He was all business now, turning back to us and waving.

I was really interested—especially about the location locators bit. I'd known several people over the years who had done this with their property and found it quite lucrative, as well as somewhat discommoding to be sure.

Yee returned during a lull. "You gals are early tonight. What's up?"

"I'm heading back to the beach and as I needed sustenance, we couldn't think of a better place."

"Good for me. Welcome again."

I asked Yee if he thought my place would make a good location for a movie or TV. I knew in advance, I'd do it only if they'd let me shoot them as they were shooting the picture. As movie companies frequently do a short subject on the filming of one of their epics, I did think this had all the makings of a plan.

"...and the money is good."

Yee was pleased at this turn of events. He liked us and would be happy to have given me a good tip. I asked for more details and he said he would get them for me and let me know.

"Call TJ, Yee, please. I'm on assignment now and will be difficult to catch, OK?"

Yee left our table after assuring us he'd pass on all pertinent information soon.

I turned to TJ. "My plans for driving home tonight have just folded. I think I'll go to sleep on time for once and get an early start. OK?"

"More than OK."

"Good. I'm set then. Let's head back to Sea Cliff."

We left the table. "Yee, it was delicious. Many thanks." TJ and I turned to leave when I remembered something.

"Your son, Yee. The older one. He's a structural engineer, isn't he?"

"Albert? Oh, yes. That is, as soon as he passes his state exams. He's with a very good firm. He's the new assistant to one of the partners. He's happy there."

"Really? That's very nice. Who does he work for?" I was holding my breath in anticipation of his answer.

"Mr. Paul Crowley. Do you know him?"

"I've met him. He teaches at Cal, too."

"Small world. Well, good night, you two."

Small world? I was choking as we left.

I turned to TJ. "Paul's new assistant? The one he's been ready to kill!"

"Oh, no!" TJ exclaimed.

"Oh, yes." We cracked up.

"What will you do. Will you tell Paul?"

"I have to. It would break Wu Yee's heart to have his son fired. Especially before he's licensed. It would be terrible. Also, he's probably just nervous. In any event, I'll see what I can do."

It is said that coincidence is God being anonymous. As we drove back to Sea Cliff, TJ and I talked about the power of this phenomenon and wondered what all of this meant. Were Paul and I on some predestined course or was it just wishful thinking? There was no knowing the answers to these musings—not at this time.

# 20

In the morning, I piled Honey and my gear into the car and climbed in amid a flurry of good-byes. I was anxious to get home and get started on the work.

"Our first over night we'll be in Santa Clara with Max. Guy wants to get a better fix on Bridget, now she'll be joining the clan. But we'll talk about all that later."

"Yes. I'm also anxious to know how the work goes and any gossip you might happen upon, along the way."

TJ was giving me a knowing look. I nodded by way of acknowledgment and we were off, heading home.

The car phone rang not five minutes from TJ's. I so seldom receive calls while I'm driving that it startled me. I use it so rarely myself, I fumbled turning it on.

"Hello?"

"Jenny. Oh, I'm glad I reached you." It was Paul.

"Anything the matter?"

"No, No. I called TJ's and she told me you'd just left. I was hoping we could have lunch before you become emersed in your work."

"Oh, I'm so sorry. I can't possibly." I groaned.

"Can you stop in town for a few minutes, now? I'll buy you a cup of coffee. Even a donut for Honey."

"What about me? I just might be persuaded if you throw in an apple cruller."

"Great. Can you pick me up? I'll grab a roll of plans and head down right now."

"A roll of plans? Oh, of course. Camouflage." Somehow it sounded better to me than subterfuge.

I pulled up in front as he was pushing through the doorway. He spotted me and waved, came straight over and hopped in, after Honey relinquished her front seat, that is.

"Good dog. Thank you, Honey. She's very well mannered, that pup of yours. Were your boys as good?"

"The dog is easier, I assure you." I was laughing remembering my two little devils.

"I have a picture of you managing the two of them at the same time. There must have been some pretty hilarious times."

"As well as times when I would have happily disowned them. By and large, it was great fun. In fact, it still is."

"I hope I can meet them both. We'll have to make it happen. Maybe over the holidays, while they're both in town."

"It would be fun maybe." I wasn't so sure. I would have to be careful about how I'd set it up, so it wouldn't seem like a set up. I wasn't used to being devious—certainly not with my sons.

"Well, we'll see if we can construct an opportunity. In the meantime turn right here and park. Over there is fine. Is Honey OK in the car?"

"Oh, sure. She'd rather be left in the car than at the house. This way she knows I'll be right back." I reached down and gave her head a pat. It was resting on the console.

*A Small Flirtation*

He got out quickly and came around to me. Before I could get out, he bent into the car to kiss me.

"There, that's better. Now, how about a really good cappuccino?"

He left his roll of plans in the car and tucked my arm under his arm instead. He smiled down at me in a very self-satisfied way.

"Pleased with yourself, are you?" I couldn't help giggling.

"You bet I am. I feel like I'm skipping school when I'm with you. It's delicious."

"We're awfully close to your office. What if one of your partners comes in or anyone from the office, in fact?"

"So what? You're my fellow instructor and friend. Don't worry, I won't disgrace you."

"Well, at least we do have several connections now."

"Several? Who? Although I could construct something with Guy and maybe TJ, if pressed."

"I'm sure you could, but there is still another one." I was having fun.

"Who, for heaven's sake?"

"Albert." I was watching Paul closely.

"Albert?"

"Yes, Albert, your young assistant. You know, the one who drives you crazy?"

"Albert Wu? My God, how do you know him?" He was astonished.

"TJ and I had dinner at Wu Yee's last night. We've all been friends for years."

"Wu Yee? I know that place. Good food. You mean that Wu is Albert's family?"

"Yes. Crazy, isn't it?"

"How'd you figure it out? About Albert, I mean?"

"Well, as we were leaving, it suddenly occurred to me that Yee had a son in engineering and I asked about him."

"And his father told you . . . ?"

"Yes, and I almost choked. He asked if I knew you. I said I'd met you and mentioned our both being at Cal. We couldn't get out of there fast enough. TJ was cracking up."

"I can just see it." We were both laughing. "So now I can't fire him, can I, without getting in dutch with you?" I was silent. "Well, I wasn't going to anyway. He's a good kid, just over-anxious, nervous about his work and his upcoming exams. The whole thing is pretty daunting for him right now."

"I'm truly relieved, Paul. You must know what this means to his family."

"Of course, I do. And really, he's quite good and will be a whole lot better when he's more seasoned. I'm not willing to give up on him. That's too easy. It's just when he . . ."

"I know. It's when he slows you down and detains you as you're leaving to meet me. That's when you're ready to kill him."

We kept up the small talk about Albert and the office and my work...inconsequential talk just to stay together. Every minute was so precious. Neither of us wanted to let go.

"It's getting late, Paul. I'm sure you need to get back, and I, for sure, must leave." He was finishing his donut and reaching for the check.

"Cheap date." Grinning.

"Wait. You've no idea—yet."

"I'll wait, happily. I see you're wearing your cowboy in the right place." I was wearing it right over my heart.

"An appropriate place, don't you agree?"

"Exactly. It's just where I want him. Right over your heart."

We left hand in hand, again. It was the least and the most we could do walking down the street in the middle of San Francisco. He shortened his stride for me and moved with such utter grace, it made me wince with a pleasurable, painful awareness of his physical being. It was hard to keep from slipping my arm around his waist. This was not going to get easier—this being together and staying apart at the same time.

Honey had taken her place in the front seat again. And as we approached, she stuck her head out the window in greeting.

"Aren't you afraid someone might steal her? That window is open quite a bit."

"The doors are locked. She may seem sweet to you." I said. "In fact, she is sweet; however, I wouldn't want to be a stranger to her and reach into the car to unlock it. No, she's no pussycat when it's necessary to be a lion."

"I like your analogy. Hi, Honey. Move into the back; I have a special treat for you."

She was so quick it was laughable. She must have known the package Paul carried contained something for her.

He broke the donut into pieces and fed them to her one by one. What a picture, and me without a camera handy.

We were at his office too quickly for me. I'd only had a small taste of him at coffee.

"This was delightful. Not easy, but delightful." He was looking at me with that frank, open face of his.

"I'm thinking the same thing, Paul. And it's going to have to hold us for sometime."

"How long, Jenny? Do you have a fix on your schedule yet?"

"Not really. But it will be this week and more. As I said before, this project has to be finished before Thanksgiving."

"We'll talk. Call me and I'll call you back if necessary. Anytime. You may even get Albert."

He laughed and bent over to kiss me when he remembered where we were. He squeezed my hand and lifted it to his lips.

"That'll have to do for now. Thanks for taking the time for this."

"It was fun." Keep it light, Jenny. "And, yes, I'll call."

"Drive carefully. Good luck on the work. Hi to Guy." Now he was doing it. Lingering, not wanting to let go. Lord, lord what are we to do? "Bye, my Jenny. Bye, Honey. Guard your mother well for me." He waved and was off.

"*Hola, Celestina. Como esta?*" Honey and I bounded into the house loaded down. Did I say bounded? More like staggered.

"I'm fine, Missy. How are you? Hi, Honey. Here, give me your basket of toys." Honey had been carrying her things, too.

Celestina and I did this all the time. I'd labor in Spanish while she'd answer me in nearly unaccented English. We had some great conversations.

"The soup is ready. I made cornbread, too, and salad. You need anything more?"

"No thanks. That sounds perfect. It seems quite warm outside. Shall we set up out there?"

"I already set up outside." She was well pleased with herself for preempting me. She often outguessed me. It made her proud. Me, too. She was a special young woman. We were friends. Happily, we still are.

"OK. Help me unload, will you?"

"Mr. Guy. Is he coming later?"

"Yes, later in the afternoon. We'll have dinner together. What have you decided to make?"

"Some black beans and rice and enchiladas. OK? Also, I bought fruit and yogurt—frozen. That's all. Enough?"

"Yes, that's just fine. How about your salsa? Did you make it?"

"Oh, *sí*, yes, salsa is ready and chips and guacamole."

"A veritable feast. Perfect." I exclaimed. We smiled in comradely, good humor. "I'll just get cleaned up. See you in a few minutes."

Guy and I got to work as soon as he arrived. So far, with the way things were progressing, it looked like we had a winner. We broke for our dinner à la Celestina and continued to work for a couple of hours more. It was a happy day and, on sum, a good beginning for this phase.

I walked around the studio yawning and stretching, "I'm suddenly bushed, Guy. I think I'll turn in. Do you mind?"

## A Small Flirtation

"No, of course not. How 'bout a little run together in the morning? Before breakfast," he asked.

"After I've had my coffee. My legs and feet won't work otherwise. And some orange juice."

"And your English muffin." He added.

I smiled at my friend, "I guess you know me pretty well."

"Yeah, happily I do. Come on, let's both turn in."

We parted at my door. A sweet hug and a wish for sweet dreams.

The days went. Productively. Lots to do. Some leisure time loafing. Some trotting on the beach. Plenty of food, too. Guy and I were satisfied with what was being produced. The project was beginning to take shape as we began to shape our plans for the much shorter trip south.

"I'd like to take you out to dinner tonight. How about it, Jenny? We can have a little celebration of work well done so far."

"That sounds great. Shall I call that place in Mill Valley we like? How's 7:30? That'll get you home rather early."

"Good. I'm going to take a run before it gets too dark. Come on Honey. Let's romp."

They were barely out the door when the phone rang.

"Hello?"

"Jenny? Paul. Can you talk? Is this a good time?"

"Perfect. Guy's out with the dog."

"And you? What are you doing, my girl? Where are you now?" He sounded so good, so near.

"I'm in the hallway just about to go to my room. Excuse the buzz on the phone. I'll change over to a regular one in a sec."

I flopped down on the down.

"Where are you now?"

"On the bed." I sighed and wriggled around getting comfortable.

"I want to be there with you."

"I know. Me, too. Come on over and join us for dinner. We're going up to Mill Valley. You could save Guy the trouble of bringing me back before he drives home." I was kidding on the square while holding my breath for his response.

"How much I want to, you'll never know, Jenny. I'd love to drop everything and simply come across to you."

"But of course you simply can't." It was a frustrating wish at best. There was no need to continue on this line. "We're leaving Monday as planned."

"Lucky man, Guy. Where's the first overnight?"

"So far, Santa Clara at Max and Bridget's."

"Do they have room for you both?" He was so transparent it was pathetic.

"They have a guest room." I wasn't going to explain.

"Oh."

"Paul, this tack is not funny anymore. Let me spell it out for you. Guy and I are not sleeping together. We are old, dear friends and, yes, we have thought about it, even talked about it."

"Jenny, please . . ." Paul protested, embarrassed.

I continued. "No, it's the truth, Paul. It would have been the easiest thing in the world to do." It had started as a joke, and now I was becoming agitated.

"Jenny, don't be upset. I'm sorry. I was stupid to say anything, ask anything. Childish."

"Well, anyway, to finish it up: We opted for a life-long friendship rather than a roll in the hay, ruining the whole thing. And that's that." I stopped abruptly.

"Is that what you think we did? Have a roll in the hay and ruin the whole thing?" Now he sounded testy.

"Paul, stop it! Right now! Before you say something we'll both regret. You know perfectly well I don't believe that. We share something unique—separate and apart from anything or anyone else. If you don't believe that, well then, we have nothing." I was furious at his ability to put me on the defensive.

"Jenny, I'm a fool. I believe in us from the very core of my being, and I admire your relationship with Guy."

"Then, let's drop it. Really, it is upsetting to constantly have to explain him in order to reassure you. And if I were sleeping with him, Paul, it's really none of your business anymore than it's my business whether or not you are sleeping with your wife!"

He didn't respond and I wasn't quieting down as quickly as I wanted to. Paul had intruded where he had no right. He'd have to know I had a life before him. Mine, too, was separate and apart, even as his life was. I took a deep breath and continued.

"I've had a busy and productive day, Paul. Totally satisfying and I'm about to take a tub and rest a bit before dinner. Tomorrow and Sunday I loaf, and the next day the work starts all over again. That's the long and the short of it."

"Forgive my blunder. Jenny, I'm glad you've had a good day. It sounds like you have a leg up on the rest of the project as well."

"I'm sorry, too. It's just hard to always have to say good-bye almost as soon as we say hello. We're both feeling the pressure, I know that and I don't want to fuss with you about anything. You're the last person on earth I want to create a tense moment with. I care too deeply already."

"I care deeply, too, Jenny. I've fallen in like with you." The tense moment passed.

"I'm going to relax now, turn on the Jacuzzi, play some music and think of you."

"Me, too, my Jenny. I'll be thinking of you as I drive."

"Home," I added under my breath. "Until Monday," I said aloud.

I slipped into the warm water and relaxed. Soon I felt the tension wash away. I closed my eyes, drifting. What was it Paul said? He believed in us and what we mean to each other from the very core of his being. There was a dichotomy here. A delicate balance was needed in this relationship. I hoped it wouldn't become a tightrope walk.

What I really needed to do was to let go and trust fate. Hadn't I just told myself if being happy with Paul is making me unhappy, I should drop the whole thing? My thinking was becoming circular. Better not to think the same things again and again. I pushed it all aside. Like Scarlett, I'd think about it tomorrow or in a week, or—never.

## 21

It was a relief to be with Guy. We always have a good time together and soon we'd be 'on the road again' He is, at once, light-hearted and steadfast. Over our celebratory dinner, we talked about the rest of the trip and were confident it would be as good as the first part had been.

He set his coffee cup down carefully and looked at me in that curious way of his—half-serious and half amused.

"Well, dear one, how's it going? Are you having any fun? I know I promised I wouldn't say another word about your little fling, but I lied."

"You lied?"

"Yes, it's not just idle curiosity, Jenny, and you know I'm not a voyeur. What I am is worried. This is not your style. Not the Jenny I know." His face was creased with concern.

"Guy, I . . ." He reached across the table and took my hand the way Paul had when he was explaining about his marriage. It was a curious gesture. One of comfort while almost commanding me to listen and pay attention.

He continued: "Have you given any thought to where this might lead? Do you know what you want from him? What you are willing to give for what you will get in return?"

"I don't know, Guy. I just don't know yet."

"I know you and TJ are having a good time with this. You're acting like schoolgirls. But, Jen, it's not a joke. It's great to keep saying 'have fun,' 'keep it light' and 'don't look beyond tomorrow.' That's a bunch of baloney and you know it." He was sounding very upset, almost angry. "I wish you could look at yourself." I couldn't get a word in edgewise. "You're practically in tears, not because of what I've said, but because of what you know."

"Can I speak now?" I tried to smile as I extricated my hand.

"Sure, Jenny, of course. I'm sounding like a bully, even to me. Go on, please."

"Everything you've said is true and every question you ask is a good one. I simply don't have the answers to it all, yet. I do know one thing I keep saying over and over."

"What's that?"

"Guy, I'm so happy when I'm with him, and so close to unhappy when I'm not." I paused a moment looking away and then continued, "When I think about it, the larger picture, that is, I tell myself to focus down on the immediate subject at hand, otherwise forget it." Guy nodded. "I want to stop looking ahead—at least, for right now. I want to focus on us, you and me, our project and make the work as good and fulfilling as any we've done. I don't want to miss the life I'm living because I'm only looking at what may or possibly could happen in the future."

"One day you'll come to clarity about all of it, Jenny. I know you will. And then you'll know what path to take. I have complete and utter confidence in you. But for now, be careful, dear one."

We left the restaurant and drove home, mostly in a companionable silence. He walked me to the door. I hadn't said a word about my phone call from Paul before dinner.

"Will you come in for a night coffee?" We smiled at our local joke: no nightcap or one-for-the-road—not on this road!

"No, Jenny. It's been a full day, and I'm tired."

I nodded in agreement. "Thanks, Guy. You are my beloved friend."

"More than that, Jen. I love you dearly."

"Oh, Guy, now I am going to cry." And I did. He took me in his arms and held me close until I quieted down. He kissed me gently and then gently disengaged from our embrace.

"I love you, too, Guy. Please know how much I treasure you. I want you in my life, all my life."

"Good night, Jenny." He could say no more.

"Good night, Guy. Drive carefully."

## 22

"I can't believe we have this entire day to ourselves. What luxury! What do you think, Honey? Want to go for a ride or shall we walk?"

Honey went for her leash and left her Frisbee behind. "OK, to the car! We'll run up to the market and fetch some goodies for you and me."

No dogs are allowed in the market according to Health Department regulations. When I see some of the people who go in, I wonder that the department hasn't got it backwards.

The first thing that hit me was all the displays for Halloween. Halloween? When is it? I turned to ask a clerk when I spotted my neighbor.

"Hi, Laura. How are you?"

"Hi, Jenny. I thought I saw Honey in front."

"She wanted a ride, and I need a few things. By the way, when's Halloween?"

"Tonight."

"Good Lord. Did it come early this year or what?" I was shocked.

"Sure seems like it. It's hard to believe it's less than four weeks to Thanksgiving. When are you and Guy taking off again?"

"Day after tomorrow." We continued talking as we walked through the market together. "I guess I'd better buy some packages of candy while I'm at it. I don't know that I have time to make popcorn balls again this year."

"The kids all love them, Jenny, and your brownies, too. I'll help if you like. It'll be fun."

Her enthusiasm was infectious.

"Not exactly the way I planned to spend the day, but with an offer like that, how can I refuse?" We made a date to meet after lunch.

By the way, "As long as I'm going to help, just plan to make extra brownies!"

"Well, Honey, you're going to have fun. Tonight is Halloween, and the kids will be coming by. I'll have to dress you up in your clown outfit."

She wagged and nuzzled in complete agreement. She certainly recognized the upbeat energy I was displaying and most certainly was responding to it.

The morning drifted by in a pleasant and leisurely manner. The sea was relatively calm for that time of the year. Brisk and clear, my favorite kind of weather—not too windy either. I'd set out the butter and eggs to come to room temperature and air-popped masses of corn, then turned on some music and actually curled up on the couch and went through a stack of magazines.

Soon enough it would be time to take off again and leave my enchanting surroundings. For now, I was luxuriating in what normally would be referred to as wasting time.

Interesting, in three in a half years I've made this place feel so mine. In spite of the fact I live here alone, as my sons were grown men when I moved in, and in spite of the fact my friends live in the city or down on the peninsula, I feel at home here.

There is some sort of magic to this little place, this community of 1200 souls. I feel I've dug in, hunkered down—whatever it is, it suits me just fine. I have come to a very peaceful place within me.

"Time to get busy, Honey. Come on to the kitchen. We'll have a bite of lunch and get to work." Halloween's a big event in our town, in fact, all holidays are. The children are safe and they know it. We all stock up on treats and join in the fun.

Laura and I spent several productive hours together making popcorn balls and six different kinds of brownies. It goes without saying they were basic chocolate fudge; some plain, some with nuts, some iced in chocolate, some with miniature marshmallows inside, some marshmallow-nut and others dusted with powdered sugar. That's six I think. Oh yes, and some with caramel sauce swirled through. Seven variations on a theme.

"You are the Master Brownie Chef of all time, Jenny. Your boys and their friends were sure lucky. Look at these piles of goodies. Enough for the throngs of Lilliputians who will be descending in a couple of hours, I dare to say."

"Help yourself, Laura. Remember, without you, there wouldn't be any at all."

She took home a heaping plate full. We promised to check in later after the deluge.

And deluge it was. Literally dozens of children—all sizes and shapes. I swear they come from all over Marin County and probably Sonoma County as well! Honey was the hit of the evening. I had made her a blouse of polka-dot satin with ruching all around the double collar, a few years back. She was really alluring and knew it. I had to keep a firm grip on her or she'd have taken her toy basket and accompanied bunches of children as they continued their trick-or-treat night. As it was, I'd no idea what all she'd eaten. And she wasn't telling.

I had a moment of deep sadness as I closed the door on the last child. It was just the kind of fun I desperately wanted to share with Paul. I tried to convince myself to phone him. All I had to do would be to place a person-to-person call. I was certain it would work. I picked up the phone and dialed his number. When I heard the busy signal, I slammed down the receiver. What a crazy thing to do. Did I really think he could talk to me from his house? I really was losing it.

I suddenly felt utterly at loose ends. I picked up the phone and called Laura. "I think it's over. What do you think?"

"Yes, I agree. We'll have to figure out how to hand the loot out jointly next year," she said.

"I was thinking the same thing. Maybe next year I'll move myself and have an adult party. In the meantime, I'm starving. How about you?" I asked.

"I could do with a hamburger at the local beanery in the village."

"Shall we?"

"Sure." She agreed.

It was a nice interlude. I told Laura about the trip Guy and I had planned. She caught me up on her latest series of children's books. Nothing intimate, nothing revelatory, just nice friendly friends.

At one point, however, during dinner, I wondered if I could tell her about Paul. I felt an internal pressure to speak of him, to blurt it all out. But I caught myself, once more. What was there to say? That I had met this divine man by accident and that I was now seeing him by design? And, oh yes, he's married—very.

What was she to do with that piece of information? And who knew? Maybe she knew Kathy or had met them both socially. The Bay area is rather spread out, but in truth, it's a very small community in many ways. I couldn't risk it, and what was the point of burdening her?

It is the kind of self-indulgence I hate when I experience it in other people. A former therapist of mine once said to me of behavior like that—it was a soft sort of dumping, that kind of 'sharing a confidence.' Toss a pillow. 'Here, catch it—it's not heavy; just be careful not to drop it' Once is not so bad—carrying around someone else's light, small pillow. Then comes the next pillow with the same admonition, then the next and the next and so on until you have become so burdened by your friendly confidante's pillows, that you can barely function for fear of dropping something.

I remembered that admonition clearly and applied it to myself.

After we said good night, I was giddy with relief when I thought about what I had almost done. Had I acted on impulse and babbled, I'd have been heartsick at my stupidity. What must I have been thinking? Very soon my concerns were to be validated in a way I couldn't have imagined.

"Well, Honey, another close call. Another near miss—whatever you want to call it. We've had a great day, you and I. Now it's time to turn in. Come on, girl. Into your basket."

I tuned into my favorite music station, set the sleep timer and shut down for the night. It was still relatively early. I could use a long, restful night's sleep. I rolled over and hugged the pillow that had been under Paul's head. At the same time wondering when and how he could be there beside me again.

## 23

I got an early start in the morning on my personal packing. It would be warmer down south and drier. Still I packed a raincoat. I'm much too much a northern Californian. Anyway, November can be tricky, I told myself. I checked and rechecked our equipment and supplies, took the time to write a couple of notes and make an entry in my journal:

*I don't know why I'm sighing so deeply. The work goes well—I love being with Guy—I don't know what I'd give to be doing this with Paul. That's the truth of the matter. When in the name of good common sense will I come to terms with this obsession? Enough! Time to focus and get on with my real life—and yet this part of the trip will be so much more difficult—we've made gorgeous love and now I'm not so willing to 'keep it light'. Yes. I want more. I want this man for my own. How do I accomplish that one? Show me the way—give me a clue. I'm calling on my Guide to guide me. Thank you.*

As I closed my journal, I glanced across the desk and noticed the red light blinking on my answer machine. Hadn't I checked it after dinner the night before? I guess not. Three messages: 1. "Hi, M'am. Happy Halloween. Hope you indulged the neighborhood again with your brownies tonight. We had a gang. Call in the morning and tell us when to expect you. Love and stuff. Max."

2. "It's me, Guy. Thought you'd be in tonight handing out brownies, Jenny. Just wanted to say I'll be up between 8:00 and 9:00 Monday morning. If you have a problem with that, let me know. Otherwise, I'll see you then, kiddo.

3. "Hi, Jenny, it's Paul. I'm calling from the car Sunday morning around 10:00. I just wanted to say hello. Sorry I missed you. I'll call early tomorrow morning."

Damn. Where was I? Oh, yes, the laundry room. I can't possibly hear the phones with the machinery going and I'd forgotten to take the portable in with me. Damn. Damn. Damn!

The phone rang as I was spluttering. "Hello?" I tried not to sound grumpy.

"Oh good. You are there."

"Paul, oh hi. I was in the laundry room. I'm so glad you tried again." It was crazy to be so happy at the sound of a voice.

"I figured you might be in the shower or doing something else noisy. How are you? Did you have fun last night?" He was doing his breathless number again.

" I had a ball once I found out it was Halloween. I really had to move it to be ready."

"Didn't you know?"

"No. I couldn't believe it. While I was at the market my neighbor told me. She offered to help, and we went to work."

"Help? Do what? Which neighbor?"

"Slow down, Mister. Give me a chance! Laura and I baked all afternoon and made dozens of brownies of every description, popcorn balls, too. The neighborhood kids and grown-ups, for that matter, have come to expect it. Without her help, I could never have done it all."

"Those great brownies of yours! You could go into business.

You'd give all those cookie and bake shops a run for their money. Ever think of that?"

"Yes, I think of it, and then take Robert Hutchison's advice and lie down until the feeling passes." I laughed at the idea of the late Dr. Hutchison of the University of Chicago baking brownies. I think the activity he purportedly was referring to was exercise.

"Did you save any? Have you put mine away in the freezer? I hope so."

"My, aren't we full of questions this morning? Yes, dear one, I saved you examples of all seven kinds."

"Seven? Good Lord. Seven? Unbelievable."

"Oh, that's nothing. I've been known to make twelve or thirteen variations on the theme. It's easy once you get rolling. Did you play treat to kids tricks, too?"

"Oh, certainly. I wear a monster mask and greet the kids with this terrible looking thing on, and they all laugh at me. It's always fun. The more kids, the better."

"By the way, where are you?" There were traffic sounds in the background.

"I'm standing outside at the car wash. It's a perfect place to call you from. You know, noisy and private at the same time." We both laughed at the idea of being so totally isolated in public. "Jen, do you have any idea when you're leaving in the morning? Would it be too early to call?"

"No, that's perfect. You can be my alarm clock." I was warmed by the prospect of cradling the phone close to me and hearing his voice the first thing in the morning—any morning.

"OK, girl, I'll call you then. Got to run. They're honking my horn."

"Don't let them get too familiar. Heaven knows what they'll try next time." He burst out laughing as I was hanging up.

That's about as light as I could keep it. My true feelings of gratitude for the call were much too close to the surface. Dismay was my primary reaction. Dismay at being so vulnerable, so willing to take the crumbs from his table and make a dessert out of them.

After I returned Max's call, I phoned Guy.

"Are you set on our plan or can we change it a bit?"

"OK with me, Jen. What's up?"

I told him of my conversation with Max and his real disappointment at our not coming until Monday. Guy said he was willing to come up, load the Jeep, and get going.

Paul. I'd have to call his voice mail and leave a message explaining his inability to reach me at 7:00 in the morning.

By the time Guy got here, everything was assembled by the door. I'd spoken to Max again and confirmed the new plan and made lunch. Not bad.

"Good show, Jen. I'm sure Max was pleased."

"Hi dear. Oh very. Laura's here. I fixed lunch. I'm sure you haven't eaten, and I'm starved."

"That's novel! Where's Laura? In the kitchen, of course."

"Of course." Laura emerged from the kitchen smiling. "Gosh, Guy, I haven't seen you in ages. You look great!"

"You too, Laura. You're looking mighty fine. Jenny tells me you're working on a new series of books."

Laura nodded, "In fact, it may become a real series. A television series, I mean. It's not for publication, yet; but I've been bursting to tell you, Jenny. I've become an excited wreck about the whole thing."

"I'm thrilled for you, Laura. Is it a done deal? Or must we put some energy on that one?"

"We're signing tomorrow. I guess that's about as done as you can get."

"I'll drink to that!" Guy had opened a beer—my kind, 0.5% alcohol. He never drinks and drives. We had one tragedy in this family. One too many.

We joined him and sat down to a big salad and a feast of leftovers folded into omelets. We'd make it through to dinner.

# 24

Sunday afternoon traffic wasn't so bad. We headed down Highway 1 along the ocean and arrived at Santa Clara in time for a tour of the garden and house while it was still light.

Daylight savings time had just ended. My least favorite day of the year. I dreaded the shortened daylight hours. I've never been able to figure out the system of changing the time. It always seemed to me one should save time of daylight during the winter months when nature makes it dark earlier. Instead, it's the other way around. Oh well, just another of life's contradictions.

Max and Bridget were glowing with good looks and good health. They also were very much in love. We had a long visit, dinner at the Pub as planned, breakfast in the morning, a long walk with Honey who seemed perfectly content to stay with Bridget and Max, and we were off once more.

"Short and sweet, Jen. Sorry your visit has to end so soon, but we'll be up before you know it." Max was leaning on the car door. "You do know that Nicky and Diane will come here first and we'll come up together later?"

"However it works best for you. Either way suits me. I'll keep in touch, dear. Take care of each other."

As predicted, the weather was a little cool and overcast on Monterey Peninsula. Bits of sunlight pushed through the clouds. It was so beautiful. How I love Carmel, the valley, the entire area.

My parents lived there after Dad retired. He stayed on, though alone, when Mother died. He said his life was well ordered and he'd rather have us want him to visit and vice versa, than our getting bored with each other. How right he was. One's identity can be too easily lost when three generations are under the same roof. He was too young to do that to himself. It would have been very destructive to his life. As it was, he knew everyone in Carmel and had a busy and active, sometimes admittedly lonely life for his remaining ten years.

I still miss him daily. Things have never been the same for me since he died.

Time flew like the birds. We wended our way south—Cambria Pines, Morro Bay, and the State Park Bird Sanctuary. Then on to San Luis Obispo, the string of beach towns, and finally Santa Barbara. It's an enchanting town, rather like Carmel-by-the-Sea, only larger. The oldest mission in California is there as well as a very fine school of photography. There was plenty to do and lots to see. We hung out there for a couple of days and just kicked back before making the turnaround and heading home.

## 25

TJ was delighted to hear from me. She wanted to know about Guy, the weather, the birds, and anything else I wanted to tell her.

"We'll be turning around soon. There's a Canadian Geese Flyway we want to visit down here first. Though, from what I heard, they aren't flying away very much."

I went on to tell her that we had talked with a man from the U.S. Fish and Wildlife Service while we were in Seattle and he told us more than we ever thought we wanted to know about geese. Apparently, they like the manicured grass of the golf courses and ample supply of water they provide, as well as the warm pools in the southwest. They've become so fat and lazy they're driving even the naturalists crazy all along the Atlantic Flyway, too! There's great diversity of opinion on how to address the problem.

"Fascinating," TJ said. "And to think years ago, there was the threat of extinction because of over hunting."

"In fact, one wildlife authority, I'm told, said they'd need a road map to find Canada anymore!" We both laughed at that picture.

"Wait until you see our pictures. You'll begin to understand what they're up against. Anyway, that's a small taste of what we're up to. I'm also ready to call it done. I'll have so few days to work before the gang arrives, and then it's non-stop until after Turkey Day."

"Are you sure you want us all up there the night before Thanksgiving, Jenny?"

"You bet I do. I want all of us to be together the night before, as we always have done. Darned if I'll be the only one getting up at dawn to have it all ready on time. In the meantime, I've got to get out of here, and I'm not even dressed."

"OK, Jen, say hi to Tom. Good Lord, Jenny, what have I said? I'm so sorry. I can't imagine why I did that. Please don't be upset."

I was breathless for a moment, struggling for composure. Finally, "Don't you be upset, TJ. It's OK. We were speaking of our days with the children. It was a perfectly natural thing to have done. I've had Tom on my mind, too. What with the boys and their significant others. It would be unnatural not to."

Poor TJ. She was in shreds. "In all these years, I've never done that before."

"Then it's about time you did. We've been talking about Tom a lot these past few weeks. As I said, it seems almost natural for you to have done that. Please, please, dear, believe me; I was startled, yes, but I'm not upset. Truly, I'm not."

"What you are is a good sport and a great friend." TJ was sounding greatly relieved

.

I ran into Guy coming into the lobby. He'd been out to the car and was ready to go as soon as I had coffee.

"I have no need to linger here any longer. Do you, Jenny? I'd like to get underway again. How about it?"

"Fine. Me, too." I was still feeling a bit edgy and thought work would refocus me. It always calmed me; made me feel grounded.

"You're a bit restless today, Jenny girl, aren't you? Thoughts elsewhere?" Guy hit the nail on the head, and I didn't want to talk about it.

"I'll be all right, Guy, once we're on the road again. I have been thinking of Thanksgiving looming up ahead beckoning me to get home. We've an awful lot to do between now and December 15th. Maybe I'm just tired today. I admit to feeling I'm on overwhelm." I sighed and gave him a crooked smile.

"We'll be heading back soon, kiddo and we'll get it all finished on time. Frankly, I think the Thanksgiving break will be good for you. Lots of commotion—with the twins at home. They're bound to drown out your thoughts. They and Celestina and the rest of us will help with the preparations, as we always do."

A nice pep talk—leading where?

"I'm sure it will work. By the way, what thoughts are the boys supposed to be drowning out?" I tried to sound casual.

"Unless you're suffering from PMS, Jenny old girl, I'll lay you ten to one this is all tied up with Paul. Holidays and family times wreck havoc on this kind of threesome. There's bound to be less contact, coupled with the desire to be together and join in the festivities together. All that can make for an enormous amount of inner tension." He was watching me closely, observing my reaction to all he had said.

"That's all true, devastatingly true, Guy. And there's still another dimension to this: Because of Paul, we've all been talking a lot about the past recently. I've also had another reason to think of Tom more than usual. Max and Nicky have women of their own now. There may be two weddings in the offing sooner than we think. And Tom's not here to enjoy all the pleasures of our two grown sons; not here with me to share in the wonder and excitement of it all." I sighed.

"I'm very aware of all that too, Jenny. Tom's been on my mind a great deal lately."

"I keep thinking I reconciled myself to his death years ago, Guy; I still think I have. And now, here I am, ten years later involved with a man I want to share this with, and he's not available to me either. There's something terribly wrong with this picture, isn't there? One man can't be and the other may not be.

Oh, Guy I've really made a mess, haven't I?" I suddenly felt wretched.

"Jenny, you've made a mess of nothing. Stop this silly self-pitying. It doesn't become you." Guy was chastising me as though I were a lovesick teenager. "So, you've fallen for a very attractive man who happens to be married. What's so damn unique about that? I told you to be careful. Well, I'm saying it again. BE CAREFUL! You don't need to be hurt again. You don't deserve to be either. Handle it. Keep it at a distance from your daily life. Treat it for what it is—and escapade. If not, run, do not walk away. RUN!"

I couldn't look at him. I didn't dare. I was so shocked by his outburst. I wanted to run and hide. I was humiliated by the situation between Paul and me. Humiliated that I couldn't hide my feelings and keep it to myself. What kind of nonsense is this?

How dare he lecture me? How dare I have burdened him with this knowledge? I had had a foreboding of this. TJ thought Guy would be accepting of it all. I had the feeling he wouldn't be and I was right.

He'd referred to Paul and me in very flippant language. Those little jabs were warning signs. I noted them, but didn't heed them. Was I arrogant or stupid or insensitive? Probably some of each. Now what? He couldn't possible retract what he'd said. That would be false, only adding to the problem. And I, what did I want him to do? There was no way I'd stop seeing Paul. Not yet. Maybe one day we'd find we had to, but not because Guy blew his cool. No, not that way.

Right now I had to find a way to answer Guy. For all the gruff and abrupt way he spoke to me, he was trying to protect me. That I could acknowledge. I could apologize for upsetting him and for wearing my heart on my sleeve. I had to. I had to salvage his ego and our friendship. Hadn't I only a few weeks ago promised nothing would come between us? Nothing must. Guy was in the here and now. Paul was a fantasy, a mythological character come to life—to my life, with very little substance to maintain his hold on me

Everything about Paul and me was future oriented, if there was to be a future for us. Our 'now' only ephemeral, dream-like—not based in reality. The only reality we had was the recognition of our souls reaching out to each other; to the love we felt so deeply and were unable to verbalize, yet. No, I'd not relinquish Paul. I'd find ways to handle it alone.

"Guy, you're right again. I apologize for dragging you into this unsavory shenanigan, as you once dubbed it." I was valiantly keeping my voice steady and my face composed. "If I'm going to let this impinge on my pleasure in the real part of my life, I'm crazy. It must be encapsulated, the whole darn thing and enjoyed as it can be, without all the emotional upheavals."

"Jenny dear, it's not a matter of my being 'right again.' I don't want to be right at your expense and I don't want you to be wrong. By that, I mean I want all things in life to be right for you from now on. That, you've earned." Emphatic.

"Thank you. Don't I wish that for myself and the rest of us!"

"Does that still include me?" The tension of the last, endless, five minutes was dissipating.

"That still includes you. First and foremost, it includes you!" We were painfully aware that these moments were not over for us. There would be many more times we'd be called upon to comfort one another in life. This was a lifetime commitment. One neither of us took lightly.

We were on the road again making our final loop. Things had smoothed out between us although I'm sure Guy was feeling a bit constrained. I know I was. It's just my timing was off. I'd momentarily lost my sense of self, that wonderful secure feeling inside that assures you you're fine.

How far I'd slipped! So quickly. My well ordered life had lurched out of balance the first moment it was seriously challenged from outside. Well, I was paying attention now. No longer would I depend on my most beloved friends to prop me up. Support me during life's tragic times, loving devotion and forbearance during stressful times, these were separate issues. Sharing joy, fun and frolic, too; but this was different—what had started as a lark was fast becoming folly, as I observed it taking hold of my life. With my eyes wide open, I'd let it happen.

I had told myself I was in charge of the 'situation' as Paul referred to us. After the confrontation with Guy, I now knew that to be a myth.

# 26

It's amazing how different the climate is between northern and southern California. Within a few hours, the scenery and the weather changed. We noticed it shortly after leaving the Santa Barbara area as we headed back up north.

"Is there a storm brewing?" I was becoming anxious. "Did I miss something on the news?" It had become quite chilly. Dark clouds were rolling in. Rain began spattering the windshield.

"There's a forty percent chance of rain this afternoon," Guy replied. "Sure looks like we're heading into something with a lot more than a forty percent chance to it." Guy shrugged and put the seat back. "I'm going to snooze a bit. Holler when you're ready to shift." He put his head back and, in moments, was snoring.

With that there was a crack of lightning followed by a crash-boom of thunder, and the rains came. My God, how they came! The windshield wipers were all but useless, and the headlights reflected back at me through the rain with a terrible glare. It was becoming foggy, too. The warmer air of the south had collided with the cooler air from the north, and 'bingo,' FOG!

I drove on for a few miles until I could barely see. The storm was raging. I was suddenly terrified. No way could I stay behind the wheel while Guy dozed. He had not even been awakened by the storm.

The cars approaching had headlights on, which told me this was no local little rain. A weather front had moved in very fast. It looked like one of those storms that could last for days. Solid gray sky, leaden, unrelieved by any break. Everything was soaking wet as water began to gather in pools in the low spots along the road.

We had driven away from the highway in search of something more interesting than freeways. Now we were, who knows where? Heading in a northerly direction; that's all I knew.

I frantically looked for somewhere to pull off that would be safe. I reached for Guy and called his name at the same time.

"Guy, Guy! Wake up! We're into a terrible storm and I'm scared to death!"

"Jenny, what is it? What's wrong?" He sat up straight and stretched. "It's only a little rain. You've been in much worse than this."

"I can't help it, Guy. I'm a nervous wreck." I'd slowed down to a crawl. "I really don't want to drive through this, and I can't find a place to pull over."

"Just stop over there." He was pointing to a fence line with a three or four-foot strip of grassy land on the roadside.

I pulled over and somehow managed to stay out of the ditch that ran along the edge of the fence.

"There now, see? You're fine. You did it just right, and we can sit here until the rain slackens a bit." Guy sounded like a scout leader assuaging the fears of one of his troops. In his eyes, my merit badge was won.

"I'm not feigning it, Guy. I'm frightened. We're not off the road completely, and in this fog, I doubt our lights can be seen forty feet. I'm not staying in the Jeep and making myself a sitting duck." With that, I reached around and grabbed my hooded jacket. I started for the door handle.

"Jenny, for God's sake, stay put. Where do you think you're going? Is it safer to stand out in this driving rain and fog with no protection whatsoever? If you think the lights won't be seen, how in the name of good common sense will you be seen?" Guy had me by the arm and was pulling me away from the door.

"Let me go, Guy. I must get out of this death trap." I was nearly hysterical and shaking like a leaf.

Guy grabbed his jacket, too, and a big torch light as well.

"You're not going out there alone, and you're for sure aren't getting out that side. Damn it, Jen, calm down or you will get hurt." He was opening his door pulling me toward him. I clambered over the console.

"Where will we go? Do you know where we are?" It was pitch black outside. I was fast losing my courage. Maybe we should stay in the Jeep.

"Will you wait inside for a few moments, please? I'll put out a bunch of flares and try to get a look around."

I was very close to him, and he finally took a good look at me—the door was ajar and the interior light was shining down on me.

"You're white as a ghost, Jenny, and you're shaking. Hey, come here." He shut the door and pulled me into his lap.

I was sobbing and couldn't control the shaking. I was, in short, a wreck.

"Shh! Shh! Dear one. Relax. I'm here. Nothing's going to harm you. Quiet down. Take a couple of deep breaths. Here, that's better." He released his hold on me a bit and began mopping away my tears with his big handkerchief.

I was still hiccuping from the hysteria, feeling, at once, like a young child being attended to by a loving older brother, and being suddenly drawn to Guy on a raw emotional tide. He saw the look in my eyes. It was a reflection of his own feelings.

He pulled me down to him and kissed me full on the mouth—a long, passionate, lingering kiss that rocked us both. We pulled back for a second; he looked at me again, and then kissed me again. This time I responded with the same force of all the pent-up emotions we felt between us.

We got all tangled up in big jackets and flashlights and embarrassed passion, and yet, we didn't stop. He slipped his hand under my jacket and surrounded me. Somehow, he'd slipped his arms out of his coat and we were locked in an embrace that had nowhere to go. We weren't used to this physical tussle in a car at our ages. And we certainly weren't used to doing this together. We struggled to straighten ourselves out, but it didn't happen, and we ended in each other's arms again. This time, much more deliberately, much quieter. He slipped his hand under my sweater and caressed me. My whole being responded with a burst of excitement that shook me back to reality.

"Guy . . . dear . . . I can't go on—this mustn't happen."

Fortunately for us both, there was no room in the car. The back was loaded with equipment, and we had too many obstacles in the front to carry on any further.

"Oh, Jenny," he moaned. "We can't anyway, there's no room to turn around. We could go out in the rain and lie down on the grass. The only problem is we'd probably roll over and drown in the ditch." He was laughing away the tension.

By now we'd untangled, and somehow I'd crawled back over the console to my side of the seat. We were both bursting. It was hilarious and so serious at the same time.

"Wow, what a tempest!" I said.

"Yeah, both inside and out. Jenny, I don't want to brush this aside as some aberration. These feelings have been building between us for a long time and they feel damn good"

"I know, Guy . . ." I nodded in agreement, "To me too."

"And I want you," he said.

"Oh, Guy, I'd never have had the will to stop if we'd been in some normal place."

"We'll be in some 'normal place' soon. I know where we are, and with the fog lifting we can go on. Crawl over here again and I'll change places with you."

I'd love to have had the scene on videotape. The rain, the tears, the passion, the crawling all over each other and all over the car. A French comedy.

"Guy, I'm so full of you right this minute. I'm almost afraid to go to a hotel with you. Maybe we should just drive all night in shifts."

"You've just given my ego the biggest boost it's had in a long time, Jenny. Why don't we just settle down for the night and let nature take its course?"

"Are you suggesting . . . ?"

"You're damn right, I am. Who's to be hurt? We're both free agents. The playing field is level with you and me, dear one. And we've promised each other a roll in the hay for a long, long time."

"A roll in the hay? You mean we're going to that barn over there?" I was laughing again and getting excited at the bizarre turn of events. Guy was right. Why not?

We found a snug place, had a decent meal and went off to our rooms. For the first time ever, we spoke of having one room and then reconsidered—we had to keep up appearances—they were connected.

I took a quick bath, brushed both hair and teeth and sprayed a little "Carolina" on myself. Guy knocked on the connecting door and shoved it open while juggling a bottle of Jim Beam, two glasses and an ice bucket. He looked fresh and shining. He was in a terry robe.

He poured us each a drink, handed me mine and took a sip of his own. "To us, to love and to friendship." We clinked.

The room had a cheap radio connected through the TV. I'd found some pleasant music and gestured to him to dance with me. We stood together very close and swayed to the music. I laid my head on his shoulder. He began to hum. I lifted my head up and looked at him. Here was Guy—sweet, wonderful, loyal Guy. Yes. It felt good. I felt loved, and it would be so easy, but I realized I'd be using my friend out of frustration.

The tempest inside me was as fierce as the tempest we'd driven through, and the tempest Guy and I had created in the car. I couldn't do that to Guy. I couldn't make him a substitute for Paul. On the other hand, I wasn't 'doing' anything to Guy that he hadn't started. We were equally culpable. Equally aroused, and enjoying it equally.

As we swayed to the music, the passion was ebbing instead of flowing. The moment had passed; but we'd never see each other in the same light again. The idea was new and light hearted. We'd uncovered the secret we'd kept from each other for years. Now we'd keep it from the world.

Life is a series of character-defining moments. This surely was one of them.

The music ended. We stepped apart for a moment, and then embraced again. We kissed—this time a loving, gentle kiss. He petted the back of my head and pressed me close again. He released me and smiled. "I love you, Jenny. And I'm going to say good night."

"Guy, my beloved, Guy."

I stared at the ceiling for some time reliving and reviewing what had been happening. The growing love for Paul and the attendant frustration which accompanied it; the recalling and reliving the loss of Tom, the only other man I truly loved; the twins on the brink of making life decisions. Is it any wonder I felt off balance? So much to evaluate and to manage, plus my work, to say nothing of the rest of my life.

And now this contra-temps with Guy. The way my body felt, for two cents I'd have gone through the connecting door. Fortunately, my head ruled. Our 'roll in the hay' didn't quite happen. What did was quite a revelation insuring our life-long friendship.

## 27

The tap, tapping on the door awakened me. "Yes? Who is it?" I mumbled groggily.

"Jenny, it's me," Guy answered. "I'm taking the Jeep in to be looked at and will be back as soon as possible."

"Come in, Guy. The door's not locked." I had pulled my robe on and was walking to the connecting door. "What time is it?"

"Hi, dear." He gave me a peck on the cheek. "It's 7:30."

"Oh well, Good morning. What's with the Jeep?"

"I heard a clunk of some kind when I drove it last night. I may have struck a rock when I pulled back on the road. Anyway, we need gas, so I'll have it put up on a rack and take a look."

"Have you had breakfast?"

"Yeah, I've had a cup of coffee and a bagel. That's enough for now."

"Well, I'll get ready and be in the coffee shop. Check there when you get back."

"OK. And Jenny, about last night—I loved every moment of it, but I guess we did what was right."

I looked at Guy and smiled. "Yes, I loved our 'moment', too, and agree we were smarter than I would have bet. And frankly, but for the weather I'm not so sure we would have been."

He was grinning, "I'll see you soon."

I think he was as relieved as I.

The car was fine, fueled and ready to go. It was still raining, but being light out made an enormous difference.

We both felt we'd done enough; had more than enough to work with, and were more than ready to beat a path homeward.

By late afternoon we were on the last leg of the journey. The storm had abated. We were looking at the clear sky and smelling fresh air—it was heaven to open the windows and the roof.

I put my head back and closed my eyes. I didn't feel like talking anymore. It had been a strenuous trip—more than any I'd taken before with Guy. I tried to put my finger on why, and the only thing I could come up with was what, to me, seemed unlikely. Guy was jealous of my relationship with Paul. It made no sense to me, and yet, it was the only thing that did make any sense.

After Tom was killed, I was busy getting my life back on an even keel. I hardly had time to date, nor did I have the inclination. Oh, certainly, there was the odd invitation or so, but nothing that had even the slightest hint of romantic interest. At least, not for me. My old friends had all my attention and I theirs. It had been a perfectly satisfactory arrangement. Then came that crazy plane ride. Since then, Guy has been super observant, and now that he's known for a fact "something's going on . . ." he's been like a watchdog—a very verbal and sometimes cranky watchdog.

Yes, I concluded. Guy's jealous. There was no doubt about it. It explained all the unsolicited opinions and commentaries, as well as his more than usual attentiveness and his proprietary attitude.

Oh well. I yawned and stretched and settled back. There's nothing to be done about it. He'll manage. We both will.

"Hey, sleepyhead, wake up. We're here." Guy was pulling up at TJ's. "You had a nice snooze."

"Whew! I must have been 'out' for over an hour."

Another yawn and stretch and I began to get out of the car.

"Here, take these things and I'll grab the rest. Ask TJ to open the garage door, will you, hon?"

"Sure." I rang the bell and heard the two dogs respond.

"Away from the door, you two. Hi, Jenny, come on in. Welcome back. Where's Guy?" She was looking over my shoulder. Both the dogs were both all over me.

"He's waiting for you to open the garage door. What with all the equipment in the Jeep, he can't leave it in the street. Hi, Honey. Come here, Poochie."

"Right away. Here, let me help you with those."

"I'll just set them down here while I receive the royal greeting from my pals."

We were at the table munching on one of TJ's great salads and devouring the best soufflé I'd had in years. The wine was chilled, the candles were glowing, fire in fireplace—and flowers, always flowers in her house—this time it was mums—bowls and bowls of them everywhere. A festive and loving homecoming. Try as I might, I couldn't help feeling that the only one missing was Paul. Paul, always at the very edge of my consciousness.

Suddenly Guy jumped up from the table: "Well, you dolls, if we've finished, I'm going to excuse myself and head home. I'll leave you two to all the girlie things you need to catch up on. Thanks, TJ. That was perfection." A light kiss.

"As for you, Miss, I'll see you late morning. Get some rest; you can use it." A light kiss for me, too. He was on his way, surprisingly fast.

"What's with the 'girlie things' he's talking about? Did that sound like a strange little means to leave early to you?" TJ was curious.

"I think we both have had it for awhile. The work was good. The weather and accommodations, what we expected. It's just we were getting a little tired."

"Of the trip or of each other?" TJ was too quick for me.

"A little of each, to tell the truth. I think Guy left early because he didn't want to talk about it and it gives me an opportunity to do so without him being here."

"This is beginning to sound serious." TJ was pouring coffee and watching me at the same time.

"Not really. It's just that he couldn't let the subject of Paul alone."

I told her that, in fairness, I guess I seemed glum or unsettled at one point, and we got off into a lot of philosophical stuff. Not wonderful. Then, there was that God-awful storm and how it got kind of heavy between us for awhile. "But we worked it through." I sounded more convincing than I felt.

"Must be the barometer. I've been pressured myself this last weekend. I've heard from clients I haven't spoken to in years, all wanting up-dates on their charts. One of them wants to sign-up for my upcoming seminar on "The Interpretation of Natal Charts". It's fascinating the way we humans are affected by the elements and yet some people still scoff at astrology. Amazing!"

"It's another version of 'don't confuse me with the facts; I've already made up my mind' department." We laughed. I had escaped telling her more about Guy and our 'moment.'

"On to the rest of life. Jen, I heard from Wu Yee. He has signed a contract with the TV Production Company he told us about. He's terribly pleased. And they do want him to portray a restaurateur as well as use his place as part of the set."

"That's wonderful!"

She went on to tell me the company was interested in seeing my place. She called them and spoke on my behalf. Told them I'd be returning to the city very soon. And that I'd call them the moment I was back, to make some appointments for immediately after Thanksgiving.

"They couldn't have been nicer. So . . ."

"So, now you're my agent! I love it!" I was excited by the idea.

As we cleared, TJ turned to me and said, "Paul called today. He's terribly anxious to see you before you are both inundated with holidays, company, etc."

"I feel the same. I'll leave a cryptic message on his voice mail right now." TJ's demeanor changed: "I'm sorry to hear about Guy's reaction to Paul and you, Jen I told you he'd be a bit jealous. 'Possessive' would be closer to what I had thought, but I'd didn't think he'd be so disapproving. You know, I haven't spoken about this part of it before, but I have been quite aware of his little innuendoes and rather snide comments. And truthfully I'm baffled by them."

"I'm so relieved. I was beginning to think I was overreacting to his every comment. I've thought and thought and do believe you were right to begin with, about the jealousy bit. More so than possessiveness, though I'm certain that enters into it, too. Maybe I was too hasty telling him about Paul. Well, I can't undo that . . ." I shrugged.

"Frankly, I'm sorry I encouraged you to open up to him. Funny, after all these years, to misjudge someone you know so well."

"I wouldn't say either of us has misjudged Guy. He's being the loving, protective friend we've always known him to be. In this case, he's simply taken all of his positive qualities to an extreme."

"I think he's sorry he didn't put his foot down before you got serious, and so he's making up for it now, maybe. I don't know!"

"Exactly, TJ. You're right. I think we've both underestimated the depth of his feelings for me." I truly didn't want to say more. What happened was strictly between Guy and me. It would only make TJ uncomfortable. Happily, we involved ourselves with other distractions. Anyway there was little else to say on the subject. "I'll tell you one thing, I'm planning to keep my mouth closed on the subject of Paul."

"You're right, and I'll do the same. He'll overcome his feelings."

"Let's talk about Thanksgiving." We were in our usual places by the fire; so were the dogs. We had our special coffee, and they had each other.

"Fine. What shall we talk about first? People? Food? Assignments? I'm all ears." TJ was putting a light face on our evening, at last, while giving me her most radiant smile. I smiled back. Relaxed. Finally.

"Food first. You know that's my favorite non-people subject, or maybe we need to count noses first. The number may bear on the menu."

"Right. Let's see: You, me, Cara and Josh, her chum, your twins and their girls . . ." TJ was out of fingers.

"That's eight already and Guy makes nine. I invited Laura, but she's off to her family in Portland. Who else?" I was thinking.

"Don't know off hand, but two or three more will show up. They always do. I think we should just plan on the usual dozen or so. Don't you?

"Oh, yes, absolutely. We've only counted our basic group and I'd like to invite a few neighbors in for a drink maybe. I don't know if that's too much to do with last minute preparations?" I asked.

"Probably so. It's always a good idea this far from the fact of doing it, but when we're out in the kitchen the last hour, I don't think you need to be planning a cocktail hour, as well. With our own gang, it's help us and help yourself time."

TJ is practical in a way I'm not. I mean, she's a pragmatist and I'm too ready to take on the world and exhaust myself. That's not exactly accurate either. TJ 'does' for everyone all the time, and yet, she can see clearly pitfalls in my plans that I'm always falling into, and then wondering how I got there. Whatever—it's not important. We don't keep score, but, I can say for certain, she's way ahead of me on getting it right!

We set the menu and decided who should do what. Typically, we gang up in the kitchen and all work at once all over the place.

Magically, it all gets done, and we end up with a grand feast and lots of laughter.

We play scrabble or monopoly. Someone is always working on a crossword puzzle and a jigsaw puzzle, too. The dogs frolic. They're happiest when people are around to make a fuss over them, and they return the compliment.

TJ and I reminisced about past holidays and moved onto our Christmas Frolic plans.

"I've made preliminary inquiries as we agreed and finally settled on what sounds like a fabulous chalet at Squaw Valley." She went on to describe the place. It sounded too good to be true: Five bedrooms and three and a half baths with a big open living room and kitchen. The hallway upstairs surrounds the Great Hall with the bedrooms opening off onto it.

"Sounds more than perfect. But you didn't mention it when Guy was still here?" Now I was curious.

"Didn't have time. He bolted! Anyway, I'm glad we had a chance to talk first. He'll love whatever we choose and ante up his share without a murmur."

"It's a great deal for us. All the perks and none of the pain of a love affair. Well, almost none of it." I laughed. TJ, too.

We decided to go up the day after the day after Christmas. It would give us five full days of skiing. I was getting excited already. It was enough time to relax and have fun, and short enough not to get on each other's nerves.

"What do you say we wrap it up for tonight? I'm a mite tired."

I struggled up out of the couch, gave a hand to TJ, and we staggered off to bed.

The morning flew as we ordered the day in our usual way. Guy came to fetch me and Honey. I bade a fond *hasta la vista* to TJ.

"I'll see you Tuesday? How's that?" TJ asked.

"That's terrific. Celestina and I can use all the help we can get from you."

As we drove, Guy and I talked through a work schedule for the two weeks in December we had before the deadline.

"It seems quite possible to get it all done, now we've discussed it," I said. I'd begun to feel pressured by time.

"No, we're on the last leg now. I'm certain we have plenty of time. By the way, has TJ lined up anything for the holidays? A place for skiing, I mean."

"Oh, yes." I repeated what TJ had told me.

"Sounds great. But, do you think it's big enough?" Guy was amused.

"Well, seriously, Guy, we do have two couples; maybe three if Cara comes with her new beau, TJ, you and me. That is five rooms. If we're to have any privacy, we'll need them all. And who knows who will drop in for a couple of days? You know Max and Nicky, they have friends everywhere, and then they'll have to double up."

"Are we sharing a room? Or are you going to be stuffy because the boys and Cara will be there?" Guy was kidding on the square. "After all, they're going to be sleeping with their girls, and Cara with Josh. How 'bout it?" He was serious.

"Guy, you can't be serious? I thought we'd agreed to leave things alone. I don't want to be on edge with you from now on. It's going to put an unbearable strain on us. You know I'm in love with Paul and we both agreed that using you as a substitute would be a mistake. It would be insulting to you. I care too much about my commitment to our friendship. I admit I went overboard night before last, and I take my share of responsibility for it. I just don't want that episode to spoil things between us. " I was dead serious. I was also rattling on in a very hyper way.

"I know, Jenny. I started to tease you and suddenly found myself getting serious. My God, it was easy to do. Get serious, I mean. Intellectually, I know it can't work. Not now, anyway. It's just, I am a man, and you only get more attractive. Sometimes I wish we weren't such damn good friends. However . . ." His voice trailed off.

"Listen, Guy, I was just as turned on as you were. It would have been very easy to slip into bed with you. Then what? I'm afraid we'd have got the giggles; we'd be so self conscious."

"We weren't the least bit self conscious the other night, and yet, suddenly I couldn't. You were so frightened, so vulnerable. Even later, I wanted you and yet felt as though I'd be taking advantage of your emotional state." He paused a moment. I waited for him to go on. "I felt like a fool after I left you, but I would have felt like a bastard if I'd stayed. I know you're frustrated by Paul's position. Frankly, I didn't like the idea of being a substitute, either."

"Guy, you're such an incredible man. You know everything about me. You don't miss a beat. It's wonderful and frightening at the same time." I shook my head. "I feel so transparent around you. But, I'm not ashamed of my feelings either for you or Paul. You have me all psyched out. All I can say is thank God you're on my side. You'd make a formidable adversary."

I felt a tremendous sense of relief having all this out in the open. Now, maybe, we could take a break from the discussion of this subject and get on with our lives.

"I'm not used to verbalizing all this emotional stuff, you know that, Jenny, but I'm glad we got it out, too. Happily, I do know you. That's just how I want it. And I appreciate what you're going through. I have my own feelings about all of it I admit it. What I said the first night I met Paul still stands. I think he's a good man and he won't want to hurt you, but he might. So again, dear one, be careful. I hope you won't need me, but if you do I'll continue to be right here. For better or for worse . . ."

"Don't finish the line, please, Guy. I don't know what I've done or what kind of karmic reward I've won to have you in my life in such a profound way. I only know I'm deeply grateful."

Guy reached over and took my hand and held it tightly for a few moments, then kissed my palm and folded my fingers around it. The same gesture as Paul.

"Save that one, Jen. It's there for you anytime you want it." He gave me a twisted smile. I could say no more.

Celestina had lunch ready. Guy and Honey took a short romp on the beach before he left. "I'll see you Thursday afternoon, Jen. Don't work too hard and don't fret. We do have plenty of time. Get some rest. You'll need it when the gang arrives!"

I was more than satisfied with our rather unfocused, rambling rehash of our near sexual encounter. It felt resolved. It was, for as long as we wanted it to be.

# 28

As I entered my studio, my private line was ringing. "Jenny Matthews here, hello?"

"Hello, yourself! Welcome back." That voice!

"Oh, hi! I'm so glad to hear your voice. How are you?"

"I'm fine, but I'll be better when I can see you." His voice took on the lighthearted, breathless quality that excited all of my senses. It's impossible to describe.

Thank God, Guy and I had controlled ourselves. Right now, I'd have been a wreck of anxiety and guilt if we'd not. "Thank you, oh special protector of Jenny," I murmured under my breath. A somewhat strange reaction as I thought about it later. Adultery was all right, but being unfaithful to my lover was not.

"I hope we can make a plan soon, otherwise, it's likely to be weeks before I, for one, can draw a breath. What's your schedule?" I asked, fingers crossed like a kid.

"Believe it or not, I'm free to come up Sunday if it fits into your plans."

"Sunday? How's that possible?" Here I go again. Damn! Don't ask questions. It's not your business.

"It's fine. I have to make a quick turn around trip to Vancouver. My choice is to come to you Sunday, early afternoon, and leave as late as possible before I fly off."

"What a nice choice. I concur." I was thrilled. I hadn't dared think about having that much time with him so soon. And Sunday! Perfect. A quiet day. Yes. Ideal.

"I'd like to spirit you away with me." He was serious. "That's my other choice."

"And oh, how I'd like to let you," I sighed.

"Really, Jenny? Just one day?" He was really serious.

"Oh, Paul, I've been away almost three weeks, Thanksgiving is upon me and I'm expecting eight house guests starting with TJ on Tuesday. Tell me how I can, and I will." Challenged, I felt.

"I know, Jenny. I'm impossible. I'm just greedy. I admit it." He was smiling; I could hear it.

"That's the way I want you to be. It's just this time I can't fulfill your wish or mine—not completely, but Sunday! What a gift."

"Great. I was worried that it was too short notice. That's why I phoned TJ. Then I got your message this morning. I was thinking about you when I pushed the retrieve button, and there you were. Fantastic!"

"Fantastic is right! When can I expect you? For lunch? Dinner? When?"

"For lunch."

"What time's your plane?"

"8:30 from SFO."

"I'll be waiting. Will you call when you're en route?"

"Of course. I have a meeting coming up in five minutes, Jenny dear. I have to run now. I'll phone you."

I saw my face in the bathroom mirror. It was shining. Every bit of fatigue was erased. What an effect that man has on me, I thought. What a glorious effect. I stopped there. Forcing my thoughts elsewhere—back to Thanksgiving plans. I didn't want to ruin my sense of wonder and anticipation by thinking beyond Sunday. One day at a time. Moment to moment, Jenny. Remember, life is a series of moments!

Saturday came and went. A blur of activity. Celestina was leaving for the remainder of the weekend.

"I'll see you Monday. Have a nice time, Celestina. And thanks for everything. It's going to be wonderful."

"*Por nada.* You are welcome. You have a nice weekend, too. When is Miss TJ coming?"

"Didn't I tell you? She'll be here Tuesday, a day ahead of everyone else. To help you."

Celestina grinned. "Good, Missy, good. See you Monday."

"Drive carefully."

"*Gracias.* Thank you. Bye."

Honey and I settled down early. We were fast getting used to being home. She and I watched TV for awhile. I gave her a pat and was rewarded by a wag of a very large, fluffy tail.

"Good night, old girl. I'm glad to be here with you."

She grinned her golden retriever grin and put her head down between her paws and watched me with that unique stare dogs give to the special people in their lives. Finally, she turned her head away, let out a deep contented sigh, and closed her eyes. So did I.

I awakened with a start. The sun was up. Every spot in the room was drenched in a glorious, golden glow. The large animal was standing over me looking down with a toy in her mouth.

"I know. I know, Honey. It's time to move it. Come on. I'll get your breakfast and a cup of coffee for me, and then we'll run!"

Honey, bounding, rushing by me and running back. I, stumbling over her laughing. My heart was full of joy, and she knew it. Something good was about to happen!

"I'm on my way. I'll be there by noon." Oh glorious morning!

Honey and I romped and played along the beach. I finally called a halt. I needed to bathe and dress. Happily, Celestina had filled the fridge with goodies. Lunch would be no problem.

The little red car bumped over the berm and came to a halt in front of the garage. I pushed the button. The door rolled up and he drove in.

He swung out of the car and me into his arms in one movement. I felt his heart pounding against my chest. His hands gripped my back and slid down. A sharp intake of breath and I was gone. I started to pull off his sweater with one hand as I reached for the button to close the garage door.

I pulled away laughing and spluttering. We always seemed to get tangled up with each other—bumping into the cars and all the other unnecessary stuff that's in a garage, in the way of lovemaking.

We pushed our way as one into the house. He even had a moment for Honey who now understood the air of excitement blooming sweet and light through the house all morning.

We were nuzzling and nibbling and laughing, tugging at clothes, dropping them along the way to bed.

"Ah! At last. My God, how I've missed you, Jenny. I ache in the pit of my stomach when I think of you." He rolled over toward me and we began to make love. Slow and leisurely, we had all the time in the world. His eyes penetrated mine as his hands moved to stroke and caress me. He moved his head and began kissing me in lingering, slow motion, grandly, lovingly, bringing me with him as the tempo and depth of our passion grew and swelled until we were unable to control the pace any longer. With a gasp he rolled on top of me. We were locked in an embrace driven by longing. Held with a fierceness, a hunger I had never experienced before.

Forget bells and whistles. The bed rocked, the wind blew and fluttered the blinds, and just like the old black and white movies, waves crashed on the shore. The only thing missing was the triumphal march from Aida! He relaxed on to me and squashed the breath out of me.

"Oof! Oh you must move over. I'm squashed." I croaked and laughed.

He moved an inch or two, bringing me with him—laughing, too. Always the lighthearted laughter. And then he rolled over on his back while still holding me. It was my turn to stare down at him and to bring him back to me. We rested awhile and, once more, slowly began to rock and move. Every one of my senses was alert and ready. I couldn't believe the suddenness with which we were both engulfed in passion, once again. Hot and heavy—fast, furious and five minutes!

We lay back panting and laughing at the wonder of us. I curled up, my head against his shoulder, and we slept—the sleep of the well loved and well satisfied. Our passion spent, for now . . . and still, no words of love passed between us.

We had moved during sleep, and when I stirred, I felt pressure on my chest. He had flung his arm out. I was pinned underneath. I tried to move it gently, but to no avail. It wouldn't bend.

"Paul, yoo-hoo! Wake up! I can't move."

"Humph. Why must you move?" He repositioned himself on one elbow, and I received a kiss on the tip of my nose and then my lips. "You really are some beautiful woman, Ms. Matthews, and sexy as hell." He grinned and kissed me again.

"You're pretty sexy yourself—for a man, that is." I moved away quickly as I said that, knowing full well he'd react—and he did. He reached out for me, but I was too quick for him.

"Come back here, you . . ." I pounced on him, and we rolled around nipping and petting and grabbing playfully at each other in high good humor.

Suddenly, Paul stopped and looked at me. The humor was gone. It was replaced by a look I hadn't seen before—a look of pure anguish.

"Oh Jenny. It's so good being with you like this. Why does life have to be so damn complicated?" He was pacing. "These moments with you are the highlights of my very existence—not this alone; all of them, the phone calls, the meals together. Riding around with you by my side . . ."

"Not quite by your side. The console keeps getting in the way!" I was trying to lighten it up for Paul. This was not a time for sadness. I'd have to cope with my own anguish after he was gone.

"Ah! Yes, the console. If it hadn't been for that crazy thing, I'd have had you in the car that first day!" He was giving me his best, wolfish leer.

"You would have what? Not on your life, Mister. You were lucky I was in your car at all."

"I know. You thought I was an ax murderer."

"While you thought I was some helpless female."

"Not quite right. Female? Yes, very. Helpless? No! Driving me crazy? Yes! Wanted to run off with you? Yes! All of the above still applies in spades. Doubled, and I'm vulnerable!" He was coming across the bed reaching for me.

We succumbed to our need of each other, yet again. Dreamily, in a languid state. We loved each other, filled each other's deepest needs, murmured sweet, passionate words to each other—we were mesmerized by the feelings we evoked. We dared to let go, to trust each other with our wants and desires knowing they would be satisfied, acknowledged by a movement, a shift of body pressure, another caress.

Oh, Lord! What ecstasy! No thoughts to spoil it. No pretense, never pretense, only raw, quivering emotion. I pulled him to me as tightly as I could and held on for dear life as we, once more, let our bodies tell each other what we were unable to put into words: we loved each other openly, deeply, with a great understanding and acceptance. Lord be good to us. Show us a way to be together. Tears were streaming down my face. I was shaken to my very soul by these stunning feelings,

We were in like, in lust, and in love. Like was easy. Lust was robust, good fun. Ah, but love? That was different. That was serious and untenable. We weren't allowed to be in love.

"Tears, Jenny? No, please, you'll break my heart. I can't bear to cause you tears."

"You and I cause them. We are so perfect together, Paul. My tears are tears of relief that come from being with you; tears of emotion so deep, there is no bottom; and yes, tears of frustration. I won't deny that." I had stopped crying. I knew it was the abundant release of sexual tension and all the rest I'd mentioned.

I was also hungry.

"More to the point than all this gorgeous lovemaking is, I'm starving. Good Lord, look at the time, and look at the sky! The afternoon is waning! Come on, we have to eat!"

"Typical female. Satisfied in sex, energized and now ready to conquer the world! While we poor males limp off to the showers!"

"Oh, *pauvre petit*." I made a face. "Throw on your sweater and jeans and come out to the beach before it starts to get dark. You can shower later."

"You are a slave driver. You do all that. I'm going to shower now, thank you." And with a firm step, strode off to the bathroom singing lustily again like the last time—which was the first time.

I did what I'd told him to do. I pulled on my jeans that I'd left on the floor and pulled a turtleneck out of a drawer. I didn't bother with under pinnings. I admired my figure in the mirror. Not bad in spite of nursing twins. My breasts were still firm enough to go without a bra when I felt like it. And right now, I felt like it. The soft touch of cashmere against my bare skin was sensuous and delightful. The tight jeans held me in a way that was exciting me again.

I was sorely tempted to climb into the shower with him, but stopped myself with the thought of saving something for 'next time.' Anyway, he had only two hours left, and I did have to feed him. Something for his stomach this time!

Reluctantly, I left him to his ablutions and went to the kitchen.

"Calm down, Jenny," I told myself. "I know it's been a long, dry period, but you can't make up for it in one day!" I smiled to myself.

Let's see: warm the bread, pour orange juice with a touch of vodka and peach nectar, set up the coffee and toss a crab and crayfish salad. The avocado and tomatoes were already sliced. Oh yes, heat the pea soup.

"We're getting boring with these salads," I said. Paul had just come in, shining and still slightly damp.

"Boring? This is great and the soup smells are making my mouth water. What's in this? It's delicious!" He was sipping the 'juice plus.'

"Careful. It's not as innocent as it looks or tastes." I cautioned.

"Just like someone else I know. Not as innocent as she looks or tastes! Here bright eyes. To us! To forever!"

"To us. To forever."

We stared at each other deep in our own interpretations of the toast.

"And now I'm giving you one more chance to drop everything and come with me, Jenny." He held out his arms to me.

"Paul, I simply cannot—aside from the impossibility of the timing for me. This is the beginning of the Thanksgiving Holiday week. We'd bump into no less than forty people we know in the San Francisco Airport. Not terribly clever, I think."

"How can you be so desirable and such a pragmatist, or is it realist, at the same moment? Of course, you're right. I was thinking only of the great pleasure of having you with me. We'll find a more appropriate time to do it. Maybe after the holidays at some point."

"Maybe." I smiled and walked into his arms. It was soon time to say good-bye. Again.

"I'll be back in a flash, Jenny. I know we won't see each other again for weeks probably, but can I phone? This week, I mean?"

"I'd dearly love to hear from you tomorrow when you're back."

"Where in the world will you put everyone? Eight, you said?" We were still in a holding pattern.

"All over the place is the simplest answer. The boys and girls will have to make dorms out of the studio and the boy's room. Guy will be in the guestroom. TJ will share mine. I never worry when it's the young. They work it out better than any of the rest of us can." My chuckle was lost in his sweater.

I looked up; he accepted my kiss and gave one in return.

"Fly safe, cowboy. Tell the man up front to drive carefully." I waited as he folded himself into the car. I stuck my head in for an extra little kiss.

"If I have time, I'll phone you from the airport. Get to bed early, Jenny. And dream of me. Thank you dear-person-in-my-life." He backed out of the garage and pulled away. We waved until we were lost from each other's view.

"Well, Honey, as we say, back to basics!" She handed me her paw and gave my hand a sloppy kiss for good measure.

"You really are my pal aren't you?"

"Woof." I laughed and rubbed her ears for a few moments. We both went inside.

After Paul left, I thought over the past few hours. We hadn't spoken of children and family responsibilities other than sleeping arrangements here for Thanksgiving. Most importantly, we were together and loving every second of it. I'd made a valiant effort to overcome my tears—my one bad moment—and then there was Paul, suddenly gone so solemn as the reality of us struck him.

The truth is, we were reacting emotionally to what we had accepted intellectually every day. We had fallen in love and couldn't do a whole lot about it. Only steal a few hours from time to time—carving out the tiniest niche for ourselves from the complex structure of our lives.

# 29

Preparations for the holiday week were moving ahead. The house was beginning to smell like Thanksgiving even though dinner was three days away.

I didn't hear from Paul until he returned from Vancouver. He'd barely made his plane. The ride from Marin County to the airport wasn't easy. The day was productive. He missed me and loved our time together. We'd talk again.

I was inordinately relieved to have heard from him. These short turn-around business trips would always make me edgy. I just couldn't prevent it. It's not that I consciously said, "Oh dear, here comes a short business trip, I have to react." No. I'd suddenly find myself anxious for no apparent reason and then the light would go on inside my head. "Of course, no wonder I'm a walking wreck!" Well, not always so extreme, but something like that.

In any event, Paul was back safe and sound. I was, as I just said, mighty relieved.

As announced, TJ arrived on Tuesday. The pace of activity increased and with it the fun. Celestina and I dragged out all the extra bed and bath linens. TJ was making her extravagantly gorgeous floral arrangements, including a cornucopia for the dining table overflowing with fruits and vegetables and flowers in the rich, ripe colors of harvest-time. Then she began cooking up specialties from her armamentarium of holiday menus.

Tuesday night I cooked masses of whole small apples peeled and cored and simmered in simple syrup made with cinnamon red-hots. My mother's recipe. I couldn't sit down to a holiday dinner without serving them. Now the entire house redounded with evocative scents of Thanksgiving.

By Wednesday morning we were ready for the thundering herd to arrive. I was elated, anticipating having my boys with me. I'd only seen Max briefly since he and Bridget moved into their newly established home. I'd not seen Nicky at all since he left for Boston in August, and here we were, four weeks from Christmas! Nor had I seen Cara, my goddaughter, in months.

The van arrived tooting its way up the driveway. The three of us, TJ, Celestina and I, ran out the door to greet them.

"Nicky! Max! Diane! Bridget! My arms aren't long enough to hug you all at once!" I was close to tears. They all looked so healthy and handsome and beautiful. They were laughing and stumbling over each other and the dogs, trying to get to each of us for a special greeting.

"You guys," Nicky said. "Back off. I want to get a hug from my mother. Gosh, Jen, you look great."

"Thanks Nicky. So do you. I've missed you a lot."

"Me, too, Mom." I got an extra squeeze.

The house was a riot of activity for the rest of the week. Cara and Josh arrived later in the day. My, she had really grown into a stunning young woman. Her 'special friend' was a nuclear medicine research fellow at the University of Oregon in Eugene. If things progressed as they appeared, there could be yet another wedding in the coming year.

"Jenny, I'm so glad to see you. It's been eons since we spent any real time together." Cara and I were just finishing setting the table. "Can we talk this weekend? I mean take a walk or something? I want to catch up."

"Can we? You bet. I've wanted to meet Josh and hear how all that's going. I was so surprised when your mother told me you were staying in Eugene. All I know is that you went up to look around for the weekend and well . . ."

"Well, I guess I wasn't as forthcoming with Mother as I should have been." I agreed, but I didn't say a word. I listened. That's what godmothers are for. She continued: "I knew Josh was going to stay there for the foreseeable future. I hadn't counted on actually staying at the time. He just persuaded me to try it for awhile. And so I did." She smiled and shrugged and looked so disarmingly young, I couldn't comment. At least not now.

"Maybe we can talk tonight after dinner, if the weather holds. Otherwise, we'll have one of our famous Cara and Jenny talks tomorrow after a Max and Nicky breakfast." We both laughed. Cara knew well what the twins' breakfasts were like.

"Either way suits me, Jen. By the way, I think the boys' women are fabulous. I'm sure you do, too."

"They seem well suited to one another, and I thoroughly like them, though, as I keep saying, that's secondary to their liking each other."

Cara looked serious. "Yes, that's certainly true, Jen. But, you must admit, it's so much nicer all the way around, when parents approve of your choice of mate."

"Very true, Cara. Are you having a problem? Or shall we wait for our walk?" I wanted to be useful, and so I let her decide what her timetable for discussion of personal matters was to be.

"Mostly, I'd like to wait. I just want to tell you, Hank is all bent out of shape because Josh and I have been living together these last few months. If you have any ideas on the subject, tell me later, O.K? In the meantime, we'd better get back to work."

Curious, about Hank. Maybe his conscience was bothering him. Or wasn't he happy in his second marriage? I'd check it out later with TJ and find out what she knew.

For now, it was getting time to gather the brood to the table. Guy would be arriving at any moment. Counting Celestina, we were ten and I was satisfied to keep it 'all in the family' this year.

The scene between Guy and the twins was touching and heart-warming. They had the most wonderful, satisfying, intertwined relationship. All of them truly loved one another. From the time they were the littlest boys they were pals.

Guy has never tried to assume the role of surrogate father with my sons. Rather, he is a trusted mentor and life long friend. I've often thought about it, this unique relationship they have, and have been grateful to Guy for his sensitivity in this area.

As much as the boys missed their father and missed out on the 'fathering' since his loss, they were too old to accept another man in that role. Rather, the role Guy arrogated to himself was perfect.

All in all, they fared quite well in that department. By and large, they found outstanding people to study with and later to become associated with at the universities. And now, they had their future wives selected. Before long, they would have their own children to love and protect and nurture.

Good Lord, Jenny, stop pushing time away. How much faster can it go? You're already fifty-three—hard to believe. Soon enough, all of these things will happen. Right now, I needed to concentrate on the matters at hand. Namely, Thanksgiving Dinner.

"Sound the gong! It's time to sit down. Shall we join in saying grace?"

I looked around the table. My nearest and dearest, save one. It was a poignant moment. Joy and happiness abounded with a tiny overlay of sadness for all the missing people in my life. But those times were past. Great memories. The moment to be enjoyed was now, with gratitude.

Celestina brought out the turkey and set it down in front of Guy. "Let the feast begin!" And begin it did. It went on for hours with storytelling, eating, laughter, game playing and finally dessert. There was one collective groan as the last bite was taken and coffee sipped.

Nicky rose at this point and lightly tapped his glass with a spoon: "Hear yea, hear yea, to all assembled. Listen up. Diane and I have an announcement to make."

We all stopped in mid-sentence, focusing our attention on this handsome young man—this son of mine.

"Raise your glasses! Give a cheer!
For the end of my bachelorhood is near.
We'll tie the knot in early September,
Come one, come all for a time to remember.
Diane and I'll join the Christmas rally,
See you at the beach and up at Squaw Valley.
But, you, too, must promise to come out our way,
To celebrate a love-in, on our Special Day."
Cheers!"

He raised his glass and took a long drink amid cheers and huzzahs. Diane was standing, too, and they treated us to a long, happy embrace.

Everyone jumped up and soon they were surrounded. Much laughter and pounding on the back by the fellows and kisses for the girls.

My, oh my! I knew it was coming but . . . I was overcome by emotion. TJ was at my side.

"Leave it to Nicky. What a touch. Pretty special young man. And Diane, look at her! Brimming with happiness!"

"Oh, TJ, they suddenly look so young." I was a bit teary.

"We were younger, Jen. And not nearly so worldly."

"Times are very different, TJ. Our generation hasn't done much to ease their way. I think we had it easier some how."

"I'm not sure. Aren't you happy about this?" TJ was scrutinizing me closely.

"I am, absolutely. I'm just feeling the press of time suddenly. That's it. And thinking one down, two to go. I feel they will all be married within months of each other. It's quite a major shift in our little family."

TJ looked surprised. "You think Cara will be, too?"

"Most certainly they'll be setting up housekeeping. By the way, has she mentioned Hank's reaction to her moving in with Josh?"

We had moved into the kitchen.

"She's mentioned that her Dad wasn't pleased with this 'rush to a decision,' I think he said. What's she told you about it?" TJ asked.

"Only that she wants to take a walk tomorrow so we can get caught up. And then she mentioned it. She's looking for ways to handle him." I stopped what I was doing and looked over at TJ. "Any ideas?"

"You talk to her, and in the meantime, I'll give it a good think. I know what I'd like to do in the way of 'handling' it for her, but I don't think that's what she had in mind!"

I nodded in agreement. "We'll talk some more later. Let's rejoin the kids."

"Jenny, what about the plan for all of us at my house Saturday? Has that been settled yet? Shall I mention it now?"

"Oh, do. I'd mentioned it in passing last night, but go ahead. I think that's great. You can't put us all up, though."

"No, Guy said he'd take Nick and Diane. I think he wants a couple of hours with them Sunday before they leave. The rest of you can stay with me. We'll manage. Don't forget the couch in my office opens, plus the guest room." We moved back into the group.

"All three of them. Look at them. Great kids." Guy had joined us.

"They're our kids. What would you expect? With you as communal Godfather, you should be damn proud, too!" TJ was including Guy in her inimitable way, acknowledging his role as male model for all three of them.

"I am, actually. They're doing us all proud." He turned to me and said, "Jenny, by the way, shall we take a few minutes tomorrow to schedule the wrap up of our project?"

"Sure, Guy. We can get it all set. I like to think we'll turn it over to the client before the fifteenth. I've got a lot of Christmas shopping to do."

"TJ, did you bring the information on the Squaw Valley house? We can look at it tomorrow, too."

"It's in my bag. I'd totally forgotten about it, Guy. Too much turkey. We can go over it all tomorrow."

The three of us were observing a scene fraught with the vigor of life. A sight to behold. The three of our offspring so close all their lives. Now, grown up. Experiencing sharing their lives with each other's chosen partners. Thus the cycles of life move. A tiny glimpse of the future unfolding. God bless them and keep them safe from harm.

The hours flew melting into each other and suddenly it was Saturday. We were blessed with good weather. There had been a bit of a blow, but it dissipated itself rather quickly. Walks were taken, talks, loads of fun. Plans for Christmas and the skiing holiday were taking shape. Work schedules—all of it dealt with. And soon it would be time to pack up and move on into the city. TJ said come anytime. Guy had driven her in earlier.

The phone rang. It was Laura. She was back and wanted to say hi to the twins.

"Come on over, Laura. We're about to 'do' a Max and Nicky brunch."

"I'm on the way."

"Hi, Laura, come on in." The kitchen was awash with food, yet again. Life certainly seemed to revolve around food in this household!

The twins greeted her warmly, introduced their girls, and we all plunged into the preparations.

"Jenny, I'm going in to San Francisco for a couple of parties this weekend. The one on Sunday should be fun for you, too. Care to join me? You'll know a lot of the people. What do you say?"

"Gosh, Laura. Thanks, but it's been a very busy time. I think I'll pass."

"Jen, don't be that way. You should go with Laura." Max was being firm.

"Max's right, Mom. We're leaving in the afternoon. Go ahead. You might just meet someone interesting." Nicky chimed in. Diane and Bridget were amused at this side of my sons.

"My sons are pushing me, Laura. 'Interesting' to them is translated 'A man for mother.'" I couldn't help feeling a little guilty, but also couldn't help laughing.

"Well, Jenny? How about it? I think they've got your number. You'll have a good time, I promise." Laura was caught up in this exercise to 'get Jenny out amongst them.'

"OK, I give up. I'll get the particulars from you before we leave. Thanks, Laura."

The phone rang as she was leaving. Nick got it.

"Sorry, Guy's not here. This is Jenny's son, Nick. Who did you say this is? Sure. Hold on a minute. Jen, a man named Paul Crowley is on the phone."

"Paul?" I suddenly choked. "Did you say Paul Crowley is on the phone?" What was the matter with me? I'd just made a mess of my composure. "Oh, thanks."

Nicky gave me a funny look as he handed me the phone. He was quite curious, and why not? His cool, assured mother was suddenly stammering.

"Hello? Paul? What a surprise." What an inane way to open a conversation.

"Hello, Jenny. You're unable to talk, I gather. I'm sorry if it's not a good time. I wasn't thinking. I just took a chance."

"Hmm," I responded.

"I thought he was Guy and identified myself immediately."

"Yes, I gathered as much." Nicky was trying to be unobtrusive by tidying up a bit

Paul was chuckling now. Having apologized, he was enjoying the situation I was in. I could happily have strangled him.

"Happy Thanksgiving to you, too. Yes, that was one of my sons who answered. What? OK. I'll check my calendar. Excuse the buzz, I'm on a portable. I'll change in my office." I was talking on and on—nothing to do with what Paul was saying. In fact he wasn't saying a thing. He was only laughing.

I escaped the eyes and ears of Nicky. I waved as I left the room—talking all the time into the phone.

In case he had left the kitchen, too, as I picked up the other phone, I said rather too loudly: "My course will be on Thursday this year. Yes, I'm beginning in January . . . next week? Let's see. We could have lunch one day early—Monday or Tuesday." I finally paused for real, and waited for an answer.

"You're formidable, Jenny. What a performance, once you regained your balance. Awesome!"

"Wait until I see you," I whispered. It was more of a hiss. "I can only imagine what a horror it must have been to be your sister!" Now, I started to laugh.

"Tuesday's perfect. Shall you pick me up? Where will you be? TJ's? Have you had a good time? How about sushi again?" He didn't draw a breath.

"Hold it! Give me a chance to answer. Yes, I'll be in town. We're all moving to TJ's today. It's been outstanding. I'd prefer Chinese. I need to talk to Wu Yee and that would be a good time to do it. Did I answer everything? And did you have a nice holiday, too?"

"It was a very good family time. Yes, thanks."

"I've got to go, Paul. I'll see you Tuesday." I was super-composed as I was heading back down the hall.

"I'll call you at TJ's Tuesday morning, OK?" He asked.

"Great."

*A Small Flirtation*

"And, Jenny?"

"Yes?"

"I wish we'd been able to spend this holiday together. I'd have loved being part of it."

"Dear, man, how I would have loved it, too."

"Till Tuesday, then."

"Till Tuesday. Bye. Bye." I felt nonplussed as I got to the kitchen. I hoped I could pass my sons' scrutiny—they, for all their talk, were unaccustomed to my receiving phone calls from men unknown to them.

"Are you all right, Jen?" This time it was Max. "You look like you've seen a ghost."

"No, dear, I haven't seen one. I've heard one." I tried to smile. It was a feeble effort at best.

"Heard a ghost? What are you saying, M'am? Who were you talking to?"

"A friend and colleague, Max. A very nice man. We were making a date for lunch. We're team teaching for part of the quarter and need to talk over the course plans."

"But, what's all this ghost stuff?" Max still seemed concerned.

"It was just something he said, Max. Believe me, I'm fine." I put down the phone and beat a hasty retreat toward my room. "Let's finish up soon, OK? And be on our way. Anyone want to drive with me?" The others were in the living room gathering up their litter.

Cara and Josh said they'd come along with me and Honey. I set a time to meet and hurried on down the hall.

I had no idea where Paul was when he called. The reception was better than a car phone. I was ready to call his house at this moment. My rational mind stayed my hand from dialing the phone. "You'll get yours!" I muttered to myself. Still, I was amused. And completely smitten by his statement. Also, impressed with my thinking quickly enough to make my subterfuge sound real enough.

My being impressed with myself was short-lived. It was replaced with remorse. I was lying by omission to my own sons! What had I come to? Whatever I had come to, dealing with it would have to be put on hold. For the moment, I had other things on my mind, like packing the kids off to TJ's, closing up the house and getting Cara, Josh, Honey and me out of there before we blew the entire afternoon.

I phoned Laura and got the information for the Sunday party. Told her I'd stop by for a bit. She said TJ would be welcome as well. I did know the people giving it and felt comfortable about a second hand invitation. At best, holidays are like that, all inclusive; at worst, people can feel alone and abandoned. I was surely blessed.

That taken care of, I returned to the task of rounding up everybody and taking off. But only after we gathered up the bowls of flowers to take to TJ. No way was I going to leave them unattended and unseen for the rest of the week

TJ did a real number that night. She pulled out all the stops. Dinner was out-of-this-world wonderful. And how we got so lucky with the weather is unknowable. Perhaps the gods were listening to my prayer: Let Diane be impressed with California and want to move out after Nicky completed his present contract at school and before any question of tenure came up. It was getting uncomfortably close.

In any event, it all went wonderfully well. The girls were getting to know one another and were having a great time together. Josh fit in after the initial intimidation of twin brothers and their best childhood girlfriend-qua-surrogate-sister who happened to be his best girl.

I was surely ready to fold shortly after dinner. Guy decided the nightcap coffee be served at his place, and although Max and Nick had seen some of my latest work in my studio, Guy had the very latest at his home. It would be the only chance they'd have to see any of it until Christmas, and maybe not then either.

"Go. Please do, all of you. I'm happy to get to bed early, for once."

I all but pushed them out the door with a surprising sigh of relief. Never had I been so eager to be alone for a few hours. "Tomorrow, when they've all left, you'll be miserable," I said to myself. "Perhaps," I answered. And perhaps not!

It seemed I'd been moving in lock step with the world for weeks, and I was quite weary at the moment. I knew it would pass, but, for now, a little peace and quiet was what I needed and wanted most. The last few days with everyone had been wonderful. The momentum had carried me through.

Now, at TJ's, no major effort was expected or required. As a result, I'd let down and allowed the full impact of my over-stimulated emotions wash over me. The best way to achieve inner balance once more was to do some breathing exercises followed by a period of meditation. It always relaxed me and allowed me to focus on matters inside myself. After that, it was easy to fall into a deep, restful sleep.

In the morning I heard all about their evening at Guy's. It sounded light-hearted and fun. I was more than happy to have escaped it.

Breakfast there would be just right. I felt rested and refreshed—eager to 'join in' once more.

"You feeling better, Mom?" Nick looked concerned.

"I'm fine, dear, really. It's, well, it's been a very jam packed few weeks and I'd had quite enough last night. But honestly, Nick, I'm super!" One of his own favorite expressions. He laughed.

"Yeah, and you have a couple more weeks of solid work from what Guy told us last night."

"Plus Christmas shopping and packing up for the snow trip. Gad! I really will want to hole up by the first of the year for awhile."

"Then your class begins. Seriously, Jen, don't get worn out. I know you work out and eat right . . ."

"Not after this weekend!"

"Well, you know what I mean. Just take care of yourself, OK? Max and I need a whole lot more of you for a long time."

I caught my breath at such an open confession of his feelings. He gave me a little hug and moved off to finish his packing.

Talk about the rewards of parenting! That sort of thing doesn't happen out loud very often. Oh, certainly, I know how close we all are, and we aren't ashamed or embarrassed about showing it. The nice thing, the special thing is to hear it.

It's the female thing, I guess. Words, words, words—while men are action oriented. Yes, yes, there is some of each in all of us. I'm simply taking a broad brush to make my point.

# PART 3

# 30

"Were we ever so young?" TJ asked.

"I doubt it. And if we were, we weren't so damned full of energy! I'm positively numb from all the activity."

"Sort of makes me sad—to feel so alien to that stage of life. But Jen, you're wrong about one thing. We had the energy. It was just directed differently. Remember we were both married and having babies at their ages—running households and helping young husbands establish themselves. No, we had energy. What we didn't have was the time and money it takes to be self-indulgent."

"How do you manage to think so clearly and say all those words, when I'm so tired?" I sat upright. "I'm heading for a little nap before the cocktail party. Are you going to come with me?"

"Yes, I'll come. It could be fun, and we won't have to worry about food anymore today!" We both laughed.

"We certainly have done a whole lot of consuming." I groaned.

"And a lot of preparing too, don't forget! See you in a couple of hours." TJ headed to her room and I to mine.

Thank God she came with me! I don't know how I would have handled what was about to happen without her.

As we walked up the stairs, we could hear the party in full swing. We both recognized several people, pushed our way through to say hi to our hosts, and found Laura helping herself to a mound of something wonderful on black bread.

"Hey, you two. It's great to see you. TJ, you look terrific. It's been a long time."

"I know. Jenny keeps me hidden away when I'm up there. She tells me you're about to have a very big leap forward in your writing career. Congratulations!"

"It's exciting and fun, and it may even be lucrative." She added. "Who would have thought when I started writing children's stories, I'd wind up a TV mogul, or whatever they're called?" Laura was suddenly distracted by a man's voice. "Over here, Bret." She motioned to someone who was squeezing through the crowd. "This is the man I've wanted you to meet, Jenny." She whispered.

TJ and I exchanged quizzical glances. The man who was approaching was quite nice looking. He had a kind of rugged, intelligent look that I recognized and found attractive. But I didn't remember Laura mentioning anyone specific to me before this very moment.

"Bret, hi. Happy Thanksgiving. I wondered if I'd see you here. Meet my friends. TJ and Jenny, this is Bret. Jenny's my neighbor at the beach, and TJ's a local." Laura seemed genuinely happy to see him, and vice versa. She also seemed pleased to introduce us.

Not a very conducive atmosphere for getting acquainted. On the other hand, there was no need to struggle to make small talk to a stranger—no matter how attractive.

Nevertheless, Bret and TJ started to exchange animated, little bits of unimportant information to keep the flow going. Laura took advantage of the moment to turn aside and tell me a little about him.

*A Small Flirtation*

"He's an engineer. I met him a couple of years ago when he was in the throes of a divorce. Not the best time in anyone's life. We liked each other, but not in any romantic kind of way. He's a bit too old for me, anyway. I'd like to marry and have a family. I'm not looking for someone twenty years older than I to father my babies."

I was a bit startled by this rush of facts about, not Bret, but Laura. It was an unlikely place for this kind of revelation voiced in a rather loud stage whisper. As she was telling me all this, I was sipping on my glass of wine while automatically scanning the crowd when my eyes locked on an attractive woman across the room looking directly at me.

We held each other's gaze momentarily transfixed by a kind of knowingness when a man approached her and noting the intensity of her stare followed it directly to me. Imagine my shock when I realized I was staring back at Paul. The expression on his face went absolutely flat. He turned to her, said something while taking her elbow and directing her to the entry hall and down the stairs. All in one swift and continuous movement, Paul left the party with his wife in tow.

My heart sank as my stomach was on a collision course with my emotions. I didn't know what I was going to do next. One minute I felt like throwing up, the next I felt an uncontrollable giggle rising in my throat. Neither was the correct response to what Laura had been saying to me. She had been trying rather too hard to explain why Bret was a good catch for me but not for her.

At that very moment I saw Paul rejoin the party alone. TJ, turning to me with the best, blank expression I'd seen in a long time said, "Bret is a partner at Crowley, Warden & Soames."

"Oh?" I was struggling to maintain my composure on all fronts.

"Yes. Do you know the firm?" Bret inquired. "Wait a minute, here comes my partner, Paul Crowley, of the firm name. Over here, Paul. Hello!"

"Hello, Bret. Jenny Matthews! What a small world . . . and TJ. How are you?" You had to admire Paul. He was cool, real cool.

"Great, Paul. Thanks. Have you had a nice holiday?" I was quick to respond.

"A really good family gathering. Thanks. And you both?" He was including TJ, now, very smoothly. No curiosity.

"Oh, yes," TJ said. "Jenny's twins were in town with their 'significant others,' and my daughter, Cara, was here with her best beau. It was quite a gathering."

"You all know each other? Amazing." And Bret did look amazed. So was Laura. I was dumbstruck. My admonition to myself had just been confirmed: Whoever knows whoever knows who? Thank God I hadn't poured my heart out to her!

She laughed and said, "Here I am trying to introduce Jenny and TJ to a few new people when I find out they know more people here than I do. I might have known it. Jenny, it's your turn, introduce me."

"Oh, Laura, how dumb of me. This is my friend, Paul Crowley. We teach at Berkeley together. It appears he and your friend, Bret, are partners."

"Is Kathy with you, Paul? I don't see her." Bret was looking over Paul's shoulder.

"Actually she and Beth stopped in for a short time. In fact they left just a few minutes ago. They're off to do some serious looking at silver and china. By the way, have I told you Beth's being married in June?" Paul was directing his comments solely to Bret, distracting him while I composed myself.

"Really? That's great news. Hard to believe." Bret shook his head. "The years are really racing. I swear, twenty-four hours aren't twenty-four hours anymore."

"You're right, you know," I chimed in. More than ready to change the subject entirely. "As it's not my field at all, I feel perfectly comfortable claiming I know more than physicists. Days are only thirteen hours and forty-five minutes, I've measured!"

"You've what?" They were all looking at me. Paul was grinning from ear to ear. He'd heard my theory before.

"I've measured! It really is very simple. I've been going as

# A Small Flirtation

crazy as everyone else with the speed up of time. The problem is no one has actually researched the problem."

"Tell us then." They were all teasing me and egging me on.

"I figure that with all the explosions of the wars this century, particularly the sonic booms of the 60's and subsequent decades, added to the rocket and missile launchings and nuclear testing—well, the earth . . ."

"Yes?" Bated breath.

". . .the earth has been moved off its axis a little bit, tilting things and making the planet twirl faster. Ergo, although twenty-four hours is still recorded on time pieces as such, in real time we have only thirteen hours, forty-five minutes per day."

"All well and good as a theory," Bret said, "but what about this measuring you said you've done?" He was half amused, half-serious and curious as the devil.

"I figured carefully what I used to accomplish in twenty-four hours. You know, driving time, meal preparation, sleep, errands work, etc., etc.; even factored in increased traffic and subsequent additional time for travel, all sorts of things, and found I could only do thirteen hours and forty-five minutes of my former routine in twenty-four hours. How's that?" I felt triumphant! "I practiced the routine over and over, remembering little things extra I'd forgotten about. And it still worked plus/minus five percent."

"Whenever did you do that for heaven's sake?" This time Laura asked.

"Oh, I checked back to eight, nine years ago one day and figured from there," I said smugly.

"Well, I'll be damned." Bret again. "I've heard about a second or so from physicists, but, I admit, I think I'll buy your theory."

"I'll drink to that and to you, Jenny." Paul raised his glass, and the others followed with laughter.

"To Jenny!"

Laura saw someone else she knew and drifted away for awhile. TJ and Bret resumed their getting-to-know-one-another conversation. That left Paul and me alone together. Out of earshot, he said he thought he'd got through the shock of seeing me there pretty well and admitted, at the same time, I wasn't so bad myself.

"We were lucky TJ was talking to Bret and warned me of his professional association just before you joined us. So I had a split second to pull myself together after seeing you leave with . . . ?"

"Yes, it was Kathy. I had no idea you'd be here, Jen, or I'd have warned you or made another plan or something to have prevented this."

I nodded, "It was bound to happen sometime, someday. It's just—I don't know—strange. Somehow we seemed to recognize each other. There was a connection, almost an acknowledgment of who each of us is. Then you appeared and I understood my feeling."

"I'm having a devil of a time not taking you in my arms right this minute, Jenny. I want to take you away from here. How do we manage that?"

We were standing too close. I suddenly remembered TJ's admonition and moved back a step. She and Bret turned to us at the same time and said it was too noisy and crowded, and why didn't we all go someplace for supper.

"In other words, let's blow this joint." Bret was taking the lead. "What do you think of the idea?"

"Sounds good to me. Paul, what about you?" I prayed silently and forced myself to ask the question: "Will Kathy and Beth be coming back here?"

"No. Later they're meeting at the house with the potential bridesmaids. They most certainly don't need me there for that."

"I think it's a great idea, Bret. We're not too far from Wu's," I said " How about some good Chinese food?"

"Any good ideas about all the cars?" TJ was being practical.

"Leave yours here, Jenny. I'll bring you back for it. Bret can take TJ in his car. OK?"

"Swell. Let's find Laura and say good night to our hosts, too." TJ was organizing our departure.

We did. She was thrilled that her introduction seemed to take.

I don't think she noticed the pairing. We bid our good nights carefully and selectively, not showing any particular attention to the men, who were speaking to others as we left. TJ and I had a hard time not acting like boarding school girls out after hours.

"Would you believe . . . ?"

"Thank God you're here with me." I gasped as I was laughing, admittedly I was still shaken by the sight of my Paul with his wife. How very odd—he and I belonged together. What was she doing in the way?

"I'll keep things away from you two. I think I can and, obviously, Bret has no idea. Being at Wu Yee's may help, too. He'll talk about his new contract."

"And about Albert . . ." I added. "It should be all right."

"I hope so . . ." TJ murmured. The two men were catching up to us.

TJ and Bret went off together.

"Thank goodness they seem to like each other. They also seem a more natural pair than he and I," I said to Paul as I got to the car.

"A more natural pair than he and you, did you say?"

"Yes. Laura, it appears, had encouraged me to come to the party expressly to meet Bret. Not that she said so earlier, although she did before you arrived. Interesting that TJ and he hit it off immediately."

"Really. That's nice. He's a good guy." Paul sounded relieved.

"In the beginning, I think she was just making small talk while checking him out."

"Does she check out all of your suitors and potential suitors to deem if they're suitable for you?" He was at his mischievous best.

"Of course. She checked you out, too. Do you forget so soon?"

"Anyway, I'm glad the tide seemed to have turned and they're talking with some real interest. I'd certainly hate having my competition be my own partner. Especially one as eligible as Bret." He grimaced and reached for my hand at the same moment. He turned it over and kissed my palm folding my fingers in the familiar way.

"Remember to hang onto that for me, Jenny."

"I will. What if he did find me interesting and wanted to call me? What would you do?" I didn't exactly admire myself for asking the question. Somehow having seen him with Kathy made it easier to do.

"There's nothing I could do, not a damn thing. I'd hate that a hell of a lot, for sure." He sounded almost angry, in the dark of the car.

I instantly regretted my unspoken childish question: 'Tell me you love me best.' It couldn't have been a clearer statement had I said it out loud. We drove on in silence for a few moments.

"That can happen, Jenny, and may well one of these days." He spoke softly. "I'd have to be happy for you, all the while, regretting it for me." He was still holding my hand and lifted it to his lips again.

"Well, it's certainly not happening now. As for someday? What will happen, will happen, without any help from us." I sighed.

This was neither the time nor place to bring up the one subject that was still 'verboten'.

The four of us converged at the restaurant. Wu Yee looked up from his reservation book. "Hey, you guys, a nice surprise. Welcome!" He shook hands with Paul and gave TJ and me a cheek to cheek 'cousin's kiss.'

"Yee, I don't think you know my partner, Bret Saunders." Paul took the lead. "Bret, this is Albert Wu's father."

"Really? How do you do? Albert's a good man. You should be proud of him."

"Indeed, I am. Thank you. I'm also pleased to meet you. What's up? You look like you've been partying."

"You're right on, Yee," TJ said. "These nice men rescued us from what was becoming a too noisy, too crowded party."

"Also, we couldn't get near the food," I chimed in.

"Not you, Jenny! No wonder you came here. Now, I'll rescue you from starvation." Yee seated us and signaled a waiter to bring some pu-pus.

The smell of pungent spices filled the place. We inhaled the appetizers and ordered much more food and beer. I like Chinese beer and mix it with Seven-up or orange juice. The rest turned up their noses in disgust. Yee explained that's the way some people drink it in China. "It makes a refreshing flavor especially in very hot weather. The British started it there and in India. I believe they call it a 'shandy,'" Yee explained.

"Well, it still sounds awful to me." Paul finally spoke. He'd been very quiet, letting the conversation flow around him. I caught his eye and nodded imperceptibly toward TJ and raised an eyebrow. He nodded with a little smile and a twinkle in his eye.

I hadn't seen TJ this engaged by a stranger in many a year—other than Paul, that is. Maybe we'd have yet another romantic interlude to cope with. Good grief. That would leave only Guy. We'd have to see about that. Mind you, I was being more than a bit premature. I'm not so sure TJ even heard Bret's last name.

Food, conversation, a lot of laughter, and then the sudden realization it was getting late. Paul called for the check, and we were ready to retrieve my car and call it a night.

"How are the TV plans progressing?" I asked Yee as we were leaving. "Any idea when they expect to begin shooting here?"

"As a matter of fact the answer is yes. They hope to get started next week. Have you had a discussion with them yet, Jenny? TJ, you did talk to them, didn't you?" Wu turned to TJ who hadn't been listening. She was having her own private conversation with Bret.

"What? Oh, the TV people. Yes, I've set a time next week for them to look at the beach house."

"Good. This could turn out to be a nice thing for all of us." Wu was delighted. "Stay in touch and let me know when they're coming up. I'd like to know what their reaction is to your place, Jenny."

"I'll be sure to call. And thanks, my friend. I'll make it all the way to breakfast because of you. It was wonderful as always. My best greetings home."

"Many thanks to you, Jenny. Good night. And to you TJ. Come soon for lunch, and we'll talk about the movies! Gentlemen, a delight to have you here . . . Welcome, again." Yee bowed slightly as he shook hands with Paul and Bret.

"Good night Wu Yee; I'll see you again soon." Paul was turning to go when Wu put his hand on Paul's arm to stop him.

"Tell me, Paul, how is Albert? Is he really doing a good job? He seems less nervous than in the beginning."

"He's good and getting better all the time as he gains in self-confidence, Yee. You have nothing to worry about. I intend to help him study for the licensing exam, also." Paul was showing his professional interest while still being encouraging to this very interested parent. Nice, I observed to myself. Nice.

"A pleasure meeting you and dining in your fine establishment. You'll see more of me," Bret said.

More good nights and we finally left. More good nights at my car. We were all exchanging pleasantries when Bret turned to TJ and asked if he could call her.

"Why, of course, yes. That would be nice. Thanks," she stammered. I was amused.

"Great. Well, good night then to you both." He helped TJ in and gave her a quick kiss before he closed her door. "I'll call you soon. Good night, Jenny."

Paul was closing my door. "I'd like to come by TJ's for a few minutes. Is that OK?"

"Yes, of course, come on over."

The two men waited until we drove off. I could see them in the mirror shaking hands.

"Whew! What a night. The circles of our lives keep getting tighter." I let out a deep sigh that ended with a choked up sob kind of sound.

"Jenny, what in the world did I miss?" TJ was truly perplexed.

*A Small Flirtation*

"I heard all of Paul's explanations, but you—you were white as a sheet when Bret spotted him and called him over."

I told her of my eye contact with Kathy and then Paul's move to her and the rest.

"How I managed, I'll never know…" The effort at the party followed by the warmth of being with Paul for the first time as a couple, out with another couple was leaving me both emotionally charged and physically drained. I was in such conflict as we drove back to TJ's; I wasn't sure how I could handle seeing Paul. Despair and joy are strange bedfellows. Still I wanted to bed this fellow now. Every nerve ending in my entire body was on the alert.

"Jenny, did you hear me? Did I hear Paul say he was stopping by?" I forced my attention back to what she was saying.

"Yes. You don't mind, do you?"

"No. No. Just wondering. It'll give me a chance to grill him about Bret."

"You seemed quite smitten—especially for a woman who has been keeping men at arm's length for years." I teased her while being unutterably pleased.

"He seems different somehow. How's that for an original concept? Bet you've never heard a woman say that before!" Always keeping it light—my friend who had been so badly hurt.

"That was some switch. Good thing Paul was there to team up with. I would have been the odd one out. I wonder what Laura thought about our little group as we left the party. Of course, she was busily involved with any number of people she knew there." I was pulling into the garage as Paul drove up.

TJ signaled him to drive in, too. That little red car was very conspicuous and, as such, seemed safer inside. She headed straight into the house. Paul and I headed straight into each other's arms.

"There, that's much better. My head was running out of things to say. All I wanted was to hold you like this." He kissed my forehead and looked down at me with that frank, open look of his. "It wasn't easy being casual with you so near."

Neither of us wanted to touch the subject of Kathy. I for one was absolutely determined to push the incident as far away as possible. Instead, Paul answered TJ's questions about Bret and then, as usual, had to leave.

Saying good night was harder than ever before. I'd seen his wife—the woman he was going home to, to bed. And even though I had heard many and varied statements about his marriage, they all boiled down to he couldn't do any thing about it—at least not now. There had been no real explanation of why not. I wondered how long I could continue this way. I prayed fervently that the gods would make it right and we could be together forever.

## 31

The day dawned windy and overcast. Our glorious holiday weather had departed abruptly. We were well on the way to a northern California winter. Not what easterners would call winter; but, nonetheless, winter to us. That is not to say we don't have sunny and warm days and then . . . oh well, I'm certain you get the idea. If there's ever to be rain, now was the time for it to begin.

Guy called. He was ready to work at his place. So was I, ready and anxious to be finished. I'd liked the project; learned more than I ever expected to about migratory birds; most certainly had an interesting and revelatory time with him.

It was evening, and it was morning, and another day dawned. Suddenly, it was time to leave the warmth of TJ's hospitality, meet Paul for a bite of lunch and head up the coast to my home.

"Is it OK with you if I keep Honey for a few days, Jenny? You'll be busy, and Poochie and I can use the company." TJ was looking exceptionally well at breakfast.

"It's fine with me, but why do you and Poochie need company?" I was more than a little curious.

"Oh well, it's Poochie, not really me. Bret called yesterday and wants to take me to dinner tonight. I just thought if Honey were here, Poochie wouldn't suddenly feel abandoned."

"Ah so! He's really a very attractive man. I'm glad you'll be seeing him, TJ."

"I'll give it a try, for awhile. I admit I think he's interesting. It seems like a worthy idea."

"A 'worthy idea'? It sounds like you're doing something for a charity event! How about 'he's cute and fun and it's been a long time'?"

We laughed and said good-bye.

"See you soon. I've had grand time."

"Me too, Jenny. It was a lovely Thanksgiving."

I picked up Paul around the corner from his office. "Where shall we go? Any ideas?" Paul took my hand and turned it over.

"What are you looking for?"

"The kiss I told you to hold on to. Just checking to see it's still there." He looked up and smiled that smile.

"After all that turkey as well as Chinese food, I, for one, could do with a California salad," I suggested.

"Do you have time for the ten mile round trip to Cliff House today? What's your time schedule?" Paul surprised me. Midweek he usually takes only an hour plus a little.

"I'm fine. TJ's keeping Honey so I don't have to circle back for her. I have plenty of time."

"Swell. Let's go out for a change. I feel like playing hooky."

"Tough to get back to work after a four day weekend, is it?"

"Especially when I can spend some extra time with you, girl."

"Want to drive?" I hadn't pulled away from the curb yet.

"Sure, I will, but you'd better pull away a bit. I am just around the corner from my office, and now that one of my partners knows you . . ."

"That was a real fluke. As we've said before, one day we'll find out we're related!"

It was amusing, all the cross connections, but it was a mixed blessing. We were no longer the anonymous couple we had supposed, and that fact alone would make these little 'pick-up' times together more difficult to carry off. Guy was one thing—and frankly, that was proving tough enough. Bret? No way! He wasn't to be brought in, to say nothing of Kathy now. Paul and I were still avoiding the subject like the plague. And that's just the way I wanted it—for now at least. Anyway, what was there to say?

"Here, Hon, pull over and we'll switch seats." I did and we did and I received a kiss on the tip of my nose to boot. We listened to music and held hands.

"Has Bret commented on TJ or Sunday or anything? You haven't said a word, yet."

We were seated by a window; the view was, as always, sparkling and beautiful.

"Haven't had a chance yet; and yes, he thinks she's someone he'd like to get to know better. TJ's the first woman he's shown any real interest in since his divorce. Fortunately, he was so wrapped up in his own comments, he didn't think to ask me how I know her."

"Good Lord, I hadn't thought of that until this very second!"

"You, I explained immediately, but TJ greeting me...anyway, he had nice things to say about you, too. Thank God she was there for him to focus on."

"Sheer dumb luck, is all I have to say." It had been some night.

"What's next on your agenda? Have you planned Christmas? Where will you be? Fill me in, please." He was doing that funny thing again. Flooding me with questions, filling in the gaps of our life together with words. We don't have enough time to be current with our daily activities, and so, we each play tell-me-more games.

"First, I have masses of Christmas shopping to do. Then I have to plan the vacation."

"Will the boys and their girls be with you?"

"Yes. I want Christmas Eve and day and the day after to be at the beach. I want to establish the family gathering as a focal point for holidays. I know that Diane has family in the east, and I'll eventually have to share the times with them, but this year they'll be here. Bridget's family is close by. I'm hoping we can do things together sometimes. We'll see. What about you and your family?"

"We'll have Christmas away this year. We're leaving for ten days of family skiing on the twenty-third and staying until after New Year's." His voice had gone a bit flat. I didn't comment. "The condition of the snow should be perfect and then there's always activity in town for those who want it," he continued.

"We're leaving the twenty-seventh until after the first. All of us. My entire extended family. We'll be skiing, too."

"Who all, and where?"

"All of us. The boys and girls, TJ, Cara and Josh, and Guy."

"Even with TJ and Bret just getting to know each other?"

"She'd not change the plan anymore than I would. She'll have a chance to see him over Christmas. If she wants to bring him up, he'd be welcome. It'll work itself out. Laura, too, for that matter. Where are you going?" I asked innocently.

"Squaw Valley. Where will you be?"

"The way the circles of life have been pulling us together, where do you think we're going?"

"Jenny, no! Not Squaw Valley?"

"Of course. Where else?"

"We're beginning to sound more like a soap opera everyday!"

"Squaw Valley!" We burst out laughing and then grew quite serious. "So near and yet so far. We'll have to figure out something, Jenny."

"Maybe you'll get to meet my twins. I'd like that. I think."

Like that? I was uncertain. It might just make things too difficult. They'd like each other for sure—like the proverbial ducks to water. Then what? Was he to turn into a family friend? I didn't think I could take that.

"Why do you say, 'I think?' I know I'd like to meet them and have you meet Beth." He was warming to the idea.

"Are we to become family friends? Is that the way this is to evolve? Right now, I don't think so. I'm not ready to hide my true feelings and become Auntie Jenny to your daughter and Kathy's newest best friend." For a fleeting moment it struck me funny, and then, suddenly, I felt anxious and uncomfortable.

I didn't know whether to laugh or cry. Paul was taken aback by the play of emotions on my face and in my voice. He wasn't sure how to react to me—or to himself, for that matter. He went for 'light.'

"Not exactly what I had in mind, dear, but it could be fun—for awhile." He was putting a happy face on this crazy maze of coincidences.

The whole idea finally struck me very funny. There was no other way to deal with it. It's not my style to remain anxious about something over which I have no control. I had, unhappily, learned long ago to accept the unacceptable and bear it. If falling apart changed any outcome for the better, believe me, I'd have done it. Instead, all that's created is a big mess with no one to clean it up, but you. No. The only way to deal with Christmas was to let it all happen as it would anyway, and not fight it.

"In the long run, I don't know; but, for the short run, I guess you're right." My tension was dissipating. "This entire relationship is based on coincidence and synchronicity anyway."

"How about a bit of serendipity while we're at it? It all must be leading somewhere; but, at the moment, I'm damned if I know where." He reached across the table for my hand. "All I know is right now I'm extraordinarily happy and, for me, 'now' is what's important.

We sat and looked at the sea for a few more minutes and then rose to go.

Paul stopped the Jeep a block from his office bent over and gave me a quick kiss and hopped out.

I was sorry I'd left the dog at TJ's. Honey was good company, especially when I felt so alone.

Not since I lost Tom had I felt such deep loneliness. It didn't take much introspection to understand what was bothering me. The twins had paired off, so had Cara, Guy was eyeing Laura and TJ was eyeing Bret.

That left me in the untenable position of having met the perfect man who just happened to be married to someone else. No wonder I felt so alone.

# 32

The next ten days we worked, ate, relaxed and also admired what we were doing. Guy had come and stayed. Even on weekends we hung in there together and accomplished a monumental amount.

"I'll go in with this mass of material tomorrow. In the meantime, let's celebrate tonight," I said.

Celestina had cooked up a storm: empanadas, black bean chili, chilies relleno with pimentos, a huge salad with pines nuts and mandarin oranges, and topped off with a silken flan. We invited Laura to join us. Guy was in his element—three women! What more could he want? We put on salsa music and he danced with us all.

By the time I got up in the morning, Guy was loading his car.

"Nice work, Jenny. A good project, well conceived and well executed." Guy was obviously well pleased. "I think we can risk saying the clients are going to be satisfied. We had a good time together, too, didn't we?" He was watching for my reaction. "There was some pretty powerful stuff going on. I, for one, found it interesting, to say the least."

"To say the least," I echoed. "Now on to Christmas and our next adventure!" We walked back into the house, talked about the skiing trip while gathering up Guy's last few things. I wanted to avoid that other 'powerful stuff' altogether.

"I'm on my way then. I've got to shop, too. Let me know when you're coming in and we'll 'do' lunch." He laughed.

I knew we'd see each other at least once before Christmas. He and TJ and I had things to arrange before then. I lingered in the driveway wondering if he'd made any dates with Laura, when I remembered she was to be away that next weekend. They'd hardly had more than two words together while we were working—private words, that is. Even so, it was obvious last night, she was happy to have a little focused attention from Guy. That told me it wasn't the age differential between her and Bret that mattered so much. Guy and he were virtually the same age.

Structural engineers are different than creative people, though they'd hate to admit it, I suggest. Their world is plumb, square and level. And it better be. After all, buildings, bridges, tunnels and the like must maintain their structural integrity. No whimsy, no flights of fantasy—these were the realm of a writer of children's books.

No, Bret and TJ were much better suited. She is a certifiable mathematical genius. Her consuming interest, astrology, as well as other esoteric philosophies, is based on mathematical certitudes. Never mind how many people think of it as 'way out.' It is the oldest exact science known to mankind. Maybe that's its problem. Had it been known to womankind, it would probably be well accepted for centuries by now. Sailors know the tides are controlled by the moon. Farmers rely on the phases of the moon as prognosticators for the successful planting of crops. Others among us seem unwilling to accept the power that guides the universe as exerting any influence over the other aspects of our lives. As so many seem not to believe in God, these days, it should be no small wonder to me they don't believe in the wonders of the power of the One who created it all! And yet I wonder.

My, my, Jenny. All of this because your two beloved friends are finding possible new romantic interests!

## 33

When you wait until the last few days to shop, you haven't the luxury of browsing; you merely buy. In the long run I do believe it's the more efficient way to deal with it—no dawdling. You can't wait until tomorrow.

Anyway, I rushed a lot and accomplished some. A few more days of this and I figured I'd be finished.

I turned the corner and headed down the street to Gumps when I felt someone was following me. Great! Just what I didn't need. Holding my bags and purse tightly in front of me, I stopped abruptly. Immediately someone bumped into me. I was jostled, but didn't drop anything.

"That was a neat move, Jenny. Except, I could have stumbled and knocked you down! You're a tough one to surprise."

"What in the world . . . ? Paul, you really are mad! I was scared to death! Don't laugh at me."

"How can I help it? You're adorable. For a minute I thought you were going to bash me with your pocket-book."

"Don't think I didn't think of it. Whatever are you doing down here?" I was pathetically elated.

"Same as you. I'm shopping. I saw you turn down here and sprinted up behind you." He was grinning, of course.

"I'm about to call it quits for the day. Want to stop for a cup of tea somewhere?" I tried to sound casual and was praying he'd say yes.

"I haven't much time. I've a meeting soon. Jen, I'm so glad to see you, but I don't think we can find a place and get out in time. My Canadian people are here on a very brief trip. I wish I could . . ." His voice trailed off.

"I do, too. I was thinking of you as I came across."

"Good. Maybe after. Are you going back over or to TJ's?"

"To TJ's. There's just too much traffic at this time of the year. And frankly, I don't enjoy an almost fifty mile round trip simply to do a little shopping. Look, dear, don't push yourself into a corner. It was fun bumping into you, but . . ."

"Literally! Let me see what I can do. I'll phone you as I'm leaving. Just, don't change any plans. I mean, don't wait, if you want to go out."

"I know. We won't."

"I've got to run, Jenny. I'm sorry."

"You can bump into me anytime!" I laughed.

We couldn't touch or anything; we were both holding packages. I stuck my head forward as he did and we had a quick kiss and almost collided again. I turned into the store as he strode off. The barest contact, the barest glimpse and my heart sang. Be still, my foolish heart!

Funny I should see him now. At this very moment I was looking for a special Christmas gift for him. I wanted some sort of cowboy, not jewelry or clothing. Something he could put on his desk, possibly. Something to see everyday.

And there it was. My cowboy in bronze. Standing in that easy, loose manner—his hat in his hand hanging down the side of his leg. His face was serene—a steady gaze straight ahead. I loved it. It was perfect. Then I saw another one. This cowboy had his hat on. He was twirling his lariat and his head tipped to the side watching what he was doing. I looked back and forth between the two. The second one was preparing to catch something. The first looked confident that he already had! Two guesses which I bought.

I had it sent to his office. Uncertain, as I was, that we'd meet again before Christmas. Just as I was turning away, I caught a glimpse of the woman standing at the next counter. I stopped mid-stride. There was something about her and although I was certain I'd seen her before, I didn't actually know her. Then I heard her exclaim:

"Paul will be so surprised. He's been lusting after this for weeks," and laughed. She was admiring a perfectly handsome barometer of antique bronze.

I held my breath. The salesman glanced over at me. I must have been staring. Had he overheard me order a gift to be delivered to this same man's office? I turned away abruptly and pretended to be engrossed in a display of maps.

"Charge it to my account, please, and send it to my house." I didn't want to know more, but I was transfixed and positively couldn't move.

"Certainly Mrs. Crowley, I'll see to it being wrapped for Christmas and send it out. And thank you very much. I'm certain Mr. Crowley will be enormously pleased. Merry Christmas to you."

She turned and almost bumped into me. We looked at each other full in the face for a split second. There was a flash of subliminal recognition and then moved on. At least she moved on. I felt paralyzed. A close encounter. For the moment, I was unknown to her.

More circles within circles.

My reaction was so intense I felt weak and sought out a place to sit down for a few moments to collect myself. "The woman is Paul's wife. That stunning, dark, sleek beauty, perfectly attired in suburban chic is PAUL'S WIFE," I kept saying over and over to myself. "The disinterested, disaffected wife. The cool, unconcerned wife." Well, she certainly didn't seem cool or disinterested while buying his Christmas present.

I was all but on my knees with gratitude that it was I who heard her and not vice versa. Timing is everything in life, so it is said. This time it was a lifesaver.

I wasn't ready for a confrontation with Kathy Crowley. And had she heard me order his gift to be delivered to his office having given his name and address aloud—a confrontation of some sort would most certainly have ensued. On the other hand it was conceivable that I was a client. A bit weak perhaps, but possible.

Shaken, I got up and left the store.

What a day! What ifs...kept cropping up in my mind. What if she'd been in the shop and was finished when I bumped into Paul out front? What if she'd seen us kiss? What if I had confronted her with "I'm Jenny Matthews and I'm in love with your husband." Or what if I'd said we are lovers? I was going in circles and I had to stop this. I'd also have to be much more careful. Telephone orders for gifts would be dangerous, also, as salespeople repeat orders aloud. No. Only hand carried in the future.

I sagged inside and continued on my way.

# 34

"You won't believe what just happened," I blurted out to TJ as she held the door open for me and my packages. "I was just finishing buying Paul's Christmas present when I spotted Kathy doing precisely the same thing."

"Kathy? You mean Paul's wife? My God. What did you do?"

"Thank God she didn't hear me. We looked at each other for a split second and moved on away from each other. TJ, she's positively stunning and exuberant and decidedly not a disinterested wife picking out a gift for her husband—who happens to be my lover. I didn't know whether to faint or throw-up, so I just hot-footed it back here before I did either one." I tried to smile. It felt more like a grimace.

"And yet another bullet dodged," TJ said.

"I can't describe how it made me feel. Part of me was ready to go up to her and…"

"And what? Introduce yourself? Oh Jenny, how awful."

"I haven't told you what could have been the worst part. Speaking of dodging bullets, I had just literally bumped into

Paul outside of Gumps, we spoke for a minute or so, kissed each other over our assorted packages, I went inside and within five minutes saw her."

"Jesus, Jenny, that could have been quite a scene. It's almost too bad it didn't happen. I'd loved to have seen Paul get out of that one" She was cracking up at her images and I was just cracking up.

I finally focused on TJ. She looked simply wonderful. "Hey, do I know you? You look familiar, but it's that glow that's different." I put my hands on her shoulders scrutinizing her. All these years she'd flourished without a special man in her life. And yet now it seemed her step was bouncier, her hair shinier. I don't know how to put it. Maybe it was the glossy, warm glow that she exuded. In any event, it was especially appealing.

She was laughing and pulling away shaking her head. "Oh, come on, I've had two dates and you've got Bret and me paired off already."

"I had you paired off the first meeting. At least, you two made the pairing. I simply observed, and am now commenting. You're too cute."

"Gad! I haven't ever been called cute. Not since I was three years old. I'm sure of that! He is a nice man. I'm enjoying our time together. It's direct and easy. What is it about engineers? Or do you suppose it's because they're partners? That same quality?"

"The openness and straightforwardness? Is that what you're referring to?"

TJ nodded, "Yes! What's your take on the subject?"

"There may be something to the professional bit. No subterfuge, no hiding the facts. I don't really know."

"Anyway, whatever it is, so far, it's been interesting."

"Interesting? Is that as excited as you can get over him?"

"You know me, Jenny. I can be frivolous and go overboard for someone else—for you. But for me, well, so far it's been interesting. Interesting enough, I might add, to want to pursue it and see where it goes." A look of anticipation crossed her face and left a smile.

"That's a strong statement for you. What's next?"

"He's coming over around six. We're all going to dinner, OK?"

"TJ, that's not right. I'll make myself something here. You two go." I was not ready to become chummy with Paul's partner. Not yet, at least. Later, if things got serious between him and TJ. I'd have to. Then, would be soon enough.

"I told Bret you'd be here. He was pleased as punch. Said he'd be delighted to escort two such outstanding female types. Do you suppose those two take charming pills everyday? Anyway, I go out with you and Paul."

"I don't know, TJ. It's different somehow. This has all the earmarks of a budding relationship. While Paul and I are an illusion—a fantasy, of the highest order, I admit; but, nonetheless, a fantasy."

"When did you decide that?" TJ had turned serious. She sensed some shift of mood in me. "Has something happened I don't know about?"

"Life happened, TJ. Every time I turn around, I'm smack in the face of life happening—his and mine; separate, but not equal."

"Has something else happened? I mean other than the contretemps you just described?" She had made some tea and we were heading to our favorite place by the fire. It was burning brightly, casting moving shadows around the handsome room. "Tell me."

"When I bumped into him in town just now, I wanted to have a few moments more and he couldn't. He can't, TJ. He never will be able to."

"True. He may never be able to. So what, Jenny? What does that tell you that's new? How long are you willing to carry on this way? Are you biding time? What do you want?" TJ was pushing like the devil. She sounded as though she'd torn a page out of a book by Guy. I didn't know what to do or to say. I was silent.

"Tell me, Jenny; please tell me how you want me to behave. How can I best be your friend? Do you want me to tell you to stop seeing him, because that I won't do, unless you tell me you're feeling guilty. Then, and only then, would I put my foot down."

*A Small Flirtation*

I was unable to utter a sound. She continued: "Are you, Jenny? Are you miserable because you feel guilty, or are you miserable because he won't get a divorce or what? For heaven's sake, say something!"

"Oh, TJ." I broke down and wept. She let me. No more words, just her arm tight around my shoulder.

Finally, I stopped. Abruptly. Sat up straight and shook my head, blowing my nose at the same time. A neat trick.

"This is absurd. I'm not guilty. Not now. And I hope I won't ever be. I am frustrated as hell. That I've said before. And I'm foolish, to boot."

"Oh?" Full of feeling, at least three syllables.

"My life was 100% wonderful before we met, and it still is. Nothing has diminished, nothing taken away. Meeting Paul has added a new dimension to my life, another facet. Only I can spoil it. And I'm coming perilously close to doing it."

"I'll do what I can, Jenny, to remind you, I mean. But truly, as you just said, it's up to you. I trust you realize that Paul's having a very rough time, too." My even-handed friend. Ever faithful ever fair.

"Yes, I do know. And I think if I weren't, he'd be better, too. Another reason to cut the baloney and stop trying to second guess what's happening." I finally smiled at my friend.

"Look, go wash your face and put a new one on. That one's worn out. Bret will be by soon and you will join us. Come on. No more monkey business. You know, whatever happens to one of us, happens to both. Whoever we get involved with has to know, from the outset, we come as a matched set. So get with the program. I'm feeding the dogs."

I went to freshen up. She was right. I needed a new face. Thanks to witch hazel, I soothed the eyes. A bit of this, a bit of that—a brush through the hair and a dot of perfume. I swear I never could make it in this life as a man. The magic of a few lotions, potions and unguents worked miracles!

The doorbell rang as I was leaving my room. I heard TJ answer it.

"Bret, hi!" A pause. Probably a kissed greeting. "Paul, what a surprise. Come in, do."

I stopped in the hall, still out of sight, and caught my breath. He'd said he'd call, and I'd forgotten he hadn't during all my drama just now. How was this possible? Had he come with Bret, or was it another ghastly coincidence? Had they met in the drive not knowing the other was coming?

Well, I couldn't hide out in the hallway forever. I had to go face it and find out. In the meantime, I took a couple of deep breaths. I heard the three of them laughing. There hadn't seemed to be any rush of explanations. That was promising. With head up, I headed into the fray

"Well, bless my soul, if it ain't them two cute engineers we met a few weeks ago at that noisy party. Howdy, fellahs!" At least my clowning got a laugh.

"Jenny, how are you? I'm pleased to see you again."

"Thanks, Bret. Me, too. How are things at Crowley, Warden and Soames?" I turned to Paul.

"Paul. This is a surprise. How are you?"

"Great, Jenny, thanks. As to Crowley, Warden and Soames, they're overworking me; otherwise, things are terrific."

I couldn't look directly at him. Bret helped me by speaking up, actually explaining. Bret had seen Paul coming out of the meeting he'd told me about. They exchanged a few words, and it was then Bret found out Paul was working late. As a result of the meeting, he had to clarify his notes and deal with some design alterations preparatory to the next meeting the following morning. Paul was going to get a bite of dinner and return to the office.

"These times with our Canadian connection are swift, short and intense. It means a lot of hours and then a lull while things simmer," Paul added.

"Anyway, I told him I was taking you two out to dinner and persuaded him to tag along. He can work later or come in earlier.

It'll work itself out. Sometimes, he's too conscientious. It didn't take too much persuasion, to his credit." Bret had a nice laugh and was obviously pleased at what he'd pulled off.

Now that I was under control, I was thrilled. Foolish girl. More crumbs. But I wasn't feeling that way then. I was loving it. It wasn't until later that I had second thoughts.

"Jenny's just finished her project with Guy and is ready to celebrate. This couldn't be better," TJ added.

"Where is Guy, Jenny? Why aren't you celebrating with him?" Paul, curious again.

"We did last night when we wrapped it up. We had a feast, a fiesta." I spoke lightly and enthusiastically.

"Congratulations!" Paul took the opportunity to bend down and give me a friendly kiss on the cheek. I felt like I turned every color in the rainbow.

Later, TJ said I was 'cool'. She was impressed for the rest of the evening.

"The last thing I want to become is the office friend." TJ and I were rehashing the events of the evening. I had become edgy by this time. "This business of his being your friend and Paul's colleague puts me in a neutral place as far as Bret's concerned. That's all well and good. But if and when things progress with you two, then what?"

Circles inside of circles.

"You're jumping the gun, dear. Don't worry, we'll plan a strategy if it comes to that."

"I'm the one who always needs to square things. You'd think I was the engineer."

"Their relationship does make being together easier, doesn't it, Jenny? I mean, they even got in a little work talk with no strain on us to keep things going." TJ was trying to sound positive and lift my spirits

"A nice plus. Most importantly, you two seem comfortable with each other already."

"And Bret hasn't a clue, beyond the fact that you and Paul teach at Berkeley."

"Even so, I don't want to get caught that way again." I shook my head. "It's a bad idea and it's totally unfair to Bret. It also puts a terrible constraint on Paul and me. In fact, I wish he had resisted Bret. You know, TJ, there are times Paul seems to be tempting fate. It makes me wonder if at some unconscious level he *wants* to get caught."

"It seems to me it's more likely he's noncomposmentis when he has you on his mind. I do agree, though, let's not look for trouble like that."

"After I saw his wife today, I must say I'm not clear what he's up to."

"What do you mean?"

"She wasn't just going through the pro forma of buying a gift for her husband and any-old-thing would do. Not on your life. The barometer was an antique and monstrously expensive."

"Come on, Jenny, it's not as though she's hurting financially. Am I missing something? I don't get your point."

"Well, it isn't only that the gift cost so much, it's more the fact that she was enormously excited about it—almost gleeful. What's more, I may not know everything about Paul's interests but if he has been lusting after this for weeks, as Kathy put it, one could imagine I would have *some* awareness of his interest in antique barometers—or any kind, as a matter of fact. No, for someone who has been cast as a disaffected wife, it doesn't parse."

"On the other hand, Jen, I've known women who buy expensive gifts for their husbands for any number of reasons."

"Such as?"

"For one, as a hint. Maybe she feels neglected and thinks a very special, very expensive gift will push him to reciprocate— you know, remind him she would like some special gift, too. There's also the I-feel-guilty syndrome."

"The what?" The tenor of our discussion had shifted entirely and TJ was being her serious/amusing best.

"You know, what if she has a lover and the expensive gift is to cover her guilty tracks?" TJ was grinning, mightily impressed with her own theories on wifely behavior.

"TJ," I was serious again, "Do you think he's still in love with her? Do you think he's not even trying to get a divorce or a separation because of that? Am I simply a dalliance—an interlude to play out his fantasies for while?"

"It's hard to imagine, although anything is possible. Enough, Jen. Don't drive yourself crazy with such speculations. If either of us is correct, in time, it all will be revealed."

TJ was tidying up. "Time to turn in? It's been a big day."

"A very big day from one extreme to the other. I am exhausted." The whipsawing in one day had been fierce—a real clash of emotion versus intellect. It made my heart feel sick to think about it.

# 35

Honey and I were off in the morning to ready the house for inspection. I had mobilized the 'troops'. Celestina and the gardener would work together. TJ would be up to supervise the discussion with the TV people, as I was no good at negotiations.

I pushed the thoughts of Paul and Kathy and their marriage to the back of my mind. Right now I had other things to consider.

"The road's a bitch, but it's worth it. This location and your house is perfect for us." The crew chief was excited by the whole set up. The long shots of the area, the drive—everything. Now, we had to talk business.

TJ took over. The negotiations had to be finalized at the production company office. It would be a nice chunk of change.

"You understand Ms. Matthews is a noted photographer herself. She'll want the right to photograph you all at work."

"We'll take a look at her work and credits and discuss the subject at the office. How's that, Ms. Matthews?"

"That's fine," I replied, "and the name is Jenny."

*A Small Flirtation*

"Thanks, Jenny. I'm Sam. To you, too, TJ." We laughed.

It was an exciting notion having something to look forward to after the holidays were over and everything quieted down. My class was only one afternoon a week, and with the bird project over, well, I'd have to find more work to occupy my time and my thoughts, to say nothing of producing income.

"Do you want to meet this week? Or wait until after the first of the year? I'm OK either way." I looked over at TJ who nodded slightly. I knew she was on track with my thinking. Strike while the iron is hot.

He explained they wouldn't be using my place until February or March. However, getting a contract in motion now would be fine. Sam was walking to his van. He motioned to his assistants. They waved back and came over.

"How about two days from now? We'll all talk, and depending on any areas of disagreement, we should be able to sign a standard contract as soon as you can have your attorney peruse it. We'll have a copy faxed to you today," he said.

"I'll see if she can meet with us at the same time. That would simplify matters. I'll call her office now." We shook hands. TJ lingered.

She continued talking with him, setting a time and place certain. All of those details were her metier. I ducked into the house to make my call.

"I can't believe my good luck. I'm sure I'll find the contract suitable."

"If Wu Yee's cousin approved of the contract for him, it will be just fine for you. You can bet on it," TJ concurred

The two of us strolled on the beach while Honey romped. It was an unusually warm afternoon for the time of year. The low lying winter sun was casting wonderful shadows among the dunes. The atmosphere was so calm and peaceful, one was hard-pressed to remember that chaos existed close at hand in our world and could encroach upon us at almost anytime. I pushed the thought away.

"Are you ready to finalize our plans for Squaw Valley? It's about time I think." TJ was getting organized.

For a moment I was ready to tell her Paul's family Christmas plans. Dangerous to be there too? I decided not. And, furthermore, why confuse everyone by trying to scurry around to find somewhere else to go at this late date? What kind of an excuse could TJ and I find that would even come close to being plausible? That's what would be dangerous. As for Paul, well, between his family and our gang, I felt protected from disaster. A little withholding, for now, wouldn't hurt TJ. She didn't have to worry in advance.

"Whenever you say. I'm almost finished with my preparations for Christmas. Do you realize the twins and Diane and Bridget will be back up here in no time at all?"

"Then we gather the troops and we're off for a week," TJ added happily.

"It's going to be great fun. I just don't know if I'll have the energy left to ski," I groaned. "It's been a hellava non-stop five months."

"No kidding?" TJ feigned surprise. "It's finally dawning on you that you've been burning the candle at both ends, has it? Good. I'll be glad to settle down a bit myself. I can only begin to imagine how you feel."

"Well, you have your new adventure with Bret, and who knows about me? Maybe I'll meet Mister-Perfectly-Available on the slopes. That should keep us busy next year." I turned and retraced my steps to the house. TJ and Honey followed.

"Jenny, I was thinking of calling Guy to come up tonight and talk about our trip. He can take me back and you can have a few days by yourself before the gang arrives. How about it?"

"Swell idea. Let's call him now. We'll eat at the Pub in the village. And later you guys can help trim the tree!"

"Splendid!" said TJ. We called. He came. The Pub was great fun. I saw people I'd been out-of-touch with for months. The place had an added holiday spirit.

*A Small Flirtation*

Back at the house we had our discussion, settled things and made assignments. All this while decorating the tree.

"It looks terrific!" Guy backed away, now, admiring his handiwork. "All set. I'm raring to go and get some real exercise. I hear the base is twelve feet already with more snow expected. The skiing conditions should be perfect." Guy was at his best.

His enthusiasm was contagious. By the time he left with TJ, I was as excited about the trip as he was. I stood quietly for a moment admiring the beautiful tree as it stood in the window sparkling and glowing.

They left early. Honey and I closed up the house and headed to my beautiful bedroom.

"Want a bath, Honey?" She lay looking at me from between her paws. "I didn't think so." I turned on music and headed into the bathroom. I filled the tub, added my favorite soaking salts, lit some candles and slipped in.

What a wonderful moment when you first feel that slightly too hot water covering your body. My thoughts drifted. I was completely relaxed for the first time in days. No shopping in crowded stores, meeting deadlines, writing contracts no nothing. Just the pleasure of a very basic creature comfort.

Some minutes later I emerged from the tub, toweled dry and slathered myself with a soft musky rose scented lotion. I was beginning to feel the first stirrings of arousal. The hot water combined with the memory of being there with Paul, and now, the feel of the silken lotion being spread all over my body. It was too much. I felt an electric warmth all over.

Instead of the usual sleep shirt and socks, I reached for a satiny-slip-type gown. Now the cool smoothness of the clinging fabric did the rest. I ran my hands down my body as I slipped the gown on, then climbed into bed and let my imagination run away with me. Whenever had I come to such a racking climax alone, unbidden? I lay still for many moments enjoying the aftermath and wondering where Paul was at 10:17 p.m.

I wish I could say the doorbell rang at that very moment and that Paul had come to take me away on his white horse or in his red car. No, that's not what happened. Instead I fell asleep instantly. Two hours later, my dreams were shattered by the insistent ringing of the phone at my bedside.

"Hello? Who is this? What time is it?" I'd opened my eyes. It was still dark.

"Jenny, are you all right?" It was Paul. "Jenny? I was so frightened, I was afraid to call."

"Paul, what's the matter? What's happened?" I was fully awake. The sound of his voice terrified me. "Tell me, Paul. Speak to me."

"I was listening to the late news in my study. There's been a terrible accident on your road up near Tiburon. A Jeep with two passengers and a dog crashed and burned. They're all dead. Oh, Jenny, I almost . . ." He let out a terrible choking sob.

"It's all right, Paul. I'm here, safe and sound. I turned in early."

"Jenny, I'm so sorry to have disturbed you. It's just . . . There was no way I'd not have called. In my soul, I knew you were all right, were safe. It was my mind that thought up every God-forbid I'd ever heard. Thank God you're fine."

# 36

The morning news was full of our local tragedy. My neighbors and I were all gathered outside talking about it. We were in shock. In a community of 1200 souls, give or take a few, the fiery death of two of our own, plus a pet, was as horrible as things can get around here.

The victims were two lively young adults coming home from a party. Details were sketchy. We knew all that mattered. They were gone and we felt sick at heart.

Laura came into my house with me. I fixed coffee and we sat and talked awhile. We were all conscious of the hazards of driving our road. However, as a result of caution, very few accidents of consequence occur.

Our conversation shifted away from the accident and onto talk of holiday plans.

"Guy tells me you're all heading to Squaw Valley for a week. Sounds great. He asked me to come up for a few days over New Year's." There was a question in her voice.

"Terrific, Laura. Come on and join our merry throng. There's room—or do you plan to share with Guy?" I decided to be absolutely frank with her. There was no need to act coy. We knew each other well enough. One plus for TJ and me would be to observe them together at close range.

"Now, that's an interesting question. We've only had a couple of dates. They've been great fun, but no heavy romancing—not yet. True, we're attracted to each other, but so far . . ." She let her voice trail off.

"Laura, please. My question was straight, but not meant to put you on the spot. We've done boy dorms and girl dorms over the years. That's never a problem. Anyway, with all the exercise we get during the day—who has the energy for sex?" We laughed.

"Thanks for the invitation and for your candor. Game playing isn't my style. I'm not sure I'll be able to come, though, but I'll certainly let you know." Nice smile. Open. Real.

"I'll leave the phone number with you in any event. By the way, will you be here or away Christmas? If you are here, will you join us for brunch?"

"Yes, and thanks, I will. And I'd like to invite you, in turn, to come over for cocktails and such later. I've sent out invitations. You should have yours tomorrow."

"Sounds grand. Thanks. Will you want us all? All nine of us?"

"Only eight. Guy already knows about it. He said he'd help bartend." She smiled a bit shyly, I thought.

"Ah ha! Plots and plans I know nothing about. I must say, Laura, I've thought the two of you would make a good pair for the longest time. I'm just not very good at pushing people."

"To tell you the truth, Jenny. In the beginning, I mean when we first met, I'd have sworn you and Guy were lovers." She was serious. Also questioning.

"Really? No, Laura, just the best of long time friends. Almost life long. Did you know he and my husband, Tom, grew up together?"

*A Small Flirtation*

"No, I didn't. I knew you'd been friends for years. Even so, you travel together and he does spend the night. I mean, what was anyone to think? Especially a next-door, friendly neighbor?"

"I guess we take each other so for granted, we've never bothered about how we look to other people." I shrugged. "It's just, we come as a package."

"And TJ makes three." She laughed. "One thing, for sure, it's fun being together with the all of you. And having you for a neighbor is a real plus."

"The feeling is mutual," I said.

"By the way, speaking of TJ, what's happening with her own, new romance with Bret? Wasn't that a riot? I introduce you, and he turns to TJ and off they go!"

"They were really smitten, and I understand. I figured it out this way . . ." I told her my theory about engineers vs. creative people. She laughed and agreed about the age thing too.

"Will he be joining you at Squaw?" she asked.

"It hasn't come up yet, but somehow I doubt it, knowing TJ. Cara will be with us, you see, and I'm not certain TJ is ready to play out that scene with her."

"Oh, I understand. Well, anyway, thanks, again. I'll let you know."

Later in the morning I caught TJ up on Paul's call to me in the middle of the night.

"What a horrible moment he must have had. God, protect us all from such happenings." TJ spoke fervently.

# 37

My mind was on the accident that roused Paul's fear. Once more, the human spirit had to persevere. Once more families were called upon to rise above tragedy and adversity. Once more called up to carry on. And once more, I asked "Why"?

My life was robust—full of energy, of creativity, of loving friends and wonderful sons. Did I need this ghastly happening to spotlight my growing discomfort with my affair with Paul? Wasn't life good enough to me? Must I always be reaching for more? What had happened to my peaceful, contented self these last months?

There were no easy answers. Had I not had my own tempering by tragedy? Been tried and come through with my head up and my reason intact?

I shook myself out of these musings. No. This was an accident—a ghastly, cruel accident. It was not a warning to me. I mustn't read portents into every action of life.

If I did, my life would soon become stultified by fear. I'd worked hard to overcome those feelings ten years ago. There was no rational reason to transfer them to my feelings about Paul.

We'd been in touch by phone. He'd called several times during this pre-holiday. He was concerned and frustrated. There was no way to see each other, no chance of a private moment. Instead, we wished each other happy greetings. I realized he hadn't mentioned the gift I'd had sent over to his office.

"Did you receive a package from me?" I finally had to ask.

"The mail is being brought in right now, as we speak. There is a rather large and heavy box, too. It's marked for delivery today."

"Good. When will you open it? Can you do it now?" This was as close as I'd come to being with him when his gift was opened.

"Wait a minute." I heard the door to his office close. "Now I have some privacy."

Next, I heard opening package sounds. "Oh, Jenny, it's wonderful! He's perfect! He even looks like me!" Paul exclaimed in a rush of feeling.

"You mean he's perfect like you?" We laughed and laughed. It was the laughter that got me into this to begin with, and it was a big factor keeping me there. Laughter and love is a very potent combination.

"Of course. That's exactly what I mean. Thank you, Jenny. I love it. It's perfect on my desk."

"That's just where I want him. I'm thrilled you like it."

We talked some more. Hoped we'd have a chance for a meeting in Squaw and then worried aloud about the risks involved. I told him it would have to happen on it's own. There were too many people involved; too many unknowns to factor in to try to manipulate something.

We agreed and finally said our good-byes amid many oft-repeated New Year's wishes.

# 38

Our double family had descended on Sea Cliff from all directions by the time Honey and I arrived. The gleaming silver bowl of eggnog was already being taste tested. I personally went to the champagne bucket. Guy beat me to it.

"You must never pour your own wine. Hasn't anyone taught you that?" He smilingly handed me a flute of the palest, bubbliest stuff I'd seen in ages. He also gave me a peck on the cheek and his most impish grin. "Thought you'd get me off your case by distracting me with Laura, did you?"

I took my first sip while looking at him over the rim of the glass.

"This is gorgeous stuff. Did you bring it?"

"Don't change the subject, Miss. And, yes, of course."

"How about some caviar?" I reached for his hand to lead him to the hors d'oeuvres table TJ had set up near the windows.

"Well, if you won't answer my question, I will. Your ploy is working. I don'tunderstand what took me so long to relate to her as a person in her own right and not simply as your nice neighbor. Who, incidentally, happens to write the most enchanting children's stories I've ever read."

I was still looking at him and not saying a word. I simply smiled.

"Don't be so damn pleased with yourself. You look like a Chessie cat." He was savoring caviar, too.

"What pleased? It's only taken you three years!"

"See's really quite a remarkable young woman. We've only had a couple of real dates—you probably know that already—but it has all the signs of developing into an important relationship. It's early but, we'll see"

I raised my glass in a silent salute. He touched his to mine and we drank.

"Guy, dear, I am delighted for you both. Our tight little triangle is opening up."

"While we're on the subject of relationships, what about TJ? Do you have any good news to share?"

"Nothing much. She's seen Bret a bit. They seem to like each other. Have you met him yet?"

"Not yet, though Laura and I will probably see them after we get back from Squaw Valley."

"Is she coming up for New Year's?"

"I'm working on it. Is Bret?" he asked.

"No. I don't think so. It seems a little 'previous' to TJ."

"With all the kids?"

"Yes."

He caught on. "Funny, isn't it? They can do their thing without a second thought, while the parents watch their own actions, as though their offspring gave a hoot!"

"It's the old one way street of parenting, Guy. It's tough to break away from it no matter how old 'the kids' are. Anyway, I hope Laura will come up. We'll all have to work on her tomorrow. We'll sic the 'brunch bunch' on her."

"Hey, you two, what are you so engrossed in?" Max flung his arm across Guy's shoulder.

"We're just talking over his new love life, Max."

"Not so fast, Jenny. I'm in no hurry."

"No, not you, 'Unc'? Who's the lucky woman? Anyone I know?"

"Max, your mother's set me up."

"No!" Unbelieving, "With whom?" Always correct Max.

"With Laura."

"You mean the dish next door?" he queried.

"Exactly—though I'm not sure she'd like being referred to as a dish." Guy grinned.

"Why not? I meant it as a compliment."

"She'd probably love it," I chimed in. "She has a soft spot for the twins, Guy. You might as well know it."

"Can't think of finer competition. Especially as you both are tied hand and foot now." Max tugged on Guy. They tussled around like kids.

"Whoa! Watch out you two. Don't knock over the tree." TJ slipped her arm through mine. "Come with me for a minute," she murmured.

"Need an extra pair of hands in the kitchen?" She nodded at the fellows and pulled me away.

"What can I do for you?" I asked as we bypassed the kitchen.

"Come to my room with me." She was being her mysterious best.

"Here." She thrust a small, beautifully wrapped package at me. "Put it away. It's for you."

I looked at her quizzically. "What?"

"Paul dropped by this afternoon and left this for you. He wanted to hide it in the tree branches. I suggested that wasn't the coolest idea he's ever had. Honestly, that man! Sometimes I wonder. He'd have stayed to give it to you himself, I swear. He wanted to meet the twins on some trumped up story. I had to bundle him out of here just before everyone came."

She was half-exasperated and half-amused. I was crushed. I could have thought of something to tell them.

"I know you think you could have dreamed up a plausible tale for everyone, but I had to weigh the possibilities of a slip up and said no." She looked closely at me for approval.

"You're right, TJ, I'm sure. Your judgment is steadier than mine in these matters. But I have to be honest, I'm disappointed and frustrated in equal parts."

"Of course you are, Jenny. So am I for you. I just couldn't put you in that bind. I hope you're not terribly upset." She was looking doubtful.

"Dear girl, you can't upset me. I understand completely and, frankly, I have to agree. It would have been insanity." We both burst out laughing at the scenario TJ would have had to concoct. My friend the lousy liar.

"Good. Now open the package. I'm dying to see what's in it." She was hovering over me.

"Don't you think I should open it alone? In the privacy of my bedroom?" I was putting her on.

"Oh come on. You need company to share it."

With that, Nicky called looking for us. "Where have you two disappeared? Mom? TJ? Some friends of yours just came for the eggnog you promised."

Nick was in the doorway looking like a Viking. Tall, straight blond hair and sea green eyes. My God, he was handsome. He's the one who has Tom's coloring. And the older he gets, the more he looks like his dad.

"Sorry, dear, we were checking on details. We're coming." I turned to TJ. "Later, old girl. We'll see what's inside, later. I promise I'll open it with you, OK?"

"OK. Come on. It's party time. The buffet should be set up by now. Jen, please check the kitchen while I go play hostess."

The evening was splendid. Much gaiety. Many old friends with some newer ones dropping by. A classic TJ party. I've often observed that her consummate interest in the stars and planets of our universe is reflected throughout her house. It was enchanting with twinkle lights in the tree and masses of poinsettias everywhere. Crystal and silver reflected the lights from dozens of candles ablaze all over the house. The fire in the fireplace had quieted down to a beautiful glow. Gifts were strewn all over. It looked like every Christmas Eve I'd ever known. A wondrous mess. Only the names of the people changed from time to time. Some gone forever; some moved away, but the core group remained intact and was on the verge of growing.

"I'm heading home. Anyone want to ride with me besides TJ?" This was the best time to leave. No traffic to deal with and I'd be settled for the night instead of staying over. "The beds are ready. Come all of you. Let's hit the road!"

So the caravan left Sea Cliff. The dogs, the kids, the about-to-be new kids and the three of us. The expanded core—is that possible? To expand the core? Never mind. It's what we were doing, possible or not.

Loads of luggage and skis and gifts and people and dogs all piled into my house and found their way to various rooms and sleeping configurations. No one was too sure who went where. We had many hugs and pats and good wishes and good nights.

Out went the lights. The doors were closed. Silence reigned. Silent night.

A burst of activity in my room brought me awake suddenly. The twins had brought me my breakfast on a tray.

"Hey, *Mamacita, Feliz Navidad!*" they chimed. You'd have thought they were little kids, not the grown up, erudite professors they'd become. They still were my kids, and how I loved them. Still do. Always will.

That morning is one I think of today when I remember the best mornings if my life.

More food later. More activity, too, and many more presents. I thought we'd decided to cut back. Sure.

*A Small Flirtation*

Good Lord. My special present was still in my purse.

"TJ, come with me and bring your coffee." I headed to my wreck of a beautiful room. "Let's see what's in here." I began unwrapping. Out of masses of ribbon and tissue emerged a suede pouch drawn together by a silken cord. I untied it carefully and extracted a most delicately wrought golden lariat twined around a heart paved in diamonds.

I was struck dumb. Speechless. I stared at it in the palm of my hand.

"Paul, oh, Paul. It's exquisite." I cried.

"And what a powerful statement," TJ added.

"Oh, where are you? And how can I reach you?" I knew there was only one answer. He was already at Squaw Valley and I had no number. I couldn't call if I had. Somehow, we'd have to meet on the slopes.

"It's so beautiful. I want to wear it right now."

"Don't do it, dear. Think again. It'll wait for another week. Then you can sleep with it on if you want to."

"I'm so touched. How did he get it made at this time of the year?"

"I think it's been in the works awhile, Jenny."

"Did you know? Come on, TJ, fess up." I giggled. "You do know something."

"Yes, I do know something, but not the entire thing. I knew he was having something made. But not what. That's all. I swear."

"Don't you go swearin' at me, young lady!" I pulled her over to me. "Help me put it on. Thank goodness it's not conspicuous or ostentatious. I mean, I can wear it with almost anything."

"The way it's wrought, you have to look twice to see what it signifies."

"So much the better."

"Just don't wear it on your sleeve!" TJ teased.

I admired it a bit longer, then carefully tucked it back in its pouch and stashed it away with my other wearable treasures. I read the note later.

"Come on. Let's join the merry throng."

Another Christmas Eve and Day was about to be history. We tidied up a bit—the house and ourselves—and headed next door to Laura's. There was Guy happily greeting her guests, meeting her friends and having the time of his life. What a difference a little romance can make in a person.

We spent a lively few hours, returned home and called it a day. At least TJ and I did. We never did know if and when Guy returned. The three young couples were roasting marshmallows in the fireplace the last we saw of them. I yawned, called out good nights and was sent sweet dreams.

# 39

We all arrived at our chalet while it was still light We stopped in the doorway and gaped. The rental agent had laid a fire and there was a gorgeous bowl of flowers in the center of the huge round dining table. All of us were pleased beyond all hopes. This boded well for the entire week.

No one 'assigned' rooms. As the natural order of things unfolded, we each found ourselves in the right place—however, sometimes with the wrong duffel bag.

We'd brought plenty of food for our first dinner. Magically, things got done. To this day, every time our whole gang gets together, chaos seems to reign supreme. And yet, when the dust settles, gear gets stashed and meals are wonderful, creative events. Everyone stays in high, good humor. Even the laundry and dishes are done without too much grumbling.

What we consider trivialities of every day living are coped with and managed with as little effort as possible. We save our energy for the big things when we are on vacation together—having fun is our first priority regardless of the venue. It could be hiking, boating, camping, skiing—whatever, we have fun. Second priority is good food—mostly 'in house.' And anytime anyone of us wants to cut out, be alone, most importantly, no demands are made. Somehow it all works.

"Who set up the coffee? It smells delicious." Guy was pouring as I emerged. He handed me a steaming mug.

"I did. Last night. I figured the aroma would be the best alarm clock. Where's everybody?" I asked.

"If, by everybody, you mean the six young people, I imagine they've hit the slopes already. They're certainly nowhere to be seen."

"Who's nowhere to be seen?" TJ was coming down the stairs. "I'm right here, you two are there, who else is there?" Big yawn.

"We were just saying the young are out already," I told her.

"Oh them. Yes, I heard them tiptoeing and laughing *sotto voce* about an hour or so ago. I just turned over and went back to sleep."

"They must have the dogs, too," Guy suggested.

"Surely, they know they can't take them on the lifts?" I was horrified.

"I don't even want to think about it." TJ, in her best dismissive manner. "They insisted on bringing them; they can deal with them. I have utter confidence in them!"

"Swell. I can tell you one thing for sure—they'll not do anything to put them in harm's way. Anyway, what's for breakfast? Who's cooking?" I was getting hungry. I headed for the English muffins and the toaster.

"I'm up for it. Look out gals! I'm about to make 'omelets paesano.' Where are last night's leftovers? Ah, yes. Out of my way!"

TJ and I took our coffee and ensconced ourselves in our favorite place, no matter where we are—in front of the fireplace. Someone had done a good job of banking the fire before turning in and it had it roaring already.

I didn't want to miss a day of skiing, on one hand. On the other, it was unutterably peaceful to have nothing I had to do and nowhere I had to be. Plus the added luxury of breakfast being made for me and being with my two closest and dearest friends . . . well, I decided whiling away the morning wasn't too slothful. After all, wasn't a vacation to be a period of exemption from work or a scheduled period during which activity is suspended—a time of respite from something? Those are just some of the things defining 'vacation' according to Mr. Webster's book. Additionally, relaxing for a while put the brakes on my wild desire to dash out and find Paul.

After our glorious breakfast I felt more human and ready to strike out for the hills. TJ and I both knew Guy was anxious to go but didn't want to desert us or leave us stranded with no means of transport. So we bundled up, gathered the gear we needed and headed out.

She and I decided we'd stick to taking walks and doing some limbering up and stretching before hurling ourselves down hill. We went in search of the young and the dogs. Guy was already heading toward the lifts.

"Don't worry about me. I'll hitch a ride with the troops. See you later." He was gone.

We spotted my van. Nicky and Diane were coming toward us, calling and waving.

"Well, good morning, sleepy-heads." We got a big grin from Nick. "We were just checking on the dogs. They're out cold."

"What have they been up to?" I asked.

"Oh, probably skiing the moguls!" TJ chirped.

"Almost. We've each taken turns romping with them this morning. They're pooped. Right now they're happily ensconced in the back of the van, snug and warm. What are you up to? Where are your skis? The snow is great." Nick was breathless, just like he was as a kid when he was excited about something.

"It's glorious," Diane chimed in. "Will you be taking the lift up soon?"

"Jenny and I are going to walk a bit first."

"Then we'll join you before lunch, OK?" I added.

"Great! We're over there. See Guy? Here he comes."

We waved and shouted. He couldn't possibly hear us, but he spotted us and waved a pole in the skier's salute. He was followed by Max and Cara. Josh and Bridget were just a little bit behind them.

Max came toward me. "Hi, M'am. How goes it? Will you be skiing later?" He was on his way calling over his shoulder.

"Yes, in a bit. Have fun, dear." I waved.

TJ and I were putting on our skies when we heard someone call out. "Jenny, TJ, over here"

And there he was flashing his gorgeous grin, looking as young as the young—but for his silvering hair—straight and tall with the grace of a natural born athlete. He took our hands in his. I had to restrain myself from throwing myself on him, skis and all.

"When did you get here? How's your place? Did you have a great Christmas? Where are the twins? When do I get to meet them?"

We burst out laughing at him. He was so funny, first asking one of us and then the other.

"Oh come on you two—give me some answers"

"Paul, Paul slow down! We got here last night—the chalet is grand—so was Christmas—Nick and Max and the other young are on the slopes—and I don't know about the other, meeting them I mean"

"I'm so happy to see you. Where can we go hide? What's your phone number?" He never stopped. I was so excited to see him on the first day; I couldn't believe my good fortune.

"Listen, I'll contact you somehow. I've got to go back up. They'll be spotting me as one of my bunch comes down. I'll call" He looked around and then bent down and gave me a peck on the cheek.

"So soon we have complications. Did you know he'd be here?" TJ asked.

"Yes, we mentioned it to each other, briefly. We said we'd not try to manipulate anything—too many people, too dangerous. Frankly, with all of our recent family activity, it simply slipped my mind"

"Imagine that. You're just much older than you look." She was shaking her head.

"I know. Awful, isn't it?

"Personally, I think you forgot it out of self-protection"

"You're probably right. In the meantime, TJ, what shall I do? I certainly don't want to meet Kathy, though am curious about her."

"Just not that curious," TJ added.

"You're darn right. Beth is a different subject. But I can't figure that one out. How do I see Paul, meet Beth and avoid Kathy?"

"I can see why you wanted to forget the entire subject." TJ was laughing at me.

"What do you suggest? Come on, TJ, be creative."

"No, not creative in the way you mean. Forget 'curious', Jenny. You and Paul agreed not to try to manipulate something and you're right—it is dangerous. Don't you realize the whole thing could blowup in your face if you're not careful? My suggestion— my fervent suggestion is that you avoid all contact and stay as clear of the entire Crowley clan as you possibly can. Don't, for God's sake, court disaster!"

TJ was, at once, brusque in her manner while trying to sooth me and allay my anxieties.

"When and if a plan does evolve, there'll be plenty of time to decide whether or not to participate. For now, Jenny dear, I repeat—do nothing." My sagacious friend.

It was the best possible advice. "Avoid all contact," she said. It was the only intelligent thing to do. I certainly didn't need to embroil myself and everyone else in high drama. I didn't want to be caught in an awkward spot where someone became curious and began to ask questions.

I had no role other than to say, let it happen, or not. Nowhere did it say I'd have to join in.

Later, I caught a glimpse of a familiar figure skiing directly toward me. He came to a halt with just a few feet to spare. TJ had turned away and was chatting with someone she knew.

"Jenny? Jenny Matthews? That is you, isn't it?" Someone had skied down with him. A woman of indecipherable age, considering her head was covered and so was much of her face. I was holding my breath.

"Yes, it's me, Paul. Merry Christmas." I couldn't think of a single intelligent thing to say. Obviously, we were to pretend we were seeing each for the first time.

"Jenny, great to see you. Merry Christmas to you. This is my daughter, Beth. Beth, Jenny Matthews."

"Hi."

"Hello." She lifted her goggles. "I just met Max Matthews at the lift. Is he your son?" Beth looked quizzical.

"He certainly is." I smiled, so relieved. She was the spitting, female image of her Dad. Also, she was not Kathy.

"How do you all connect?"

"Well, to begin with, Jenny and I teach together at Berkeley," Paul started.

"When did you arrive?" I broke in. I didn't want to make further explanations.

"We came up Christmas Eve. We're at North Star, and you?" Paul asked carrying on the charade.

"Just yesterday. We're such a crew this year, we couldn't face hauling all of Christmas up here, plus the gear." I wanted Beth to go away so I could talk to Paul. She stayed.

"I'd rather have stayed home for Christmas, but the folks decided to do it this way, once. So we all agreed to try." Beth smiled up at her Dad.

"Probably not a good idea, after all. It was a bigger job than we anticipated." Paul and his smile.

*A Small Flirtation*

"It always is. It falls into one of my favorite categories—great ideas that don't work."

Beth burst out laughing. "What a perfect way to put it! That's exactly right." She had Paul's laugh, too.

"We barely avoided it, but the twins wanted Christmas at home. That saved us."

"Twins? Max is a twin? Wow!" She giggled like a kid.

"Yes, but not identical."

"You mean boy and girl?" She asked still laughing.

"No, no. Both boys." I, too, laughed. "Just not identical. Mind you, they're both handsome and winning, of course."

"Of course," Paul chimed in. Obviously delighted by the quick interaction of his daughter and me.

"Here comes Nicky now." I waved and hollered. He saw me and came our way.

"Here's the other one. Hi, dear. Nicky, this is Beth Crowley and her father, Paul." I'd never have got through the encounter so easily had I planned for it. Somehow this spontaneous combustion was working just fine. What I didn't know was what to do next.

Nicky and Beth began to talk about snow conditions and such after he established how Paul and I knew each other. TJ turned back to the cozy little scene and tuned in immediately. It all happened very quickly, much more quickly than it takes to tell about it.

"Hi, Nicky." TJ turned to Beth. "I'm Nick's Aunt TJ, and you're . . . ?"

"This is Beth Crowley and her father, Paul." I chimed in quickly.

"Hello and Merry Christmas" He had taken the cue. There wasn't any logical way for Paul to know TJ. Thank heavens, that was over. Now, TJ and Guy and Paul had met and now I had met Beth –TJ had, too and the three young ones had met each other. Whew! What a crazy puzzle. The only element missing from the equation was Kathy. I could wait for that for a good long time.

The subterfuge was complete as far as it went. Max could easily meet Paul, now. The other young would have no interest in the interactions and machinations of this other group. They were uninvolved.

Tying it up so neatly made me apprehensive, for some unknown reason. It was all working out much too easily for my comfort. Neither Beth nor Nicky showed an iota of curiosity about Paul and me. We obviously were well acquainted and extremely pleased to see one another. It must have been the time, place and circumstance.

Ordinarily, from what I'd heard about Beth and knew of Nicky, each of them was much too astute to miss the aura that surrounded us. Nicky and Beth were ready to take off again. So much for my worries

"Good meeting you, Beth. I'm sure to see you later." I waved.

"Bye, Mrs. Matthews."

"Jenny, will do fine."

"Thanks. Bye, Jenny." She waved back.

"Well, that's over!" I sighed.

"Seemed easy to me," TJ said. Was she kidding or what?

"To me, too." Thanks a lot, Paul. That left me, the only one even slightly unnerved. The two of them seemed to count on me being the one who worried about these little details. Therefore, they felt free to be relaxed.

"Anyone for a hot chocolate? I could use a drink!" I wasn't kidding.

"Sure. I'm always ready to avoid exercise," TJ nodded.

"I think I'd better get on back up. Maybe we can set a time to meet and make it happen tomorrow or even later today."

"No, Paul, it's impossible. This worked, and maybe it will again. I don't know how to 'make it happen,' as you put it." I was serious. I didn't want to plot along with planning.

"Yes, well, I do understand. We'll just see what happens by itself. At least I got to meet Nick. He's a handsome guy—seems easy too."

"He and Beth certainly hit it off quickly. She's a real beauty. Looks like her Dad. Sounds like him, too, when she laughs."

Paul nodded, "She's a good kid, a good sport, too. She also knows me very well and is perceptive as the devil. I'm afraid I really have to go. I don't want to raise any eyebrows. Bye, TJ. Bye, Jenny." He pushed off and headed for the lift.

TJ and I headed for a hot chocolate. I wanted to get inside, away from all of that confusion for a few moments.

"Are you feeling all right, Jenny?" TJ was looking at me closely.

"I'm OK, TJ. It's just these unexpected confrontations are not easy for me. I'm all right when they're happening, but afterward...really, I've said it before. It's not my style."

"I know, Jen. It can't be easy. I just hope all of this isn't going to spoil your vacation. That would be a crime."

"Nothing can spoil it, if I don't let it. You know that."

"Sounds good. How does it work?"

I took a deep breath and tried to explain, "I'm here with my nearest and dearest people in the entire world. That hasn't changed. I love being here with all of us together. Nothing can spoil that. I wish to God Paul could be part of it. But he isn't, and can't be, so what am I to do? Nothing. He understood and accepted it, too. You heard no argument on his part. Neither of us is ready for a family confrontation. God forbid!"

"Feel better now?" TJ was finishing her drink. "I'm serious. You look better. The talking it out—ventilating and a hot drink seem to have done the trick. Shall we go ski?"

"Yes," I nodded in agreement. "Let's head up, so we can come back down and start all over again." We both laughed and went out to put on our skis, again.

It was close to noon. The sun was high, the snow sparkling. The entire scene was dazzling. No time to ponder the exigencies of life and love. That would have to wait.

## 40

Back at the chalet, Guy was reporting on his call to Laura and her plans when the phone rang. We jumped a collective foot. It rang again as we each looked at the other like a bunch of dummies. I finally pulled myself up out of the couch where I'd plunked down for the evening.

"I guess someone should answer the thing." I caught it on the fourth ring. " Hello?" I fully expected one of the kids. "Bret! How are you? Where are you? Merry Christmas!"

"To you, too, Jenny. I'm in San Francisco and I'm fine, thank you. Is TJ around?. And are you having fun?" He sounded great.

"Yes, to both questions, thanks. Here's TJ."

She came back from the phone with a broad grin on her face. "Looks like we'll be doing the share-a-room plan we discussed before."

"Oh?" I waited for more.

"Bret's coming over on the same flight as Laura. He'll have to return on the first, though."

"What a neat coincidence. Or was it?"

*A Small Flirtation*

"No, Jen, it wasn't. He called Laura to find out what her plans were vis-à-vis us, and she talked him into it. Safety in numbers, I guess." TJ was eminently pleased.

The only sound Guy made was a humph.

"So much for a solo run to the airport, Guy."

"At least I'll finally get to meet this miracle man," he grumped. "Does he know anything?" Guy looked first at TJ and then at me.

"Nothing," TJ answered.

"Nothing? But you all had dinner with him, you told me."

"He knows we teach together at Berkeley. So far it's been easy."

"I'll be damned. What in the name of good common sense are you going to do now, Jenny?"

"She's not going 'to do' anything, Guy. Just let her be. You know it is tough and getting tougher."

"I'm OK, TJ. Guy and I will keep going round and round on this subject till one of us tires of it. Frankly, I already am, but he's not."

"You two have me all 'psyched out,' as though I'm picking on you. Jenny, you know damned well I'm not. What I am is puzzled beyond belief."

"By what, Guy? By the cosmic jokes? It does seem I'm being bombarded, doesn't it?"

"Jenny, girl, I'm about to apologize again. It does seem I'm sounding off a lot lately . . ."

"You certainly are," TJ jumped in.

"Stop it, you two! Stop the haranguing. I'm going to have the last word. Let me remind you, Guy, Laura knows no more than Bret does and she lives right next door to me. And she works at home. That could lead to complications that boggle the mind. It's all getting too much for me. I can't decide whether to have another toddy or just go to bed and hide!" I jumped up and was striding back and forth across the room.

"Sorry, old girl, but that doesn't sound much like a last word statement to me. I'll fix the toddy. You stay where you are and cogitate."

"Cogitate. Great! On what shall I cogitate? Personally I'd rather get drunk. If I didn't have to face a bad night and worse morning, I might even consider it."

"The trouble is, Jenny, you don't really drink. I'd think of something else, if I were you." TJ was lightening the conversation. "Look, you two, we've been over this before, when there were no other involvements. Well, now there are. I don't know anymore than either of you. I simply know I will support you, Jenny, in any way I can. As for Bret, we'll see each other if and as we do. He'll know nothing from me. It's really none of his business. And honestly, but for our friendship, none of mine."

"You have my word, Jenny, as well. I will never say a word to Laura. You can count on that."

"This is all too much. You two are pledging me your friendship? What is this anyway? Some kind of fraternal ritual? We must all be crazy to carry on like this. Listen to me: Go about your business, see Bret and Laura, make your plans and do your number. What happens to Paul and me is a totally separate issue. We can't go and do what we please, join you as a couple, none of the good stuff. We know that. So kiss and make up and get me out of the middle of this muddle!"

We looked at one another scowling at each other and burst out laughing.

"Nice little alliteration, Jenny. Well, somehow we'll muddle through and still be intact." With Guy's statement, we turned down the lights and turned in. We still had a day and a half to figure out what if anything needed to be said or done. I, for one, was ready to let the entire matter unfold in whatever direction it wanted to, and the devil take the hindmost. I simply couldn't think about it anymore. Within the framework of our expanded group everyone had met everyone else. There was now an established, legitimate connection between and amongst each of us.

Except for Kathy—

So be it,

And the days passed . . .

# 41

Laura and Bret arrived in time for an afternoon of skiing. They joined our small mob without making a ripple. I was avoiding the slopes as much as possible and rather took my time shooting pictures, reading and trying my strength at cross-country. I knew what I was doing—so did TJ and Guy, and they both left me alone. The rest were having such a terrific time; frankly, I wasn't missed at all. Besides, I played with the dogs, thus relieving others of sharing the responsibility.

We had decided not to extend our stay but to go back home after New Year's Day as originally planned. Hopefully, we'd find time for a long weekend in the snow a few weeks hence.

As for my state of mind, I wanted to be alone. I felt a growing need to write, to explore through the wonderful medium of pen to paper my thoughts and feelings. I had neglected my journal for weeks and it was beckoning me.

Paul made no effort to be with me alone. We passed a few pleasantries when we found ourselves together in a crowd. Once I spied him playing Frisbee with the kids and the dogs. I watched for a few moments and turned away. It was better that way—frustrating as the devil, but better. What could we have done? Have a little roll in the snow? Hardly. Made dinner plans? No. What we did was the best we could under the circumstances. A very simple statement covering a multitude of emotions. I hated it.

And then the New Year's Eve plans were discussed. The kids all wanted to be together. Our chalet was larger than the condo at North Star and would it be all right to have a joint blowout right here? There was no logical reason to say no.

Guy and TJ exchanged glances. Each was waiting for my answer. I looked at them helplessly.

"How many?" Guy broke the ice.

"Around eighteen or twenty, I guess," Nick responded. "That is including all of us and all of the Crowley's, too. If they come."

"And maybe a few more," Cara joined in. "Josh and I saw some friends and invited them." She looked sheepish. We laughed.

"Max? No extras?" I was warming to the idea.

"Sure, M'am, a couple of the guys I saw from school."

"Why not?" TJ queried. "A real old fashioned New Year's Eve bash."

"Go ahead and plan it anyway you like," Guy took the lead.

Bridget, Cara, and Diane all chimed in to say they'd take care of everything with the boys, and not to worry.

I just looked at TJ and laughed. It was finally time to let it happen. Step aside and let the kids have at it.

Under different circumstances I couldn't have been happier at the idea. However, now I was afraid Kathy and I might finally have to face one another. She, being the innocent in this scenario, suspected nothing. Was she the least bit perceptive? After nearly thirty years of marriage, how could she not be? Would Paul and I give ourselves away just by being in the same room?

And what of their daughter, Beth? She and her beau were definitely to be part of the gang of young people. Wouldn't she sense something was awry with the picture? Then, last but, hopefully, not least, how about me? How was I supposed to behave in front of my entire family—extended and otherwise? No-no-no! There had to be a way to avoid it, at all cost—never mind arousing the curiosity of the young. Much better that they have an errant thought about it and forget it the next minute than participate in a disaster that found a place to happen.

After dinner, Cara sat on the floor in front of the fire, looking like an angel in that soft light. Josh was with her acting as a backrest, one arm draped over her shoulder. The others, too, were all curled and cuddled up in various places around the fireplace two by two by two by two by one. It was such an unaffected, unabashed love scene, it made me wince. Even the dogs were a pair of good, old friends. Honey sensed my mood. She got up and came over to me and handed me her paw. I could have wept.

I rose out of my chair, and started up the stairs. Max spotted me about halfway up. "Turning in, Jen?" I waved and nodded. "Well, good night, then. Sweet dreams."

"To you, too, dear." I blew a kiss. I was fighting back tears, overcome by so many conflicting emotions.

It was thrilling to witness our little miniature Noah's Ark downstairs. It was more than a little painful to be upstairs by myself.

The focus the following day was on skiing. The party would take care of itself. TJ and I had done our bit and relaxed into the swing of things.

At one point that afternoon, I spotted Paul at the foot of the run. I wanted to wish him Happy New Year and find out, if possible, what he and Kathy were planning. I needed some lead-time if they were actually coming over.

He turned away from me and toward a woman who was off to the side and ahead of me. As I stopped, I could see them in earnest conversation. I started to turn away. Suddenly Paul called out, "Jenny. Jenny Matthews. Over here. It's Paul Crowley."

"Hi, Paul. I wasn't sure it was you." Where do I come up with these inane comments?

"It's me, all right." He was coming over to me, talking all the while, looking very directly at me. "Jenny, this is my wife, Kathy. Kathy, Jenny Matthews."

"Hello." My heart sank.

"Hi, nice to meet you. Paul has mentioned you and I've met your sons. Beth thinks they're 'super'."

"Thanks. I've met your daughter, Beth, and her finance. They're a terrific couple. And she's a beauty." Now, what was I to say?

"Jenny, Kathy and I won't be coming by tonight." The expression on his face was very bland, trying to remain neutral. "You see, we're giving a small dinner party ourselves. It's an annual thing," I got a quick smile bestowed on me.

Good Lord, can't we end this conversation? Kathy was just standing there with no words in this dialogue. I was rapidly running out of them, too.

"Well, have a great evening and Happy New Year to you all."

"You, too, Jenny." She had a nice smile.

"Hey, Jenny."

"Hi, Mom."

The twins were approaching fast. I moved a little so I could watch them better as they came toward me. What a blessing for them to arrive at this moment. What a gift! Paul and Kathy were heading toward the lifts. I couldn't have taken much more of that scene.

"Isn't that Paul Crowley and his wife, M'am? Max queried me.

"Sure is," I replied.

"Are they coming over tonight?"

"No, Nicky. They are giving a dinner party at their condo."

"Too bad. Are you coming up again?"

"No, I don't think so." TJ was ahead of me and said at the top she was finished for the day. I told her I'd meet her at the Sweet Shop for a coffee or something. "What about you boys?"

"We're going to keep skiing a bit longer." They still speak in chorus. They don't make a conscious effort to do so; it simply happens that way.

"OK, you guys. See you back at our chalet." I was on my way to meet TJ when I saw her coming out of the shop.

"Where the heck have you been? I thought you were right behind me?" She seemed agitated. "Are you all right?"

"Of course, I am. You'd have heard some sort of commotion if I weren't. Things happen. I'll tell you inside."

We were sitting over our steaming mugs when I told her about my seeing Paul and Kathy. She was curiously silent as I related the short, but powerful encounter.

My tale ended with: "She has a nice smile."

"Well, I'm certainly glad of that," TJ countered. "I'd hate to have her scowl at you."

"It did help the situation . . ." I trailed off lamely.

"Honestly, Jenny, you can be such a pain. I truly don't give a damn how either Paul or Kathy looked or what they said to you. I want to know how you feel, now you've met her."

"How can I feel?" I said sadly. "She has stepped out of the shadows and become a real person. True, the encounter was fleeting, but the impact was fierce and is likely to last a long time. I don't mind telling you I'm shaken. I can't imagine what Paul was thinking, doing such a mindless thing to both Kathy and me. To see them standing next to each other was almost more than I could bear. Oh TJ, I didn't want it to happen—to have to look in her eyes! I mean, I don't want to know her, to recognize her."

"Did you? Recognize her, I mean?"

"Yes. Remember? I saw her fleetingly at that party where you met Bret over Thanksgiving. And you know about my near miss with her at Gumps and I've seen her here in the village at the market. She was alone. She didn't seem to recognize me, though."

"Personally, what I recognize is that Paul could have damn well spared you this!" TJ was vehement.

"How? I was right there." I was defending him.

"You just told me, you saw them and were turning away to avoid contact when Paul spotted you and called out."

"True."

"He should have had the decency to ignore you. He could have avoided the entire scene. Men! I sometimes wonder, and other times I'm sure." She was being protective of me, and as furious as I'd seen her in a long time.

"I know one thing, TJ. It's becoming increasingly clear that one day I will have to give Paul up. He's making no move to change things, and I'm treading water."

"Relax, Jenny. It's not the end of the world. Although your feelings haven't changed on the subject of you and Paul, you've been terribly conflicted from the beginning. And now, meeting Kathy has made her real, no doubt about that. I'm so sorry, dear; you didn't need this."

"That's for sure. Well it's done now. The only good thing to come out of our encounter is they aren't coming to our party. I'd been wracking my brain for a plausible way to get out of the entire thing. Thank you oh-special-protector-of-Jenny."

"A perfect example of the support of nature you think? Anyway, I think it's time to head back to our digs? We can begin to put together some things for tonight. That'll give us a break from all this. The rest of the gang will find a way home; there are only nine of them!" She laughed.

"They'll love us for that one. I could use a bath and a little snooze before we're descended upon. How about you?" We got up to leave.

"Great idea. We'll get the dogs fed, a bit of tidying and crash!"

Being with a beloved friend under stressful circumstances, someone both bold in her thinking and so straight that being totally open, totally exposed is completely safe, is a blessing beyond measure. Loyalty and sincerity are the two most important ingredients in friendship. As subsets, humor and acceptance come next. TJ and I have an abundance of each of these. That's why we've been friends for these many years.

Hours later, we gazed at the great, round dining table in utter amazement. The young women had produced a sight for all senses. What an array of delicacies. There was also a huge pot of white bean turkey chili. I knew who was responsible for that.
My brownies were piled high on the sideboard along side TJ's outstanding dark, dark fruitcake. Champagne was cooling in the fridge, for midnight. Cider and beer would be the drinks of choice early on.

Guy walked up behind me and whispered to the back of my head, "Thanks, dear one, for giving me a gentle Jenny push. Laura's the best thing that's happened to me in years."
"Happy New Year, Jenny." Laura stepped between Guy and me while we were talking and she slipped her arm through Guy's. A bit possessive? Maybe. At least she wasn't watching us with the curiosity she had in the past. These few days with Guy and Laura were proving to be curiously revealing, I for one, felt a little pang even as I was pleased seeing Guy have so much fun. He'd been jealous of Paul. Was it now my turn?
"Happy New Year to you, my friend. May the days ahead bring good fortune to all your endeavors."
"Thanks, and same to you."
"I'll drink to that!" Guy was ladling a wonderful, spicy, warm cider into mugs for us. "Here, TJ, Bret, have a drink, too. We're about to have the last for this year and a first toast to the new one!"
"To life, to love, to friendship. May they flourish for us all!" We chorused and clinked.
What seemed like a hundred young people came and went. They stayed awhile and drifted on to other gatherings. The rotation through the parties went on for hours in high, good humor with lots of loud music.

I was in the kitchen setting up glasses for the champagne when the phone rang. It was getting on to midnight. Just as I reached for it, Beth picked it up.

"Oh, hi, Dad. Happy New Year, too. It's great! Oh, I answered because I was standing right next to it, and here you are! Say Happy New Year to Mother and the rest for me. OK? I'm glad you called. Mrs. Matthews, that is, Jenny's right here. You can tell her yourself. Bye, Dad. Don't wait up." She laughed and handed me the phone with a nod and a smile and took the tray of glasses I'd set up and walked away.

"Hello, Paul. Happy New Year." I was trying to sound up beat. "The same to you and yours. Yes, we're heading back on the $2^{nd}$. We'll desperately need tomorrow to get organized. And you? Same deal? Well, it's almost midnight. Make a wish, but don't tell until next New Year. Then you can disclose what it was, and whether or not it was fulfilled!"

"That's a new one on me. Is it one you just made up?" He was laughing.

"No, no. That was from my Swedish grandmother. It's totally real."

"So are you. Can you talk freely for a moment? Or just listen?" All at once he sounded serious.

"Yes, for a moment. What is it?" My heart skipped.

"Jenny, I must apologize for today. In no way did I intend to set you up like that. I wouldn't have done it for the world. It was strictly reflexive. When I spotted you as you were turning away, I called out because I was so happy to see you. All I could think of was to shout out your name. I could have bitten my tongue in the next second. I'm really sorry."

"Yes. Well, I'm all right now, although, admittedly, I was a put off at the time. It wasn't my idea of fun, although I can understand how it happened." And I could. I just thought faster than he at that particular moment. "But, please, no more," I added.

"I had to clear it up before the New Year begins. No left over, unfinished business between us. Dear heart, there are no words to tell you what I wish for you and for us. They are all buried deep down inside of me."

"Thank you and same to you." I could hardly speak.

"I know you can't talk, but we will soon. I'm going back inside now. I'm on a cellular phone outside and it's freezing!"

"Go back now. I must go, too, and thanks." I hung up as TJ and Bret came in to get the champagne.

TJ looked at me with squinty eyes and said nothing. She quickly engaged Bret in the activity of the moment to distract him and give me a moment to compose myself. Others came in carrying things to the sink, refilling bowls and trays.

"It's three minutes till midnight. Turn on TV and let's start the count down. Come on, Jen." Max was leading me into the center of the room. "I want to toast my mother, my wife-to-be, my family and friends. To you all, greetings! Bridget and I have made the monumental decision to beat Nicky and Diane and tie the knot in July. I'm not the poet my brother is. I just know I love Bridget and she loves me and we want you all to witness our first kiss after the official announcement! Here's to life, to love, to friendship!" He went to his girl and folded her into his arms. I wept for pure joy. What a truly Happy New Year this looked to be. Yes and no—in the end.

Horns and bells, hurrahs and yells. We saluted the glorious, young couple and the brand new year. Hugs and kisses mingled with high hopes and aspirations.

Let it be a good one, Lord, for the world and for those I love and cherish. Thank you.

TJ slid her arm around my waist and gave me a sidewise squeeze. "One more to go, kiddo. I have a feeling Cara and Josh will put it off a bit longer, but I do think they're great together, don't you?"

"I think they're great. You're all great. Even I'm great. Thanks for recognizing the moment in the kitchen."

"It was all over your radiant face."

"He apologized for today's episode. Calling out to me was reflexive; he could have bit his tongue."

"Have some champagne." The subject was closed. She was still a might miffed.

I reopened it. "He didn't want to start the New Year with a blotch. Wanted it cleared away prior to midnight. I kind of liked that."

"I like the concept. I may yet forgive him." TJ was being magnanimous.

"The slate is clean, then. Here's to us, old girl. Forever friends."

"Forever friends, Jenny dear. Forever friends."

The group was forming a quiet circle, swaying to the music. We started singing, one by one.

"Should auld acquaintance be forgot . . ."

# PART 4

# 42

The next few weeks flew. What is there about being away that makes coming home so sweet? Surely not the dirty laundry. Most definitely not the accumulated mail, the empty larder and all the rest. No, it's the familiar, the sense of envelopment in one's own particular place in the vast universe. Every pretense is dropped at the door before entering. Not having to accommodate to the outside world.

Whether it be peaceful and quiet or noisy and boisterous, it is the safe haven called 'home'. At least, for a few minutes. Oh yes, the life-is-so-daily world encroaches soon enough. Too frequently the tranquility is shattered almost before one settles in.

I've endured those times. Now, my moments at home are blessed. I feel I'm where I'm supposed to be, in the scheme of things for now. And for now I busied myself in my studio and darkroom cleaning away, sorting and filing any number of things from the bird assignment. I threw myself into the project full tilt and allowed myself the luxury of taking as much time as I needed to do it right.

My phone rang infrequently. I, too, made few calls. My guess is everyone was busy as I, closing the book on the old year and taking a long look at the new one.

I'd heard from Paul once. He called me. I wasn't ready to make any overtures. The holiday episode was still getting in my way and causing some tension within me—not unwarranted. I was willing to cool it a bit and wait to see Paul until our first faculty meeting at Cal. He said he'd be there and asked about my immediate plans.

"Won't you be coming into the city at all before then?" He inquired. "No shopping? No visiting TJ?"

"No. I've done quite enough of that for awhile. Besides, I'm very engrossed in my clean-up program up here."

"I don't honestly see how I can come over to you. Right now it's a madhouse around here," Paul explained. "If you change plans and come over, let me know, please?"

"Of course I will, Paul. It's just between the working full tilt up here and all the company, well, I've got a lot of real work to do to get this place even orderly again." I sighed.

"Yeah, I can imagine. It must seem a bit empty at the moment, though."

"Frankly, it's a nice time. I need the quiet and the space to organize myself. There's something about orderly surroundings that soothe me and allow my creative juices to flow."

"Same here. I can't work surrounded by chaos. In fact, I work best late at night when there are no distractions. After everyone's gone home, I can finally concentrate on some intricate problem that absolutely defies resolution when others are around."

"Then you understand why I'm staying put awhile. But, believe me, if I change my mind, you'll be the first to hear about it."

"Before the fact, not after," he laughed, and then sobered, "I miss you, Jenny. More than you can know."

"I do know, Paul. I miss you, too. It's just I need some re-entry time."

*A Small Flirtation*

"I understand, Jen. Surely you know it wasn't easy for me either."

"I understand that, too. Anyway, we'll see each other at the faculty meeting." My spirits lifted and so did my voice.

"Maybe they'll let us sit next to each other at lunch." His good humor was returning, too.

"We'll have to behave."

"Wear your sunglasses!" He chuckled. "You know what TJ says about the sparks that fly between us."

Good. Things were taking a lighter turn. The pull was greater to be together when things were light. Conversely, I could say good-bye now with a happier heart and on a note that said all's really well between us.

And, so we left it at that—satisfied we'd see each other soon. Dissatisfied that we weren't together at that moment. Always the same.

# 43

"Hi, Kiddo. How's it going up there? Are you ever planning to come to town?"

"Oh! Hello, Guy. I'm really happy to hear your voice. How are you, dear? When did you get back from Los Angeles? How's Laura?"

"Last night. Laura's still down south with the TV people. She'll be there a few more days," he replied.

"How's it going for her? Is she having any fun out of it all?"

"Yes, some. It's a totally different world down there, you know. Writing charming children's stories is one thing; dealing with studio types is another."

"I'm sure. But she'll do fine. She'll hold her own. Laura is no shrinking violet. Nevertheless, I'm glad you were able to be with her for the first week. I'm sure it was a help for her to have you there," I said.

"I suppose it was. From my point of view, I'm glad to be back. Things seemed to be going smoothly when I left."

"Good. How about you? What does bring you back?"

"Family business. I have to look at a few pieces of land that have come on the market. But how about it, Jen? When are you coming down? No one has seen you since we came back from Squaw. Were we really that bad that you've disowned us?" Guy was fishing. I had little to offer.

"As a matter of fact, you were a pretty awful lot. But I forgave you on the spot!" I laughed and so did he. I was glad to hear his voice. No kidding about that. "Right now, I'm thinking of coming into San Francisco from Berkeley after my first faculty meeting of the upcoming semester. It's Thursday, I think."

"Check it and let me know, OK?"

"Hold on, I'll do it right now."

I went looking for my appointment book—always in some mysterious place.

"Yep, it's this Thursday, all right. I'll give TJ a call and see if my room's available. Maybe we can all have dinner."

"Swell. I feel better now. Not so disconnected," he said.

It had been quiet up here, what with Laura away. Even before that, she and Guy were being busy together. I'd seen them once but held back as they appeared deep in a serious conversation. They needed private time as did TJ and Bret. Luckily, I actually did have more than enough to keep me occupied.

My biggest problem—my only problem—was how much I longed to be with Paul. No matter what I told myself, no matter how much I occupied myself, his voice rang in my ears and his great grin greeted me from every corner of my mind.

I'd strung up prints of him in my darkroom and found myself talking to Honey about him.

The time was approaching faster than I wanted it to . . . the time to make or break the relationship. I couldn't confront it yet. I wanted more time together, more to hold, to remember, to treasure. Because I wasn't kidding myself, no matter how many times I'd been told to 'hold on,' there would be no 'making the situation work.' Not for me, not for us.

Paul was making no move and I was no closer to understanding why not. I had no clue to what was holding him. And why he couldn't break away from his marriage. Oh, certainly, I could speculate—especially as I had met Kathy and observed them together during the ski holiday. Even at a distance it was obvious there was sharing of the moment and a subtle kind of caring for each other. Body language bespeaks volumes. I ducked the big question as much as I could and still it came at me: Was he having a fling with no real intention of freeing himself from his marriage?

I wanted to believe in him, in all he'd said to me over the months. I couldn't bear the thought that he was deceitful—it didn't fit the persona of the man I loved. And yet, we were at an impasse, going around in circles. Repeating our actions with no forward movement to resolution.

"I'll be in touch later and see you Thursday night." I was ready to hang up, thankful to have escaped any comments about Paul, when Guy suddenly asked, "How's Paul? Will you be seeing him at the faculty meeting?"

"Far as I know, he's fine and, yes, he told me he'd be there, too. We're going to be team teaching one course, remember?" I almost elaborated, but decided to answer only what I was asked. It was safer that way.

I had broken the cycle of constantly talking about my contacts with Paul and had no intention of falling once more into that pattern.

"Maybe he'll stop by for a minute at TJ's if we meet there, that is," Guy suggested.

"Maybe," was all I responded.

"Well, whatever," Guy went on rather lamely, "We'll be together, and that's what I'm looking forward to, Jenny."

"Me, too, Guy dear. Me, too," I sighed.

"So long, Kiddo. See you soon."

What had begun as a welcomed call left me in a funk. Damn. I'd tried so hard not to project any further than the meeting at Cal and maybe a coffee on campus after it. Guy wasn't to blame that it took so little to set me off.

The late afternoon was spent on the phone. That occupation always cheered me. Nicky and Diane were great. It had snowed in Boston. Even though their wedding was eight months away, plans were in formation. When could I come out?

Ditto, Max and Bridget, except their plans wouldn't move till we could meet here and go over things together soon. I was humming "Here Comes the Bride" by the time I'd finished those calls.

Then TJ called me. "Guy and I are ready to welcome you Thursday. How 'bout staying the weekend? I've been suffering this lousy weather alone!" My best pal. It was quite obvious Guy had told her I wasn't talking about Paul.

"I'll be ready to stay over. I hate that long circuitous route to campus from here. So much so, I'm seriously thinking of quitting the course after this semester." I surprised myself by the charge I put on the statement.

"I tell you it's the weather," TJ responded cheerily. "No wonder you've been content to hole up, up there."

"One thing for certain, Honey will be glad to see her boyfriend and I'll be more than happy to see you. It seems a long almost-three-weeks."

We ended the conversation on an upbeat. Each of us looking forward to a long weekend of catching up with one another. There was no mention of Bret by TJ and no mention of Paul by me. Nor did either of us make any inquiries of the other. Just as well.

## 44

Thursday morning looked more promising. The cloud cover didn't seem quite so dense somehow. Honey and I took a long walk before breakfast. We came back in time to hear the answer machine pick up. It was Paul. I grabbed the phone.

"Oh, hi," was all I could say, partly because I'd run the last few yards and sprinted to the phone. Mostly, because hearing his voice always took my breath away.

"Jenny, dear. I'm so glad I caught you. You and Honey been out walking?"

"More of a trot. It's down right nippy out there this morning." I laughed. "I needed to keep moving."

"Yes, I'm sure. It's been cold here, too. Listen, Jen, I had a brainstorm this morning. That's why I called."

"What is it?"

"How about you driving into town and leaving your car in my building? I'll drive you to Berkeley and bring you back here. At least we'll have some time together. What do you think? It'll cut your driving, too," he added.

"Now, that's a real incentive."

"I thought I'd catch you with that one," he chuckled.

"You have." I didn't drop a beat. "But how did you know I'd be coming into town?"

"Just good sense. I know you haven't been in since the holidays and figured this would be a good time for you and TJ to get together. Right?"

"And Guy as well. Right."

"Great. The meeting's for lunch, isn't it?" he asked.

"Yes. I'll leave in plenty of time. We're just having our breakfast and will pack up and be in by 11:00 or before."

"Phone me when you're on this side of the bridge. I'll meet you in the garage."

"Wonderful. I'll be there."

We rang off and I was smiling from ear to ear. I gave Honey a big, happy hug and she washed my face in appreciation.

"Here we are." Honey bounced over to him. I was more restrained in front of the attendant.

"My car's over there. Here, let me have the leash. I'll put her in back."

I suddenly thought of the cramped space in Paul's little car and offered to use mine.

"Swell idea. If I'd thought through this grand scheme of mine, I'd have brought my station wagon. Sure, let's take your Jeep. Much better for our furry friend. Right, Honey?"

"Woof!" She somehow always understood her role in any query.

Back to the Jeep and we were out of there! What joy to be with him again. My heart sang as he took my hand in his and raised it to his lips.

As we wound our way through the San Francisco traffic and on up to the Bay Bridge, we said little. Simply held hands in contented silence.

"Oh, by the way, I found a note from Wu Yee in my mail

when I got back home. He wants me to photograph the TV crew as they film at his restaurant."

"Fantastic! You will do it, won't you? How often will it be and when do you start?"

"Whoa! There you go inundating me with questions." He filled me with such happiness I couldn't stop smiling. "First, yes, I'll do it. Second, I'm not certain how often, although from what Yee says, probably three or four days a month for awhile. And last, probably next week will be the first time."

"A great excuse to eat Chinese food for lunch." Paul reached for my hand again. We both laughed like a couple of kids.

"I don't think the shooting will always be during the lunch hour, Paul. It hasn't been worked out yet."

"Well, I'll work out something once I know your schedule. Do you plan to photograph each session?"

"Oh, no. That's much too time consuming for me and would be intolerably expensive for Yee, even with a massive discount on my part. No, I think twice a month should do it, but I can't say until I start. It probably will take longer in the beginning."

"You're not planning to shoot the actual action, are you?"

"No, no. That is, I can shoot stills of the action and video the prep work behind the scenes. I'll have to work out some sort of balance. It depends on how Yee wants to use the final product."

"I have a feeling he'll hang some blow-ups in the restaurant," Paul suggested.

"You're right. I'll be working in black and white, of course. A series down the corridor wall from the entry is what I've suggested. The video will be for his own private use, probably."

"Will Guy be working with you?" Finally, no charge on the question.

"Not on the restaurant part. There isn't going to be room for all of them and two of us. It'll be tricky enough for me to keep out of the way. He'll probably join in when they start using my place. That part will be a breeze. We both know the very best viewpoints."

"Will you be at Wu Yee's for Chinese New Year? Albert has invited Bret and me to attend the banquet."

"Yes, I'll definitely be there shooting the entire event. I'll probably do it in two parts. The food prep during the afternoon, and then shoot the actual banquet that evening. Or maybe the prep one day, have dinner as a guest, and film the banquet the second night. I haven't worked out the details yet."

He looked at me closely. "Will it make a difference in your work plan if Kathy and I attend?"

"I'm afraid so. As I said when we were all at Squaw Valley, my idea of fun is not becoming the newest family friend. If you're coming, I'll shoot the banquet and prep in one day, probably. Just let me know as soon as possible."

"Jenny, I'm sorry to hold you up on your plan. I'll see what I can do in the next week. OK?"

"Of course. Sure. We'll work out something." I sighed, quietly I thought.

"Big sigh, sweet one. I know just how you feel." What could I say? He knew what he could know. And I knew the rest.

"Oh, by the way, Jen—the latest with Beth and Dan is they'll be married in May instead of June. There's a flurry of activity at the house now everything's been moved up a month."

"Good Lord, I can relate to that. With Max and Bridget's wedding coming up in July, I'm already feeling the pressure. What brought about the change?"

We'd crossed the bridge and were wending our way through Berkeley to the campus. Lunch was being held at the Faculty Club. Quite fancy for us.

"Dan's office is sending him to Japan and Hong Kong for three weeks in June. The kids decided to move the wedding date and consider the trip their honeymoon. The company is gladly picking up the tab for Beth, as they've caused a rather large change in plans for them." A rush of words and lots of information.

"It sounds divine to me."

"It's a professional break for Dan. I encouraged him to make any adjustments necessary."

"You're right, of course. It seems to have paid off for them in all ways, already."

And so on and on. We covered the time and space between us—learning more, exchanging ideas, loving being together. It was these kinds of times, so called 'normal' times where there was no subterfuge, no cover to deal with, that made separating without a future plan so much more difficult. Each time it happened, I'd feel great when we were together and increasingly devastated when we parted. It was the simple, wonderful times that made me want more and more.

I kept remembering both Guy and Paul saying don't look beyond tomorrow. One scoffing at the idea as though I was crazy to think I could keep to that admonition. The other holding on to the phrase for dear life, knowing the way he could cope with the situation was to hold to that notion. It was tough—a conundrum.

The meeting went well. We had a coffee alone afterward and were heading back to town when Paul said, "I'd love to show off my Oakland project while we're on this side of the bay. It's downtown near Lake Merritt. It's fairly well completed" And so we spent the afternoon climbing around construction sites.

We wound up the tour walking around what was fast becoming a beautiful low-income housing project near downtown San Francisco. It turned out to be one of his favorites, as it combined the social aspects of living in community with well-designed housing.

Paul spoke to any number of subs about various aspects of the job. At the same time my professional status was a perfect foil for picture taking. I planned to work the best of them into my course at Cal. Admittedly, I enjoyed the admiring glances of the guys while Paul with obvious discomfort attempted to explain who this woman was and what she was doing there on the site. I chuckled all the while watching.

It was getting late when we returned to Paul's office building. We saw Bret heading for his car as we drove into the garage.

"Paul, there's Bret. Surely he'll see us. Now what?"

"Don't worry, Jen. We have every reason to be together. I'll just tell him where we've been. Stop worrying."

He slammed the car door, came around to my side, and assisted me out with an impish bow.

Bret was walking toward us with a quizzical expression on his face. "Playing hooky, are we?" he said as he clamped a hand on Paul's shoulder and gave me a peck on my cheek.

True to his word, Paul glibly got us through a few uneasy moments—at least for me. The guys seemed completely at ease.

In the meantime my car was being driven up. Bret left us with a hearty "Good-bye. See you soon." I smiled and waved and was left with the same empty feeling I get every time Paul and I say good-bye.

"This isn't the way I wanted to end this great day, Jenny. I'd much rather have had a chance to be with you alone someplace."

"Me too, Paul. It was exciting to see the projects and be together all afternoon, but where to we go from here?"

He looked startled—by my directness, I guess—and right there standing in the garage of his office building, I threw my arms around his neck and whispered, "Come home with me now."

Of course he couldn't and he seemed so saddened by my challenge, I was almost sorry I'd done it. We'd had a great day together and I went off and spoiled it at the last minute—or so it seemed. But on the other hand, hadn't he spoiled it by pulling back, offering so little beyond the easy?

"Are you spending the weekend with TJ?" Paul, changing the subject.

"Yes. She and Guy and I are planning to have dinner tonight. The rest of the weekend is totally unstructured."

"How's the romance going between TJ and Bret? We've been so busy at the office, we've hardly talked at all, though he seems happy enough."

"So far, so good. They're having an easy time. Not so intense."

"As us?" he laughed. "That's what you mean, isn't it?" Of course he was right.

"A bad comparison. They're fine from what I know. We haven't seen each other, you know. We do need to catch up."

"Will he be over tonight?" Curious. Envious? Maybe so.

"I've no idea. Why?"

"I could stop by for a bit after the office. If it's OK. What do you think?"

"Well, you've just told Bret about the faculty meeting today. It would make some sense for you to drop by and say hi to TJ and Guy. Just give me fair warning if you're coming."

Honey had had a nice romp on campus and was contentedly asleep in back. She lifted her head to receive a pat good-bye. I got a quick kiss while no one was around.

"Call me."

"I will."

"Bye."

"Bye. Bye." And we left him standing there in the garage. He waved and turned away.

My stomach turned over. I hated this.

# 45

I drove off midst gathering clouds. The sun was low pushing streaks of light over the water. We were in for a blow and some rain. The weather reflected my mood, precisely. A wonderful day with a man I love and now what—or as I said to Paul, "Where do we go from here?" Well, I know where he went: Home to Kathy—home to his wife.

Since my encounter with her while Christmas shopping and later during our ski holiday, I had become increasingly uneasy. Paul and I were being seen together more and more often in one place or another. This time, Bret. Who next? Then what?

Maybe, just maybe, Kathy would get wind of what was brewing and take the hint bringing everything to a head. It would save my running her down in the street! I had to laugh at that one. I wasn't usually taken by such evil thoughts. How about a nice skiing accident or one while sailing?

Jenny, pull yourself together! *You* laughing at such thoughts? Anger, jealousy, envy are bad enough, but hoping someone has a fatal accident simply to serve your purpose? What's happening to you? Wasn't one such event in your life savage enough? Are you feeling guilty? Is that why you're killing her off in your daydreams? Pay attention, old girl, there's no karmic reward in that kind of thinking.

"My gosh, it's good to see you. It feels like months. Gloomy outside, isn't it?" TJ, all in one breath.

"Me, too. And, yes, it's awful. Pretty in Berkeley, though. You'd think it was the other side of the world."

"Well, it is the other side of the Bay, and there are those of us who consider it the other side of the world."

"Snob."

"Of course." We stacked my stuff and headed to our place by the fire. It was more than atmospheric. That day, it was a necessity. "How's Paul?"

"Fine. He wants to know if you're expecting Bret to join us tonight? Would like to stop by en route. What's the plan?"

"No plan other than corned beef and cabbage. Think he'll stay for that?"

"In or out?" I queried.

"Oh, in. I don't want to go out one more time today. If Bret decides to join us, there's no problem with Paul and Guy here, is there? I mean, he does know you teach together. Why, we're practically one big happy family." She grinned impishly.

"Thanks a lot. Just what I told Paul I don't want to become."

"How'd that come up?"

"Oh, we were talking about my project with Wu Yee and Chinese New Year and all that."

"Are they attending the banquet?"

"Probably. Paul's not certain which night. I absolutely don't want to be there at the same time." I was vehement

"I absolutely couldn't agree with you more. You're shooting the banquet, though, aren't you? How will that work?"

"It's two nights. We'll work it out."

"Good, because that would be awful for you. And Paul, too, for that matter."

"For this matter it would be worse for me. Anyway, you and Bret are going, I presume?" My question was really a statement.

"Absolutely, and I want to know which night you'll be there."

"It'll be great fun. Guy and Laura, too?"

"Oh, yes. No doubt. We'll have a ball." TJ was warming to the subject.

"Guy said she's doing well in Los Angeles. I'm a little concerned about Guy, though. He seems almost too excited, too exuberant at the way it's all going. What's your take on it?"

"It's all too funny. Three years and they finally looked at each other as people. Amazing." TJ shook her head. "I admit, at times, he does seem a bit excessive in his praise."

"Another 'wait and see' item."

I phoned Paul. He said whatever Bret decided to do, he'd work it out. TJ invited Bret, who accepted, and then she phoned Paul to invite him, too. He'd call Kathy and be with us, and 'thanks.'

Guy arrived shortly after 5:00 bearing a wonderful pate and two bottles of his favorite Pinot Grigio. He was ready to celebrate something.

"I thought we should celebrate being together. It's almost three weeks since we've seen each other. Hi, Cutie. How the heck are you? Give me a hug and kiss." Guy grabbed me with his free arm and swung me into him and whirled me around laughing all the way.

"Hold it, Mister, or I'll be on the floor."

"With me on top this time." Still he laughed.

"You're such a bad boy, Guy. Poor Laura, I really didn't warn her strongly enough. I am, in spite of your craziness, happy to see you, too."

The dogs were only slightly bewildered by these antics. They'd each known Guy all their lives.

"I know I saw you last week, but don't I get a little attention anyway? After all, I am cooking tonight. That should merit some slight consideration."

Guy positively swept TJ off her feet with a bear hug.

"Good grief, you maniac, put me down before one of us gets hurt! If this is what having a new romance does to you, I can only imagine what being married will do!"

"Okay. Okay. I'll behave. But you both have to know how happy I've been. I'm dating a real woman who has some substance, and I'm finding it amazingly satisfying." I listened to him choose his words carefully—'amazingly satisfying' didn't sound too romantic to me. More of a clinical analysis.

"Do I hear wedding bells in the offing?" TJ asked pointedly.

"I wasn't going to bring this up tonight, but what the hell? I have both of you as a captive audience..."

"What gives, Guy?" His entire demeanor had changed.

"My, TJ, you're at your subtle best today." I said.

"Well, I don't see any sense in beating about the bush with Guy, Jenny. He certainly never has with either of us."

"I know, but . . ." I trailed off. Couldn't think of an answer fast enough.

"It's OK, I'll answer the question. No. Not yet, anyway. Maybe never. Oh, hell you two, who am I kidding? She hasn't the dimmest clue about the 60's. She graduated from college in 1985! I'm 56. You do the math, TJ."

"I looks to me, if you were to get married immediately and had a baby immediately, you'd be pushing 80 by the time the child graduated from college."

"To say nothing of graduate school." I burst out laughing—Guy was suffering and I was being no help at all.

"Cut it out, Jen, I'm serious."

"Sorry, Guy, I truly am. I'm 53 and my twins are about to be married. It's just such a picture of contrasts."

Guy attempted to continue, "We've only really known one another for a few weeks."

"In the biblical sense?" TJ being coy.

"Mind your own business, TJ." Guy kidding on the square.

"It is my business. You are, at least. Anyway, you've always minded Jenny's and mine. I frankly think a little friendly prying is absolutely called for."

"A little taste of my own medicine? Is that it?"

"You bet. Any way, go on, you were saying that you are serious. Jenny and I will try to behave"

"I have a real problem. Laura is in love with me and she has every rationalization in the book to combat my arguments against marriage."

"Do you love her, Guy?"

"Truthfully, Jen, she's a darling—bright, talented and kind and I do have feelings for her. But do I love her? I'm not sure. The one thing I am sure of is, I'm not willing to start a family at my age. It's a commitment I'm determined not to make," He sounded grim.

TJ and I sat in stunned silence. No matter, we each had some concerns; we hadn't a clue Guy was wrestling within himself to this extent.

"TJ, Jenny," he looked from one to the other of us. "You know who my family is: You two, Nick, Max and Cara. I don't want that to change and it damn well would."

"If you love each, maybe being together the way you are now…"

"No, Jenny. I should let go of her. And give her a chance to meet someone closer to her own age. It won't be easy, but it's the right thing to do." He turned and looked at me directly. "Then there's the you-and-me thing. It may never work the way I want it to, but I'm here and I sure as hell intend to stay around. We need each other. That's the truth of the matter."

"Well, I must say!" was all TJ could muster. I was struck dumb

"OK. Enough for now. All this talk of Laura and me, is this by way of a diversionary tactic so I won't query you on the Bret connection?" Getting it out—ventilating—had lifted his spirits and he was Guy once more.

"Of course. And that's all I'm saying, except that he's joining us for dinner."

Once more, Guy looked crest-fallen. "What happened to our little threesome? Is that forever lost to us?"

"Not at all. We've got an hour to ourselves. We'll eat all the pate and drink at least one bottle of that gorgeous wine before they come."

Guy said: "They? What's the 'they' part? I thought you said Bret was coming over."

"Paul. I invited Paul to stay to dinner."

"Stay? What stay? First, you have to get someplace before you can stay. What's going on? Am I dense or have I missed something significant?" Guy looked quizzically from one to another of us.

"Oh, nothing's going on, Guy. Good grief! You know Jenny and Paul were at Berkeley today. All I did was ask if he'd like to join us for dinner after I found Bret could come. It's a pleasant and easy way for the two of them to extend the day without making a big deal out of it. That's it."

"It'll be good to see him. He's a very nice man and a hellava engineer, I'm told. Come on, you two, let's break open this bottle and raise our glasses." He poured and raised his. "To us, the 'Three Disgraces.' Long may we flourish." So much for discussing Paul, or Laura, for that matter. The telephone rang as we polished off the pate. TJ reached for it.

"Oh, Paul, hi! Not coming? I'm sorry. Everything OK? Good. I'll let you talk to Jenny."

I took the phone. "Hello? What's the matter, Paul? Oh, I see. Well, of course I understand. I'm sorry, too. Yes. I'll be here tomorrow. In fact, as I said earlier, I'll be here all weekend. Sure. I'll speak with you tomorrow. Drive carefully. Bye." I hung up and attempted to balance my feelings before turning to my friends.

"What happened?" was written all over Guy's face, but he said nothing. TJ, who on the other hand was busying herself setting the table, looked up and said, *"Que paso?"*

"Simply put, Beth and Dan are coming to dinner to discuss a myriad of things pertaining to their wedding plans. The date's been changed. They're being married a month earlier. Obviously, Paul needs to be there, and he wants to be there, more to the point. Furthermore, I agree he must be. He's sorry, and says hello. End of conversation." I got up to help TJ.

Guy looked at TJ and shook his head. I turned my back. I was fighting for composure. Bret came. Dinner was incredibly delicious, as only corned beef and cabbage can be. TJ and he were very cute together. Quips were flying amongst the three of them. They were so happily engaged, they barely noticed how quiet I was. I observed my old friends. The new one looked as though he would be part of the picture for a long time. A nice addition, I decided. My inside thoughts were elsewhere down the peninsula.

# 46

Sometime later I heard from TJ that Bret had mentioned bumping into us. He commented on what an attractive woman I am and mused about Paul and Kathy's very offhand relationship.

He'd said Kathy was a pleasant enough person if somewhat cool and distant at times. Certainly no match for Paul's high-energy dynamism. He often wondered why she seemed to make little, if any, effort to be with him for a bite of dinner or lunch on days he worked late. It wasn't such a distance to travel. I, of course, was fascinated by all this.

TJ went on: "Bret also commented on how you two looked together—more like lovers than colleagues."

"He actually said 'lovers'?" I was startled.

"Yes he did. Listen, Jenny, I've warned you before."

"I know, but..." I stammered.

"But...nothing. Even in a poorly lit garage, I've told you, you two glow in the dark." She laughed and I grimaced.

She went on to tell me Bret also feels Kathy better pay attention because, although he never has known Paul to stray, it now looks like more of a distinct possibility if not already a fait à compli.

"Did he say anything more about Kathy?" I couldn't contain my curiosity.

"Actually I asked Bret myself," TJ admitted. "In fact I urged him on and it was then he dropped a bombshell."

"A bombshell? What did he tell you?"

"Brace yourself, Jenny. Paul has rented an apartment here in the city."

"He what?" I gasped. "Has he actually moved out?"

"No, but he has rented an apartment. Bret found out today. Bret's take on it is Paul has been working late on the Vancouver job so many nights, he's decided to take a small place in town and cut out all the traveling back and forth up and down the peninsula—just to sleep and turn around and come back up."

I was bursting. "However did you keep a straight face—or did you?"

TJ said she nodded a lot and said "hum" a lot and couldn't wait to get Bret out of her house to call me.

"Do you go along with the reason he gave, TJ?" I suddenly sobered.

"Don't be a simpleton, Jenny," was all she'd say.

"Finally. I can't believe it!"

We hung up after more speculation. I was berating myself for beginning to think Paul always took the easy way out.

The idea of having a real place to meet in the city, not just stare at each other across the table of some restaurant or other. I wondered how or when Paul would tell me. As it turned out, I didn't have long to wait.

"Jenny," I was getting used to the nighttime telephone calls. "Will you come be my 10 o'clock snack?"

I burst out laughing, "That's some delicious invitation."

"Could you come across? Will you—please?" He was pushing hard.

"*Que paso?*" As if I didn't know.

"Just say you'll do it. I'll meet you in the garage in one hour. Jen—please."

"I'll be there. I'll phone when I'm on your side of the bridge."

"I love you, Jenny."

It didn't take me fifteen minutes to leave the house. I had the foresight to put a toothbrush in my bag along with a few other necessities "We seem to have a penchant for meeting in parking lots and garages." I laughed as Paul helped me out of my car and took me into his arms in one continuous movement.

We clung to each other for several moments, backed off and embraced again. This time there was no doubt about where we were heading. I was already ready to be with him. I'd had fantasy after fantasy as I drove down to meet him.

As for Paul he was backing me against the car and pressing himself against me hard.

"I hope you know I'm keeping you with me all night. Come on up to my office while I gather up a few things." He took me by the hand and led the way. I was in shock. I'd never been near his office and found this an odd time for a tour.

It wasn't what I imagined engineers' offices would look like. I was accustomed to the ones on campus. The suite was stunning. Great care had been given to color systems, which continued throughout, coordinating all the furnishings, artwork, projects and photographs.

Paul took evident pride in showing me the entire place including the drafting areas, desks, and computers. The ambient lighting was soft with task lights punching holes into the serene background. One had the sense that the space was a great place within which to work.

Eventually we got to his own office. Very unpretentious, very much a work space with drawings on the walls and on his drafting table.

*A Small Flirtation*

"I love seeing all of this, Paul. It makes me feel even closer to you."

"That's just what I want right now—to be closer to you." He walked over to me and once more pulled me to him and kissed me with a deep and growing passion. His hands were pressing me to him and I felt we'd be on the floor in the next second when the phone rang.

We both jumped like guilty teenagers having the living room light turned on by Dad.

"Don't worry, Jenny, I'm not answering it. The night switchboard will record it. Come to me. I want to make love to you in my office—it will give me something to think about when I'm here alone and stuck on some design problem." He was grinning like a kid. "Later I have someplace to show you."

He was unbuttoning my blouse with one hand and cupping my breast with the other. He bent over and kissed me all the while he undressed me. I went completely wild. We pulled at his clothes and mine and stumbled to the couch under the window. We stopped for a moment and gazed at each other with such a mixture of love and lust. It was both joyous and heartbreaking.

I don't know how long we spent there playing out the entire scene of mounting passions in quiet fulfillment. We finally came to the awareness that we had to pull ourselves together and leave before we fell asleep. The idea of being caught by the early staffers threw us into convulsions of laughter.

Paul led me through the maze of offices back to the elevator and down to the garage.

"Oh, Jen," and once more he took me in his arms. This time gently, softly enfolding me. "Let's go," he murmured into my hair, "I've got to show you my surprise."

"It had better be good," I teased, "to get me off that nice, soft couch."

The flat was all I'd hope it to be and much, much more. It turned out to be a *pied à terre* in Cow Hollow near Russian Hill.

We entered through a gate into a tiny, walled garden manicured within an inch of its life. Agapanthas lined the flagstone walk. Rhododendron and huge camellia bushes were against the wall. There was even a tiny table and chairs. I was overjoyed by its beauty showing through the dark of night. I knew I had entered into my very own secret garden. And luxury of luxuries, the place came with its own garage—unheard of in much of San Francisco.

"Paul, it's perfection's self," I said as I stood in the doorway. A perfect set piece: living room with the obligatory fireplace flanked by tall, narrow bookcases. A small dining area and a Pullman kitchen.

In the bedroom the bedding was heaped on a chair. "I thought we'd make it together. Do you like my selections? My choice of colors?" Paul flung his arm across my shoulder. Surprised you, didn't I?"

"I'm speechless."

"Not you, Jenny." He laughed with sheer pleasure. "Never speechless. Maybe slowed down a bit, I must admit. But never speechless!"

"It truly is perfection. However did you find such an enchanting place? And when did you do all the design work, the setting up?" I was smitten with the entire place.

"I told you once I don't telegraph my surprises. While you were thinking bad things about me, I was selecting colors I love seeing you in. It was tricky as hell when you asked me to come home with you the other day and were so obviously upset by my not taking up your challenge. I had an appointment with the owner's agent to go over some last minute details and almost let it slip." He was looking very pleased with himself.

"It's divine. I'm more than impressed. I had no idea your capabilities included interior design."

"As a designer of systems that support structures I'll admit I felt somewhat daunted as I selected various shades of mauve and jade green. White-white was simple. The raspberry and black touches for accent were a bit of a stretch, but I managed to get my way. All in all, it's been fun."

"And now you have to be careful I don't just move in."

"You've read my mind precisely. It's not just mine, Jenny, it's for us—it's our place."

I couldn't answer. It was pointless to list all the road blocks that would have to be cleared away before that day would actually come. Not tonight.

We made the bed; we made love in our wondrous ways and slept in each other's arms in our fantasy.

# 47

The primary sociological construct of San Francisco is the ability of the people to mind their own business. You see, that's precisely how we got away with our new arrangement. I had a key, Paul had a key and no one knew about it except TJ, and even then, I didn't disclose to her every time we were together. It was pointless to enmesh her in this aspect of Paul's and my relationship. We were far from our boarding school days when we all told all to everyone we considered a friend.

Bret must have sensed what was going on because he rarely suggested getting a bite of dinner together on a night he knew Paul was working late. He and TJ and I continued to see one another fairly routinely.

Once when I was dining out with them I excused myself and said I'd have to be getting on. Bret was surprised and asked if I wasn't staying with TJ and all I said was "no, not tonight." I smiled sweetly, gave him a little peck, a hug to TJ and left.

I had asked her to avoid the subject of Paul and me with Bret at all cost, to simply change the subject. Deflect...whatever. And here I had left her with all the explaining to do. Apparently she said nothing and did deflect questions, thus saving us yet again.

Bret brought up the subject of Paul later that same evening. TJ told me how Bret described his fierce loyalty to Paul and what Paul meant to him. During Bret's darkest days, Paul had been his sole anchor in the wind. He had utter confidence in Paul's friendship and wished nothing more for him than happiness and satisfaction in his life.

TJ told me she sat transfixed and said very little. Bret went on to say he didn't know much about Kathy and Paul's marriage. The subject had never been broached between them. What he did know is Paul is a very private man and yet, after seeing Jenny and Paul together a few times, one would have to be blind, deaf and dumb not to notice his close friend had found excitement and serenity elsewhere.

He went on to describe her behavior in public. One time she would be the soul of propriety and another time she'd be sullen and uncommunicative And if she did speak, it was to criticize Paul. No one was able to count on her behavior. It was a terrible embarrassment and a continuing source of tension at company gatherings—to the point that the other partners and their wives could have cared less whether she socialized with them or not. The subject was never broached between Paul and him.

Now I was fascinated and surprised in equal measure. TJ and I both felt Bret was saying more by omission than he realized. Something was wrong with this picture. Something was going on quite apart from the fact Paul had made a lifetime vow. I, for one, vowed to get to the bottom of this even as I knew we'd end up apart. At least I could have the satisfaction of knowing why.

I was rapidly finding out more and more about Paul. Experiencing his work place in the daytime—once when I brought pictures of projects for him to see—ostensibly for use in my course—gave me another view of this man I'd fallen head over heels in love with—really at first sight. He was so at ease in his surroundings—the way he always is with me at my house and when we're out and about. His colleagues and staff treated him with warmth mingled with a kind of good-natured respect one is hard pressed to find these days.

I knew him to be attractive and spontaneous and bright and passionate with me. I didn't know how he was in his professional life, other than the way he handled Albert during his crisis in self-confidence.

Every time we spent the night together, every time we didn't spend the night together I longed for more. I wanted him to divorce Kathy and marry me. I wanted to know why he hadn't. It was becoming obvious that I wasn't going to get that—not now and maybe not ever. I was biding my time, but was more and more aware our time for confrontation was coming soon. Yet our longing for each other became the upper most thought in our minds. When we weren't at our hide-away we were 'drowning in down' at my place. We hungered for each other, for time uninterrupted by other duties neither of us could deny. This went on for weeks midst a frenzy of activities in both our lives.

The wedding of his daughter was coming closer and the demands on his time were beginning to interfere with our time together. I too was busy with my twins' planned weddings, my own work and travel plans. And yet, whenever he called I continued to drop everything that I possibly could and would run to him to meet at our proverbial love nest for a few stolen moments or for a night of prolonged lusty love-making.

How we were unseen, if we were unseen, only heaven knows. And heaven must have really protected us because we simply couldn't be casual in public anymore.

# 48

Max called me and asked if I could meet him at TJ's early in the morning. He wanted to talk. I thought there might be trouble at home with Bridget. No way. He wanted to talk about me. Seems he'd seen Paul and me on campus recently when he was at Cal for a seminar. He was about to call out to us when he observed Paul give me a quick kiss by the car before we drove off. He was 'startled and yet not surprised,' was the way he put it. He'd seen us together only briefly at Christmas at Squaw Valley and 'sensed' rather than 'knew' something much more was between us than co-teaching.

I was dismayed and at first made an attempt at dodging the issue. "Max, he and I are colleagues, friends. We . . ."

"Mother, please let me finish," he stayed me with his serious tone. "I know you and your friends kiss each other in greeting. I've seen you and Unc embrace forever. I wasn't stopped by the kiss. I was stopped by the look on your face and the way he held both of your hands. No, it was no casual cousin kiss. There was deeper meaning to it."

"Max, dear Max," I sighed deeply not sure where to go with this. "I'm on unfamiliar ground and don't know what to say to you."

"Look, M'am, I'm not trying to tell you what to do or how to live your life; I just want to make sure you know what you're doing. Just don't get hurt, OK? We wouldn't like that for you."

I didn't tell the entire story to Max. That's not what he wanted. He was interested in confirmation of his belief and information regarding my emotional state. Of course I told him the truth. To his credit he was supportive and loving. He only worried about any possible pain and disappointment I might encounter along the way.

Admittedly, I was moved beyond all expectation. My son was a man. A compassionate, understanding man. He would tell his brother. I didn't have to deal with that, not yet. Certainly Nicky would be in touch and I'd handle it at that time.

TJ came home from a meeting as Max was leaving. He was, of course, asked to stay but he begged off saying he had a department meeting at noon at the university.

"What was that all about?" TJ turned from seeing Max off. "He looked mighty serious and anxious to get away."

"You're right on both accounts. We've been talking about Paul and me."

"How long has he known?" was her only response.

"He saw us on campus—said he wasn't surprised." I told her the whole story and added how moved I'd been by his responses.

She nodded, "Does he know about Paul's place in town?"

"No. That seemed unnecessary, at least for now."

"Good. I agree."

"I wonder how many others have seen us but simply haven't mentioned anything. Not to either of us anyway." Admittedly I was a little unnerved at the thought.

"Not me either. But it concerns me for you. How much longer can you participate in this half-life, Jenny?"

"Oh, TJ, I just don't know—it's so wonderful to be with him, to have hours of uninterrupted pleasure. I can't be there every time he decides to stay over, although I wish I could. It's probably just as well that I'm across the bridge or it would be a terrible temptation."

"Back street wife isn't your role in life. You said it yourself over six months ago." She was dead serious now, no longer simply curious about Max and his reactions to the Paul story.

"Don't put me on the defensive, TJ. I know how vulnerable I am."

"How shall we spend the rest of the day?" TJ switched the subject.

"I'd thought I should stop at the TV Production office downtown and go over some details about the picture taking at Wu Yee's. Also get some tentative dates for their use of my house, and then we could have lunch at Yee's. I'll take a hard look from the point of view of picture taking. Yee said he'd take the time to talk it over with me. How does that suit you?"

"It sounds perfect. How about going out to a flick later? Make a real day of it?" TJ sounded pleased.

Frankly, I didn't want to make time to talk. I was full of myself and had no room in my head to hear about Cara and Josh or talk about the twins or anything else. Enough of lovers and weddings. Selfishly, I wanted to take care of me and my projects and be with TJ with no strain. She understood this clearly.

I got the OK to do a behind-the-scenes shoot along side the crew at the restaurant. There were all the caveats one would expect on both sides of the agreement. Also, tentative dates were set in March and April for them to come to my home after the semester ended, and Max and Bridget's wedding was behind me.

We got back to the house and were just putting up our feet getting ready to look through the calendar section of the paper when the phone rang. TJ answered. Bret was off on an excursion with his kids and was calling to say thanks for last night and good-bye and "we'll talk Sunday."

"Have a great time. I'll say hello to Jenny for you. Drive carefully, old boy, and 'enjoy', as we say in Chinese." Bret was laughing at that one, but would have to wait for the origin of it until later.

Paul phoned two minutes later with the thought of a stop-by-for-a-short-visit.

"Sorry, Paul. TJ and I are just heading out to a flick. The timing would be off for the entire evening." I was serious.

"Gosh, Jenny, that's too bad."

"We'll find time one of these days, but not fifteen minutes that will get you on your way on time and upend TJ's and my entire evening."

"Ouch!"

"Sorry."

"It sounded more like 'too bad', or am I reading too much into this conversation?" Paul asked.

"Yes and no. I didn't mean to hurt you. And I don't like being seen *en passant*. We need to carve out some time for each other, Paul. It's just . . . it takes planning."

I told him spontaneity is great if there's enough time involved. I was getting all convoluted, but think he got the message. I simply wanted more than he'd planned for tonight. "Not this time. Oh, Paul. It's too hard to be honest with myself and not make waves."

"Jenny, we'll have some time soon; probably within a week or so. I can't promise exactly when, yet, because we're so jammed up here at work. I need to be with you, too. In the meantime, have a nice time with TJ whatever you two do. OK?"

"OK, I will. Talk to me next week. And I'll see you at school, at least."

We hung up on a painful conversation. Not the first, nor was it to be the last, by far.

"Jenny, Jenny, what can I say to you?" TJ was looking so sad.

"Not much I'm afraid. The signs and portents are coming at me from all directions. Including, I might add, that phone call. I'll be damned if I'll become the quick-kiss-on-the-way-home-to-my-wife person in anyone's life no matter how hard I've fallen for him." I'd been disappointed before. Now, I was furious.

"Jen, I feel partly responsible for your distress. I should never have encouraged you that first weekend. We could have had a brief chat and pushed him away with a thanks-but-no-thanks. It's just, he was so attractive, it wasn't difficult to be beguiled by him."

"You're not the least bit to blame. Even with the teasing about the meeting and ride to your house, I was happy to go along with the whole program. Oh, I protested, and at some level I meant it. I must tell you, had he left and not called again, I'd have been devastated."

"But, in an entirely different way. We would have talked and talked about the 'what if's', and all that. However, in the long run, you'd have got over it quickly and had a funny story to tell at cocktail parties. In short, you wouldn't be hurting as you are right this minute."

"I'd also not have experienced the most remarkable man I've known since Tom. No, TJ, I don't regret that part, not one iota. I regret my inability to keep it light and enjoy him on a more offhand level."

"I fear you've gone well beyond that point, at least for now."

"What do you mean 'at least for now'?"

"Well, maybe one day, somewhere in the future, you can become, what you term, 'a friend of the family'." TJ looked uncertain.

"Good Lord, TJ, do you really think it could come to that?"

"There are so many little connections already, it would be an almost natural thing to occur."

"What a joke. What a colossal, cosmic joke! I can see it now. Dan and Beth become best friends of Max and Bridget and suddenly the forbidden love of my life is the father of my grand-baby-to-be's God-parents." I burst out laughing. It was laugh or cry, and that day I was wearing mascara—not the water-proof kind.

"Let's go out as we started to. Come on, Jenny, it's time for your popcorn."

The weekend sported somewhat nicer weather. No rain, though it was still chilly and damp. We were treated to the sun breaking through in the late afternoon on Saturday, making silvery and golden streaks across the deep gray water. Quite dazzling. I grabbed a couple of shots while it lasted. I'm a sucker for that view. I must have dozens of variations on the theme. Maybe one day I'll put them in a book "Sun and Moon on Water." Who knows? I did a collection of moon-gates sometime back. It was very successful.

Sunday we talked some more and walked the dogs and just relaxed. We talked to all of our young and were satisfied with what we heard. We also joined some old friends for brunch, after which, I packed up and headed back up the coast with Honey at my side.

I had much to attend to at home and was ready to tackle the tasks. Laura would be back and would provide a diversion when needed. Happily, the uncertainty of her relationship with Guy hadn't effected our neighborly friendship.

Over the bridge we went. "Home again, home again, jiggety jig. Right, Honey?"

"Woof!"

More time flew by.

Chinese New Year was a complete blast. Paul and I avoided meeting as it worked out. We'd thought of all sorts of plans, none of which materialized. He did have lunch at Wu Yee's one day when I was there.

The public meetings were becoming easier. In this way our 'little connections,' as TJ called them, were working to our advantage. Another time, Bret came with Paul in the late afternoon. It was getting downright clubby around there. I winced at the thought.

Only once during that time did Yee throw a look at Paul that would have wilted bok choy. I had another protector.

Paul had automatically draped his arm across my shoulder while we were standing and talking to Bret and Yee.

Later, Yee told me he felt that could compromise me in Bret's eyes, possibly. Yee had run interference, distracting Bret while giving 'the stare' to Paul. He got the message and unhanded me immediately. He commented to me quietly as he moved me away from Wu and Bret, "Wu knows." A statement.

"Yes," I acknowledged.

"Has he said something?"

"Quite a bit, in fact."

"Oh?"

"He warned me to be careful." I smiled wanly.

"Damn. I'm being offhand and sloppy and you're being lectured."

"Right. It's the gender gap, old dear. Haven't you heard of it? You may know it by its common name."

"What's that?" he asked.

"Double standard!" I blurted.

He looked dismayed. We rejoined Yee and Bret. They left and I turned to my friend. "Thanks. He got the message."

Yee bowed slightly. "So I noticed."

I got back to work.

We saw each other occasionally and taught a few classes together; shared lunch with colleagues. Paul even came across to Stinson one afternoon. We had a short, romantic time together. No unhappy moments. True to his word, he had carved out several hours to spend with me. Celestina had made a pot of his favorite split pea soup with Italian sausage and quietly left before he arrived. She too 'knew,' although nothing was said.

The distance and time involved was simply too great for those kinds of afternoon/evenings to continue, especially as he was needed increasingly at home, now the wedding was approaching. Even when he took a day and a half turn around to Vancouver, he left directly from SFO. It was just too difficult to dream up excuses to leave home long hours before the plane. The 'situation' was wearing thin for both of us.

Too often it became: "Can you . . . ?" "No, I can't." "Will you . . . ?" "No, I won't be able to at this time. Sorry." Over and over. Until he and I became less and less willing to make suggestions and attempt to rendezvous.

In the beginning, I had had high hopes for our pied à terre. I naively fantasized it into becoming Paul's full time residence when he left Kathy. Once again, I was so wrong. Our time together was still as sweet as always when it happened. Nonetheless, parting continued to be a heartache accompanied more and more frequently by the realization that we were drawing apart. Imperceptibly, at first. Then, as the demands of my work at school, at home, at Wu Yee's, with my son and his bride-to-be, added to similar demands on Paul's time, we recognized, without saying it in so many words, we were on hold for the foreseeable future.

# 49

I was leaving the house when the phone rang. I hesitated for a moment and decided to let the machine pick up, screen the call and not bother if it wasn't important. After all our scheduling problems, Paul and I were at last to have an evening together—meet at our place at the end of the afternoon. I didn't want to be distracted by issues peripheral to my plan for the day.

"Jenny. Jenny, are you there? Damn." It was Paul. He sounded desperate. I grabbed for the phone before he hung up. "What is it, Paul? What's the matter?"

"Thank God you're still there." He let out a low whistle.

"What is it?" I repeated.

"It's not going to work tonight" He sounded uptight—even distant.

"What's not going to work?" I asked. We were to meet before dinner. I'd planned to surprise him and cook.

"Our getting together. Sorry I can't make it."

"Sorry you can't make it? You sound very off-hand, what gives?" I was trying to match his mood. Admittedly, I suddenly didn't feel off-hand.

"I'll tell you what gives," I could feel his scowl through the phone, "If you really must know, Kathy and I had a hellava blow-up this morning."

Apparently, before he left for the office, Paul told Kathy not to expect him home—he'd stay in town over-night. "She lashed out at me with 'What now? Clients, meetings, work or play?' I was dumb-struck."

He told me he flashed back with something to do with her evenings so filled with her own activities, he didn't think she noticed whether he was at home or not. And on and on. He said—she said. It was fast becoming bitter.

"I told her stop before she said things that couldn't be unsaid and then she challenged me to bring work home the way I used to"

"Before me—us?"

"Yeah."

"So?"

"So I said OK, I'd try to get a report written at home tonight—just to cool things off."

"Oh." Deflated.

"For God's Jenny, don't you go into a sulk on me. That's all I need"

I rose to that one in a hurry, "Listen, Paul, I think you'd better stop before things get out of hand here too. I'm not exactly the one to listen to your soul-searching and I'm in no mood to hear how you're planning to placate your wife."

Paul didn't answer for a moment. Then: "There's more—worse."

"Now what?"

"Kathy's in town with Beth doing some pre-wedding shopping and they want to…"

"…to meet you for dinner. That figures'" I sighed.

"Worse than that. They want to see my city digs."

"Oh, No."

"No, is right. I don't know how to stop them."

"No, they simply can't. Good Lord, Paul, we have things there—pictures, clothes—"

"Christ, Jen, how can I stop them? It's not as though I stay at the 'Y' or in some hotel. Whether we like it or not, they do know I have an apartment here in the city. After all Kathy is my wife and Beth is my daughter." He was beginning to sound defensive and agitated, again.

I was furious—how dare they invade my most precious and personal space? Was nothing sacred? Foolishly, I had never given it a thought—that Kathy would know about Paul's place. Was there no part of this relationship that was to be mine, solely mine? I could have wept in frustration.

"Just exactly what do you expect from me?" I asked coldly.

"Help me, Jenny—can you meet me there in an hour? We'll clear out some things?" I'd never heard him like this before. He was pleading. It was not his best moment.

"Do you plan to hire a moving van?" I know I was being sarcastic, but truly more than my Jeep was needed to depersonalize the place—and surely more time than we had.

"Jenny, don't. I know it's unfortunate but please. I'm asking for your help."

Unfortunate? That's the under statement of the century.

This wrangling went on for several minutes back and forth until my fury dissipated and I went numb. I couldn't believe what he was proposing. Clear out some things?

"Really Paul you've lost it. They simply can't go there. I refuse to participate in this madness."

"What are we to do?" he interrupted.

"Every time Kathy decides to come to town are we to dismantle the place? If so count me out—I mean it—O.U.T.!" I was on the edge of hysteria. I almost 'lost it' myself. It suddenly struck my funny bone—it was so ludicrous.

"Tell them you just found out the owner had the place tented today. It's being fumigated; in fact he's going to do some remodeling and you're considering finding someplace else. For God's sake, Paul, tell them anything, but don't let them in there!"

"Jenny, you're a genius. I knew you'd come up with the solution. It's perfect—fumigation! You're a flaming genius." His relief was palpable. I was still annoyed that he couldn't come up with something plausible and not have made such horror for me.

"I was in such shock, Jen, I couldn't think straight—but it still does put an end to our plans. Going with your scenario, I have to go back home tonight."

"Well, maybe between now and the next couple of hours you'll think of something better. I'll be having dinner at TJ's. She's expecting Guy and Bret. I may just as well join them." He was so relieved, he failed to recognize my exasperated tone of voice.

"Great idea. Thanks, Jenny. Thanks again. I'll let you know and be in touch somehow." Relief, pure and simple.

"Sure Paul," I said, "Be in touch." I felt like a deflated balloon. Fate had stuck a pin in me.

A narrow escape, one neither of us had ever fantasized needing to make. The thought was so repugnant, so utterly revolting to me, I was dumbfounded by my reaction. I was ready to 'bar the door' to prevent them from entering. I was also ready to commit mayhem on Paul. And above all, I was furious and disgusted with myself. How demeaning. How shabby. How did I get myself into this sordid mess? And more to the point, how was I to get out?

For God's sake gather your wits about you. Balance, Jenny. Tom was killed and you carried on, surely you can manage a love affair that's crumbling at the edges.

I dressed for the city, determined to proceed with my plans for the day—without Paul. That is, I went to the city and to 'the place.' I was exhausted and depleted and needed the surcease of its warmth to replenish me before facing my friends. No, to answer the obvious question, Paul took the easy way out—he used my plausible excuse and went home after dinner... trailing his tail behind him.

As I pushed open the high gate and entered, I was once more overcome by the beauty of this miniature garden. The scent of spring was in the air. The plants were leafing out, the roses beginning to bud and the tulips were pushing up through the rich soil. It's only a tiny place, but absolutely breathtaking. A secret garden, indeed. I felt that about it when first I entered it months ago. Can it only have been three months? Time stands still in this enchanted place. It could have been forever.

On the small, black lacquered Chinese chest next to the couch was a package. It was tied up in purple velvet ribbons with jade green silk flowers tucked in and around the bows. A small card was propped up next to it—"To my love, my Jenny. Forever, Paul." I was hard pressed to open it—I was still shaken by the earlier call and subsequent upheaval. But finding it there, waiting for me made my heart both ache and sing and I could not resist.

In the box was an exquisite silver frame holding a picture of me playing Frisbee on the beach with Honey. Oh Paul, seeing, remembering that glorious day makes me hurt less and makes me miss you more.

"What am I to do," I wailed in despair, pacing up and down the room. I was riddled with jealousy envisioning Paul with his wife, and although my anger had dissipated itself, somewhere between the phone call and my arriving at our place, I was still filled with pain and foreboding. The end was in sight—the end of my precious dream. All the portents were in place.

Suddenly I stopped pacing and went into the bathroom to gather up all my cosmetics, unguents, perfumes—all the sweet things I loved coming in and finding there. All the accouterments that spelled 'Jenny loves here.' The closet was one we shared, and when I walked into it, I burst into tears. I touched each of the things we had left there—a robe, a gown, a few garments that carried the lingering scents of our bodies.

In one motion I separated them by sweeping them apart on the rod. A pathetically few pieces which bespoke of the duality of our lives.

No longer could I leave them there. They didn't seem safe any longer. Two trips to my car and I had all but 'sanitized' the place. But somehow, I couldn't bring myself to remove the picture Paul had left me to find. In turn, I left it on the little table for him to find—whenever he returned.

The day had been so emotionally charged and I had expended so much energy trying to cover my unhappy state of mind, both during the contretemps with Paul and later with my friends at dinner, that when I finally did fall into my own bed I was totally spent. I slept the sleep of the dead.

Early the following morning he phoned. I was startled out of my sound sleep. "Good morning." He waited a second for my response, presumably to test the water.

"Oh, good morning," I yawned and stretched. "Where are you? It seems terribly early."

"I'm at our place." The 'our place' sent a chill through me. "I couldn't sleep, so I came here. I especially wanted to see if you were here yesterday and found your surprise."

"Yes, thank you. I . . ."

"Jenny," he interrupted, "you got your surprise and left me an even bigger one. You took all of your things. Why?"

"They didn't seem safe there anymore," I said simply.

"Damn. I know I bollixed up yesterday. I was totally unprepared, and I am sincerely sorry."

"So am I, Paul—sorry it happened, that is."

"Please dear one, bring back your things—I love walking into the bathroom and smelling the fragrance of your dusting powder, and the closet—it's so forlorn in there. The entire place is forlorn without your presence."

# PART 5

# 50

Two months before Beth's mid-May wedding, I received a message from Paul to call him before 5:30 at his office. Now what? Things had been tense between us since the fiasco surrounding Kathy's demanding to use 'the digs', as she referred to our lovely space.

"Mr. Paul sound very anxious to have you call him." Celestina recited the message verbatim.

"Thanks. I'll drop these supplies in the studio and call him from there. Are you leaving now?"

"Yes, Missy. I'll see you tomorrow. *Hasta mañana.*"

"*Hasta mañana*, Celestina. Drive carefully."

"Paul Crowley," he answered on the first ring.

"Jenny, here. How are you, Paul? What's up?" Keep it light, girl. Don't say how it warms you to hear his voice. Keep calm. Stay cool.

"Jen, I'm glad you got my message. I've got a plan in mind and I hope I'm giving you enough notice to agree to it." He was his dear breathless self. My resolve to stay cool, if not aloof was melting swiftly.

"Tell me more. I'm waiting with bated breath."

He laughed and went on: "I've had an urgent call from Vancouver. I'll need to be there two or three days next week. I want you to come with me. It's been so hectic here, we've had no real time. Can you? Will you? Please say yes."

I was shocked into silence.

"Jenny, have you passed out from shock? Are you there?" Now he was chuckling.

"I'm here. I nearly did. When exactly?" I was stalling for time.

"Monday and Tuesday for certain. If you come, I'll stay over to Wednesday and return that night or maybe come back Thursday morning. A perfect four day holiday."

My brain was whirling. This is what I'd wanted months ago—a real block of time to spend together. Now I had a terrible sense of foreboding. What would the backlash be when we separated? How were we, at least, how was I to deal with the anxiety that was sure to follow?

"Oh, Paul. I don't know. Do you really think we can carry it off? What with airports, hotels, the whole thing?"

"I've checked it out. I'm sure we can. I'll be dropped off. You'll park your car. We won't be seen together. Should we know anyone on the plane, so what? People do sometimes bump into acquaintances. Don't worry. We'll do it.

"Also, the hotel I want us to stay in is not in the heart of town, but a bit out of the way—more residential and quite charming. We'll work out any other details you want. Just, please tell me you'll come with me."

Who was I kidding thinking I could say no?

I took a deep breath and plunged in. "Of course I'll do it! I've the time to do some shifting of appointments and such. I'll have to get someone to cover my class."

"Me, too. Who will take care of Honey?"

"I'll see what Laura's up to or TJ. She'll do it for sure."

"Maybe TJ is better, Jen. Less to explain to Laura. Don't you agree?"

"I hadn't thought of that, but you're right, of course. I'll check it out with TJ. Thanks for sounding a cautionary note."

I was so overjoyed; the fact we had to plan carefully didn't dispel my excitement.

"This nose is going to be stuck to the grindstone all week to get ready for my meetings, but we'll talk. Call whenever you want to. I'll call when I can. Jenny, I can't tell you how happy I am. We'll have a great time. You'll see." His enthusiasm was palpable.

"By the way, will you be in meetings all day? Do you know yet?" I needed to plan my time, too.

"Only some of each day. Probably much of Monday. Will you be OK?" He sounded concerned.

"Of course. I'll have time to see the city again and take some pictures of Stanley Park and that whole area. I've never been satisfied with the totem pole ones I've taken in the past. I'll be more than all right."

"Good. Well, dear one, I've got to get cracking. Call me soon."

"I will. You, too. Anytime." It was like it had been in the beginning—no strain, no tension, lots of happy anticipation. The week was a blur of activity.

TJ was delighted, with reservations. She, too, sounded a cautionary note. "Jenny, please, don't be oblivious to those around you. In the past, you two acted as though you were the only intelligent creatures on the planet. Don't be the only unintelligent ones now. Look over your shoulder from time to time. I know this isn't the tourist season yet, but not everyone you know will be staying at home because you'd like them to."

I couldn't get a word in edgewise.

"Bring Honey down. Poochie will love it. We were going to plan more time for them to be together anyway."

"Thanks. If it's OK, I'll come down Saturday and stay over. That'll have me in town and ready to meet Paul at SFO without the long drive from home."

"Absolutely. It's the only thing that makes any sense. We'll have dinner and part of Sunday, too. Good planning."

"You're right and I accept."

"If it's a pretty day, I'll set up on the terrace. How's that? Then we can watch an old movie."

"Only perfect. Thanks, dear, in advance. I'll see you Saturday. Oh, by the way, shall I stop at the market for anything?"

"Would you mind stopping at the Bait Shop and Grocery in Sausalito and bring some of their wonderful bread?"

"With pleasure. Anything else?"

"No, no. I've plenty of everything."

"I'll toss a bag of kibble into the car, too."

I turned around to see Honey going to fetch her leash. Honestly, one day soon I expect that dog to speak English!

"Not yet, Honey. Tomorrow we'll go."

Sometime later Paul called. I told him my Saturday plan.

"OK, Jenny. I'll phone you Sunday morning at TJ's. I just hope I don't forget to take my briefcase and drawings with me. Remarkably, my mind is on other things."

"I'll remind you Sunday, if you promise to remind me to take my camera case."

"With or without the cameras?"

We both laughed and then reluctantly let go. Smiling happily, I broke the connection first. Suddenly his voice echoed in my head. "Bye, Jenny dear, see you soon." A slight shudder ran through me. I shook myself. Would I ever overcome the stark terror that phrase created in me? "Bye, Jenny dear, see you soon" were the last words I ever heard Tom speak. Ah, yes, I was still reacting.

We crossed the bridge as I sang the praises of my beautiful city—Tony Bennett and I.

Dinner was on the terrace as promised.

"These past few months haven't been the easiest on you emotionally, have they, my friend?" TJ was scrutinizing me closely.

"They've been great professionally, though, and right now things are looking up in the other department."

"Just remember my admonition to stay on the alert. Have you a story, if you do run into someone you know?"

"We'll work it out. By the way, I'll give you the hotel and phone number before I leave. You have my beeper number. I'll have it with me at all times."

"What are you telling Laura? Obviously, she'll know you're away. And Guy? What about him and the twins?"

"Stop it, TJ, or I'll end up canceling the whole thing. As far as anyone is concerned, I'm going on a short shoot for Sunset Magazine—a first segment on Butchart Gardens for the early spring flowers. I've already mentioned it to Guy."

"Oh? He hasn't mentioned it to me, yet."

"Actually, I have been in touch with the editors at Sunset and they've shown some interest in an article, kind of 'Four Seasons at the Gardens.' I've covered my flank by telling them I'll submit 'Early Spring' and they can take a look."

"It doesn't hurt that they know you there. Not too many people can simply pick up the phone and get through to an editor. I'm impressed. How about Vancouver? What are you doing there? Stanley Park and the totems?"

TJ stopped in the middle of all her admonitions and burst out laughing, "We didn't plan this carefully in college when you and Tom went away on your first overnight."

"And if we'd been caught, Dad would have come after him with a shot-gun. You'll remember, Dad was not impressed by the early 60's."

I wiped my eyes—a mixture of tears from laughter and remembrance. "Never mind all that, TJ, what am I going to take to wear? You know I sleep in T-shirts and crew socks most of the time. And my clothes, all tailored and casual. Nothing, you know . . ."

"Sexy? Seductive? You seem to be doing all right with what you have." She laughed again.

"I haven't a thing like that. I haven't shopped with a man in mind for so long . . ."

"Just dress as you always do, Jenny. Don't become a stranger to him. He loves you as you are. On one thing I would suggest—leave the sleep shirts at home."

"Oh, TJ, just let it be all right with the gods this time," I blurted.

"Be all right with the gods?" TJ asked quizzically.

"That I be happy."

"I've run out of admonitions other than to say: Have a sweet time." We turned on a movie and turned off talk.

"We'll be back Thursday." I was packing the car as we talked.

"I'm expecting you to stay over. If you go straight home, you might get a case of the bends."

"The bends?"

"You know, decompressing too rapidly."

"Very funny. So long, Poochie. Bye, bye, Honey. Have fun with them, TJ. I'll call you."

"OK, Jenny. Travel safe now and then, too."

# 51

The flight was uneventful and on time. We had waited until the luggage was stowed in the rented car and were on our way before we roared with laughter Two kids playing hooky and presumably getting away with it.

Luck was with us. The hotel was lovely, the staff courteous, and appropriately distant. Paul had been exceedingly sensitive to my position and booked two rooms—adjoining, mind you. In that way, I was registered under my own name, could receive calls and messages, charge things if I wanted to, whatever, without compromising anyone. I needed my own receipts, anyway, as it was a legitimate professional business trip for me.

"Jenny, dear Jenny, I can't believe we're here." He put his arms around me and pressed my head against his chest. "I love you so." We both sighed as if our hearts would break. I finally tipped my head back for a kiss. He looked into my eyes for a long moment before he bent his head to kiss me. The rush of feelings was so strong we had to lean against the wall to steady ourselves.

"The earth moved and all I did was give you a kiss."

"And all I did was kiss you back."

What sheer luxury to contemplate time to just 'be' together without the constraints we'd had to deal with on every other occasion. After freshening up, we opted for dinner in the hotel and a walk around the grounds.

Before heading back to our rooms, we picked up a schedule for the ferryboats to Vancouver Island and the city of Victoria. I would spend my first day there 'on assignment,' while Paul worked, and still be back well before dinner.

Once back in our own rooms, I drew a tub in my bathroom. I luxuriated in the warm water, feeling the fatigue of travel ebb away. I could hear my beloved singing in the shower on the other side of the wall and wondered if he always sang in the shower or only when he was with me. I'd never know, because I sure as the devil wasn't going to ask and he'd never say. Anyway, it was grand to hear.

We met in the doorway connecting our two rooms. I'd slipped into my satiny slip of a gown of the softest candlelight hue. It did wonderful things to my skin. Paul had draped a towel around his middle. It didn't stay on long. Neither did my gown.

He gave me a low whistle as he reached for me. I couldn't speak. I was allowing my feelings to guide me as I stretched open my arms. He wrapped himself around me and ran his hands down the smooth fabric until he suddenly lifted it and let his towel drop at the same time.

I gasped, engulfed in sheer passion. I moved as one with him kissing and stroking until we tumbled into bed still in an awkward embrace that was broken by our having to adjust ourselves so we'd not dislocate some parts of us. We spluttered and laughed, regrouped and continued.

I've no idea how long we made love. We luxuriated in our needing and our wanting each other. At once gently petting and holding each other quietly; then aroused magically by a small movement or a tiny kiss to an urgent coming together in an electrifying lust. Spontaneous and erotic. We were overwhelmed by the magnetic field we created.

There were no words, only the sounds of loving, and finally we rested. Paul turned to me and smiled. He touched my face and gave me a kiss on the forehead.

"Any second now I expect you to tell me you're hungry."

"Don't mention it, or I will be." I giggled.

We both had the same idea at the same time. He headed to the mini bar and raided the goodies. We ate cheese and crackers and candy and nuts and washed it all down with Perrier, laughing all the while.

What a pair of crazy kids. Only we were, supposedly, responsible adults.

"Do you feel like a responsible adult or a crazy kid?" I asked.

"I feel like a crazy-kid-in-love-adult."

"That's a nice blend. I like it. Can I be one, too?"

"An adult or crazy?" Paul asked.

"No. I want some of each, like you."

"Ah, but you're missing something. You see, you have to have you to love to get that way," he explained.

"I have you, doesn't that count?"

"Not exactly."

This time when we climbed into bed we hugged, sighed, and slept. We both awakened early and decided to go for a jog in the early morning mist. We found a place open and had a cup of steaming cocoa with a buttery croissant dripping in homemade strawberry preserves.

"Now, this is the way to start the day, in my view," Paul said.

"And what is your view?"

"You, my dear. You are my view, and the way to start the day."

"Thank you, sir. I couldn't agree more," I responded.

"Don't tempt me," he chided.

"I already have," I said soberly.

"I'm afraid you have. That's so."

He came over and gave me a hug to dispel whatever sobering thoughts were arising. It worked for the moment.

For three days our mornings began that way and for four nights we loved and laughed. In between, we worked diligently—each in our own way. We were, at once, effective and light-hearted, and relaxed into a routine that we'd have happily gone on with into forever.

Our final night, we dined at The Raintree. We'd heard it was the preferred place for *tete-à-tete* dinners. The setting was perfection. From the elegant candlelit room gleaming with silver and crisp linen to the view of Stanley Park across the bay-shore end-water in the foreground with a sweeping view of the north mountains in the distance. It was breathtakingly beautiful. The food was excellent and the service impeccable. All in all, the perfect choice. As usual, the staff recognized the aura of love we moved within and rose to a level beyond there own high standards.

Over dinner we were told a most wonderful story about the owner: On Canadian Thanksgiving Day she closes the restaurant to the general public and opens it to the homeless and destitute of the city for Thanksgiving dinner. Over the past several years, she has solicited fellow restaurateurs, and five or six more have joined in, with the list growing. She's now working toward repeating the practice on Christmas all over the city. We were most impressed. By the time dessert was served, one would have thought we were the owner's bankers. Paul and I always got a laugh out of those happenings. We loved it and decided the world loved us. We were their newest best friends, and they ours.

We were especially tender that night savoring every moment together. Conscious that it would be our last night until who knew when. The coming family events in our two lives were upon us. There would be no time or opportunity for any extra 'off-schedule' activities.

Sleep came, as we lay in each other's arms, content. As I was drifting off, Paul's admonition came to me: "Don't look beyond tomorrow." I couldn't. This time was too precious, too perfect to mar. These days were to be encapsulated whole and put aside—not to be discussed, analyzed, or pulled apart in any fashion. I was also to look at the entire time as an entity unto itself and enjoy it in my conscious memory and in my dreams for long months ahead.

Breakfast. Packing. Last minute phone calls to the office. Check out. Off to the airport. Good-bye, Vancouver. Good-bye, glorious holiday. Thank you, Oh-special-protector-of-Jenny for these precious days.

We said little on the flight back. Mostly we held hands and occasionally looked at one another and smiled. It was useless to try to talk about what we'd done. Each of us was immersed in our own thoughts. What we did know for certain is that we were deeply in love.

TJ was right about the "bends." It was difficult enough to drop Paul at his office, say good-bye there and head straight to my beloved friend. I could never have dropped him off and gone home to my empty house.

## 52

The entire bay area was gloriously clear and bright. I wouldn't have wanted to cope with a gloomy day.

TJ was at the door almost immediately that I rang. "Hi, traveler! How are the spring flowers and the totem poles?" She was all smiles.

"They're great. The early flowers are unbelievable. I spent hours walking around and savoring the sights and smells before I shot a single picture. It was a glorious day. I never get over the thrill of seeing all those massed blooms."

"And you? How are you? Are you fine? You look fine." She was giving me the once over.

"Yes, thank you. I'm fine and Paul's fine, too. It was a perfect time."

"That's all I want to know."

"That's all I'll tell you, in that case. I hadn't intended to say much more. Only that there were no mishaps."

"Thank God for favors small and large." She let out her breath. "Are you willing to eat out one more meal? Wu Yee called and invited us to supper. Are you up to it?"

"Yes, indeed I am. In fact, I think it's a splendid idea. I'll go change now." I headed to my room as TJ answered the phone.

"Yes, she's here and looks great. How are you, Paul? Good. Everything here ran smoothly, thanks. Let me tell her you're on the phone. Jenny! It's Paul."

"Thanks. Hello?" It was I who was breathless this time.

"Hello, Jenny. I just wanted to speak to you and to hear your voice again. Those were incredible days, Jen, and nights, too," he added with a chuckle. "I'm having a terrible time trying to put my feelings into words. I simply know I'll never forget this time. It will be with me forever. That's what I want you to know. And I didn't want to end this day without telling you."

"Paul. Oh, Paul." It was meltdown time again. "Thank you for calling just now. I couldn't bring myself to call, and I wanted to. Time is what I wanted, and time is what you gave me. A very precious gift, and I'm grateful."

"I gave you nothing more than you gave me, Jenny. The time with you is always precious to me. You must believe that. And why couldn't you call? I've told you to anytime. If I can't talk, I'll tell you. Don't worry."

"I didn't want to seem, I don't know . . . needy. Now I feel silly trying to explain. As you just said, feelings aren't easy to put into words." I was suddenly timid.

"You're right on that score, but terribly wrong on the other. You must never not call. Please believe me. It is a joy to my heart to hear your voice anytime, any day, Jenny. Own that."

"I love you, Paul."

"Now, that's what I wanted to hear. That's more like it. I do, too, Jenny dear. I love you."

"The next few weeks will be crammed for both of us. I'm sure we won't see each other, but you're right, we can talk often, and I promise I'll not stop myself. I'll need it . . . the contact. I know I will by the way I feel right this minute."

"Call to your heart's content," he said gaily. "I'll love it and

I'll need it, too. What are you two up to tonight?" A determined shift of subject.

"We're having dinner at Wu Yee's and coming straight back to the house. I've had a long day."

"We've had a long day. In fact, we've shared a long day. And I must ring off now and end it for myself. I'll talk to you soon, my Jenny. And once more, thank you."

"It's hard to say good-bye, cowboy, but I'll let you go . . . for now."

"What was all that about?" TJ had been standing in my doorway for the last minute or so.

"Just reassuring each other. Neither of us wants to be cut off, and suddenly we are. That's the bottom line."

"That's what I warned you about last week. You've got the bends, and apparently, so has Paul."

"The worse part, my friend, is the better it gets between us, the harder it is on us. The fascinating thing is I can be content to talk on the phone or see him out somewhere, when that's all that's possible; but after we've been together alone for any length of time, it's sheer hell to say 'good-bye' not knowing when we'll see each other again. The anxiety is horrendous."

"Just exactly what I was afraid of," TJ said. "I'm also afraid you're going to have to learn to cope with it, because it isn't going to go away. You know, Jen, it might even get worse." TJ was looking sorrowful.

"Don't look so sad, dear. It's lousy, but it's lousy because it's wonderful. I know I sound slightly crazed, but it's the truth."

"Jenny dear, I understand. I simply don't like seeing you miserable. Mind you, I can't think of a blessed thing to do about it."

"Well, let's just let it lay. I'll get changed and meet you in front in fifteen. OK? Call Wu Yee and tell him we're on our way." I managed a smile.

# 53

One more class and the spring semester came to an end, accompanied by all the ceremonies, the parties, the conferring of degrees—in short, the traditional Rites of Passage.

Paul hadn't been around for the last couple of sessions, nor at our school's last celebrations of the year. I spoke to him a few times, and in spite of the fact that I'd been in the city once or twice, it was impossible to meet. By chance, I caught him on his last day in the office before Beth's wedding.

"Kathy's a wreck and she's making Beth so nervous, I decided it's time to go into my balancing act."

"Balancing act? Oh, you mean exert a steadying influence?"

"Something like that. Anyway, it'll afford me some extra time with my daughter before I have to give her away." He sounded a tad wistful.

"You're a good father, Paul. It's equally important to Beth, you know, to have some special time with her Dad."

"It's a wild and wonderful and somewhat confusing time of life. Don't you agree, Jenny?"

"Most definitely," I replied.

"Yeah. I feel like a school boy around you, and at the same time, my daughter's getting married and, quite frankly, I'm already looking forward to grandchildren."

I laughed. "Don't rush things, old dear. Time races by fast enough. Just enjoy these moments to the fullest. Be a happy Dad and have a wonderful time. I'll be thinking of you." I tried to keep a smile in my voice, for I meant the sentiments completely. I also missed him terribly and was increasingly frustrated by our inability to be together.

"Thank you, Jenny dear. I'll be thinking of you, too." He sounded serious. "I miss you, girl. And I can't figure out when we can be together."

"This isn't the time to plan anything, Paul. We can talk after the festivities and make a plan."

"That's what I mean, dear. We can't."

"What do you mean? We can't?"

"I guess I haven't told you, but Kathy and I are going to take off for a couple of weeks right after the wedding. I haven't had a free day since Christmas, and she can certainly use the break, too." He was rushing on with explanations and justifications.

"Of course. Where are you going?" I was rapidly losing my cool. What was this . . . I guess I didn't tell you . . . business? Was I a child? I didn't like it at all. Suddenly, I felt degraded and was sorry I'd called. Paul was speaking. I tried to refocus and pay attention.

". . .some old friends were planning a barging trip and mentioned it to us. It sounded like fun and the timing's right."

"Where are you doing this?" I was being as offhand and casually interested as possible. Pretend it's your hairdresser talking about a summer holiday.

"In the south of France. We'll fly to Paris, spend the night and then take a hired car south through Dijon, et cetera . . ." He was warming to the subject and I was freezing cold around my heart.

*A Small Flirtation*

"Well, I guess you did forget. It sounds quite wonderful. Have a great time and, once more, happy wedding and my best to Beth."

"Thanks again, Jenny. I'll call as soon as I return."

"Yes, you do that. Safe trip." And I hung up. He was too distracted to notice my abruptness.

My eyes were stinging with unwept tears and my stomach was one large spasm of apprehension, anxiety and jealousy. Not a pretty or comfortable combination.

The intensity of my physical, as well as psychic reaction to Paul's news, startled me. I suddenly felt completely alone and miserable. Justified and unjustified in equal parts.

## 54

The entire saga of Paul and me had lasted less than nine months. In all that time, we'd spend a precious few hours together totally alone. We spent hundreds of hours thinking about one another and hours talking on the phone and fantasizing. Now, I felt a tremendous gap opening between us. A rent in the fabric of our relationship. It was the beginning of the end, and I felt it keenly. We were unraveling. And I understood it completely. At the same time, I was devastated.

We were to have kept it light and made no demands. I now knew how totally unrealistic that was. I'd told TJ the better things got between us, the harder it was on us. All my foreboding, all her admonitions, and all of Guy's dire warnings were coming true. Yet, I could and would say nothing. I still needed time to sort out all the disparate parts of our puzzle. Time to own my decision with as few recriminations as possible. Self-recrimination, that is.

I called TJ immediately that I hung up. I packed a small bag, grabbed my camera and Honey's leash.

"Come on, girl, I need some help."

By the time Honey and I arrived at TJ's, the troops had been called in. TJ had lost no time. Guy had already arrived. Wu Yee was sending over food and would join us a bit later. The wagons were circled. I hadn't realized I'd sounded so desperate.

I was met at the door by Guy. He took me in his arms and simply held me close for a few moments and said nothing.

He released me, looked at me long and hard, and said, "You look terrific. Yes, you do. You'll do fine. I know you." He pulled me close again and kissed the top of my head.

All I could think was why couldn't I be in love with Guy? It would be so much simpler.

Guy called out to TJ, "She's here!" And to me, "Let's sit down and get the talking part of this over."

"First, tell me how you and the new garlic plants are." I wanted to compose myself and hold my own tonight.

"The plants look promising. More about them later. Time to stop the distracting techniques, at which you are a master. Come sit down, TJ, and let's get the full picture."

We gathered around the table on the terrace. The two of them just looked at me. I began by bursting into tears. They were dumbfounded. It was such an uncharacteristic thing for me to do. So much for being composed.

While you pull yourself together, dear one," Guy said, "you might begin by facing the reality of your daily life head-on this time. OK?"

"I don't know!" I blurted. "What I do know is I'm jealous of the time Paul spends with her, Kathy—his wife!" That remark came from my very soul. "I know it's crazy, but it's the God's honest truth. I am also disgusted with me. At the same time, I feel taken for granted, and it's demeaning. It's all too idiotic. I hate being in this position!" I was furious. My inability to control the tears only made me more angry.

I jumped up from the table and started pacing.

"It's no good to berate yourself at this point, Jenny. You took some chances, risked little and had a lot of fun. The only problem is the two of you blundered right smack into the Law of Unintended Consequences."

"The what?" TJ looked quizzical.

"The Law of Unintended Consequences," Guy repeated.

"Meaning? Oh, I get it—We fell in love."

"Exactly. This happens to people everyday. They fall in love." Guy was still watching me closely. Looking for some reasonable reaction. "And he'll never leave Kathy. That you must know. Certainly not while you're giving him what he wants."

At that moment, I stopped pacing and looked at TJ, who hadn't uttered a sound, and then at Guy. "I feel like having a tantrum. If I were a small child I'm sure I'd have one—on the floor kicking my heels and yelling at the top of my lungs."

The image was, at once, so vivid and so ludicrous we all collapsed in laughter. I guess that's what eventually saved the day. I'd fallen in love and in laughter, and now I'd use the laughter to maintain my equanimity.

"Sounds like we're all a bit manic-depressive today." TJ was wiping her eyes. "What's the next step, Jen? Is there anywhere to go from here?"

"Can you tell us? Do you know why this happened today? What I mean is, why this incident? What made it different than, say, seeing them together at Squaw Valley? Or hearing about plans before?" Guy was pushing me to face the facts.

"I can't say exactly, Guy. Maybe it was the proverbial straw, the last drop of water before the spill, I don't know. I just know it's not the way I want it to be for me. I want a life with Paul, a real life, and I can't have it. And I can't continue with this half-life or quarter life. It's not even that much. It's so minuscule; it can't really be measured. No, it's not for me."

"Does that mean you will release yourself from the dream as well as give up the minuscule part of the dream you have?" TJ asked.

"A rather convoluted question, TJ, but yes, I have to. It breaks my heart to have been so close to perfection for me and then to have to walk away. But, what other choice do I have?"

I was gathering strength from this give and take. "To this point it's been pure joy. I don't want to spoil the good by suddenly becoming demanding. It would only force a terrible confrontation with no possible solution."

Guy watched me closely, then said, "I don't really understand you, Jenny. You've argued that you don't want to 'spoil' things between you and Paul by becoming 'demanding'. And so your solution is to walk away entirely? You don't call that spoiling things? What have you said to Paul, up to this point, that would give him the first clue you're thinking of breaking off?"

"But Guy, I don't want to end it with bad feelings between us."

"Do you really believe that walking away will end it without bad feelings? It will be hell for Paul. I know how he feels about you. He will be bereft. I know the truth of what happened, Jen. A mild and fun flirtation turned into the grand passion of your lives. I was there. I watched it develop," Guy said with a great expansive gesture. "The lunacy is Paul being unable to make a commitment to you knowing how he loves you."

"You kept sounding warning bells and whistles. I heard them and chose not to listen," I admitted. "What can I possibly do now?"

"You're acting like a Victorian, Jenny. What the hell's the matter with fighting for what you want? Right here? Right now?"

He stopped pacing and sighed and took my hand. "Frankly, I'm both sorry and glad about this at the same time. Maybe I should take my own advice and fight for what I want. I love you, Jenny girl; I guess I always have, and I know I always will." Guy turned to TJ, "You may be right—we may just be a bit manic-depressive today."

"Come sit on the terrace. The weather is still delicious. We'll have coffee out there." TJ led the way with Wu Yee in tow.

"TJ, you have *I Ching* interpretations, don't you?" asked Wu Yee.

"Yes I do, Yee. On file in my office," she was on her way.

"I think a little consultation is called for concerning Jenny's situation. How about it, Jenny? What do you think?" He was already taking three pennies out of his pocket.

"It's a lot cheaper than a visit to a shrink," Guy chimed in.

"Why not? It's always fun and often illuminating. I might even learn something." I was ready for some fun.

"It's better for each of us to use our own coins. Less confusing vibrations for the oracle," Yee explained.

TJ, Guy, and Yee each took a turn reading, commenting, and interpreting. Then it was my turn. I wrote out my question remembering to thank the oracle in advance. I lingered over the coins before I threw them, focusing on my intention as well as on the question. Then I tossed them—six times. Noted the positions each time and interpreted them according to the instructions in the book.

"What hexagram did you receive, Jenny? Wu Yee asked quietly.

"Number fifty-four: Subordinate, without change."

"Read aloud, part of it. That is the "Marrying Maiden," is it not?"

"Yes," I answered.

He nodded solemnly.

"Read." TJ and Guy were watching and listening intently.

I read:

*"The balance of forces at work at this time are wholly inequitable. You are completely dependent on a situation for reasons of circumstance, while the situation can get along quite well without you."* I looked up and continued:

*"If you try to be assertive or make yourself indispensable, you will meet with misfortune. It has never been easier for you to make mistakes, since everything you do is inappropriate. You are not in control of a single thing, with the exception of your ability to perceive your difficulties and react accordingly."*

"Good Lord!" I stopped reading and looked at Wu Yee.

"Go on," he said. "Only, skip the parts about jobs and political matters."

I glanced at TJ and Guy. They both nodded encouragingly.

I continued: *"In the original Chinese text, this hexagram was called the "Marrying Maiden" and referred, metaphorically, to the difficulties of a non-privileged concubine who remained subordinate to the recognized marriage..."*

"I can't read anymore of this. I think it's rigged."

"You skipped a line, I believe."

"Yes, Yee, I skipped a few, but I got the message. I've never read this before."

"It has never applied before either." He smiled. "But, do go on, Jenny. Read the explanation of the trigrams."

"All right. Let's see: *"The powerful upper trigram Chen 'arousing movement,' usurp the energy and influence of Tui, 'openness below.' When subordinate is received without change..."*

"You did receive it without change, didn't you say?" Yee interrupted.

"Yes."

"Go on."

*"...without change, it suggests that the path you have chosen, regardless of where you imagine it may lead, is actually a circle. You will end up where you began and will not transcend your current role. If you see this as unfortunate, then trace back to the beginning. This is where the situation was created and the only place where it can be changed.*

"I'll be a dirty name!" TJ's most extreme expletive.

"You and me, TJ," Guy concurred.

"I'm not the least bit surprised," Wu Yee chimed in.

"So, now what? I'm confused. Do we, Paul and I, have to go back to the previous lifetimes in which we've known one another to set this straight or only to the airplane ride from Chicago?" I was half-serious.

"To the beginning of the relationship," Yee explained.

"In other words, skip it?"

"Not exactly. But to the beginning of intimacy. That needed to be avoided. Isn't there something more you skipped about the future?"

"Yes. It says to develop and cling to a long-range ideal. It goes on: *"This will take you beyond this difficult time, with few mistakes and increasing clarity of purpose."*

"That sounds hopeful."

"The dynamics of life are such that every negative or difficult situation can be looked upon as hopeful; for in time, everything changes," Yee commented.

"It's inscrutable. What can change?" I was intrigued.

"Just hold to the truth, wait for the future to unfold, and seek clarity of purpose. The unknown will make it self knowable, in that way," Yee explained.

"You have a very beneficial effect on me, Yee. I may need to see you for reinforcement."

"Anytime, Jenny, anytime. And now, I, too, must leave. I have a restaurant to attend to, at least the closing up part." He smiled and took my hand. "Do not be tempted to consult the *I Ching* everyday. It could cause some confusion. Once a week is sufficient, even less, as you will be concerned with asking the same question, or version of it, over and over. If you are interested in doing it with me, I'll do my best to expand the interpretation for you. However, my advice would be to skip it for awhile."

"Thank you, my friend. I will take your advice. I don't think I could handle the interpretations everyday. It will be a challenge to do what I must, as it is."

"Yee, we'll drop off the food containers tomorrow, OK? They're too messy to deal with right now."

"Just put them in the box they were delivered in .TJ, my pot scrubber will take care of them. Come have Dim Sum with me tomorrow, anyway. I'll have some special ones for you to taste test. About 1:30? How's that?"

"Perfect. We'll see you then."

"How about you, Guy? Can you tear yourself away from your garlic long enough to join in?"

"Sorry, Wu Yee, another time. I'm heading down to the ranch at first light tomorrow, but I'll see you soon. I'll bring you some of the new garlic for you to test."

"Wonderful idea." He turned to me again. "Be strong, Jenny. Be calm, steady, and open. It will help you through this. I feel strongly that destiny is at work here." He gave me a peck on the cheek, said good-bye to us all and left.

"Destiny at work, eh? I don't know, yet . . . Wu Yee's a pretty savvy guy." Guy turned to me and asked, "Do you have a time frame in mind?"

"For the denouement?"

"Yes."

"It will unfold of its own accord, Guy. In any case, I'll not have the time or desire to face up to it until after Max's wedding."

"And destiny?" Guy kept at it.

"Destiny will have a hand in the timing, Guy. The manner will be up to the two of them. I have great faith in the process." TJ smiled at me. "Anyone ready to turn in besides me?" She was ready to put an end to what was becoming a useless discussion. I nodded my thanks.

"Let's take the dogs for a little walk first. How about it, Guy? Want to join us?" I reached for my jacket and the leashes.

"Next time, Jen. I have to be on my way to the ranch early. I'll stay in touch, though. Be fair to yourself, dear one."

"Good night, Guy. Thanks for being available."

"That's part of the deal, Jenny, being available."

"I'm keeping her here for a few days, Guy. I need some help cleaning the garage." TJ grinned, amused by her own idea.

"Great idea. Send her over to me when you've finished. I need some help in the studio."

"Thanks, fellahs. I know, strong back—weak head." We laughed and left the house together. The dogs were scrambling to beat us out the door.

"I'll bring back some garlic for you to try, TJ."

"Don't forget you promised some to Wu Yee, too."

"And I want some to take to the beach." I wasn't to be left out.

# 55

Somehow I'd have to get through the next few weeks. There were to be more shopping trips with Bridget and meetings with her mother. Details kept multiplying. Lists gave birth to more lists. It was distracting and absorbing. I was, after all, getting ready for my very own son's wedding. This was my real life—no fantasy here.

My free time was spent putting together a very special album of family pictures for Max to have and share with Bridget. It took some doing, but in the end, all the sorting and duplicating and mounting was worth it. It was quite outstanding. Now, I'd have to make one for Nicky as well.

Paul phoned with a brief report on Beth's wedding and to say good-bye.

"She was a beautiful bride. Everything went smoothly, and now they're off on their Far East adventure. How are you, girl?"

"I'm glad to hear that all went well. You sound pleased." I avoided answering his question. "When do you leave?"

"Soon. In three days. Damned if I know how I'll be ready,

but that leads me to the next part of my call. Jenny, is it possible for us to meet at our place tomorrow? I really want to see you."

Predictably, in spite of all I'd just been through when I heard about his upcoming trip with Kathy et al, I agreed to his plan, in awe of his ability to manipulate his life and the people who populated it.

He phoned early the following morning to cancel our date. So much for meeting at 'our place' where we were to spend a quiet evening getting caught up. Our various family obligations had been keeping us apart. For one thing, his daughter's wedding had consumed every spare moment. There was no room for me in that scenario.

He sounded a bit vague and uncertain and I got that old sick feeling in the pit of my stomach.

"Oh Paul, I really am disappointed. It's been so long since . . ."

"I know, Jenny, so am I, believe me. I'm stuck with clients for dinner."

"Come after dinner," I urged. "I'll be waiting. We can have some time and at least we'll be together. Dinner doesn't matter." I startled myself by pleading.

"It won't work tonight, dear. I simply can't." He put such a strong period to what he said, I couldn't argue further. "Look, we'll talk tomorrow and I'll tell you about Beth's wedding and the pitfalls to avoid for Max and Bridget. But right now I really have to move it. It's going to be a day and a half."

It was obvious he wanted to end the conversation as quickly as possible. His explanation was plausible and yet I continued to have a queasy reaction to it all. He had been as frustrated as I because we hadn't had time for each other and then after all the shifting and reshaping of schedules, we'd made tonight our night. What had happened? I shrugged and sighed again. Another pothole in the road we traveled.

In spite of my disappointment, I had to go into the city as planned. My hair needed cutting. I'd made the appointment over a week ago and intended to keep it. Also, I promised myself to take a look at a newly mounted photography exhibit at the Museum of Modern Art. And maybe my mother-of-the-groom gown was ready to be fitted. In any event there was plenty to do. In fact, I decided to call Guy and see if he would meet me at Wu Yee's later.

The day ran on and while the uneasy feeling persisted, I managed to accomplish a great deal and was feeling quite well satisfied when I decided to drop by our place, never mind Paul wasn't going to meet me there. I'd make a few calls and relax a bit before deciding how to wrap up my day. Guy wasn't available for dinner. He was in Gilroy at the ranch. And TJ was up in Oregon for a few days with Cara. Oh well.

The Jeep was left on the street as I had totally forgotten to put the beeper for the garage door back where it belonged after I had changed the battery.

Stepping into my magic garden inside the gate, I sensed something wasn't quite right. I moved slowly toward the door, pausing every few steps to listen to—I don't quite know what. Then, just as I was about to slip my key into the lock, I heard clearly Paul's voice coming through the door. My hand jerked back as though burnt.

"Come on, Babe. Hurry it up. I'm due back at the office right now. I warned you before we came I didn't have much time."

A woman answered him: "Who do you have to explain to? Aren't you the boss?" And then she laughed. It was a rather short, harsh sound.

"I'll pull the car out and meet you in front," is all he said. I was transfixed for a moment when suddenly he pulled the door open. We stared at each other for a split second and then I fled back across the garden toward the gate. Reflexively, I turned and looked back and saw him for an instance as he pulled the door shut. He must have fairly sprinted as he almost caught up with me at the curb. I dashed to my car, jumped in, and was pulling away as he was calling my name. "Jenny, Jenny, stop. I can explain . . ."

"Explain what?" I asked myself as I drove blindly away heading for the Bridge. Paul was there with another woman on the day he had broken a date with me. What more was there to say?

I don't remember the drive home. My mind was racing off in all directions. All I remember is the phone rang unanswered over and over throughout the evening. I was enraged and wild with hatred and had no one to rail against except myself. At once I was furious for turning tail and running away and then I asked what possible good could have come out of a confrontation with Paul had I stayed? The woman—whoever she was—would have been embroiled in it too. What a great show that would have been for the neighbors! That one image, that bit of comic relief broke my mounting tension.

Eventually the phone stopped and so did I. There was nothing to do, no place to go, and no one to turn to.

I screened all my calls the following day. Paul must have left a dozen messages.

"Jenny, please for God's sake pick up the phone. I must talk to you. I'm about to leave town . . ."

I paced up and down, past the answering machine. As he spoke, I became more and more sick to my stomach. "Jenny, please . . ."

I finally broke into the conversation he was having with the machine as I picked up the phone.

"Hello, Paul."

"Jenny, my God, I've been going crazy—I need to explain about the other night."

"There's nothing to explain. You made your choice for the evening and it was quite obvious I had no place in that little scenario."

"No, Jenny, you have it all wrong . . ."

"Women always do, Paul."

"Jenny, please let me tell you what it really was. Please listen to me." My heart was pounding in my ears as I stood rigidly holding the phone. I said nothing. He rushed on sounding more and more desperate: "The woman you must have heard through the door was Kathy."

"You really don't have to go into this. I don't need to hear a lengthy explanation. It was quite clear to me that you didn't want to tell me the whole story when you broke our date, and now I know why."

"Jenny, I did have dinner with clients as I told you."

"I know, you went with the available truth and omitted the rest of it."

"What would it serve to have talked about Kathy's plan?"

"But Paul, over all my objections, she was there at our very own place." I had begun to calm down when that part of it hit me again. "Tell me, how often has she been there? Have you slept with her in our bed? Tell me, Paul!" I was trembling so, I had to hold the phone with both hands.

"Damn it, Jen, that's crazy. Never before. She wanted to freshen up and demanded I take her there."

"Paul, Paul," I said with a deep sigh, "Just drop it please. This is exactly why I haven't wanted to talk to you."

"It's just—Jenny, I didn't want you to think I was there with some other woman."

"You were, Paul," I muttered under my breath.

I waited for him to suggest we meet, even for a coffee before he left. Any thing to take the sour taste out of my mouth from the episode the night before, but the invitation wasn't forthcoming, so I changed the subject completely by asking about his upcoming trip.

"It has turned into a three week jaunt what with the travel time and a couple of days in Paris." His attempt at being off hand didn't quite come off, not for me anyway.

"I'm not surprised," was all I could muster to say. "You have had a rough time lately between Vancouver and Beth's wedding, it is good you're getting away." I tried to sound sincere. The tension between us was barely beginning to ease off.

"You've no idea" he exclaimed with such vehemence, I had to laugh. In spite of myself.

He tried to make small talk for a few more moments, asking about Max etc.

"The plans are well under way for Max and Bridget's event. It's coming along soon." I ended lamely. "Thanks for asking."

I had nothing to say of unimportance. Small talk was the last thing I had in mind, and the important matter would have to wait.

"That's great. I just couldn't leave without making contact before I leave, Jenny. I miss you and I'll be thinking about you."

"I miss you, too, Paul. Go and come safely."

"I'll call as soon as I return."

"Yes. Good-bye, Paul."

"Take care of yourself, Jenny. Don't push too hard. The kids will have a good marriage even if the shade of roses isn't exactly as ordered for the wedding."

"Oh, dear. That bad, was it?"

"Almost. But as I told you, it all did go well, in the end."

"I'm glad, Paul. I really am. Well, good-bye again" I couldn't, upon pain of death, wish him a great trip. I hung up without any further comment, either by me or from him.

I was shaken by the call. Admittedly, I was relieved to find out there was no 'other woman' just the same old one I was up against daily—his wife. That was some small consolation. The enemy you know vs. the unknown enemy. Yet, I couldn't completely shake the feelings of betrayal. Paul had used my goofy idea about the building being fumigated to keep Kathy away before. Why couldn't have come up with something on his own this time?

The last we'd spoken, I'd wished him a happy wedding and good trip. I surmised we'd not talk again until after his return. And now I was left with his voice ringing in my ears, yet again. The lilt, the sweetness was impossible to brush aside. It always got to me. This time there was no laughter, though. Only the barest chuckle when he mentioned the slightly off color roses.

I can't be certain he sensed something was wrong. I only knew that our next meeting would have to be planned with complete privacy in mind. It would be utterly impossible to discuss anything serious in a public place.

My journal had been neglected for some weeks. Now, I was writing something everyday. I struggled to get a handle on the matter, to understand the meaning of it all. The *I Ching* was right. I kept going round and round in circles. And always ended up where we began, with nothing resolved. "The unknowable will become known," Wu Yee said. I could only ask to balance, meditate, and accept and expect that I would come to clarity before Paul and I met again.

## 56

The usual end of June weather had cleared leaving a soft light reflecting off the water. The sea was quiet, the tide low. I sat staring out of the window mesmerized by the changing colors of the water. I was day dreaming surrounded by photographs I'd piled on the couch. It was a quiet day, a lull before the storm of activity about to descend on me the last two weeks before Max and Bridget's 'great do.'

The photos were for the album I'd promised to Nicky—much like the one I'd recently completed for Max.

It's always amazed me what going through photographs does to people. We live life everyday forgetting much of what goes on—remembering some of what has caught our attention or piqued our curiosity. We're seriously engaged in all manner of activities and projects from morning till night and, many times, beyond into the following day. We're focused on the events of the moment and barely give a thought to what's gone on before.

Then someone opens and old photo album, and before you know it, half the day is gone looking at pictures, reminiscing, commenting on people and places seemingly long forgotten and instantly remembered because of one glance at some faded, old snapshot. And the day is enriched by connecting once more to our past, carrying forward the richness of experience while sharing it with others, if possible, or simply enjoying it alone.

My reverie was disturbed by the phone. I tried to ignore it, but it rang on and on insisting I pay attention. The answering machine wasn't picking up.

"Yes? Hello?" I wasn't listening particularly intently, so I didn't recognize the voice through some cellular phone-crackling disturbance. "Hello? Who is this, please? Who do you want to speak to?"

"Has it been so long that you don't recognize my voice?" The line suddenly cleared.

"Paul! How funny." My head felt light from a sudden rush of emotion.

"If it weren't for the lousy connection, I'd consider being insulted. How are you, Jenny?" He was laughing.

"I'm fine, thanks. Busy beyond busy, but fine. And you? How was your vacation?"

"It was splendid from top to bottom. The only thing missing was you."

"That would have been a bit awkward, having me along, don't you think?" The idea amused me, while my insides did flip-flops.

"Just a bit, maybe. Oh, Jenny, it's so good to hear your voice. When can I see you? What's your schedule this week? Or next or when?"

Questions on questions. I had to laugh.

"One at a time, please. My schedule is a nightmare after today until after the wedding. In fact, even then, it's tight. The TV people will be here almost immediately, and shortly after they're finished, I head east."

"I understand about the time before the wedding, but right after we'll have to find some time. Maybe you'll come up to Vancouver for a few days. I'm sure you'll need a change of pace, and I'm going to be there for awhile my next trip. How about it, Jen? Will you join me after Max's wedding?"

"No, Paul. I can't possibly." My heart sank. I wanted to say yes and knew I couldn't. "I told you the TV people are coming almost immediately. What little time I'll have will be spent unjunking the place. No time."

"Even for a quick coffee? I just want to see you, Jen. Won't you be in town at all?" He urged me to acquiesce.

"Of course, I'll be in. I simply can't before the wedding. Afterward, I'll see. Call me in a couple of weeks; I'll know better then." I know I sounded very offhand and totally disinterested. My heart was pounding in my ears. "Steady girl," I said to myself. "Balance." I had to get through this somehow.

"Jenny, I'm underwhelmed by your response to my invitation. I accept the timing is off, but 'call me in two weeks.' What's that about?"

"It's about business here at my house. And getting myself ready for the next event."

"I'll take you at your word, but I'd still like to have you join me. Maybe just for two days, after the wedding. Would that work?" He was trying to keep the conversation going. "I'm going to be spending a lot of time there," he explained.

"One day when I'm in town after the festivities, maybe. Please understand, Paul. It's an incredibly busy time, right now."

"I know, but . . ." His voice trailed off.

"I'm truly sorry, Paul. You'll have to accept what I'm saying. I know too well, it's not what you want, anymore than I, when you're not available. It's our lives; the way it is and presumably will always be." I instantly regretted adding that.

"So that's it. I've been gone, and before that, tied up; so now you're retaliating. Jenny, that's not like you." He sounded half angry and half defeated. I felt awful.

"You can't believe that of me, Paul. I've given you no reason to react this way."

"Until now, Jenny."

"Stop this, Paul. Don't spoil things. Please!"

"I'm sorry, Jenny. I'm making a mess of this call. It's just . . . I'm disappointed."

"Then 'be' disappointed. You must know I'm in a happy, exciting time, deeply involved in my two sons' weddings. I can't believe you expect me to drop everything and run off, as enticing as it may sound. On the other hand, how about joining me in the east before I leave for Scotland? That I can do."

I know what made me spring that on him. I hadn't planned it that way, but I was becoming irritated and felt like challenging him on his own turf, so to speak.

"Scotland? When's that?" Surprised.

"After Nick and Diane's wedding. I've a shoot."

"For how long?"

"I'm not certain. The company has plans beyond those for me. It's open-ended at the moment." I was calming down while warming to this shift of focus. "But you haven't answered my question. How about it, Paul? A few days on the Cape in early September? You've plenty of time to plan it." I held my breath, and then exhaled softly.

"There's no way I can break away at that time. I know it already, Jenny. I'll be spending an inordinate amount of time in Vancouver these next few months." He heaved a big sigh and continued past my silence. "I get it now. You're asked to shift plans and make room for me, with little or no pre-planning time. While I say I can't, even with months to plan."

"Listen, Paul. Let's just drop it. I know what you're up against. It would be a perfect time for me, as I said. And if by some happenstance your schedule changes, well, let me know. In the meantime, I'll phone, if and when I'm coming to town, and perhaps we can meet for a coffee or lunch. I promise."

Why did I add the 'if your schedule changes . . . ' bit, when

I fully intended to have the entire matter over sooner than later? I was being ruled by heart, again. It's too difficult to push away a loved person who loves you in return.

"Make it possible, please, Jenny."

"I will." I meant it.

"Have a happy time, my girl. Please. I'll call, if I may?" Never had he asked before.

"Of course."

"My best to Max and Bridget. My love to you, Jenny."

"I'll tell them. Mine to you, Paul. Bye."

I stared at the phone for several minutes. Afterthoughts, things I might have, even should have said, flooded my brain. I had a terrible time reconciling the two opposing facts: first, Paul had just returned from a three week vacation with his wife which, in his own words, was "splendid from top to bottom" and second, almost immediately upon his return, he calls me and wants, almost insists, I go away with him. What had become of this wonderful sensitive man's head...his thinking? Had I become such a 'sure thing' that all he had to do was beckon and I'd come running? Not a time for games.

For now, my time and energies had to be focused on my son.

I don't know how I did it. In my heart I wanted to drop everything and run to Paul. In my head I knew I had to toughen up. I yearned to be with him—again, alone. But there was no way I would relent. Circular. Round and round. Never changing. No. Eventually we'd end up feeling trapped, unsure. Our love dissipated by anxiety and uncertainty. No. It had to end, before disaster struck.

# 57

Oh happy day! The sun shone bright, the sky was clear, the bride radiant, the groom handsome. The flower girls didn't forget to spread the rose petals, and the best man had the rings ready at precisely the right moment. Champagne flowed, the orchestra played, delicious food was artfully displayed, and every possible blue, purple, pink, and white flower known to the botanical world was gathered in the garden of Bridget's parents. In short, it was a feast for all the senses. Dazzling!

"Did you ever see such a sight?" TJ asked. She had come up beside me sipping champagne and munching on some wonderful shrimp-in-dill thing set on a thick slice of cucumber. "Yum. This is good. I'll have to remember to do these soon again. Anyway, as I was saying, it's all so gorgeous. Those beautiful young people all done up grandly, they're making me swoon with delight."

"Swoon? Good grief, TJ, what have you been reading? Jane Austin, again? But yes, they are an extraordinary sight. The lavender and celadon organza dresses and those floppy garden hats—too much! It does look like a different time and place. I hope the video comes out well."

Max and Bridget and Nicky and Diane were having the most glorious time together. They switched partners and danced and laughed and switched back.

"Too bad we're not identical," Nicky said. "That's the one thing we've missed out on as twins—confusing our girlfriends."

"It's just as well, Nick. You'd have won my girls away," Max retorted.

"But not your bride!" Bridget slipped her arm through Max's and smiled up at him with such tenderness, I thought I'd swoon.

He bent his head down and kissed her and hugged her tight. I thought of Tom and me and winced inside. Tears had sprung unbidden to my eyes, and I had to turn away, lest I be seen.

After the festivities, rather than stay with TJ, she came up with me to the beach to help get my place ready for the TV crew. Anyway, she wanted to be there, too, for the fun of it, and I was, of course, more than happy for her help and particularly for her company.

Poochie hadn't been up for ages and he and Honey frolicked and played like a couple of puppies.

Guy would be coming in time for the shoot. In the meantime, the advance crew arrived to look over the place thoroughly, checking the best viewpoints and all that is involved in setting up. They asked if the dogs could disappear for a few days. TJ and I looked at each other and decided she and they had best go back to her home. We'd make better plans for the next shoot, so she could participate in the action.

On the way to town, I told TJ I had promised Paul I'd call him if I were coming into the city.

"Did you reach him before we left?" TJ asked.

"No. I didn't try. I'm so torn, TJ, facing him over a table—experiencing that lovely man again while holding to my vow, seems impossible." I was wretched just thinking about it. "You know he wanted me to go to Vancouver with him this week. I thought my heart would break into little pieces when I said no."

"You poor kid. It must have been awful." TJ was clucking and shaking her head. "How I wish I could come to some solution, but I'm very much afraid, Jen, there isn't one at hand. Not unless you're willing to push for divorce. His silence on the subject speaks volumes and I'm at a dead loss about that one. Why hasn't he?"

"All I know is he keeps saying 'hold on' and 'it's not the right time yet'...all the cliches. And I'm not ready for the divorce scene on my own 'yet'. I know we must break it off, there's really no other way. In the meantime, I'll meet him if he's available and take it from there."

"Oh, he'll be available. I can promise you that. He'll make it happen. Do you want to ask him over? At least you'd have some privacy to talk. I can make myself scarce for a couple of hours with no problem."

"No thanks. Meeting him out will be better. I'm not prepared for more today, although I feel the time approaching fast."

"Whatever you say."

We did meet. TJ was right. He canceled appointments and rescheduled a staff meeting for the following day. He asked if I'd pick him up and could we have a late lunch at Cliff House.

"Do you remember the first time we were here?" He reached across the table for my hand.

"Of course I do. You sat with your back to the view exactly as you're doing now." I smiled.

"The view was in front of me, exactly as it is now." He kissed my fingertips. I drew my hand back. It felt burned. "Tell me about the wedding and the TV show and Nick's plans and what's all this about Scotland?" Covering the time between us in a flood of questions. Making contact, catching up. The technique was so familiar by now I couldn't keep from laughing.

"Which answer do you want first? And how much time have you?"

"As much as a whole life, Jenny, if I could." He looked away for a moment and continued. "Just keep talking. I love hearing your voice." He smiled that same smile that melted my heart almost a year before. I could barely stand it. Inside I was shouting, "you can . . . get a divorce!"

And so instead, I told him about my beautiful son and his beautiful bride and my other beautiful son and his soon-to-be-bride and got teary.

"Jenny, Jenny, how I wish I could have shared those days with you, even as I wanted to share Beth's day." His voice dropped and he was not smiling. "It's tough, girl, very tough." He shook his head.

"And there's nothing to be done?" I asked. "Nothing, Paul?" We looked into each other's eyes and looked away. It was too painful. He simply couldn't address the question. And I was incapable of pushing any further.

"I can't believe it, Jenny. You haven't finished your crab." Paul was trying to lighten up a bit.

"I guess for once in my life I'm not hungry. Anyway, it's getting late and I must drop you and head back very soon."

"Tonight? I thought you'd be staying over."

"No. I have to be in place in the morning. The TV people will be there bright and early."

"I'm leaving day after tomorrow, Jen, for the rest of the week. Can you possibly join me on the weekend? Surely they won't be working then?"

"Paul, please try to understand. I can't do it. I must take care of things at home those two days, and then they'll be back on Monday for the entire week. Soon, I'm off to the east with TJ to visit friends and join in Nick's pre-nuptial festivities. Oh, it's a busy time."

I tried to sound enthusiastic and upbeat. It was tough to do at the moment, and yet I was truly happy in that other, orderly part of my life. My real life, my life-is-so-daily life.

"I'm happy for you, Jenny. Life is full and good for you. I only wish we could share more of it."

"Well, it's just not that way." I put on my best brusque voice and firm face. It didn't hold up. "Paul, that's just another reason I can't join you. It only makes me want more when we have that kind of precious time together. It's become too difficult to part, to keep saying good-bye. Oh damn! I didn't want to go into all of this, here, at this moment." I prayed for self-control.

"Jenny? Are you saying what I'm afraid you are? If you can't tell me now, when and where are you planning to?" His face was creased with anxiety.

"Soon, Paul. We have to talk privately, soon. Somehow, we'll find time when you're back, before I leave . . . sometime. I've even thought of writing to you or sending you pages from my journal." I let my voice drop.

"No more, Jenny. I don't want you to go on, please. Let's go. You've a long ride ahead of you and I don't want you upset. Come on."

He all but pulled me up from the table and we headed up the road to my car, his hand on my elbow guiding me as he had done so many times before.

He took me in his arms beside the car and we both held on for strength and dear life. We released each other and kissed lightly. I got in. He drove. Neither of us could utter a sound.

At the garage, where I dropped him, Paul sat a moment behind the wheel before trading places with me. He took my hand and kissed the palm before he got out. "Move over, lady, and drive carefully. We'll talk, Jenny."

"Yes. We'll talk. Travel safe, Paul."

I pulled away without looking back. Tears were rolling down my cheeks. I remember nothing about my drive home. The bridge, the road down to the beach—nothing. How I managed it, I'll never know. Mere words cannot begin to describe what I felt.

# 58

**G**uy joined me, as planned. Working with him on any project was always gratifying. His professionalism mixed with his light touch made any set of circumstances surrounding work bearable. In the case at hand, those attributes made it remarkably good fun, as well.

We dodged camera crews while taking our own pictures. All hands were busy and, at times, it got a bit chaotic, but good humor prevailed. Celestina provided the good food.

In spite of the good time we were having, my thoughts were in Vancouver. I fantasized the days and nights Paul and I could have had. My heart regretted my decision not to join him, while at the same time, my head knew I was right. Very soon it would be time to face Paul.

As soon as he returned from Vancouver, he contacted me. He wanted to set up a date that included spending some hours together at my house. My reluctance was evident as I tried to dissuade him. I didn't trust myself alone with him.

In the end, I realized I'd be better off in my own home. More secure in my own surroundings as we talked our way out of our dilemma and out of each other's lives.

"The crew is still here, although I think tomorrow will be the wrap-up day. They've said, barring any mishaps, they'll be out of here by noon."

"Great! I'll phone you from my car and check on what's happening. The worse thing that could happen is we'd overlap a bit."

"I'd planned on having lunch for them . . ." I began.

"Go ahead. I'll join you," he interrupted.

"No, I started to say I'd planned it, but they said they'd rather have me join them for dinner at Wu Yee's Saturday night. So instead, I'll provide the usual coffee and donuts."

"And maybe even some brownies?"

I laughed and said, "And maybe even some brownies."

"Then it's OK to come around noon?"

"Yes, and remember to call from the top of the hill."

"I will, and Jenny, thanks." In the end, I doubted he'd be thanking me.

Paul didn't ask and I didn't say what I'd do about Guy. As luck would have it, Guy decided to go back to San Francisco that very night. I heaved a sigh of relief. It meant I didn't have to enlist him as a co-conspirator. I asked if he'd be at the wrap up dinner at Wu Yee's Saturday night.

"I wouldn't miss it, Jen. I'm going to the ranch tomorrow and plan to return in time to be there."

"Don't forget to bring some garlic to Wu Yee." I felt more relaxed again and I decided not to say a word about my plan for the following day. He'd hear about it soon enough. I needed neither encouragement nor advice. I could blunder through on my own.

## 59

The morning was hazy and overcast. The weatherman had a rather cavalier attitude about it. He said that it could sprinkle a little or not—take your choice. Apparently, the weather patterns were crisscrossing and almost anything could happen. He did predict, however, that it would straighten out by early afternoon and not to worry. It was not "earthquake weather." That was a relief.

I pondered the cost of weather satellites as I often had in the past, and wondered, yet again, why it was always so hit-and-miss. Frequently, they'd say we might have 'scattered showers' when any fool could tell, merely by looking out the window, it was pouring outside. I guess they don't have windows in studios.

Sam and his crew didn't seem to mind the sky. They were finishing up with extra footage of a particular area of interest to them. They even suggested Honey and I could walk or trot through if we wanted to. It gave us something to do besides hang around the coffeepot.

I threw a stick for her, and then we played 'frisbee.' She

probably wondered why we were romping at this time of day, but she asked no questions and had a great time.

They had just finished loading up their vans and were saying good-bye when the phone rang. I waved them off and hurried into the house.

The machine had picked up and I heard Paul's voice tinged with worry.

"Jenny? Jen? Are you there?"

I grabbed the phone. "Paul? Hi. I'm here. I was just saying good-bye to everyone. Where are you?"

"I'm half way down the hill, Jen. I'll be there shortly, OK?"

"OK." I was murmuring affirmations by the time I hung up. Thank you for strength of purpose. Thank you for equanimity. Thank you for this being the highest good for all concerned.

I splashed cool water on my face, added a bit of lipstick, brushed my hair and retied it. By then I was a nervous wreck. The doorbell sounded.

"Come in, Paul." I stepped aside as Honey bounded to him.

"Hi, Honey. I'm glad to see you." He patted her and looked up at me. "You, too. I'm glad to see you, girl." He straightened up and looked around. "It's been awhile. It's good to be here."

We were both under terrible strain. The space between us was thick with tension. We each knew this was to be difficult at best, devastating at worst.

We were still standing in the entry when Paul started to talk to me. "Jenny, there's no sense in skirting the issue I came to discuss with you. I won't even try, but do you think we could sit down someplace and maybe have a drink of something before we get too serious?"

We laughed and broke the tension for the moment.

"How about iced coffee? And some pasta salad? We can sit outside, now it's clearing up," I suggested.

"Great. Here, let me help you." He went to the drawers and took silver and napkins, reached up for plates and glasses, too.

He was comfortable here. He fell into step with the rhythm of my preparations in his usual way. An observer would have thought we'd been going through the same routine for years. He was his easy self again.

We carried things outside, set up and sat down. Not before he took me in his arms. I let him without any reluctance. I needed to feel that embrace once more. It would have to last me for a very long time.

"Now, that's better," he said. "I don't feel the executioner is about to arrive." He tried to smile, but looked anxious instead. We picked at our salads and made small talk for awhile. Finally, I put down my fork and looked at him. "Paul, I don't know exactly where to begin . . ."

"Just anywhere, Jenny. There's no right place. But I have to tell you first—you look so good sitting there. Serious and perplexed and beautiful. I wish I could make the uncertainty vanish for you."

"Aren't you ever uncertain about us, Paul?"

"No, not really. You see, I'm certain about the most important part of it. About wanting you in my life. What I am uncertain about is how to keep you there without hurting you."

"Doesn't it hurt you? Don't you ever want more?"

"Of course, I do. I've told you over and over I could go on with you forever the way we are together. The way we are right this minute."

"Do you ever consider what this whole thing is doing to your marriage? Doesn't that bother you at all?"

"It's not doing anything, Jenny. I assure you. Kathy knows nothing. She goes about her business taking everything and everyone in her life for granted. I simply 'settled.' Most people eventually do, you know. Settle, I mean."

"Yes, I believe that, too," I said.

He continued: "For me there would always be a void. I'm a romantic and I'm a high energy, highly charged male, which, by the way, is why I work so hard and such long hours. I've sublimated my desires for years. I've told you all this before, Jenny."

I nodded. "When you came into my life, it was as though I'd been struck by lightening. My fantasies, my wildest dreams were standing there before me. I had to act or lose the chance of experiencing them, forever. And so I acted, without guile, without thought of consequence and without guilt."

"Paul . . ." He reached for my hand.

"I have done my best to protect her, to shield her from any fall out from our relationship. That part hasn't always been easy for me. You've heard about a few of the blow-ups we've had. But, truly, she is oblivious to my emotional needs. She blocked them out years ago completely, for lack of any desire on her part to understand. I'm not speaking only of sex. I'm speaking of intimacy as you and I know it—experience it. Kathy is frightened by the mere thought of it. She feels too vulnerable to trust feelings, to share them openly." He stopped abruptly and looked away. He turned back to me and said, "It makes me sad sometimes, but guilty about us? No. I don't feel guilty."

I took a deep breath and began my well-rehearsed statement. "Sometimes, Paul, I feel old and out-dated, literally guilty for feeling guilt pangs about our relationship. No matter what you say about your relationship with Kathy, she is your wife now, in the present, and the present is all we have.

Paul started to speak. "Jenny, I . . ."

"No, this time let me finish. You've said your vow to her on your wedding day doesn't permit you to divorce her, and yet you are eagerly breaking another vow you took that very day. I just don't understand it. As long as the 'till death do us part' stands, the 'keep myself only unto you' can be broken? Without remorse?"

Once more he started to speak. I held up my hand to stop him and continued: "I, on the other hand, was parted by death and kept myself only unto my husband until I met you. Tell me, Paul, do you think of yourself as standing on higher moral ground than I?"

"My God, Jenny, of course not."

"Then I don't understand how your application of religious prohibitions squares with what we're doing, and I am increasingly uncomfortable because of it." I stood up and was pacing about. "This, simply put, is not my cup of tea."

We faced each other directly. Paul was agitated. "Surely Jenny, you can't think it's all fun and games for me? What's wrong with you? Don't you know I'm being torn apart by this? Not your cup of tea? Well, it's damn well not mine either! I know it doesn't make sense on the face of it. It's just something I feel and feel very strongly . . . in the now, as you put it. That doesn't diminish my feelings for you in any way. I care. I care deeply." His voice broke with emotion. "I wish I weren't so conflicted, but, in truth, I am. You say you want more, and I know it. I want more, too, and I can't do it, not now, and maybe not ever. I can't say. And I can't try to keep you by pretending otherwise, much as I want to."

"No, that's no good. We've been too honest to start lying now." I stopped pacing and looked directly at him.

"Lying has never been a strong point with me, Jen." He smiled trying to lighten the burden of this arduous conversation.

We were getting nowhere as we sought a common ground on which to maintain our relationship. I, for one, felt completely overwhelmed and could say nothing.

Paul spoke again. "It has been pure joy for me until very recently. I thought I could encapsulate us, keep us separate. It hasn't worked. You invade my thoughts every day."

"For me, too, Paul. No pain, only pleasure. Now, I can't deny my feelings any longer and so," I was struggling, "we must put an end to this. I've said I don't want to become a family friend. I don't know yet what, if anything, I'll be capable of sustaining." I was crushed inside.

"Jenny, Jenny, I don't want to hear you say that. I don't want to lose you." Paul was in shock. "And I have no right to ask you to continue." He had jumped up and was standing holding my hands.

*A Small Flirtation*

And so we decided to part. Each of us broken-hearted. On my side there was a strange sense of release. I'm sure Paul felt the same. Not virtuous, no way. That didn't enter into it. It was far too late for virtue. Relief. At least for this moment. The stark reality of our decision would come later. Soon enough we'd have to deal with it.

"Leave now, Paul. Please. Before I lose my courage. You know I'm a devout coward. I'll never be able to replay this scene." I tried valiantly to smile. I failed miserably.

"I'm going, Jenny. But tell me one thing—if what we're now doing is so right, how come I feel so utterly devastated? I can barely speak. Somehow, someway, it will work out. It has to."

"Maybe. Someday."

And he left.

My journal became the place to pour out my feelings. I couldn't speak of them to anyone. Neither to Guy nor TJ nor my sons. Nobody was to know the depth of my despair. No one. Not yet. I had to pull out of this on my own. After all, I got into it on my own, and it was my choice to end it. I'd overcome it alone, too.

I wrote into the night:

". . .and so now it's over. Or is it? My soul knows yours—you—so well—over and over through eons of time we have been together. What is the meaning of this heart wrenching unrequited recognition? This strange coming toward one another only to stay apart. What the lesson? When our time? How? Why? It seems so unknowable.

Is there an answer? Do you know it? Share. Please.

Care always.

I do."

# PART 6

## 60

"Max, Darling! Are you back? How's Bridget? Was Maui wonderful?" What a relief to hear his voice.

"Oh, Jen, it was wonderful. Super! Terrific!" He quieted down when he said, "It's very different. Being married, I mean. Isn't it?"

"Very." I winced inside.

"Having an affair, even living together—it's just not the same."

"You're right, of course. I'm fascinated you've discovered it already. It's the commitment, you know."

"Yes, that's it, of course. I find it in all kinds of little ways. You're right; it is fascinating. Anyway, how are you, M'am? How'd the TV gig go? When do you leave for Boston or is it New York first? Tell me, tell all." His enthusiasm was infectious. It was exactly the lift I needed from the right person, too.

"Well, let's see. The 'TV gig,' as you put it, just finished a few days ago. It was interesting and I learned quite a lot. In fact, it was great fun in the end."

"In the end?" he asked.

"Well, I admit it did take some little getting used to. Having all those strangers all over the house—inside and out, to say nothing of the heavy equipment. I must say it did cause quite a stir in the neighborhood." I chuckled.

"I'll bet it did."

"As to when I'm leaving? TJ and I will go to Boston and on to the Cape for a week. That way, we'll be available for Nicky and Diane's pre-nuptial festivities. By the way, you do remember I'll be going on to Scotland from the east? So after the wedding, I'd thought of stopping in New York for a few days, but I've begun to reconsider that part."

"Why is that?"

"It seems like too much. The city will be quite warm and muggy by then. And the time frame for meeting the production crew in Edinburgh is such, that if I skip New York, I'll have a couple of days to adjust to the time and reacquaint myself with the city. I love it there and haven't been back since your father and I were there together. It must be twelve or fifteen years ago, hard as it is to believe."

"Your new plan sounds better to me, too. Are they going to keep you busy all fall?"

"Looks that way. By the way, Diane's parents are already planning Christmas for all of us. Would that suit you two?" I was beginning to understand the push-pull of family holiday times from a first person singular point of view.

"Would it be OK if Bridget's folks have Thanksgiving this year, then? Including TJ and the rest, of course?" he asked.

"Oh, Max. It's going to start getting complex, isn't it? Good Lord—from the three of us we've really grown!" It was an exciting prospect.

"You've always said the more the merrier, Jen."

"You're right, of course. Don't fret about it the first day back from your honeymoon, Max. It will all work out. It always does." Except when it doesn't.

The conversation went on and on. We loved talking, my boys and I—always. It was decided they'd make the drive up in a few days. They each had some time before job commitments took hold of their lives again. They'd stay up during my packing and closing the house, too. Then they'd drive me to TJ's the day before she and I were to leave. Nice. A neat plan.

I had discussed nothing of my shutting down Paul's and my affair. Thank God for the sensitivity of my sons and my dearest friends—no one had broached the subject, even obliquely. Max and Nicky were enmeshed in the new configurations of their lives. In any event, neither would have dreamed of asking about it. They would have considered it a gross intrusion and they would have been right

There would be ample time during TJ and my travels together to talk about it. Frankly, I wished she could be with me abroad, but it didn't work for either of us at this time. Maybe on another jaunt. In the meantime, she would take over the complete care of Honey upon her return. The dogs would be in 'summer camp' while we were gone. Everything was falling into place nicely. Everything, but my heart. It was falling apart.

# 61

September in New England is a very different setting than July in California. It was still softly summer, though the burning edge was gone. Everyone looked tanned and healthy. The wedding plans were in full swing.

This time my contribution was an old-fashioned clambake. Oyster stew, steamed clams, boiled lobsters, corn on the cob, gallons and gallons of beer and quarts of melted butter.

The rehearsal had gone as well as could be expected, what with the twins high jinks. Max made a big deal about teaching Nicky proper bridegroom decorum. He took Nicky's place, and at the end of the rehearsal grabbed Diane and held her in a backbreaking bend to show what a real 'you may kiss the bride' embrace should be.

We were in high good humor and went about eating and kidding around afterward into the wee small hours of the morning.

"What a wrinkled, buttery mess I am! Your grandmother would have said this kind of meal should be eaten in the privacy of one's own bath tub!"

"Boy, she was right, Jenny. I sure wish she and Pa were still with us." Nicky smiled sweetly and gave me a sticky hug.

"Me, too, Nicky. They'd have loved all of this and be proud of you two, besides."

"I don't think I'll ever get clean in time for the ceremony," TJ moaned. "I've never seen such a glorious mess! Can you imagine we ate mud pies on top of all that stuff?" She groaned.

"Come on, gals. I think it's time we roll ourselves out of here and let the really young carry on for as long as they like. I, for one, need my beauty rest." Guy waved to the assembled group, took TJ and me in hand, and headed us back to the hotel.

"Thank heavens the wedding is still over twelve hours away. If it were a morning ceremony, I think I'd need a seeing-eye dog."

"Make that two seeing-eye dogs, TJ, and I'm the mother of the groom! I can't imagine why I'm wearing that funny, taupe chiffon dress."

"You're wearing it because it's positively divine on you with your coloring. Even after carousing all night, by 2:00 p.m. tomorrow, you'll have recovered."

"The excitement will carry you through, Jen, and I promise not to take any of those lousy grab shots of you that you hate. How's that for a concession to friendship?" Guy laughed.

"You're too kind, Guy. I promise to return the favor in that case."

"You two never get tired of needling each other, do you? Give it up for this night and let's get some sleep. Good night, Guy." She was pulling me down the hall.

"Good night, my favorite female types."

"Jenny, come on, or I'll lock you out."

I was on the edge of hysteria; I was so wound up. I think it's known as over compensating. And, boy, was I doing a whole lot of that. Well, it was seeing me through a rough time. What was it Paul had said that last time we were at Cliff House? "It's tough, girl, very tough." Yes. It was tough. Very tough. Paul, Paul—where are you right this minute?

"You've managed to pull yourself together very well, Jen. Witch hazel eye pads really do a job, don't' they?" TJ was being solicitous.

"All I know is I'm glad I've a couple of days in Edinburgh to recover from all this hilarity before I have to do anything productive. Come on. Let's go see what's going on, where."

Another gorgeous garden setting. More beautiful young people decked out in all their finery in autumnal colors. Happy friends and relatives. My eyes and ears were filled with sights and sounds I'd carry in memory for the rest of my days.

"Come dance with me, Jenny." Nicky handed his beautiful bride over to Guy, took me in his arms and swung me out onto the dance floor and back in time over thirty years. He looked like Tom; he smiled Tom's smile; he even danced like Tom. I missed him more acutely than ever before.

These are the moments of bittersweet memories that come upon one at the happiest times in life. "Nothing is ever allowed to be perfect in itself," I thought and instantly corrected myself. The moment of perfection is still perfect.

How often I've had to relearn that lesson.

Guy cut in and waltzed me away from the crowd, after returning Diane to Nicky. They moved away as one.

"Break it up you two. You look far too serious." Max was shining with pure pleasure. "My bride would accept a dance with you Unc, if you asked. I want to try some fancy stuff with M'am to that Salsa music." And off we went.

"By golly, M'am, you're really a knock-out!"

"My gallant son!" I was pleased beyond pleased.

"No, I mean it. You're terrific."

"Thanks, Max, you're pretty terrific yourself."

We stopped hopping about. I went for the iced champagne punch. Max had the straight stuff.

"When do you plan to be home, Jen?" he asked.

"I'll be back for sure for the Thanksgiving and Christmas holidays. Then I'll probably be off again."

"Will you enjoy work without Guy?"

"In fact, I hope he'll join me at some point in the next several months. It will depend on how projects go at the ranch. Anyway, I expect I'll have plenty of help along the way. I'm rather excited about the notion of working in television. It's an entirely new experience."

"Hey, look, they're about to cut the cake!"

## 62

TJ and Guy saw me off before returning home. Guy felt a pinch in his heart for not accompanying me. I assured him I'd be fine and that he could catch up with me anywhere and anytime he chose.

The trip was pleasant and uneventful. "The Flying Scot" from London up to Edinburgh was still a crack train with an excellent dining car in the old manner. Oxtail soup and turbot with boiled white potatoes and Brussels sprouts. Who could forget it? Oh yes, and a raspberry fool for dessert.

I spent my first two days revisiting old familiar places. The Festival had ended and the fall school term had begun. Tourists left. Things were returning to normal in that wonderful old city. The pipers still marched up Prince's Street everyday at noon sounding their drones and playing their rousing songs.

I walked the castle grounds one early morning in my Gordon kilt and was greeted by a tall, gaunt Scot, "Good morning, clanswoman. And how are you this fine day?"

"Ah, well," I answered, "and you, sir?"

He saluted and strode on. Where, but in Scotland? I was refreshed and couldn't wait to get to work.

The time there was fascinating. Those of us in core crew traveled together, adding local pros as needed along the way. We started in Edinburgh, then up to Fort William and onto Inverness. Down the west side of the country to Troon, where some of the die-hard golfers knocked off early to experience one of the game's toughest world-class courses. We worked our way on down through Ayrshire and Robert Burns country.

We ate kippers and herring and bangers and orange yolk eggs. Had short bread and strawberry jam and marmalades so thick and dark I couldn't relate them to anything called by the same name in the states. Oatcakes and Scotch broth and haggis. Well, I didn't eat haggis, but others did. And Chinese food like no other, served by Scottish-Chinese who spoke English with Scottish brogues.

We ended up in Avimore before returning to Edinburgh. A ski resort in off-season, it was decided, would make a rather interesting and almost spooky location without crowds of vacationers. The episodes were moving into a more mysterious genre. They played on the superstitions rife in Scottish lore.

I'd fallen into a nice, easy relationship with my fellow artists of the lights and cameras. A companionable, comradely atmosphere surrounded our work. We actually had very little to do with the others.

Quite frankly, I was just as happy Guy hadn't joined me. No one knew me; therefore, I had no one to listen to my sad story, no one to commiserate with me. The distance helped as I labored to gain some perspective on the subject of Paul and me.

We'd broken up before we caused each other unnecessary pain and damage. I hated being so sensible, and fought against calling him, more than once.

Return trips home for the holidays were made, as promised. There were new family configurations coupled with new ways of celebrating and a wish now and then for the old ways. Always the yin and yang of life. Always new learning experiences.

When I was home, I was busy catching up on the various family and friends, paying bills, playing with Honey, and generally enjoying my house. And then I'd get a call and be off again. Little time to mope and ponder. That is not to say I didn't feel bereft from time to time. And sometimes angry at the whimsy of fate. I'd had enough of cosmic jokes. Occasionally I would think I saw Paul. Amazingly I never did.

Once, when I returned to Vancouver Island, I almost called to see if he was in town. Tho' sorely tempted, I resisted. My idea for the Sunset Magazine piece on the gardens had been bought, and I returned for "Winter in the Garden."

I wandered around the city reliving my glorious days there with Paul. By now, these months later, I wasn't even certain he'd be receptive to a call from me. I'd have died at politeness. That, I couldn't have handled. I continued to resist and returned home.

# 63

Every year I seem to be playing catch-up. I'm never ready for the change of month, let alone the change of season. January is spent getting over November and December. It also is useful for becoming accustomed to writing the New Year on one's checks. February is so short it doesn't exist for me, except for Valentine's Day. March is the month I usually put away my Christmas cards and get ready for the April property and income taxes, so it's a bust.

May is my month. May and September—these are the months I wait for all year. May, breathlessly awaits summer as its flowers unfold in all their lush, young beauty. Daylight savings time has been with us for awhile and the lingering effect of sunlight gives a special glow to early evening skies. Summer comes and goes in a flash, and then September. Maybe, because it's my natal month, but somehow September embodies everything I love about life. The seeds have long since been sown and the harvest is upon us. Late summer fruits are at their luscious best. Grapes are firm and ripe, filled with rich juices. The fields are being mown, and young children are returning to school with renewed vigor. The days are still sweet smelling and warm with the barest hint of autumn in the air. And then the gallop of days through the fall festivals and holidays, and suddenly another year has gone.

TJ and I were having lunch at the Cliff House shortly after I returned from an assignment. We'd not had much time alone in a very long time. This was an afternoon we'd set aside strictly for ourselves.

"I can't believe it will soon be a year since Max and Bridget's wedding. How is it possible? I know I've been extremely busy, but an entire year?" I was incredulous.

"You most certainly have been busy, Jenny. The first few months following both of the weddings were an absolute blur of activity. In truth, this entire year plus has been."

"I know, and it's been perfect for me that way. I'd have died of remorse if I'd had nothing to do that really engaged me. No, the activity, the new aspects of my professional life has been my best antidote to a broken heart." I sounded a whole lot more matter of fact than I felt.

"What's next on the agenda? Is there anything in the offing?" TJ asked.

"Maybe a trip to Alaska and the Arctic Circle; but, I'm not so sure I want to take it. It sounds very cold." I laughed. "The other choice may be somewhere in China including river trips. I'll know soon. The company has been working on a plan and filling out forms, etc. But enough of my travels. Tell me more about you and Bret."

"We're doing very well. Better than I'd ever thought possible. He's a lovely man and I'm quite fond of him, really."

"Wow! That's a huge expression of passion! Quite fond? How quaint. Whatever happened to 'madly in love'?"

"You're so easy to put on, it's positively pathetic, Jenny. Bret and I are in love and we're considering his moving in and living together. How's that?"

"More like it, TJ. I'm thrilled!"

"Don't worry, though, your room will be intact and you'll come and go as always, at will; that's part of the deal."

"I'm very touched, and I'd be more than put out if it was to be any other way. Tell me more. How are things at work? Is he busy?"

"Do you mean what do I know of Paul?" I shrugged. She smiled. "Bret doesn't say too much. They work on different projects, you know. I gather Paul's practically been living in Vancouver. The job's taken on a life of its own and he spends much more time there than was expected. Other than that, I don't know much."

"Does he ever contact you, TJ? I mean, do you ever just talk?" I was longing for news. We hadn't broached the subject in months.

"Not really. Other than the time you know about, after I returned from Nicky and Diane's wedding. You'd gone on to Scotland and I came home with Guy and the others. I'm sure you remember?" TJ queried.

"Yes, of course, I remember. He was having his own bad time. Have you seen him?" I persisted.

"On rare occasions Bret and I see him for dinner."

"With Kathy, too?" I couldn't seem to help myself.

"Once or twice at business parties. Evidently, she still doesn't come into town very often." TJ shrugged and made light of it. "How do you feel about it all now, nearly a year's gone by since you called a halt?"

"Well, to give you a quick bottom line, I think Wu Yee's comment last year that destiny was at work here, hasn't panned out. At least, not the way I'd wanted it. However, the grief has dissipated. Only the sense of loss is still so great that it tends to overwhelm me from time to time, when I let it." As I seemed to be doing now.

TJ shook her head. "I haven't figured out, yet, why you two met. There had to be a karmic reason. It hasn't unfolded entirely, yet. I think that's what Yee was referring to," TJ explained. "The coming together overtook both of you precisely the same moment. Synchronicity, plain and simple. It was out of character for you and for Paul."

"It is almost a year since we 'called a halt.' One year and probably not one whit closer than we were when we met."

"But how could you be? How could you know more than you did with that first flash of recognition?" TJ asked.

"Was it ancient memory, TJ? Or fantasy fulfilled? Is there a difference?"

"I don't know, Jenny. Perhaps they are one and the same. Perhaps fantasy fulfilled is tied to ancient memory," TJ conceded.

"He literally flew into my life." I laughed at the memory.

"As you flew into his," TJ nodded.

I continued: "Timidly, at first, I admit, and amused. Somewhat abashed, maybe. Laughing and, yes, a bit scared. And daring, too. When had I ever dared such a thing before? To say and be. Mostly just to BE with each other—who we are. Then, with fantasies flying, we linked arms with Fate."

"And soon you became dear to each other, out loud," TJ interrupted, "for all the world to see. You two terrified me in the beginning. You seemed to be protected by an aura of anonymity that screened you as you were oblivious to your surroundings." She shook her head in disbelief at the memory.

"Oh, TJ. How I prayed for it to work out for us. I remember early on hoping with all my might that one day he'd tell me he wasn't really married—that he was separated or some such thing." I sighed. "One day I'll understand, but now all I can be is sad and, yet, grateful to have experienced him even for a little while."

TJ nodded. "Gratitude for a taste is a paltry substitute for an entire life."

"At least I found out I could love again, I wasn't sure. You can't choose who you're going to love. Would it were that simple. Now tell me about Guy from your perspective." I wanted to change the subject. It was still too painful for any more discussion.

"I've seen him only briefly this month. He seems quite good

to me. It was the thought of marriage that had him spooked." TJ laughed. "It's just as well Laura and he rethought the whole thing"

"Why don't they live together for awhile? Like you and Bret? No one's pushing them."

"I suggested it, Jen, but he said no. Laura is really committed to marriage and children. You know Guy always says our three kids are his family." She shook her head. "Six months ago, I'd have sworn we'd be caught up in plans for their wedding. Instead, right now she's deeply involved in the promotion of her children's TV series and Guy has lost himself in more garlic."

"It's only my opinion, TJ, but I think Laura pushed too hard. I can understand his being scared off. She's never been married and he had that early, disastrous, short-lived one."

"It's hard to believe now, isn't it, Jenny? Will you ever forget that New Years Eve? I still shudder whenever I think about it" TJ winced at the memory.

Guy had a fling with the ranch foreman's daughter—never mind the old 'farmer's daughter' jokes—it's the truth and the whole disaster ensued. They'd known each other since they were kids. The problem was neither set of parents approved of their budding romance and tried to break it up. The predictable thing happened: We were all at this New Year's Eve party, had too much to drink and after some kidding around on our parts, Guy and his girl ran off and got married in Arizona.

The police found them in a motel in Yuma. There were hysterics and recriminations—the humiliation was overwhelming. In the end, Guy left the ranch and entered graduate school at UC Davis where he continued his studies in agronomy. The rest is history.

"TJ, do you imagine the memory of that party had any bearing on Guy's sudden break up with Laura? It did happen shortly after the New Year? It was a nice interlude for them and they seemed to be building something permanent." I shrugged.

"Who's to know what the real story is? You know Guy's still in love with you, Jenny, and as time goes by, he seems more content than ever with his work at the ranch plus his involvement with you in the photography department."

"I admit I've missed that part of it while he was romancing Laura. Also, our times together weren't the same. Bret fits into our pattern. She's just…"

"Too young? That's my take on it. She was never fully comfortable with all our history. It does tend to be somewhat exclusionary. One thing, for certain, their romance kept him off your case and mine too for awhile!" We both laughed at that. "By the way, Jenny, will you stay over with me tonight? I need your opinion on some things I want to do at the house. You could shop with me for some fabrics and maybe we can get Guy to join the three of us for dinner." Enough gossip and speculation, it was time to move on to other matters.

"I'd love to, TJ. It's been too long since we've had that kind of day."

We finished our lunch and were leaving Cliff House when I saw a little red car pull up in front and hesitate.

I reflexively grabbed TJ's arm as I stared.

"It's not Paul, Jenny. Relax. Oh dear, your startle-reaction is quite overwrought."

"I'm afraid so. It was so unexpected and yet this is a favorite place of his, as well," I said ruefully. All the same, it was good to be back in the city, even for a bit.

## 64

We went through TJ's stunning house room by room as she insisted things were past worn out and out dated.

"What all have you in mind to do?" I was looking around at a perfectly beautiful living room. "The place is flawless."

"I'll walk you around again and show you. It only looks flawless to you, Jenny, because it's tidy and you're at home here."

"Could be part of it, the comfort of the familiar. But, believe me, TJ, it's still flawless." I walked up to a bowl of purple tulips and butter yellow freesias casually arranged with the utter abandonment of nature. "Gorgeous!"

"Thanks. Having established that, come and I'll show and tell you what I have in mind."

We went from room to room, she talking about everything from bedspreads to bookcases while I thought of Paul as he showed off his handiwork that first night in our enchanted place.

Bret called, said he'd be by, or could we meet him at Tadich's? He'd get in line for a table while we were en route. It would be faster. We said, of course, and got ourselves pulled together, fed the dogs, and left.

"Jenny, we haven't talked about you and Paul in ages as we have today." TJ had a habit of watching me as I drove.

"That's quite true. It's been much too painful, and I'm grateful you haven't pressed me, TJ."

"I know that, too, Jen, and I've been considering telling you something all day and have decided I should."

"What is it, TJ? Is Paul all right? Has something happened?" I was suddenly frightened.

"No, no, Jenny. He's fine. Oh, I've made a mess of this."

"Go on, then," I urged.

"When you asked so much about him today, I ducked, thinking that was the way it would be best and easiest for you. Now, I'm not certain it was right for me to talk past your questions." I waited for her to go on.

"It's true, we barely see him. Probably, as much because of me and my connection to you as because of work. Wu Yee sees him at the restaurant, but not just that. Remember Albert? He's a very perceptive young man. Seems he'd noticed some changes in Paul and reported them to his father who, in turn, called me, if you follow that." She smiled her funny crooked smile.

"I follow. What kind of changes?"

"Somewhat absent-minded and unfocused. But after all the time he spent in Vancouver, he seemed better to me. Yee reported he seemed better to him, too. Paul even called Guy to have lunch and literally pumped him for word of you."

"When was that?" I inquired.

"A few months, I'd say," TJ replied. "But the latest is he called me today."

"Today?" I asked. "What made him call today?"

"He'd heard via the grapevine that you were in town. He wanted to know what I thought about him calling you." TJ looked awful. I felt awful.

*A Small Flirtation*

"Go on, TJ. What did you say?"

"I told him I thought it was a totally rotten idea. I said, yes, you were in town and were getting ready to leave again soon. I told him to let it lay, that you needed more time to heal and that you were moving on with your life."

"Did he say anything about Kathy? Has he made a move to leave her? Was there any sign of that? Oh, TJ, I'm a wreck. Tell me more," I pleaded.

"No sign of any change, Jen. None. That's one reason I discouraged him from getting in touch. It was the right thing to do, wasn't it?"

"Maybe so, but not what I want. Frankly, I don't love the idea of your making that kind of judgment in my name, 'for my own good'." I felt peevish—frustrated.

"Then call him yourself, Jenny, and get finished with the agonizing."

"I don't know, TJ. I'm so afraid we'll fall right back into the old pattern and that I couldn't take—that's for sure."

"This whole thing is crazy." It was TJ's turn to sound annoyed. "He's churning inside while you're miserable and sitting here hoping I'll tell you I'll call him for you and set up a 'chance' meeting. Well, I'm not going to do it."

"TJ, I . . ."

"No. Listen to me. You've simply pushed aside the emotions and pretended it's resolved. Well, I can tell you, it is not! Think about it, Jenny." She turned and smiled at me. "Come on. Let's get some good food. That always makes you feel better."

We found Bret still in line waiting for a table.

"How are my two favorite girls . . . I mean women?" Bret gave me a peck on the cheek. TJ got a real hug.

"We're having a great time. The only problem is we can't seem to finish one subject before we're off on a tangent." I was very happy to see him. "You look great, Bret. It must have something to do with the news of your impending move."

He just grinned and took TJ's arm. "By the way, I saw Paul

Crowley as I was leaving and invited him to join us. He's been caught up in that Vancouver job so totally, I've hardly seen him. He sent his greetings, but won't be coming."

"Oh?" TJ.

"Said he'd had a late lunch and wanted to push through and get home. Something about a local event he'd promised to go to with Kathy."

"Too bad. It would have been nice to see him. It's been awhile."

"That guy works too hard. Conscientious is one thing, but day and night is another."

"I prefer your attitude." TJ gave his arm a hug.

"Me, too," Bret smiled at her.

I kept quiet, very quiet and then changed the subject. I'd consider all TJ said, later.

## 65

"Paul Crowley."

"Paul, it's Jenny . . ." I hesitated and he jumped in.

"Jenny! Jenny, my God. I can't believe it. Where are you? Are you in town? How are you? Jenny? Can I see you?" And on and on. He didn't draw a breath. And with it all, he took my breath away. I couldn't speak.

I was right to be worried about starting up all over again. If I could only have reached through the phone.

"I'm at home at the beach. I'm fine," was all I could manage.

"Jenny, you'll never know how I've missed you. When can I see you?" He rushed on in his old familiar way. I had to stop it before he assumed more than was true.

"Hold on, Paul. That's why I'm calling. To make a time to see you."

"Anytime, Jen. Where? When? Shall I come over?"

"No, not here. I'll come across," I responded quickly.

"Where then? At TJ's? Tell me, Jenny, can we meet now, today? I'll cancel the rest of my day."

I hadn't really thought about 'when' and I wasn't quite prepared for his 'now'. But decided to take advantage of his reaction to my call.

And so we decided to meet immediately. Yes, I agreed to meet him for lunch. No, not Cliff House, rather someplace in the Embarcadero near the ferry docks.

"It's such a beautiful day, I'll leave my car in Larkspur and come across by boat. I can be there around noon, I'm sure."

"I'll be at the dock waiting."

My mind was racing ahead of the ferry. What shall I do and say? I suddenly forgot every word, everything I'd planned as an approach to the subject of us. The closer I got to the dock, the more panic I felt. If I could have jumped ship, I believe I would have.

I saw him scanning the passengers as we debarked—my cowboy, my love—handsome as ever with an anxious look on his face.

"Paul! Over here," I called, waving. And he came running, pushing his way through all the other ferry passengers to get to me. He threw his arms around me lifting me off my feet. We struggled to maintain our balance as he put me down and drew my hands to his lips.

"Jenny, Jenny—all these months—My God, how I've missed you."

He pulled me to him again and I melted again, overcome by that same overwhelming desire I felt so many times before in his arms.

He placed my arm under his as we started walking toward a restaurant down past the Ferry Building—a place we've been to many times.

"Let's grab lunch right here in the Embarcadero. OK?" Paul asked with a knowing smile. "I'm sure you're hungry. It's close to 1:00."

So far, I was only grinning like an idiot and listening to my heart pound.

*A Small Flirtation*

We were given a window table at the far end of the room, away from the noisy lunch crowd seated around the bar. A seagull perched on a pier and stared at me. In some weird way I identified with it. Both of us were waiting for a crumb to be tossed our way.

"Did TJ tell you I phoned? I'd heard you were in town. She thought my phoning you was a lousy idea. Frankly, I felt foolish asking for what amounted to permission to contact you, and since talking to her I've felt like a damned fool for not calling you—it's just, she was so adamant, I was afraid those were your instructions to her." He looked down at me quizzically. "In fact, that's why I declined when Bret invited me to join up with you at Tadich's"

"No. No instructions. As a matter of fact, she did tell me and I was more than a little annoyed with her deciding what is right and what is wrong for me. She ended by telling me to call you myself if I wanted to talk to you. I thought about it for awhile and—well, here we are."

As we sat together sipping some lovely wine, it was so tempting to simply forget my vow and enfold myself in the warmth of his being. Would that be so wrong? Almost a year without each other and nothing had changed. The time that separated us collapsed and all that mattered was we were together again.

"Jenny, you haven't heard a word I've said," Paul was frowning. "What's the matter? Where are you, girl?"

"I'm right here, Paul." I smiled. "I was just thinking about the strangeness of time. Just how it's evaporated, the months in between, I mean."

"The months in between our being together? They seemed an eternity to me, Jen."

"But now they're gone, aren't they? It's like they never happened."

Suddenly he got up from the table, "Come on, Jenny, let's get out of here—take a walk in the park. We can't really talk here." He took my arm and led me out.

As we left, I turned and said, "Come this way, Paul, let's ride the boats. It's such a beautiful day, and we can have all the privacy we need."

He agreed. We took the ferry past Treasure Island and Alcatraz and the Golden Gate Bridge, as awesome a sight as any in the world. Truly the world is no match for San Francisco Bay on a fine day.

We caught up on the year filling in the blanks: My work was exhilarating. The Scottish trip enticing. I missed him terribly. For Paul, work and more work. The Vancouver project had taken on a life of its own and was blessedly very engrossing. He missed me terribly.

I gazed out at the beauty of the bay, gathering my strength to face up to the matter at hand with no more circumlocution

"What are we to do Paul?" No preamble—I plunged into the heart of the matter. "We can't pretend all is well between us and slip back into an impossible situation again." I turned away from him as he reached for my hand. "Perhaps this was a bad idea." I was thinking aloud.

"Seeing each other again? No, Jenny." He looked perplexed.

"I don't know, Paul, maybe it would have been better if I hadn't called—if I'd left well enough alone."

"No! There's nothing 'well enough' about our being apart, Jenny. It's been sheer hell. There hasn't been a day I haven't thought of you. You have no idea what a battle it's been not to contact you. I thought of a million great excuses to call."

"But you didn't..." I knew I was pushing. "Tell me, what was so different about last week—when you did call TJ?" I was curious.

"I don't know—I seemed driven to call her. I wanted to talk about you—to hear news of you..."

"That's it? That's why you called TJ?"

"That's one reason . . ."

"And?" I couldn't resist.

"And I wanted to see you, to be with you so badly—I thought if you were in town I'd get some encouragement from TJ. Instead,

I hit a blank wall." He grinned the famous Crowley grin, and my resolve started melting again. "Jenny," Paul was suddenly serious, "why did you phone me? What's the real reason? I'm sure it's not just because TJ challenged you." The anxious look was back on his face.

"The truth is, Paul, my calling you, our meeting here at this moment is meant to see if we can break the impasse between us. I want to know where you stand—now."

"Jenny, I love you as much as always. I know it's difficult for you to understand. It's just not the right time yet." He looked miserable. I felt miserable and foolish and sad and disappointed. My heart sank. I walked away from him. He followed and took my hand, but didn't speak.

"Why do you keep saying that? Why can't you level with me once and for all? When will it be 'the right time'?"

He was standing very close and suddenly took me in his arms. "I do love you, Jenny. Oh my girl. How I wish it were different. Someday, Jenny. Hold on. Please, hold on. It will work out."

"Hold on to what and for how long? You'll be 60 in a couple of years and I'm pushing 55! What's the mystery? What miracle am I to wait for?" I felt so frustrated.

I pushed back out of his embrace, took a deep breath and let it out slowly. I had to get a grip on myself and not break down in front of him. What a monumental mistake I'd made. He wasn't about to make a move. That would have been obvious to a blind person. Had he been so much as thinking about it, he'd have said so now. No, I was still the love of his life, but not to be in his life. He had truly 'settled'.

He couldn't even respond. I said instead, "We'll be docking in Larkspur in a few minutes. I'm going to get off there. It's pointless to go on with this. I'm so sorry I stirred everything up again, no matter how good it is to be with you." I pulled on my jacket.

"Jenny, no. Don't leave like this. Please. I'll get off, too. Please, Jenny . . ."

"No, Paul. This was my last, best shot."

"Jenny!" He wanted to stop me. He reached out. "How can I make you stay. What can I say?"

"At the very least, you can tell me what's going on, because something important is missing in this equation. You owe me that much."

Paul turned his back and walked away from me. He stood by the railing staring out at the sea. When he turned around, he had an odd expression on his face—almost angry.

"I never wanted to tell you this. Maybe I was unfair not to, but I was protecting Kathy. That may sound crazy. Sometimes I felt crazy." He shook his head sadly.

"What are you telling me? Go on," I urged.

"When I first talked about my marriage, I didn't tell you the whole story." He got my full attention with that statement. I waited for him to continue. "After Beth was born, Kathy went into a depression. The doctor thought it was the common post-partum blues and that it would pass as the condition is basically self-limiting. Well, it didn't. In fact, it got worse—much worse. I had to call on her mother to come help with the baby and finally hired a full time nanny. In the meantime, her doctor consulted with a colleague of his, a psychiatrist who recommended short term therapy and prescribed some medication."

At this point in the recitation, I interrupted Paul: "Sadly, that is an all too common tale and while it must have been terribly difficult for all of you, it took place over twenty-five years ago. Forgive me if I've missed the point. What has all of this got to do with us?" I was becoming irritated and sad at the same time. That couldn't be the reason Paul was allowing me to walk out of his life.

"Jenny, let me say it bluntly. Kathy is bi-polar—in other words, she is a manic-depressive and has been in supportive therapy all these years. When she takes her lithium regularly she's in a fairly balanced state as long as she can keep stress at arms length."

"And if not?"

"She crashes—either up on the ceiling or through the floor. At those times added medication must be given. She has had to be hospitalized several times in the past. It's been damned hard. Her episodes are one of the reasons I had to break dates with you. And why I spent so much time being the good father you once commented on, with Beth before her wedding."

"Why in the name of God haven't you told me this before? What was there to hide? At the very least, it would have given some reason to your constantly telling me to hang on." I was losing control and yelling at him "Oh, I know I was a willing participant for a long time. Frankly, for a long time, I was afraid to hear your reason. But, Paul, I could have made rational decisions based on fact instead of exhausting every avenue of thought to try and figure out what was the matter with me." The wonders of female logic—'what was the matter with *me*?'

"I'm truly sorry, Jenny. I just couldn't bring myself to tell you—don't ask me why. Somehow it seemed unfair. I thought Kathy deserved some modicum of privacy. Besides, how would you have taken this information—poor Paul stuck with a mentally ill wife or maybe you'd have doubted me? I don't know Jenny.

"Believe me I have tried to break away. I tried even before you and I met. She pleaded with me not to leave—swore she'd commit suicide if I did. It was hell. What was I to do? I knew I couldn't leave Beth alone in such a potentially dangerous situation and I didn't want Kathy's blood on my hands. So I backed off...I stayed." Suicide, my God! I was dumbstruck and stood there quietly while he continued.

"Then you came into my life. I hoped we could continue with our plan to see each other without any promises," he shook his head. "It was impossible. I fell in love with you and desperately wanted to keep you in my life while I tried to make sense of the other part of my life—my marriage. I swore I'd get out of it and be free for you, for us." He broke my heart he looked so sad.

"I have met with her psychiatrist any number of times over the years and many more since our time together. He's never commented on Kathy's therapy but he listens to what I have had to say and works with whatever part he feels is important and might, in the long run, make a difference. That's the reason I keep saying 'please hold on'. You must know, Jenny, no psychiatrist can guarantee a patient will not commit suicide" He sagged in abject defeat.

I nodded. I had my answer. He'd never leave and I couldn't play the role he had cast me into. "The tyranny of the weak. How they make life work for themselves. They manipulate and hold the strong ones hostage."

We had reached the ferry dock when I turned away and left him standing there on the deck. When I turned back he hadn't moved. I waved one last time and walked away—tears rolling down my cheeks, but determined not to break my stride. At my car I waited and watched as the boat pulled away. Still he didn't move.

I was devastated. I drove home alone. I'd lost everything.

# 66

"What day do you leave, Jenny?" Guy was having a cup of coffee with me in my studio while I put my camera cases together and packed up extra gear I'd need for the trip.

"We fly on Friday. We'll arrive in Beijing Saturday night, get settled in and have Sunday to get our bearings. We're being met by our counterparts and shown around a bit before we start work on Monday."

"Three months in the PRC! This is one trip I envy you."

"Guy, have you considered coming over and joining in for awhile?"

"Not really, Jen. I've got a lot to get settled at the ranch with the new crops we're developing on the added acreage. No, I won't join you this time, but I will again. You know our joint ventures are important to me. We'll work it out—but later."

"When I get back from this trip, I plan to ease off a little. I've been going full tilt for a long time." I stretched and sat down.

"We haven't really talked, kiddo. Not for months. How's it going?" Guy had turned serious.

"I'm all right, Guy. Admittedly, I still get blue from time to time. How could it be otherwise?"

Guy nodded, but kept still, sipped his coffee.

I continued, "I realized we were heading for trouble when I began to want more and more—to long to be with Paul constantly. Did you know I had pictures of him I had taken hanging all over my darkroom? When I started talking to them, I decided enough fantasy life. It was time to get on with my real life, and my reality didn't include Paul. Not married," I added, shaking my head. "Not married."

"A very sensible attitude, Jenny, but how do you make it work? You were very much in love."

"TJ asked me precisely the same question a very long time ago. I can't remember my answer at the time. I can only tell you that it isn't easy. It's taken me a long time to talk about it even to you two. You see, I still am very much in love with him."

"I know, Jenny. And you know how I wished it could have worked out for you. As I said all along, Paul is a very good man. My concern was never that he was some kind of bastard and would hurt you without giving it a thought. No, it was that you two had fallen deeply in love, and I could see no way out of your dilemma—not without great anguish."

"And you were right, my dear. You were right." I had told neither TJ nor Guy about my most recent devastating meeting with Paul.

They would never know, if I could help it.

# 67

San Francisco to Tokyo and on to Beijing. So much to grasp and absorb. All the pictures in all the books come to life. Tien an men Square, the Forbidden City of Crimson and Gold. The Summer Palace with the wooden and white marble, non-floating house boat. The gigantic stone statues of animals guarding either side of the road on the way to the Ming Tombs. The Great Wall! All the pictures I'd seen of it hadn't prepared me for the enormity of the reality.

Crowds of Chinese were everywhere enjoying the tourist attractions, along with the foreigners. They outnumbered us ten to one, at least.

X'ian and the warriors entombed in clay for the first time. Up to that time, each emperor had his personal army buried alive with him upon his death. Acres and acres of clay statues and horses, no two exactly alike. An awesome sight housed in enormous field house-like structures.

On to Dazu and the gigantic Buddha lying on his side with hundreds of other Buddha carved into the walls and standing all around "Big Foot."

The drive through Sichwan province was marked by hills terraced and sculpted into flooded rice paddies. Planted and tended as they had been for centuries by water oxen with peasants walking behind, guiding plows, over ankle deep in water.

We took the Yangtze River trip leaving from Chungqing and traveled past the Three Gorges on to Wuhan. We visited Fudan University and met the president who had suffered house arrest and beatings by the Red Guard during the Cultural Revolution. She was left crippled in body only and carried on her work, having rebuilt her university into one of the finest in all China.

Nanjing, the old capital of China and the city where Sun Yat Sen was buried in a most impressive tomb rising some 450 steps. Hundreds of the faithful and the curious climb those steps daily to gaze at the preserved body of their hero.

It was in the hills above the city that Chang Kai Shek was captured by the Communists.

What a time in history. What a journey I was having!

We went on to visit the garden cities for a few days respite. Wuxi, Hangzhou, Suzhow, and then for the *pièce de résistance*, Shanghai, the Li River, the Zoo with the pandas, the circus, the puppets, the museum and the restaurant in the Blue and Green Park that serves only dumplings. I felt like a stuffed Chinese teacake, myself, by the time I rolled out of there. So much to see—and to experience.

After a few weeks you forget the people are Asian, and the old cliché and stereotypes of all of them looking alike drop away as you become aware of the same faces, head shapes, expressions, body language we know so well among our own people.

We visited factories of weaving and jade carving, schools with beautiful bright-eyed children, 'the flowers of China'. Fortunately, we didn't have to be involved in anything political. We were steeped with the culture and admiring of the ancient and the modern living side by side in some disharmony from time to time. But so little of it when one considers the enormous number of people who have to be dealt with daily.

## A Small Flirtation

My way of getting a handle on the size and number of people was to tell myself that China has approximately the same size land mass as the United States and an excess of four times the number of people. In other words, picture oneself alone with another person at home. Then picture the same set—that is the same room with the same two people—and then add six more people to the same scene. That's China. Four for dinner equals sixteen in the same amount of space. As the numbers increase in that little exercise it begins to boggle the mind.

That's why virtually every square foot of empty land is used for growing food. That's why most flowers and ornamental plants are grown in pots. The ground bears food.

All in all, this trip had to rank as a peak experience in my life of travel. At every turn, I wished Paul were with me to share it. I kept copious notes, took many personal pictures, and wrote in my journal nightly . . .

". . .So much has been done. So much yet to do. They seem to have the will. Can they find the way peacefully? Twenty-first century—here they come all BILLION plus of them! Look out world!"

There were days I felt I was living in the middle of a painting. What a beautiful country. Monumental efforts were being made everywhere to bring themselves into the present and to provide for all those people. So hard working. So patient, so long-suffering, and so proud, it made my heart both sing and ache.

Then it was time to leave. I'd been virtually incommunicado, dropping notes and cards along the way. Never being any place long enough to receive mail. Contact with the states and with home was minimal; mostly made by the production people. We were kept up to date by the "People's Daily" newspaper. No personal news reached me other than by a birthday phone call which I made to each of the boys with firm instructions to call TJ with greetings from me.

Over and over again I wrote in my journal of my feelings, my longings to be with Paul and to share the glories of the trip with him. I often sat up till the small hours of the morning composing letters to him as though he were mine to come home to. I'd weep alone and scold myself for hanging onto such fantasies.

## 68

On the return flight I slept fitfully, tried to read, reread my notes and my journal, made more entries and slept again. There were always movies to watch and food being served. Still, I felt unsettled my mind racing backwards to China and ahead to home. I'd visit with one or two of my fellow fellows on the crew as I walked up and down the aisles doing little exercises to limber up.

Finally, the last four hours I slept. I awakened with a start to the smell of fresh coffee and the sounds of people stirring. I don't know why, but my first thought was of Paul and the smell of freshly brewed coffee that first morning after he stayed over. The smell of breakfast being served only enhanced the memory of walking into my kitchen and finding him in the throes of preparing our breakfast.

"We'll be landing in San Francisco in a few minutes. Please turn off all portable electronic equipment you may have been using, bring your seat backs up to their upright position and lock your tray tables in place. Make sure your seat belts are fastened . . ."

After immigration and customs were cleared, I was on the way out with my baggage when I turned and saw a tall, handsome man striding toward me smiling.

"Excuse me. Do you need a ride or are you being met?" He inquired.

"Well, I'm not sure exactly..." I stammered.

"I have my car. I'll drive you to town." He reached for my camera case. "I'll carry it for you. It looks ... it is heavy," he said as he took it off my shoulder.

I still hadn't moved an inch. I think my mouth must have dropped open, because he began to laugh. This oh-so-familiar stranger put his hand under my elbow and guided me to the exit.

He stopped half way to the door and pulled me away from the crowd. He carefully put my camera case on the floor, relieved me of my raincoat and purse and folded me in his arms.

His sigh ended in a shudder. I was smothered against his chest. He released me, bent down, kissed me on the forehead and placed a kiss in the palm of each of my hands.

I started to cry.

The surprise—the impact of his embrace was too much for me. I was both exhilarated and exhausted from the exciting and arduous assignment I'd been on. And, now, to be greeted this way ...

"Jenny, my Jenny, I have so much to tell you and ask you." I smiled and sniffled and nodded in agreement.

# AFTERWARD

On the ride home and long hours into the night Paul told me what had happened. He went crazy with grief at the loss he felt, knowing that I'd never call again. Even worse, he understood I'd never wait again to hear from him.

He was certain I'd accept the teaching position in the east he heard I'd been offered, move, meet someone else, etc., etc. The whole nightmare would come true. He had every scenario worked out—every fantasy in the book. Each one ended the same way: I'd left him for good.

Up to that indisputable point, he had placated his fears by deceiving himself into believing what he so often had said to me: "Someday, somehow it will work out for us. It has to." At that point, he even questioned whether he had preferred living out a fantasy.

His final decision was made as he took a hard look at the reality of his life: He had been held hostage by a mentally unbalanced woman for over a quarter of a century. For him to continue to remain in an empty loveless marriage and throw out, toss aside, and destroy a deeply passionate love was impossible.

It became clear that there was no hope of salvaging anything unless he moved and moved quickly. In the end, he couldn't understand what had possessed him to let me get off the ferryboat without him; and yet he realized it was *that act* that woke him up to the fact that it was over and he had lost me forever. That fact was unbearable.

He had indeed been made victim by the tyranny of a weak, controlling woman. Kathy had claimed his time and attention far too long. Now, she would have to deal with her own life. He refused to be held hostage any longer by her threats.

He was determined to build a complete life with me—a life based on the intimate relationship and mutual respect we already felt so deeply for each other.

He moved into our place in the city almost immediately after I left and found himself a level of inner peace he realized he hadn't truly experienced in years. He attributed much of it to the warmth of his surroundings, the 'good vibes' which we created there with our love.

Now at last, we were to have the time to work on all the unknowns of our relationship—to come out into the open and experience each other in the fullness of our love.

For Paul, there was much to settle—obstacles to over come. Arrangements for Kathy's uninterrupted care to be as seamless as possible, would take time. And time is what we had. There was no need to rush. We had the rest of our lives to enjoy each other.

Paul's decision to meet my plane was a stroke of genius. He had been planning it for weeks. He told me how he rehearsed his lines with TJ and even ran them by Wu Yee. He learned from Guy that it was Wu Yee who had said, "destiny is at work here." Indeed, the *I Ching* had foretold the truth: All was to be circular, round and round going no place until we went back to the beginning and started over.